Special Thanks

Special thanks to the creative team that assisted in the making of this book: Ruth Hall and Chasity Neivel; cover artwork, Candace Brown administrative support and editing, Nettie Perham-Lynch, editing. We wouldn't be here without all of you.

Chapter One

As he neared the house, he thought about the dealer and how he was treated by him. He hoped the woman would be there this time. When she was there, she kept the man from yanking him around and treating him quite as rough as he did when he was alone.

Approaching the house, he could see a dim light in the only room he had ever been in during the transaction. Except for a small table in the corner of the room, there was no other furniture.

Greg walked up the sidewalk to the side door of the house and knocked. When the door opened, the man grabbed his arm and yanked him through the door, pushing it shut behind him.

"Well, if it ain't the snotty-nosed brat. It's about time you got here. Did you bring the money?" "Can you think of any other reason I'd come anywhere near you?" Greg glanced at him with contempt, as he took off his coat, exposing the harness-like vest he wore. The straps came over his shoulders and connected with the strap around his lower chest, buckling in the center.

"Watch your mouth with me kid, or you'll be picking yourself up off the floor." He grabbed the vest before Greg had freed his arms from the straps, throwing him off balance and into the sharp corner of the table.

3

As the man unzipped a compartment on each side of the vest, removing the packets of money, a woman walked into the room. She was tall and slim, her long blonde hair swinging loosely across her shoulders. Her face was round with dimples flashing when she smiled. Greg liked her. At least she was always nice to him, which was more than he could say for any of the other people he was forced to deal with in this rotten business. He wondered why she would want to hang out with this guy.

"Well Ray, I see we have company." She smiled at Greg. "Yeah, Gert, company," Ray said sarcastically. "I'll get the order and you can stuff the vest while I count the money." He took the bundles of money and left the room, only to return almost immediately with a small box filled with plastic bags.

"How have you been Greg? I haven't seen you for a couple of weeks." She seated herself at the table.

"I'm okay, I guess." He watched her carefully place the bags evenly around the inside of his pocketed vest.

"You don't like this business much do you, Honey?" she asked sympathetically, glancing at his gloomy expression. "No," Greg said emphatically, "I hate it."

"Awe, you can't take life so seriously, Sweetie. You just have to go with the flow, I always say." Reaching across the table, she patted his arm and smiled.

"You don't have to entertain the brat, Gert. Just do the job and get him out of here," Ray called from the adjoining room.

When she finished, she helped him into the vest and buckled the strap around his waist. He put his coat on over the vest and walked toward the door.

Holding the door open for him, she reached out and touched the sleeve of his coat. "Greg." He stopped and looked up

4

at her. "Be careful won't you, Sweetie," she said. He nodded and started down the walk. *She's the only one who seems to care*, he thought. The rest, including his own mother, were only interested in the safety of the money and the drugs.

Yes, be careful. He knew the drill very well; how to look, how to act, how to walk. He had been thoroughly coached on the merits of avoiding the police and how to act if he was stopped for questioning. He had been told the terrifying stories of what would happen to him if he was caught. It was forever imprinted on his mind and he lived in fear. Even with all the information, it wasn't the police that worried him. It was the drug dealers who slashed, maimed and killed with little or no reason, that caused him to worry. He knew if he was ever caught by the police, the drug dealers would find a way to end his life.

Greg lived in a rough neighborhood and had been plagued by the neighborhood gangs many times! They were older and bigger than Greg and thought it was great entertainment to beat, kick and trip him, until he was able to scramble away from them. He soon learned to avoid them, even if it took him blocks out of his way. His mother considered his size to be an asset because she seemed to think he could go anywhere in the city without drawing attention from the police.

When Greg arrived home, he removed his outer coat and hung it in the hall closet before entering the kitchen. Dora Roberts stepped to the doorway, watching him as he unbuckled his vest and handed it to her.

She was close to six feet tall, slim and beautiful. Her dark shoulder-length hair curled softly around her face. As Greg moved past her into the kitchen, she said, "Stop for a minute Greg, I need to talk to you."

Now what did I do wrong, he wondered. *I suppose I'm in for another beating,* he thought. His earliest memories of his mother were of anger and beatings. There had never been any love or caring on her part toward him, only violent anger. He hated her.

Pulling a chair away from the table, he sat down with a heavy sigh and waited. Dora sat down opposite him, watching the expression on his face. It infuriated her that he never looked directly at her when she talked to him. She was aware of his antagonism, but she knew the reason for it was fear. It was with this fear that she controlled him, but when he refused to look at her, she knew there was a part of him she hadn't conquered. If not by now, she probably never would.

Dora pulled the vest toward her and began removing the packets, silently counting them. Looking up, Dora said, "I've been house hunting for quite some time now and I finally found a small place in Carson Cove. We'll be moving out of the city next week." Watching his face, she waited for an expression of surprise. There was none. She had to admire his self control. After a few seconds of silence, Greg said, "I suppose the drug business will be moving with us." Sarcasm was evident in his voice as he made a slight motion with his hand toward the packets lying on the table.

"No," Dora frowned. "Not right away, anyway; I've got to get away from it for a while, but the main reason to do it now is that I'm pregnant."

For an instant Greg's face registered the surprise Dora had been looking for. His eyes grew big and he looked directly at her, but she was busy with the packets and missed it.

Chapter Two

It was early November when Dora Roberts and Greg moved to Carson Cove. It was a large town, thirty-two miles from the city, situated on the Waseka River, which flowed into Lake Andrew. The town was bordered by the lake on the west and the river on the north. The result was two well-kept beaches with a large number of summer rentals and a few privately-owned cottages scattered along the northern and western shoreline. This added to the prosperity of businesses within the community.

Now that summer had passed, the tourist season was over and the people who lived year-round in Carson Cove could settle back into a more relaxed and quieter lifestyle as winter approached.

During the ride from the city, Greg tried to imagine a life without running drugs. He could hardly remember any other time in his short life. He enjoyed thinking about his freedom. It seemed as if he could fly, he was so happy. They were almost to Carson Cove before he remembered she had said she would have to get away from drugs for a while, which indicated the misery would be back eventually, but at the moment he was happy and it was easy to push the thought of drugs away.

Their new home was situated on the southern end of Carson Cove and was in the center of a wooded area on a hill, some distance off the main highway into town. Dora had chosen it because it was secluded. Although there were other homes in the vicinity, the surrounding wooded area gave it privacy. It was small with two bedrooms, but it would serve their needs adequately. Greg noticed the rooms were smaller than those in the apartment, but he wasn't about to complain since he would no doubt be responsible for cleaning them, just as he had been at the apartment.

As far as Greg was concerned, he was happy with Dora's idea of a no-frills existence. With the exception of her bedroom, the apartment had been furnished with the absolute basics. He was never allowed to go into her bedroom for any reason. The door was closed and locked whenever she left the apartment, but he didn't care as long as he didn't have to keep it clean.

Dora had parked her car to one side so the moving truck could pull in close to the back door. Soon after they arrived, the truck pulled into the yard.

As the furniture was brought into the house, Dora instructed them as to the location for each piece. When she changed her mind, the men were glad to accommodate her. They set up her bed while she stood aside, watching and flirting with them.

Greg wondered why she would give so much attention to flirting with the moving men when she would probably never see them again. Maybe habit, he thought.

When the movers had gone, Greg went to his room where the pieces of his bed were piled on the floor and the mattress leaned against the wall.

While he struggled to put the frame together, he whispered the endearing words Dora had said to the men. "Why, thank you so much for doing all this heavy work for me. You are so kind. I just would never know the first thing about where to start," he mimicked as he finally shoved the mattress into place.

When Greg finished, he stepped back and smiling sweetly he placed his hand over his heart and said, "Thank you so much. You boys have been such darlings to help me this way," and he wiggled his rear first one way, then the other.

When he had occasion to see her interact with people, it made the way she treated him, seem even more severe for some reason. He didn't dwell on it, but it did cross his mind now and then and he wondered why she hated him so much.

The next morning, Dora told Greg to get ready and she would take him to register for school.

As they drove into the circular driveway to the school parking lot, Greg noticed how small it seemed in comparison to the city school. The grounds were neat and the short bushes that lined both sides of the entryway had been trimmed for winter.

"May I help you," the secretary asked as they approached. "Yes, we're here to enroll my son." Dora had her hand on Greg's shoulder and looked fondly down at him. "I'm Dora Roberts and this is my son Gregory Roberts."

As always when they were in public together, his mother became an effective actress.

"How nice to meet you. I'm Margaret Kever, the school secretary." She pulled a chair up to her desk and motioned Dora to sit down. "I'm afraid there's a great deal of paperwork to be filled out," she smiled apologetically.

After what seemed, to Greg, an hour, they had finally answered all the questions and filled in all the blanks.

"Did you bring a transfer from your other school," Mrs. Kever asked.

"No, they said they would send it."

"All right, there's one more thing. Since you're outside the mile limit, you will be riding bus number five. Jason Ennis will be the driver.

"Oh, no, Greg will be riding his bike or walking to and from school. He loves to walk, don't you Greg?" Dora smiled down at Greg.

'Some kids have imaginary friends, but I have an imaginary bike,' Greg thought, nodding.

"In case it's raining or snowing, you might want to ride, so if that happens, just stand at the end of your driveway and bus number five will pick you up about eight-fifteen."

After another glance over the finished papers, she said, "Well, that about covers it, so now I think we should go meet your homeroom teacher. Her name is Mrs. Lymen." Turning to Dora, she smiled. "You're welcome to come too, if you'd like, Mrs. Roberts."

"Oh, no, I think I had better get on home. There's a lot to do getting settled in."

"Yes, I'm sure there is. It was nice to meet you. I hope you will like it here in Carson Cove."

"I'm sure I will," Dora turned to Greg, "I'll see you later, honey," she said as she bent and kissed him on the cheek.

It amused Greg to watch his mother's transformation when she was forced into interludes of careful refinement. *How does she do things like that with a straight face*, he wondered as he walked down the hall behind Mrs. Kever.

School for Greg was relaxed and comfortable. From the time he first started, his mother's lifestyle had isolated him from his peers and as a result it made little difference to him what school he attended. Since happiness didn't depend on their attitude toward him, it gave him a certain freedom to enjoy being his own creation. Whatever he accomplished was to please himself. His mother cared little about his scholastic aptitude as long as he brought no problems home where it would reflect on her. In spite of his mother's lack of interest, he was an excellent student. He was an avid reader, achieving far beyond his grade level. School meant an abundance of reading material, with a great variety of subjects from which to choose.

Although he made no effort toward forming friendships, knowing what the result would be, his attitude seemed to stimulate the other pupils' curiosity and they were drawn to him. All the warnings he had received over the years were forever imprinted on his memory. He knew there could never be a blend of home and school. Any friends he made in school would have to remain in school. Many of the boys participated in after-school activities and moved freely in and out of each other's homes, but he knew this would never be a part of his life.

Eventually, as had happened in the city, they would stop asking. Sometimes he felt the sharp edge of loneliness, but he had been forced to come to terms with it long ago.

When he arrived home that afternoon, there was a bicycle leaning against the porch. He felt excitement rise. Conquering the impulse to touch it, he thought there must be some mistake. His mother had never bought him anything except the bare necessities before. There was no use kidding himself, if it was for him, there would be a hundred obligations that would kill any joy he felt. He entered the house cautiously. Maybe it belonged to a visitor. As he walked into the hall, his mother met him. "Did you see the bike?" she asked.

"Yes," he nodded, trying not to look too eager.

"I bought it for you, but remember, all the same rules still apply. No kids are to come here, ever and you are not to go to their homes."

"I won't forget. Thanks, thanks a lot," he answered as he ran back to the yard.

Dora followed him and stood watching from the doorway as he looked the bicycle over from the handlebars to the tires.

"It's for you to ride to and from school. You still have your chores to do and if you have extra time, you can look for jobs if you want. But let me remind you again, the jobs are not to interfere with school. I won't have any school personnel nosing around. Winter will be here soon enough and then you'll have to put it away and walk. A little walking won't hurt you." Turning back, she picked up her purse, buttoned her coat and as she walked by, she said, "Get as much of that stuff put away as you can tonight." She drove her car out of the driveway and was gone.

Greg was so pleased about owning a bike, he didn't care that all the boxes were still as they were when he left for school; it was as he had expected. He wasted no time in learning the techniques of forward motion and balance. The reason for the rules didn't bother him, nor did the rust spots. He was thrilled to have something of his own.

There had not been any measurable snow during the month of November, but Greg had taken the opportunity to knock on doors looking for snow shoveling jobs. He had no trouble finding work, although there were some questions about his size. All his jobs so far were on the dead-end road and within two blocks of the school. He would just get up early.

Since his mother celebrated no holidays, one day was about the same as the next. He was careful not to interrupt other people during a holiday, fearing it would result in questions. Quite often after a holiday such as Thanksgiving, someone might ask if he had a big family dinner with turkey and all the trimmings and he would smile and say he had. Sometimes there were questions about toys after Christmas. He had become quite inventive, which saved him from trying to fabricate a plausible explanation why he didn't receive presents. He wondered what it must feel like to have a tree decorated with colorful lights and ornaments like he saw in other people's windows.

As he grew older, he could have bought himself toys and even a pretty ornament to hang in the window, but he told himself someday he'd be an adult and he would be able to do things differently. He had, over the past few years, earned quite a large sum of money to do it successfully. There was never any doubt in his mind that he could leave and when he did, it would have to be fast and far. The drug people were not about to smile and wave him happily on his way. He knew if they ever found him they would kill him. He knew too much about them and their operation.

Through the winter months, Greg settled into a comfortable routine of housework, school and his new snow shoveling jobs. He always had a stack of books from the library. Dora came and went each week, almost unnoticed, leaving him money for groceries. He was always careful to have coffee and creamer on hand for his mother. Other than that, the money was used for food for himself because she never ate any meals at home.

Even now, during her pregnancy, Dora was out until the early morning hours and slept most of the day, but she almost always left before Greg came home from school.   This arrangement was agreeable to them both. He had grown accustomed to this lifestyle and dreaded the weekends when she was home and awake because she usually found a way to badger him for some form of misconduct or neglected chore. Although since coming to Carson Cove she seemed to be less critical and there had been no beatings. The days when Dora was home, she washed and ironed her clothes and cleaned her bedroom.

Early on, she had initiated a sparse diet for Greg and since it was the easiest, he still bought a variety of prepared dinners. As he grew older, he had added a variety of vegetables and meat if the cooking didn't take too much effort. He had even ventured into easy baking mixes from a box now and then, such as brownies or cookies, but not very often.

Before leaving the house each morning, he measured out the coffee into the filter along with five cups of water, if he hadn't done it the night before. When Dora got up in the morning, all she had to do was plug it in. He had learned his lessons well.

By most people's standards, Greg's home life would seem dull and lonely, but he could not remember a time in his life when he was happier. They were out of the drug business.

They had lived in Carson Cove for over four months. Signs of spring were everywhere and Greg was able to ride his bike to and from school once again. Most of his snow shoveling jobs had turned into yard work. Even Dora, who was showing her pregnancy now, seemed happier.

As winter had begun to wane, there had been one sad event. It was from the people on Tyler Road where he had obtained all his winter work. The woman who lived at the end of Tyler Road had died. Greg was saddened by this. Although he hadn't known Mrs. Kincade very long, he would miss her kindness and loving ways. After he finished her lawn work, she always invited him to stay a little longer and seemed to be genuinely interested in his school activities. She often made useful suggestions for his homework. It was during this time that she shared some of the events of her childhood and they often shared some of the diversity of their education. This special time had always involved cookies and milk. It had surprised him a little that she enjoyed his company as much as he did hers.

He couldn't help but think of the differences between the people here in the Cove and the people he worked for in the city. Maybe it was because the people here were older and didn't seem quite as busy.

Chapter Three

Dora Roberts sipped her coffee impatiently, tapping her foot against the table leg, waiting. She glanced at her watch. It was early yet, but she was eager to get started. She had given the idea much thought and now that she had decided to tell Martin, she was excited. This pregnancy had slowed her down some, but after the first two months, she had been feeling good again.

Dora smiled, thinking about Harold. He had told her that he was sterile and when she became pregnant, he declared it couldn't be his. When she asked him to be tested, he refused.

When she said that she would take it to court, he had paid plenty to get rid of her and the baby. It certainly would have ended his career if the voting public found out their mayor was playing around with a prostitute, to say nothing of his marriage.

Dora had planned to have an abortion since Harold had been very generous. There would have been a substantial sum of money left over after the abortion, but Martin had talked her out of it. He knew this lawyer who, on occasion, made big money for himself and for the mother of the baby, when he found the right buyer. There had been days she thought she must have lapsed into insanity to agree to such a thing, but now that she was feeling better she had a lot of time to think. With the money from selling the baby and the money from Harold, she would be able to carry out her plan.

Although she had done well with the drug trade in the city, she would like to cut out the middle man in a new operation. Too many hands were taking the biggest share of the money. Now all she had to do was convince Martin, and he was not noted for his innovative ideas.

She eased back into the window seat and sipped her coffee. Her mind slipped back to the early years. Dora smiled, thinking of Judy. It was because of her that she learned the art of manipulation. After her mother died, Dora had been taken away from her stepfather because of his sexual abuse and the county facility became her new home. It was a small orphanage funded by the county. A small percentage of the children had relatives who, for whatever reason, made arrangements through the county to have them live there.

Mrs. Anderson was the superintendent and was responsible for all the people who managed the different departments within the orphanage. Departments consisting of the preschool, K-6, the cafeteria, housekeeping and business office. She had chosen the heads of these departments very carefully, with attention not only to their ability, but also for their compassion in dealing with the children. It was her intention to erase the sad image of orphanages of the past.

Soon after Dora arrived, a small girl was brought into the orphanage who spent most of her time crying. Her name was Judy Collins. They were both the same age and Dora had chosen to share her room with her. After the first week, Dora became more than sick of her crying, although she realized the reason for some of it was because of her small size. The bigger boys were bullying her every chance they found. Dora was large for her age and didn't have that kind of problem.

One day, Dora was walking down the hall leading to the cafeteria when she saw a boy step over to Judy and trip her. Dora reached out, grabbed the boy and slammed him against the wall.

"If you ever hurt her again, I'll stomp your head into the floor. You got that?" When she noticed a small crowd had gathered, she added, "and that goes for all of you, in case you have any ideas." Dora then turned and helped Judy up from the floor.

Dora's statement sent the spectators hurrying on their way, but it proved to be very effective. There was no more bullying and Judy became Dora's shadow.

During the following years, the awakening of Dora's new-found power became her ruling force when dealing with other people. It was flattering that Judy depended on her for every decision. She took excessive pride in her control, not only of Judy, but of other people as well. She quickly learned the art of diplomacy and quite often managed to turn ordinary circumstances to her advantage.

Judy had an uncle who lived in the same city as the orphanage. He came to visit her occasionally during the first few years. Judy hated him because he always wanted her to sit on his lap while he caressed her. When the visits became more frequent, Judy complained to Dora.

"Tell him to keep his hands off you and stay as far away from him as possible," Dora instructed her.

When Judy did as Dora had told her, the old man's visits became shorter and less frequent. Their lives were smooth as they progressed into their teen years. By the time they turned fifteen, both girls were active, well-developed young girls; each in their own way. Judy was petite with naturally blonde hair and arresting blue eyes, while Dora was tall with dark brown hair and eyes. Both girls had figures that drew considerable attention.

One day after the uncle left, Dora found Judy in their room, crying. "What's wrong?" Dora asked, alarmed.

"He says I'm old enough now to go live with him. He says he has been paying for me to be here and now it's time for me to go live with him." This brought on another bout of sobs.

Dora was thoughtful for a few seconds. "Why don't you want to go?"

Judy's face expressed the loathing she was feeling. "Because he looks at me like I'm a piece of meat or something and he's always trying to get his hands on me," Judy shivered.

Dora hesitated a moment. "We could go and see the superintendent and tell her what you have told me, but you've got to do something about your vocabulary."

"I don't know what you mean."

"You can't say he looks at me funny or he tries to put his hands on me, that's too feeble. I'll tell you what to say." Dora knew from her own experience the words that were needed.

While Dora was explaining to Judy what she should tell Mrs. Anderson, Judy burst into tears.

"Oh, Dora, I can't say those things," she sobbed.

"Maybe she'll let me do the talking. I'll say that it's what you told me and if she asks you if it's true, you'll have to say yes. Do you think you can do that?" Dora asked, with a little sarcasm creeping into her question. Judy nodded.

Mrs. Anderson was aware of the close relationship between the two girls. She listened to the story Dora told, while being assured it was what Judy had told her. She could see how upset Judy was by watching the steady flow of tears.

When Dora finished, Mrs. Anderson leaned back in her chair, frowning. "It's true, she finally said. "He made arrangements with the county officials for you to live here."

She hesitated, thinking. "About the only thing I can think of to do would be to call him in and try to talk him out of taking you away from here. I will remind him that it is a very complex and challenging situation for a man to take a young girl into his home. I will explain the danger involved if the girl reports anything she considers or implies any form of sexual misconduct on his part. There could be serious consequences for him along with the adverse publicity. It may be enough to change his mind. Let's hope so. If not, our only alternative would be to turn it over to Child Protective Services."

Mrs. Anderson walked over to where the two girls were sitting and put a comforting hand on Judy's shoulder. "Don't worry any more. This will be taken care of properly, one way or another. If there is any part of his convoluted brain still working, I'm confident he will reconsider. Now you two run along. I'll let you know how it turns out."

Less than a week later, Mrs. Anderson called the two girls in and informed them that Judy's uncle had reconsidered and she would be staying at the orphanage. Judy's uncle made no more visits. Within a month of his last visit, his lawyer contacted Mrs. Anderson with information that the uncle was very ill and would be taken to a nursing home after he was released from the hospital. He had suffered a serious stroke and could no longer care for himself.

The same year that the girls were preparing to leave the orphanage, the lawyer once again contacted Mrs. Anderson and Judy was brought to her office.

"This is Mr. Warren," Mrs. Anderson said. "He's your uncle's lawyer. He asked to see you."

"How do you do, Miss Collins," he said, extending his hand. "I'm afraid I have sad news for you. Your uncle died last night. You are his only living relative. You will inherit his estate. His funeral arrangements have been made. He ordered a cremation with no calling hours or services. His wishes will be carried out. Do you have any questions?"

"Yes. I would like to know if I have to leave here now."

"No, you are paid to the end of this year and Mrs. Anderson tells me you are of an age when you would leave anyway. Since that is only a month away, it will give me some time to get things in order to turn everything over into your name. There will be an official reading of the will and at that time I'll have everything ready for you to sign. If there isn't anything else, I'll be on my way."

Mrs. Anderson followed him to the door. "Thank you for coming."

"You're welcome and you'll be hearing from me soon," he said.

The next few weeks were busy for the two girls with finals, graduation and their preparations for leaving the orphanage.

Finally, the will was read and the estate including the deed, bank accounts, interest earning stocks and bonds, along with other assets were transferred to Judy Collins. She was astounded. She had no idea her uncle was wealthy.

The lawyer told her he would continue as her advisor while she became more knowledgeable with the demands of her fortune. He suggested it would take some time.

"As things come up I will contact you and help you with due dates of taxes, insurance and such things until you are ready to decide if you want me to continue to be your lawyer."

"My uncle must have been satisfied with you, so I don't see any reason to change."

"Thank you. What I'll do is get a ledger and we'll make an appointment so you can learn what you need to know to manage your funds. Let me ask you something else. Did you plan to go on to college?"

"I hadn't thought about it. Before all this came up, I wouldn't have had the money. I majored in business courses in high school, so I guess if I wanted to further my education I would go to one of the business schools."

"Well, there certainly isn't any rush. I'd advise you to take your time and think about it, consider it later. I'm sure you'll want to get yourself settled in before you rush into something new. Your uncle owned two cars. They are locked in the garage. He was not one for anything flashy, but they are good automobiles and well cared for. The checking account is ready for you, so don't be afraid to use it for anything you need." He handed her the keys to the house.

"When you are ready to leave here, call me and I'll take you. We'll go to the bank and withdraw cash for your everyday needs. Since you won't have transportation until you get your license, I will make a list of phone numbers for fast food delivery places and taxi service. I'm sure this will be inconvenient, so I would advise you to take a quick course in learning to drive and get your license as soon as possible. I guess that about covers it, so I'll be on my way." He handed her his card.

"If you have any questions, call my office and I'll get back to you when I can."

"Thank you so much for all your help," Judy said. After the lawyer had left, Dora heard all the details of the conversation from Judy.

"It's nice you won't have to worry about money or a home when you leave here," Dora said with sadness edging her voice.

She knew Judy well enough to know what her response would be, but she wanted to hear it from Judy.

"Oh, Dora! Don't be silly. I don't have a home to go to. WE have an estate house to go to and WE are rich." Judy did a little dance. "What's mine is yours too, didn't you know?"

Of course, she did know, but it irritated Dora thinking she would be obliged to Judy and wouldn't have unlimited access to the money.

A short time before the girls were ready to leave the orphanage, Mrs. Anderson contacted Dean Warren and set the time and date for him to take them to their new home. Warren hadn't told them anything about the house. They had no idea what to expect.

The house was situated on the edge of the city in a residential area. When Warren turned onto the cul-de-sac, the girls were alert, watching as they passed well-kept houses on both sides of the street and a small park. When he came to the end of the cul-de-sac and turned into the driveway, the big rambling house came into view. He glanced at the girls' awestruck faces as he parked the car. Neither girl moved. He laughed.

"Come on you two, let's go take a look inside."

They had a good time shopping the city malls for their new wardrobe, although their taste in fashion was very different. Judy chose the quieter colors and reserved styles, while Dora bought the more elaborate and bold fashions.

Judy chose the smaller car and enrolled in an adult driving class, while Dora chose the larger vehicle. She drove it around the yard a few times for practice and went for her license and passed.

Under Dora's directions, the second floor was renovated to be Judy's private space with a spacious living room, two bedrooms and a bath. The first floor was similarly arranged for Dora. Although it hadn't been Judy's choice to have the second-floor apartment, they were both happy with this arrangement. Both floors had their own entrance.

They shared the kitchen duties, although it pleased Judy to do most of the cooking and grocery shopping. They hired a cleaning agency to come in once a week, alternating the cleaning of one floor each week and a grounds keeper came to care for the lawns and shrubs one day a week.

The first year was busy and exciting for both of them. The lawyer scheduled a number of conferences with Judy. She learned the finer points of accounting, along with the rules and limitations of being rich. During one of the early sessions, she set up a separate account for Dora, with a generous allowance to be deposited each month.

Meanwhile, Dora spent her time planning and supervising the renovations of the house, but as the work neared completion, she became restless and began looking over the city's night life. She began touring the higher-class night clubs.

Judy had found new confidence in making her own decisions and refused to accompany Dora. As Dora patronized the various clubs, she had no problem finding male escorts among the patrons. Dora explained to Judy about the pleasure she derived from her ability to manipulate a man into doing what she wanted.

Judy had seen Dora in action, practicing on every man she encountered, whether it was a president of a company or a ditch-digger. She told Dora she was uncomfortable with this type of manipulation.

"Oh, Judy," Dora said, "don't be foolish. It's all part of a game men and women play. It's harmless."

In conversation with her escorts, Dora became aware of the potential of these club visits. It seemed that many of them were in the city temporarily for a company conference, political meeting, or sales people making contacts with executives of large enterprises. All were well-to-do and many were wealthy.

After a few weeks of experience she decided that most men, with their thinly veiled propositions, had a sexual agenda in mind. Why couldn't she cash in on their weakness? To Dora, it was the first step toward success and the power she longed for. If they were going to get into her bed, they would pay her the exuberant price she was asking. Finally, Dora was prosperous because they willingly paid her price. She had her long-hoped-for power.

Judy never told Dora the circumstances of how she met Martin. During Judy's business school training, Dora saw very little of Judy and shortly afterward Judy announced she was going to move in with Martin and they would be married soon. Dora was shocked since Judy had never mentioned him. Close to a year went by with only short messages from Judy. Dora worried she might want to reclaim the house after she was married, but she decided not to spend much time thinking about it. She could now afford to buy a house of her own, but her customers were accustomed to her location and she assumed they liked the fact that it was in a secluded area.

One night, less than a year later, Judy was back to re-occupy the upstairs flat. She told Dora the wedding was off and she was pregnant. She would not explain further, but she wanted nothing more to do with Martin. Dora had to admit that, despite the fact Judy disapproved of her business, she did stay out of her way.

Shortly after the baby was born, Judy began talking about buying a Bed and Breakfast. It would give her something to do and she would still be able to care for her son. While Judy was in the process of finding a Bed and Breakfast, she became sick. As she grew weaker, she was forced to face the fact that something was drastically wrong. After many doctor visits and numerous tests, she was told she was dying. She had possibly a year to get things in order. Judy's biggest concern was her beloved son, Greg. What would happen to him?

It hadn't taken Dora long to realize that here was a well-managed fortune at her disposal and the trump card, she knew, was Greg. What would happen to him? She began paying a great deal of loving attention to him and hinting to Judy that she was looking to get away from her vocation.

As her illness progressed, Judy went to her lawyer and planned Greg's future. After providing for Greg's college fund and setting aside a third of the interest-paying stocks for his twenty-first birthday, she turned everything over to Dora as long as she got away from her prostitution profession and took care of Greg.

The lawyer advised her to contact the boy's father and tell him he had a son. Judy did not agree but said she would think about it. About a week before she died, she told Dora about Martin and that she didn't want Greg around his illegal drug connections,

She said she had it set up with her lawyer so Martin couldn't take Greg. Dora was to contact Martin to come to the hospital and she would tell him about his son.

Dora wasn't as sure as Judy and she wasn't about to put the money in jeopardy if the law decided in Martin's favor. Dora had purposely waited until Judy was in a coma before contacting Martin. Despite Martin's many hours spent waiting for Judy to regain consciousness, she died without talking to him. Dora wasn't about to tell him that Greg was his son.

As time passed, Dora learned of Martin's thriving drug business. He spent his spare time with Dora and Greg. Having left prostitution, she decided to add selling drugs to her money-making agenda and asked Martin to help her set it up.

Dora Roberts was finally making it on her own. She felt the power. Dora stood and stretched, getting the kinks out of her body as she reminisced.

Martin Delmont glanced at his watch. There wasn't any doubt in his mind Dora would not only be ready, but probably waiting. She was never late and demanded promptness from everyone doing business with her. There were other less attractive peculiarities about her, but he suffered them in silence because of her abilities in other areas where he was weak. This fact indicated, at least in his mind, that they made a good team. She had an acute work ethic and knew intuitively how to handle most people to her benefit. This was extremely valuable in their operation. The knowledge she gained from her prostitution days taught her that her good looks were often the key to opening doors. She was difficult to cope with, yet he considered himself lucky to have her as his partner. Even so, he didn't deceive himself. He knew her to be ruthless when it came to her goals. She allowed nothing and no one to stand in her way where money was concerned.

It had always baffled him the way she treated Greg. Martin was drawn to this boy because he belonged to Judy. Dora had told him she had taken the boy in at the request of his dying mother. He must have come with a large sum of money; otherwise, Martin doubted she would have agreed. The only thing she ever cared about was money; it showed in her every undertaking.

Dora said she was fond of Judy and they were almost like sisters. It was certainly obvious that Judy had been generous in her dealings with Dora. Anyone might think Dora would have felt some fondness for the boy, if for no other reason than he was Judy's son, but it apparently never happened. It annoyed Martin that Dora had never told Greg she wasn't his mother or told him anything about Judy. Martin supposed his own undying love for Judy influenced his thinking. He had never loved any woman, before or after, the way he did Judy.

Martin often wondered who the boy's father was and why Judy hadn't contacted him to take the boy instead of Dora. Of course, at the time Dora wasn't dealing in drugs or he was sure it would have been a different story. It was the drug business that had driven Judy away from him.

Greg seemed to be a good kid, a little sullen sometimes, but who could blame him the way Dora treated him. He had run drugs for them since he was a little tyke and without a hitch too. Dora felt the only way to keep him in line was with beatings and fear. Maybe she was right. Most dealers felt the same way.

As Martin turned into the driveway, he wondered what Dora was up to now. They had been working the local bars and other gathering places to pick up new customers, but recently he had sensed a growing restlessness in Dora. Once each week he had been going to the city and getting the supplies for his customers and he and Dora were delivering them. For some reason, this seemed to disturb Dora. He chalked it up to her being pregnant.

He heard that women were moody at times during pregnancy. He sighed. He didn't suppose he'd ever understand her moods, pregnant or otherwise.

Dora stood in the window watching as Martin drove into the yard. *He's a pleasant diversion*, she thought, but she didn't picture him in her future plans. He didn't have the kind of drive it takes to make it big in this business, but for now she needed his connection with Frank Brant. It wasn't the right time for her to start up with someone new. Until after this baby thing was completed, she'd have to go through Martin. Besides, she needed his money to get her new plan started.

Martin tapped on the door and walked into the kitchen. "Hi, how's it going?" he asked.

"Fine," she said, sitting down at the table. He walked to the cupboard and took out a cup and reaching for the coffee pot, filled his cup. He walked to the table and sat down across from her. "So, what's up?"

"I want to start with our new customers now instead of waiting. Do you think Frank would deliver out here?" Martin's face registered surprise, "You want him coming here to the house?"

"No, I'll explain more in a minute. I just wanted to find out if you thought he would deliver the goods out here if you asked him to."

"Well, depending on the circumstances, I've no doubt something could be arranged with him, but more to the point is why would you want to start now? I thought you wanted to wait until after the baby situation was settled before we went all out."

"Well, after giving it more thought, I don't see that it would cause a problem with the baby deal. We have more than fifty customers lined up to add to what you already have. I understand from talking to them, the leaders of these small groups are going into the city to pick up their supplies. Most of them are dealing directly with Brant. They seem to be getting more fearful of this direct contact and would welcome someone else making the dangerous trips. We wouldn't be cutting into any dealers' territory, but we would be taking a percentage of the profit from Brant. It might be worth it to him to have someone else doing the lion's share of the work and getting out of the police spotlight. So, what do you think?"

"Of course, I can't speak for Frank, but I would think it would be more convenient for him, even though he'd have to deliver out here once or twice a week."

Dora nodded, "Good. Now that brings me to the second part of my plan. A short distance behind the house, there's a side road that's a crossover from the main road to the north beach. It's seldom used. Greg and I could clear a path and we could have Frank deliver the supplies to a designated spot at a set time. Greg would be there waiting and bring them back here where we could pick them up and deliver them."

Dora waited for Martin's reaction. Martin whistled. "You really have been doing a lot of thinking." He hesitated, sipping his coffee. "Of course, again it depends on Frank's approval."

Dora smiled, "Now for the third proposal. What do you think about opening a tavern somewhere near here? Would you be willing to be partners in it? We would have a place for our customers to come to us instead of meeting them all over creation and we'd have a legitimate business for cover."

"Wow," Martin said, "that's sure something to digest. Do you have any money to invest in a deal like this?"

"Yes, I can spare about twenty-thousand to start and then later, after I get rid of this baby, there will be more. One of the reasons I want to start now is that I can't see letting that money go to someone else when we could use it, if we go into this plan."

"Have you contacted the lawyer yet about the baby deal?"

"Yes," Dora shrugged, "he had a customer booked already. He's working with them on the price. He thinks they'll go for a hundred grand. I've been working on him to give me sixty percent instead of the usual fifty-fifty split. He finally agreed."

"The baby is due in June?" Dora nodded.

"Do you have a place in mind for this tavern deal?" Martin was pensive.

"No, but I figured we could start looking right away, if the plan was agreeable to you."

"There are quite a few details to be discussed before we get too far into this, but the first thing I have to do is talk with Frank and see what he thinks about the drop point and get that worked out. If all goes well with that, I could start with the real estate agents and see what's available locally. I could probably weed out a lot of the unlikely prospects and save you some time and energy. Then, if I think any of them have potential, we can go together to check them out." Martin's voice carried an edge of excitement.

"That sounds great to me," Dora sighed with relief, "but be sure to let me know as soon as you hear from Brant."

Nodding, Martin stood, preparing to leave. Seeing movement out of the corner of his eye, he glanced out the kitchen window. He spied Greg standing beside his car, looking it over. "Greg's home," he said.

Dora nodded, glancing at her watch. "School must have had an early day." She would have preferred Martin was gone before he came home, but no matter, she shrugged.

31

Greg walked up to the car. He had to admit it sure was a beauty. Business must be good, he thought ruefully. He recognized the car belonged to Martin Delmont. The memory stirred the dormant fear that was always with him. He walked up the steps to the back door and through the hall into the kitchen. Greg glanced at the well-dressed man standing next to his mother, but said nothing.

"You know Martin, Greg, say hello." Dora's tone held a warning.

Greg said hello without looking at him. Martin extended his hand toward Greg, who ignored it and walked past him to his bedroom.

"We have been discussing my new job." Dora exchanged a knowing glance with Martin.

Greg stopped and turned back toward them. "Your new job? How can you work?" he asked, motioning toward her protruding stomach.

His mother laughed, "Don't worry, I'll be able to handle this job without any trouble. You go along now and change your clothes. We'll talk about this later."

As he walked to his room, his intuition told him if Martin Delmont was nosing around, you could bet there would be drugs involved. When he heard the car leave the driveway, he went out to his mother. "Drugs again, isn't it?"

"None of your business what I decide to do," she raged. She reached out and slapped him hard across the face, sending him reeling away from her. "That's for your insolence."

Anger blazed in his eyes as he turned back to face her. "I have every right to ask anything I want to. Who is it that always ends up doing your dirty work?"

Shock registered momentarily on her face. He had never stood up to her. She reached out, grabbed him by the front of his shirt and yanked him toward her.

"Where do you get off yelling at me, you loathsome brat? You'll do as you're told and don't you forget it." She shoved him away from her, then walked past him out the door.

Greg pulled himself up to a sitting position and leaned against the wall. *I've got to get away; anywhere away from here*, he thought, but he couldn't just walk away. He had certainly thought about it often enough, but he hadn't figured out how he would be able to get away with it. He knew all too well that the drug dealers would move mountains to track him down and kill him. He knew too much about their operation for any fond farewells. If only he were bigger. Nobody believed that he was twelve. How could he try to pass for older? How could he be so small, since his mother was just under six feet tall? Of course, he never knew his father. Maybe he was small too. With the kind of business Dora had been in, his father could be anybody. It was possible even she didn't know, but whatever, it had nothing to do with the predicament he was in right now. He needed more time to plan some kind of permanent escape. He'd just have to go along with whatever they had waiting for him this time. What else could he do? He wrapped his arms around his knees and leaned his head against them, only to feel a sharp pain. He quickly pulled his head back and carefully felt a raised bump on his forehead where he had fallen against the door frame. *Oh damn*, he thought, *another bruise he would have to explain away to the teachers tomorrow*. At least being in a new school, they hadn't heard any of the old excuses he had used in the city school.

Martin had talked with Brant and he was agreeable to delivering the supplies to Carson City. Dora wasted no time getting things in motion. She wanted to get it started by the weekend.

The next morning, Greg was surprised to see his mother at the breakfast table, sipping her coffee. She was never up before he went to school.

"Good morning, Greg," she said cheerfully. Greg made a sound that sounded more like a grunt than a greeting of acknowledgement. He went about getting his cereal and toast ready for his breakfast. Now and then he glanced in her direction as if she was some strange apparition that he hoped had disappeared while his back was turned. Sitting down at the table with his head bowed, looking into the bowl, he began to eat.

"Greg, I'm sorry I lost my temper yesterday," Dora began, her voice gentle and contrite. "I know you hate doing this, but I have to make money to keep this house going, especially now with the baby coming. There will be extra expenses. Besides, there's much money to be made and if we don't get it, someone else will, so why not us?"

Her words sounded stiff with her attempt to be patient. "Keep in mind," she continued, "it was money from the sale of drugs that paid for this house. I thought you liked living out here in the country."

"The reason I like it here is because there hasn't been any drug business," he said flatly. "Most people can make money without selling drugs and other things," he said sarcastically. He had emphasized the word 'other' as he raised his eyes in time to see the anger rising in her face.

"Ok mister high and mighty, whether you like it or not, you will do as you are told," she said through clenched teeth, "and when you come home from school today, you will learn what has to be done and do it."

Greg pushed away from his half-eaten breakfast, picked up his backpack and walked to the door before turning toward her.

Looking directly at her, he said in a flat, even voice, "I hate you." Slamming the door, he left for school.

Dora Roberts sipped her coffee. It hadn't escaped her notice that Greg was becoming increasingly belligerent as he grew older. It was difficult for her to control his aggressive attitude. Then, too, there was her own short-tempered reaction. She was sorry to see the bruise on his forehead, knowing how jumpy school officials are about child abuse. Not that he didn't deserve it, with his smart mouthing, but she didn't need any more problems right now. Dora sighed, there wasn't anything to worry about anyway. Greg was used to making up stories to cover his bruises and he'd do it this time too, if he knew what was good for him.

They were on the brink of changing this nickel and dime operation into something worthwhile. Maybe if things worked out, she could get rid of the miserable kid once and for all. Of course, now everything was more or less on hold until after the baby business was behind her. She must have been crazy to let Martin talk her into this situation, no matter how much money was involved.

She signed. It would be over soon, but right now she had to think about this new business. It had been a relief when Martin told her that Brant had okayed the idea. One step at a time. She smiled. Now she just had to test the timing for delivery.

Later that afternoon, when Greg got home from school, they went out to the field.

"All right, then go," she said, giving him a little nudge and glancing at her watch. When he returned, she wrote down the time.

"Now, there's one more thing to do and we're finished." She handed him a brown paper bag and a small hammer. Greg looked into the bag, frowning.

"These are reflectors. Divide them equally and attach them to the trees facing you along the path and on the way back do the same thing with the other half of them. When you're finished, come into the house, I'll be waiting for you."

Greg glanced at her, anger flashing in his eyes as he realized he would be running through the woods at night. He was tired and he resented her huffy attitude. She hadn't told him this was going to be a night operation, but why would she bother telling him anything? After all, wasn't he just her slave to be ordered around?

When Greg returned, he walked slowly into the hall as Dora walked in from the kitchen. She stopped in front of the closet. Retrieving a key from her jacket pocket, she unlocked the door and handed him the key. Pointing to the lowest shelf, she said, "On this shelf will be a package. You will take it to meet the pickup car. You will never touch the key at any other time. You are to stand behind the last tree on the edge of the woods until a car comes and stops. Do not break cover until the car has completely stopped and rolled down the window."

Greg wondered how the person in the car would know where to stop, since the path was not visible from the road, but he wasn't going to give her the satisfaction of asking. He didn't care if the car never found the right place to stop, but he was curious.

"He will take your package and hand you another one, which you will bring back here and set on the shelf, then you lock the door." Dora looked down at him, wondering if he was paying attention. She felt like slapping that contemptible smirk off his face, but she continued.

"You will leave the house at eleven forty-five at night. Here is a flashlight and you already have the alarm clock. Do not be late or it will be the sorriest day of your life. I will come and pick the package up at twelve-thirty. After you have finished the run, you are to go back to bed. Another thing, don't think you can miss school the next day because you're too tired. I don't want any problems with school officials." She glanced down at him again. "There won't be a pickup every night, so you will look in the closet when you get home from school and if there's a package there, you'll know you have a delivery."

Wonderful, Greg thought, *a package of money for a package of drugs. All neat and tidy, just as it was in the city.* Greg did not speak to his mother for two days. He did the things she told him to do and nursed his hatred. Dora was growing impatient with his morose silence, but she hesitated to challenge his behavior, fearing it would induce a difficult situation. With this new operation just beginning, she didn't need any problems.

"Maybe we could agree on a substantial allowance, if this thing works out the way I think it will," she said, thinking to pacify him. He turned toward her, glaring, "I don't want any of your stinking drug money. I'll work for my money as I always have."

Since he had been going to school in Carson Cove, a boy in high school had died of an overdose. He couldn't have felt any guiltier than if he had handed the boy the drugs. It had been some comfort to him to know he was out of the drug business at the time, but now they were ready to start again. His conscience was already gnawing at his insides.

Chapter Four

Martin had searched the area with one real estate agent after another, trying to find a suitable building for their business. Finally, he had found one with real potential. He was excited. It sat back from the road some distance in a wooded area, which he considered to be a distinct advantage. Of course, as he expected, it would need extensive alterations, but he knew this wouldn't be a problem.

There were no houses within a mile in either direction, which meant they wouldn't have to contend with irate neighbors complaining about noise. Now, if only Dora would agree.

He glanced at his watch to be sure he would be on time arriving at Dora's house. They were to meet the agent at the house in question in a half hour.

When Dora was seated in the car next to Martin, he asked, "How are you feeling?"

"I'm all right I guess. I'm beginning to bulge some now, which is normal for six months I guess. I'll have to go shopping for some maternity clothes soon. I know the worst is yet to come."

Martin smiled at her gloomy expression. Dora abruptly changed the subject. "Have you been through this place?"

"Yes and I'm very hopeful. There are many things right about it and the things that aren't right can be easily changed, I think, I don't want to say anymore until you see it for yourself."

They turned off the main highway onto the long driveway. The trees were dense along both sides, forming a sheltered arch over the narrow road. Rays of sunlight danced here and there on their way through the foliage. They drove close to a hundred yards before the driveway curved gently to the right into the clearing where the house stood. It was a large two-story square building with four windows across the front and two on the second floor. In the center was an entrance into the main floor and on the left side there was a small porch with steps leading to a door.

Dora was impressed, "It's in a fantastic location. You couldn't ask for better than this with trees all the way around and room on either side for parking, plus the parking area in the front."

Martin laughed at her enthusiasm. "Do you think we ought to go look at the inside of the house? The real estate woman is waiting."

After the initial greetings and introduction, the real estate agent unlocked the door and took them from room to room through the house. The direction her sales pitch had taken indicated her assumption that they were looking for a home. They said nothing to correct her.

As they moved along, both were visualizing the possible renovations needed to turn it into a place of business. Dora took notice of the three large rooms across the front of the house, which had been the living room, dining room and den. *Perfect*, she thought, *for the bar room with the kitchen behind the dining area*. There were four big rooms upstairs and Dora was particularly interested in them. The real estate agent was offering bits and pieces of information while Dora wandered around the rooms, her mind occupied with restructuring the four rooms. Her mind was occupied with restructuring the four rooms to accommodate two offices, a sitting room and possibly a small bar. As she opened the second door to one of the rooms facing the back, she found a double staircase. She was standing on the landing when Martin and the agent joined her.

"This is interesting," she said.

"Yes," the agent nodded. "The staircase to the left goes down to the side of the building and the one to your right leads down to a storage room behind the kitchen. If you're finished up here, we can go down and take a look."

As they paraded down the stairs, Dora's mind suggested a double escape route for her customers. As the agent led the way down to the first floor, she lost hope for a sale. They had almost nothing to say, nor did they ask any questions.

"Here we are, back where we started. Now would you like to go down to look at the basement?" she asked.

"Yes, we would," Martin replied.

The agent went ahead and switched on the light, showing a spotless full basement. Dora stayed on the landing while Martin followed the agent down and examined the foundation, hot water tanks and furnace. Upon reaching the main floor again, Martin asked the agent, "Could we have a few minutes alone?"

"You sure can," she beamed, hope for a sale rising once again. Maybe they were interested after all. "I'll be outside. Take all the time you need, I'm in no hurry."

When the agent closed the door behind her, Dora became animated. "It's absolutely perfect," she said. "The three rooms across the front would be the bar room with the archway and the petition removed. The two bathrooms could be on the end," she said, pointing. "We'd have to put a door to the outside at the foot of the stairs so our other customers wouldn't have to go through the bar unless they wanted to and upstairs we can each have an office adjoining a waiting room like a regular business. What do you think?" she concluded.

"To begin with, I know for a fact you were paying attention. Yes, I do think it's perfect for what you want to do, but you do realize there will be quite a few renovations, don't you?"

"Oh yes, of course I do and I also know there are a lot of other things involved before we sign any papers."

Martin rubbed the nape of his neck, squinting. "I figure we could bring the price down some and make a purchase offer. It will give me some time to check with the zoning board since this was a residence, we need to find out if we can have a business here. If that flies, I'll see about a liquor license."

"It sounds good to me. Did you mention the water situation?"

"It was one of the first things I asked when she first showed me the house. It's supplied through the town, so we're all set there."

After a date was set for the next meeting with the agent, they started for home. Martin could see Dora's mood had improved considerably. Glancing at her face, he could almost hear her mind at work.

"How about a little celebrating?" Martin asked, "We could go over to my place, have a few drinks and later go out to dinner. What do you think?"

"Sure, why not? But I better lay off the drinks if I'm going to get through this pregnancy. I don't want to end up with a defective baby. There wouldn't be any money down that road. We could work on a floor plan and the changes we want to make."

Great idea! By the way you were talking, I see you agree we should keep the drug business away from the bar and use it as a front."

"Definitely. The fewer people involved with that end of it, the fewer chances of problems."

At Martin's apartment, he mixed himself a drink and poured Dora a glass of ginger ale. Dora looked around the large room. She had to admit, he had good taste. Everything was color-coordinated and the furniture grouping made the large room look cozy and warm. For a moment, she longed for something like this room. She was going to be moving up in the world soon and then she'd have the best of everything. Right now, she didn't need any extra baggage. Martin handed the glass to her and sat down beside her. He reached across the coffee table and pulled a small stack of papers over in front of her.

"Last night, after finding the house, I was excited and couldn't sleep. I was thinking of ways we could expand our business and this is what I came up with." He handed her a sheet of paper on which he had drawn a rough map of the surrounding area. Dora took a sip of her drink and leaned forward to look closer.

"There are five towns around us," he said, pointing at the map, "a kind of irregular wagon wheel of towns and we're the hub. Here's Port Selma on the east end of the lake, Fort Bardin on the southeast corner; Scofield on the northwest; Donelville on the north and Hylandburg on the southwest. Carson Cove is roughly in the middle. Most of them are around ten miles from here, except Scofield, which is closer. He leaned back, sipping his drink.

Dora frowned, "And your point is?"

"My point is, why couldn't we be the suppliers for these towns? They could come to us after we have the tavern up and running, sell them their drugs and we take the commission. What do you think?"

"Oh sure, Martin. I supposed you think these dealers are going to smile and shake your hand while you take over their territory."

"No, you don't understand. We wouldn't be taking over their territory, we'd be selling to the dealers from those towns. They would still be dealing with their customers. Knowing most of them, I could contact them after we're set up for business and see what I could do. I know for a fact that Brant supplies them now. Of course, Brant would have to agree, but he delivers to us already. That way, instead of them all running out separately to buy from Brant, he could make one big delivery to our office and we could do all the work for him. Of course, his commission would come from selling the drugs to us, just as it does with our orders."

"Have you talked this over with Brant?" Dora asked.

"No, I figured on leaving things the way they were until we get everything organized. Besides, I wanted to talk to you about it first; after all, we are partners in this business."

"That's true, we are." Dora was amazed. She would have to give Martin credit, he had never shown a spark of initiative or shown this kind of bold thinking before.

"You must have confidence that Brant will go for this idea." Martin looked thoughtful, "I've tried to think of all the angles. Of course, it would mean some of his profit would come to us; but, on the other h and we'd be doing most of the work. He'd deliver it in bulk to us. We'd do all the measuring and filling the orders. The dealers would have no personal contact with him. This would be an advantage for him as far as he is concerned. The last time I talked with Brant, he told me the law had been giving him too much attention lately. All things considered, I think he will go for it."

"Do you think we should go ahead with buying this place before we talk to Brant?" asked Dora. "Suppose he doesn't like our idea?"

"How would we be any worse off than we are now? He has already agreed to make the trip out here in the middle of the night. If he doesn't agree, we'd still have an office for our own buyers to come to instead of us setting up meeting places to go to them. Even if we only have our own small operation to deal with, it would be neater." He laughed, "And who knows, we might be making money on our bar business as well."

Chapter Five

Greg's school and jobs kept him away from the house most of the day. When he went home after school, it was only long enough to change his clothes and grab a snack before he was off again.

There was no more snow shoveling with the end of winter. His jobs now consisted of raking lawns and cleaning up the flower beds, readying them for a new season or possibly new plants.

He seldom went home much before dark, but today, after he changed his clothes, he sat gloomily on the top step of the back porch. He should have come to terms with his feelings about dealing drugs a long time ago. Except for the location, selling drugs was selling drugs, whether it was in Carson Cove or in the city. He was never going to like it; but for some reason, starting up again was plaguing him almost to the point of sickness. He should be used to his nagging conscience by now. Why was it worse out here than in the city?

When his mother had first forced him into carrying drugs, she had instilled fear; fear of beatings, fear of the police, fear of the street gangs and most of all, fear of the dealers he had to contact when he picked up the drugs. At the time, he had been very young and his fear had been more about the physical pain and even fear for his life more than anything else.

As he grew older, he understood the full meaning of what he was doing. Now he knew exactly what the drugs were doing to people. His conscience took over, resulting in his obsessive hatred for the drug business.

Preoccupied with his thoughts, he left the steps and walked into the woods. Since he had cleared the path, he hadn't walked the distance in the daylight. About halfway through, he stopped and sat down on the ground, leaning his back against one of the big trees. Sighing, he shut his eyes, letting the quiet peace of the forest surround him. He listened to the low moaning as the spring breeze stirred the still-barren tree branches and he tried to analyze his feelings. He realized he would never feel comfortable with his part in the drug trade, but here in Carson Cove, the way things were set up, it should be a piece of cake. There was nothing to worry about with the police as there was on the city streets because he didn't carry drugs on the streets out here. There were no street gangs nor any drug dealers to contend with since the only one he ever saw was the one in the delivery car and he hadn't even spoken to him! What was the problem?

The time before the drugs started up again had been the happiest time of his life. He loved the people he worked for. In the city, people had been so distant and impersonal, but here it was different. The people in Carson Cove were open and friendly. They acted as if he was smart and they enjoyed talking to him. It was almost like they thought he was doing them a favor whenever he came around. For the first time in his life, he had felt good about himself.

Suddenly it came to him; it was him! Now the drugs were back and the person they liked and admired didn't exist. He was a fraud, an impostor. He was deceiving them every time he went near them. It was like he had an incurable sickness he would always have to carry with him as long as he had any part in the drug business.

Greg sighed heavily and stood. He began walking out of the woods toward home, his shoulders sagging with the burden of what he knew.

Chapter Six

It was the last day of June when Dora Roberts went into labor. Moving down the short hall to Greg's bedroom, she entered and as she reached the bed, shook him awake.

Greg sat up, "What?" He squinted as she turned on the light.

"I have to go to the hospital now, the baby's coming." Greg watched as her face grew pale with the onset of another pain. He said nothing, waiting until her body relaxed and the pain subsided. He experienced a twinge of pity as he watched the pain come and go, but he had received too many painful blows from her hands to want to share any part of her pain now.

"When will you be back?" he asked.

"I don't know; maybe in a couple of days if everything goes all right. I just don't know," she said impatiently. At the door of his room, she turned back, "And another thing, you are never and I mean never, to mention this baby to anyone. Is that understood?"

He nodded. He wondered what that was all about. Of course, she had warned him many times before about saying anything to anyone about what went on at home, but he couldn't imagine why talking about the baby would have anything to do with her precious drug occupation. Well, he thought, she had nothing to worry about. He wasn't about to have anything to do with that baby.

He stood at the window watching her drive down the long driveway. Maybe after the baby is born she might have to give up her contacts with drugs. He could only hope.

During the time she was gone, Greg heard nothing. Shortly after noon on Sunday, he heard the car coming up the driveway. He watched from the window as Dora carried the baby into the house. She set the carrier down on the kitchen table, walked down the hall to her bedroom and unlocked the door. Curiosity brought Greg out of his bedroom to the kitchen table. He moved the basket enough to see the baby's face. His eyes were wide open and seemed to be looking directly at him. Greg stood in awed silence. It was the first time he had ever seen a newborn baby. There was no doubt in his mind that this was the most beautiful thing he had ever seen. He was so engrossed that when the baby moved its hand aimlessly, Greg was startled and involuntarily withdrew his hand. A flood of yearning and love swept over him. "It's looking right at me," he whispered.

As Dora returned, she heard Greg's response to the baby.

"A baby can't see anything except shadows when they are first born," Dora stated flatly, "and 'it' is a boy."

It might be true that other babies couldn't see, Greg thought, but not this one. He reached into the carrier. Taking the tiny hand in his, he ran his thumb over the soft skin, marveling. The baby's fingers curled around Greg's. In that moment, the bond between the two boys was forever forged.

"What's his name?" Greg asked, not taking his eyes away from the baby.

"Aaron," she replied, her eyes narrowing as she watched the effect the baby was having on Greg.

"How did you come up with that name?" Greg wondered, finally pulling his eyes away from the baby.

"Oh, I couldn't think of a name so I let the nurse name him." Greg nodded, but said nothing, though he thought it was a little odd to let the nurse name your baby.

Dora Roberts studied Greg's reaction to the baby closely. She now had the weapon to bring him back under her control. Even though it would be temporary, it would be long enough. Her mind reeled, calculating the possibilities.

After a few seconds passed, she said, "I think I'm going to have you put the crib in your room. With me working nights, you'll have to take care of him." She waited for the sullen objections, but none came.

Greg turned to her, "I'm afraid I might hurt him. I don't know how to take care of a baby."

"Oh, don't worry, you can learn," Dora said, "I'll be here for the next two days and I'll teach you."

"How's that going to work on the nights I have to go for pick-ups?"

"He'll be here when you get back."

"What do you mean, I should leave him here alone?"

Well, I don't imagine he'll go anywhere, do you?" her words were lightly sarcastic.

During the next two days, Greg learned the fundamentals of child care. At first, he was slow and awkward handling the baby, but as time went on he became more relaxed. To Greg, the tiny boy was a kindred soul; someone to cuddle and love. He could not imagine his mother ever loving him. He poured all his pent-up affection into the child, considering him to be the most fantastic gift he would ever receive. The baby brought meaning to his lonely life. Aaron belonged to him.

Dora didn't do anything for the baby. Greg couldn't understand his mother's indifference, although it didn't surprise him. It was beyond his comprehension as to how anyone could not love Aaron. As far as Greg knew, she neither held him nor looked at him. Two days after she came home from the hospital she went back to work. She left for work at three in the afternoon and rarely came home before four in the morning. If there was a pickup, she came home long enough to take the package and leave again.

Greg had his yard work in the mornings and early afternoons, which now took on new importance. Where once he was saving money to get away from his mother and the drugs, now his plans included Aaron. If ever he left, it wouldn't be without his brother. As far as he could see, it wouldn't bother his mother if they both were gone. She sure didn't spend a lot of time thinking about either one of them.

Now, with Aaron, he couldn't think of a way he could leave. About the best he could figure was he'd have to wait until he was out of high school, which meant another five years. It seemed a very long time to wait, but at least during that time he would be there to protect him. He was sure of one thing; he'd never allow his mother to treat Aaron the way she treated him. He'd kill her first.

Now that school was out, Greg arranged his schedule around Aaron's feeding time and rode his bike home between jobs. Although his mother was there in the house sleeping, by now he realized she wouldn't get up to care for the baby. In spite of such a worrisome situation, everything seemed to be going smoothly. As long as Aaron was fed and dry, he slept most of the day. After his mother left each day, Greg would put the baby clothes into the wash, he did the few dishes were in the sink and his other household chores. It was Aaron's time to be awake so Greg buckled him into the carrier and took him from room to room as he did his chores. He kept a running conversation going, stopping often to play.

After his chores were finished, he bathed the baby and dressed him for bed. At ten o'clock he gave him his last bottle. After the first two weeks, Aaron slept all night, taking some of the worry out of his delivery nights, although Greg never felt easy about leaving him alone. Despite frustrations connected with the drug running trade, Greg was reasonably happy.

Greg had to line up his summer yard work. Through the last few years he had saved a considerable amount of money, but now it looked like it might be years before he could leave. It would cost more because Aaron would be involved.

As he accepted new jobs, he kept Aaron's schedule in mind, since the work now had to fit certain time slots. Toward the end of the winter, he had lost two of his customers. Mrs. Potter, needing more care, had moved in with her family and Mrs. Kincade had died. He would like to find jobs to fill those two empty slots.

On Saturday, as he was finishing Mrs. Talbert's yard, he noticed a car in Mrs. Kincade's driveway. If someone was going to move into the house, maybe he could get his summer job back.

When Mrs. Talbert came to the door to pay him, he thanked her for the extra she always gave him.

"Oh, honey, it's no more than you deserve. You do such a good job for me." She looked around the yard as though someone might hear and lowering her voice, she added, "all my friends are so jealous, don't cha' know; they have to put up with the job their husbands do." Greg smiled as the old lady chuckled at her own little joke.

After a moment, Greg asked, "Do you know if someone is living in Mrs. Kincade's house, up at the end of the road?" Greg nodded his head in that direction.

"Well, I don't know if she's living there, don't cha' know, but there has been a pretty young lady coming and going up there quite often lately. It might be Martha's granddaughter. Whoever it is drives a small blue car. She might be up there now. Seems like I saw her go by early this morning."

Greg nodded, "I think I'll ride up there and check it out. She might need some help getting the yard back in shape."

He waved at the old lady as he rode out of the driveway. As he neared the house, he could hear the murmuring of the Little Weseka River as it whispered its way along the edge of the yard. The Kincade house was the last house on the road; the north side of the yard sloped down to the river's edge. He loved the beautiful location of the house. He used to fill the bird feeders on the back lawn for Mrs. Kincade. There was continuous activity as the birds flitted back and forth between the feeders and the trees bordering the yard. The feeders were quiet now and the yard needed work.

Greg rode up the driveway; lowering the kickstand on the bike, he left it standing at the edge of the driveway. As he looked around, he thought it would take a lot of catchup work to get it back in shape. Before he had a chance to go to the door, a tall, slim young lady opened the screen door and stepped out onto the porch.

"Well, hello there," she said as she smiled down at him.

He said nervously, "Hi, my name is Greg Roberts. I was down at Mrs. Talbert's and thought I'd stop to see if you might need some help with the yard work. I used to work for Mrs. Kincade."

"Yes, Mrs. Kincade was my grandmother and she told me about you. My name is Elaine Colby. Come sit beside me here on the steps for a little break." She patted the steps beside her and moved over to make room for Greg. He sat down as far away as he could without falling off the steps. Elaine smiled to herself. She hadn't meant to embarrass him.

"The house is still in quite a mess or I'd invite you in." As she half turned toward the house behind her, her long hair moved gently across her shoulders.

"That's okay, I just stopped to see if you wanted some help with the yard work."

Elaine laughed, "I'd say you got here just in time. I think the neighbors were about to throw me out of the area. I haven't had any time to spend on outdoor work, as you probably can tell. I only come out on weekends and there's a great deal of work to be done inside." She paused, "Guess that's taking the long way around to say, yes, I sure could use some help on the yard. Do you have Saturdays free?"

"I work for Mrs. Talbert Saturday mornings, but I have three hours in the afternoon, if that's a good time for you. I might be able to work an hour now and then during the week until I get it back in shape and then go back to just the three hours on Saturdays, if that's okay with you."

"I sure would appreciate the extra effort and thank you. Do you remember how much my grandmother paid you?"

When he told her, she nodded solemnly, "Since the lawn and flowers are in such bad shape, I think I'll have to give you a raise."

"That's really nice of you, but you don't have to. I really liked working for Mrs. Kincade; she was such a nice lady." Greg looked down at his hands, trying to decide whether to tell her about the cookies and other treats Mrs. Kincade had given him, but decided not to, thinking it might sound like a hint.

"Are you going to be living in the house all the time or just weekends?"

"Just weekends for a while. I'm afraid I won't be able to move in totally much before the first part of October. I don't suppose there's any hurry, except I love this house so much. I wish I could come tomorrow. I have a job as librarian at the high school starting in January, so I'll probably be seeing you there too." Greg was pleased she had thought he was old enough for high school. No one ever guessed him to be older than his actual age.

"I'm only in seventh grade, but the middle school is just across the road from the high school, so I might see you around anyway."

Greg stood and turned toward her. "I have to go home now, but did you want me to start today?"

"Sure, if you don't have any other plans."

"I have to run home and tell my mother where I'll be first, then I'll be back." He knew his mother wouldn't be anywhere near to getting up yet. It was Aaron who would need his attention.

"I'll see you a little later then and I'll unlock the garage for you. No doubt everything is right where you left it. I'm sure you know what needs to be done better than I do, but if you need anything, just let me know, I'll be inside."

She stood and stretched her weary body as she watched him ride away.

Chapter Seven

Now I've got myself in one heck of a fix, Farrell Dunn thought as he lay on the ground flat on his back. His crutches were well out of his reach where they landed when he fell.

"Well, Lord, I'm thinking I'm going to need some help here," he said aloud. He pushed himself up on his elbows, but that was as far as he could go. Maybe he could crawl over to his crutches, but then how was he going to get up; or maybe he could crawl back to the house? It looked quite a lot further away from this vantage point than it did from a standing position.

"I know Lord, I get myself into these things, but with this cast on my leg I can't seem to figure my way out of this one. So, if you have any ideas, be sure to let me know; I'd appreciate it."

As Greg rode by the house, he saw what looked like someone lying on the ground. He turned around and rode back to where he could easily see. Greg leaned his bike off the road and ran across the lawn to where the man was lying.

"Are you all right?" he asked.

"Well, no I'm not. I'm in something of a bind; with this gal-darn cast, I can't seem to figure out a way to get back on my feet. Maybe you can help me, if you would please."

"Sure, I'd be glad to," he said, walking the distance and picking up the crutches. "Just tell me what you want me to do."

"Well, if you take one crutch and hold it straight up, maybe I can pull myself up on it."

Greg looked at him doubtfully. "I don't know if I'm strong enough to hold it when you start pulling up on it."

It's worth a try," Farrell said. He pulled the knee of his good leg up as far as he could and pointed to where he wanted Greg to place the crutch. Farrell took hold of the crutch and pulled his body forward. Greg put his body behind it and it held. Farrell raised himself part way, but fell back to the ground.

"I think we've got the right idea," he said, "but maybe if we move the crutch this way about four inches and I move this stick of a leg over some, we'll try it again." After the third try, Farrell was on his feet. He took the crutch from Greg to steady himself, while Greg hurried to get the other crutch.

"Hey, my friend, we did it. I'm sure grateful the Good Lord saw fit to send you my way. What's your name?"

"Greg Roberts."

"How do you do, Greg Roberts, my name is Farrell Dunn," he said, extending his hand. "I see you riding by almost every day."

"I do some yard work for Mrs. Talbert and others up that way. I did work for Mrs. Kincade too, before she died."

"Ah, yes, fine ladies all. Now, if you'd be so kind as to keep an eye on me until I get back to the house, I'd appreciate it."

Greg walked beside the tall, thin man. His hair was thick and white, curling around the edge of his neck and ears. His eyes were dark and alert, with wrinkles at the corners.

"Were you doing something out here in the yard?" Greg was curious, wondering what that would be, with a cast from mid-thigh to ankle, besides being on crutches.

"No, I had a hankering to get some fresh air and I thought I'd take a little walk around. Not one of my better ideas, I'm thinking." He looked around the yard. You know, some people credit you with wisdom you haven't earned, just because you're getting old, but unfortunately, as you may have noticed in this situation, intelligence doesn't automatically show up at any age," he chuckled.

As they approached the house, Greg noticed a slanting ramp leading up to the porch, eliminating the use of the steps.

When they reached the top step, Greg said, "Well, I better be getting on home now. It was nice to meet you."

Farrell extended his h and "I thank you and I thank God for your help. You seem to be a nice sort of fellow. Do you think you might want to stop by again sometime? I get mighty sick of my own company. Not only that, I might have some work for you if you aren't averse to a little housework."

"I had planned on checking on you anyway and I know how to do housework. How long do you think it will be before you get the cast off?"

"Oh, another couple of weeks yet, so they tell me. Then they plan to make me jump through hoops with therapy for a few weeks after that. The therapist will come here to the house so I'll be here most of the time. You would be welcome any time you'd care to stop by."

"He took a step toward the door, then turned back to Greg, "Have you stopped to see Marge Keller, up there across from Mrs. Talbert's?"

Greg shook his head, "I have been going to stop and see if she needs any help with the yard, but I haven't yet."

"Well, you should. She mentioned the other day she'd like to get somebody."

"You know her then?"

Oh my, yes. She brings me down some of her fine cooking and baking now and then. She bawls me out from time to time for some of the trouble I get into, but a good and caring woman she is all the same."

He turned toward the door and stopped again, "Oh and while we're on the subject, if you do get to talk to her, I'd just as soon you didn't mention this little episode to her. If she finds out about it, she's apt to raise the hair right off my head."

Greg laughed as he walked out of the yard to his bike. "I'll see you later," he called, waving.

As he rode homeward, his mind wandered through the many friends he had made since coming to Carson Cove. He thought how fortunate he had been to find such nice people and now Mr. Dunn. He hadn't had all that much luck with people in his life, especially men. His earliest memories were of men who knocked him around and hurt him. The only man he had contact with who had been reasonably good to him was Martin Delmont, but he wasn't about to cut him any slack; he was up to his rear in the drug business. However, this Mr. Dunn seemed different and kind of funny too. Greg liked him, but maybe he should reserve his opinion until he knew him a little better. He had been kicked around too often to make any quick judgments. Still, he had said

Mrs. Keller liked him and she apparently must know him fairly well to be taking him things to eat. It seemed to him as if these people were like the families on television programs. If his mother ever found out about how nice these people treated him, she'd put a quick stop to it, no doubt. He hurried on toward home and Aaron.

Chapter Eight

The next two months of summer seemed to fly by. Elaine had the house ready for her move to Carson Cove, but she still had her job in the city until the first of October and her lease on the apartment until the end of October. This would give her a couple of free weeks to move and get settled in.

During these weekends in Carson Cove, she had become friends with Greg and she had learned to love the quiet young boy. They spent long periods outdoors together discussing the house and grounds. She was interested in his opinion of his school since she would be starting her new job there in January. They had a common interest in books and as they talked she realized he was an avid reader. It didn't take her long, however, to realize he was reluctant to discuss anything pertaining to his home life. She didn't force the issue, although she was curious.

She often walked around the yard with him after he finished his work, complimenting him on some of the finishing touches and discussing the flower beds.

On one of their journeys around the yard, she said, "These tiger lilies seem to overshadow this small bush behind them. Do you think we should move them?"

"Well, actually," he frowned down at the graceful branches with their delicate blossoms, "I think it might be better to move the bush. Your grandmother bought it last year so it's very young, but eventually it will overwhelm everything around it."

Elaine looked at him, astounded, "Do you know what kind of bush it is?"

"Sure, it's a mock orange. It has white flowers along about the first of June. It will be much prettier when it's full grown."

Elaine nodded, "Do you have any idea where we could put it if we dig it up?"

"I planted it here because it's where Mrs. Kincade wanted it, but I think it would do better when it grows bigger in the bare spots between the two windows in the front of the house," he said, gesturing toward the spot he was describing. "It would have lots of room to spread without crowding anything around it and it wouldn't block either window. When it's full grown it will fill the entire space."

"Wow, how did you learn all this information?" Elaine was impressed.

"I've been doing yard work for a long time and if I don't know what something is, I ask the people. Some of the bushes and shrubs I was asked to plant had tags on them. In the spring we received catalogs and I learned from them."

Elaine was continually amazed by the boy's intelligence. From bits and pieces of information she had gathered over the summer, she thought he must spend a lot of time alone. She knew he read a great deal since they discussed books more than any other subject. She hoped he had fun with his friends too, but she wondered whether he could find the time.

After starting to work for Elaine Colby, all his spare time was taken up with getting the place back in shape, but now with just the regular hours, he had an extra time slot. He would like to get one more job, preferably on this road since it was so close to home. Once again, the Keller property came to mind. The name on the mailbox read Ms. M. Keller. The lawn was mowed once every week, but as he rode by he noticed the flower beds could use some work and the trimming was seldom done. Mr. Dunn said she had mentioned getting some help and by the looks it wasn't too late.

When he knocked on the front door, an elderly lady stood behind the screen.

"Yes dear, what can I do for you?" she asked.

"My name is Greg Roberts," he said, realizing his voice was a little too loud. He was always a little nervous with someone new. "I see your lawn is mowed, but I thought maybe you could use some help trimming or in the flower beds. During the winter, I also shovel snow."

"Oh say, I know who you are; you're the fellow who works for Mrs. Talbert, aren't you?"

Greg nodded, "Yes, I do and I have been working for Mrs. Colby for a couple of weeks," he pointed toward the end of the road. Greg noticed she was a little rounder than Mrs. Colby. She had pretty gray hair and wore an apron. He liked the way she looked. He thought it might be the way a grandmother might look, although he didn't have one to make a comparison.

"Thank you so much for stopping." She smiled down at him. "Could you come in for a few minutes? I'd like to talk further to you." When he nodded, she held the door open for him.

As he followed her through the rooms into the kitchen, he noticed they were neat and orderly with a lot of bright colors, not crisp or sharp like pictures in magazines, but soft and cheerful as if happiness had been built into the rooms. He couldn't help but think of the desolate surroundings he and Aaron lived in at their house and a deep longing swept over him with such force it brought tears to his eyes. He quickly brushed them away and entered the shining kitchen.

She motioned him to a chair at the table while she sat on the opposite side.

"Well, I have to tell you," she smiled across the table at him, Mrs. Talbert thinks you're about the greatest kid on two feet. She can't say enough good things about the way you work."

Greg was embarrassed by the compliment and looked down at his hands. "Mrs. Talbert is a very nice lady," he said.

"Yes, she is," Marge Keller readily agreed. "What I want to talk to you about is this. My son is the one who has been taking care of my lawn, but he has his own life too. Mind you, he never complains, but I know young people have better things to do after they get done working all day, or on their days off, than to come over here and do more work. I know he'd be glad if I found someone to take over. Besides, I would enjoy having a nice-looking young fellow like you around. So, if you could do it, I could let him off the hook, so to speak." She smiled, looking at him expectantly.

"Sure, I can do it. When would you like me to start?"

"How about this next week; what day of the week do you have free?"

He hesitated, thinking about Aaron's schedule. "I could come on Wednesday afternoons and work until three if necessary. If you need more time, I can figure it in later."

"Very good, I'll see you on Wednesday then," she said, walking him to the door.

"I stopped down to see Mr. Dunn the other day. He's the one who told me I should stop to see you. He said he knew you quite well."

"Yes, he's one of the nice people in the world. I enjoy visiting him now and then. He's very intelligent and fun to talk to, but he sure is a total mule. No common sense at all." She smiled, thinking about him. Greg smiled too, thinking of the incident with Mr. Dunn and what he had said Marge Keller might do if she found out.

During the summer months, Marge had learned to love the sober young boy. She often worked with him or sat under the big maple tree chatting with him as he pulled weeds and loosened the dirt in her flower beds. They often discussed his school subjects and topics he felt different about than his teachers.

She noticed he was always willing to consider the different theories she had but wasn't shy about presenting his point of view. She admired his thought process. It seemed odd for a child of his age. Sometimes, after they had deliberated on a subject, he would say, "You know, I think you're right; I never came at it from that direction before."

Sometimes they walked together the two blocks down to the park across from the intersection where a vendor parked a small trailer during the summer months and sold ice cream treats.

She confessed that she loved ice cream and was glad he was there so she could come down to get ice cream cones. He was puzzled, "Why can't you go get one by yourself?" he asked.

"Well, how's it going to look," she said, "an old thing like me standing around licking on an ice cream cone all by myself? If I've got someone like you to stand here with me, it looks more respectable."

Most days she invited him in for cookies and milk after he finished his work. One day, upon entering the house, Greg noticed the screen door scraped on the porch floor as she opened it ahead of him.

"What's wrong with your door?" he asked.

"I don't know what's gotten into it lately."

As she continued into the kitchen, he opened the door wide and noticed a screw had pulled out a ways from the casing. He went to the garage for a screw driver and tightened all the screws, bringing the door back to its original position.

Marge came back to see what was taking him so long. He demonstrated the ease with which the door swung back and forth.

"Say," Marge said, "you're a handy fellow to have around. I don't suppose you'd consider marrying me, would you?"

Greg giggled. Marge placed both hands over her heart. While leaning her head back dramatically, she sighed. "I suppose that means no. I just don't know how I'm going to handle such rejection." Greg doubled over the porch railing, laughing at her antics.

One day over their snack, Marge said, "I have a son you know, but he's a little too slow to suit me."

Greg was now puzzled, "What do you mean, slow?"

"Well, here he is all grown up and he knows I've always wanted to be a grandmother, but darn it all, he just doesn't seem to get down to it. He has girlfriends off and on, but he doesn't seem to settle down," she sighed heavily. "He thinks he can get away with it by saying he can't find anyone like me."

Greg smiled, "You'd make a nice grandmother."

"Thank you, I think so too. Do you know what I do sometimes? I pretend you're my grandson."

"You do?" Greg's eyes grew big with astonishment.

"Yes, I do. In fact, I miss having someone like you around to feed cookies to and maybe get a hug from once in a while." She sighed again, "But then, I suppose you have enough grandmothers to hug you already."

"No, actually, I don't have any." Greg looked away as he munched the last of his cookies.

"Oh, I'm sorry," Marge said, glancing at his sad face. "Grandmothers are great huggers."

Greg glanced in her direction over the rim of his glass. After finishing his milk, Greg stood, saying, "I have to go now. Thanks for the cookies and milk." He took two steps toward the door, turned back and went over and hugged her.

She held him a few seconds before he pulled away. Moving toward the door, he stopped again. Looking at her, he said, "Sometimes I pretend you're my grandmother too." He pushed through the screen door, ran to his bike and was gone.

Marge took a tissue from her pocket and wiped her eyes. Looking heavenward, she said aloud, "You watch over that child, you hear? And thank you for sending him to me."

From that day on, a hug was part of every departure.

As the summer moved toward September, it seemed to Marge that Greg became less somber. It was a red-letter day for her if she could make him laugh.

Chapter Nine

Martin Delmont sat in his new office upstairs over the tavern and listened to the work in progress below. When he had checked on the workers that morning, they were doing finishing work.

We ought to be able to open the tavern next weekend, he thought. The remodeling had taken much longer than he had originally anticipated. His mind reviewed the plans Dora had drawn for the closets between their two offices, with the long narrow room down the middle between the two. It was Dora's idea and she supervised the work in every detail. She told the workmen that the reason for such a room would be to have a place for the account books and records as well as extra stock and supplies for the tavern and refreshments for friends and business acquaintances. The truth was that the room between their two closets with the sliding panels would be used for measuring drugs and storing the needed equipment. When the passageways were closed it would be extremely difficult to detect the room and it would be even more obscure once they brought the clothes in to hang in the closets.

He had objected to the added expense of the room since they hadn't yet approached Brant about giving over control of his customers in this area. As things were now, the drugs came all measured and ready to be distributed and there was no reason for the room. But, Dora had convinced him that it was a great idea. Listening to her, he realized that she aspired to much higher goals than their small drug business. He was aware of her ruthless nature and usually gave in to her ambitions, but he also knew she wouldn't let anything or anyone stand in her way when the opportunity came to climb higher. He had no intention of allowing her to do her climbing at his expense, but he had to admit, the room could be invaluable for protection later on if the police came looking around. The more he thought about it, he realized it might be added incentive for Brant to accept the idea of them taking over his customers.

Sometimes listening to Dora talk about their drug enterprise, he regretted telling her about his idea until after he had cleared it with Brant. Still, she was his partner and he felt they should agree on procedures before they took them on. He would expect the same from her given the same circumstances. Although he didn't trust her, he recognized her excellent business sense.

Only a few days ago she had tried to get one past him without discussing it. She had rushed in waving a typewritten paper for him to sign. He was supposed to hurry and sign it because she was late for her appointment with the lawyer. Shoving the phone across the desk toward her, he said, "Well call him because you're going to be a little late. You didn't actually think I was about to sign something without reading it, did you?"

As he was reading the document, he began to feel a little guilty for his misgivings. Most everything was written nearly as they had agreed, but as he came to the last paragraph, he realized this was the reason she wanted the agreement in the first place.

It read, 'Upon the death of either partner, the business would automatically become the sole property of the other partner.' He rose slowly to his feet, anger rising. Tearing the paper into small pieces, he faced her, "What a cozy little agreement," he said sarcastically. "If I signed that piece of trash, you could then get rid of me at your leisure, when I was no longer useful to you. Is that the way it was supposed to go down?"

"Oh, Martin, how can you even think such a thing. Most partners have similar agreements to protect their investments." Dora looked sad and hurt.

"I doubt it, but if they do, they don't have a partner who is forever scheming some kind of double-cross."

Dora sighed, "It hurts me deeply to think you distrust me. We have known each other for so many years and I thought we were friends. You should know I would never do anything to hurt you, physically or through the business.

"Word gets around very quickly in this business, Dora. You're a climber and you are aiming for the top, no matter who gets trampled in the process." Martin sighed, "There's no such thing as a friendship in the drug cartel. You should remember that when you are working on your next scheme."

Dora stood and walked through the door into her adjoining office, slamming the door.

Eventually, Dora made a truce with Martin and they decided to postpone discussion of an agreement to a later date. In spite of Dora's explanations disclaiming any concealed agenda on her part, Martin could not bring himself to believe her. It only reinforced what he already knew. He would proceed with caution with his partnership, but he decided there was nothing to be gained at this point by open warfare, so peace was restored.

Another thing that disturbed Martin was the baby situation. He had initiated the meeting between Dora and the lawyer. He had known George Becker for many years and was aware of similar deals in the past, but now the baby was more than two months old and the deal still hadn't been closed. When he talked to Dora about it, she had been vague and a little evasive.

Although Dora had paid about a third of the cost on the tavern at the time of purchase, he had paid for all the renovations. Dora promised to pay her share with the money from the baby deal. He hadn't been excessively worried about it because he knew the drug business was strong enough to give him back his share, but he was curious.

Reaching for the phone, Martin dialed.

"You have reached the office of George Becker, Attorney at Law. How may I help you?" the secretary answered.

"Hi Marla, this is Martin Delmont. Is George in?"

"Yes, just a moment please." Martin heard the buzz of the inner office phone. "Martin Delmont is on line one."

"Hi Martin, how are things going?"

"A little slow but coming along," Martin said.

"I thought you'd be open by now," George said.

"So did I, but we will be opening next weekend if all goes as planned."

"Well, that's good to hear. Good luck. Now, what can I do for you?"

"I was wondering what's been going on with the Roberts baby deal. I thought it would have been done and over with by now. Dora intended to pay her share of the renovations with the money. I was wondering what the holdup was."

George Becker hesitated, "You know Martin, I shouldn't be talking to you about this; client privacy and all," George laughed.

"Oh, don't give me that George, what's going on?" Martin asked.

"Since you are the one who sent her to me, I'll tell you." George and Martin had been friends for many years.

"I had it pretty well set for the week after the baby was born, but when Dora upped the price, I thought we'd lost the prospective buyer. It took some fancy talking on my part and they are back into the deal again, but they asked for some extra time to get the money together. Now, the deal is set to close in October."

"Thanks George. Dora's been a little evasive about the whole thing and I was wondering if something had gone wrong."

"Hey, you know I could get into a lot of trouble with this thing, so I'm depending on your silence about this little talk."

"Certainly George, you know you have nothing to worry about from me," Martin said, hanging up the phone. He should have known that it was Dora in the middle mixing things up, trying to get top dollar, he thought.

Martin walked out of his office into the waiting room. It looked more like a comfortable living room with its soft carpet underfoot and color-coordinated overstuffed chairs arranged in groups of three with coffee tables in the center of each group. It had been Dora's idea to keep the room light and airy with vertical blinds at the windows and only a valance at the top. Martin walked to the window and looked down the road onto the yard. Glancing at his watch, he knew that Dora would be arriving soon.

The landscape people had done an excellent job clearing away the fallen branches and trimming the trees bordering the parking lot. The white picket fence added a country look. They had planted flowering bushes across the front of the building; although they were past their flowering time, they were attractively trimmed. Along the entire front of the hedge, there was a foot-high concrete curb to protect the building from drivers with poor judgement.

Martin was pleased with the results. As he watched, he saw the work crew loading up their tools and clearing away any left-over waste material. Finally, it was over; the men had finished the job. In spite of the extra time it had taken, he knew they had done a beautiful job and he was proud.

Martin could only hope he hadn't forgotten anything important now that the opening was on the calendar. His mind automatically began going over the last-minute details still to be done. The bartenders had been notified to report to work for the next two days in preparation for the grand opening. The shipment of various alcoholic beverages and mixers were still in their cases in the back room and would have to be set up in the proper order on the shelves behind the bar. All the different companies supplying various products had been notified and these and the racks to hold them had already arrived. The two waitresses would be in tomorrow to get acquainted with the bartenders.

Martin thought it necessary to have the bartenders and all the waitresses there for the opening weekend in anticipation of a large crowd. There certainly had been ample advertising to encourage a busy weekend.

When Dora arrived, they walked around the premises together. She was generous with her praise of Martin's accomplishments. She had distributed the drug orders at night while he dealt with the work crews and the ordering, besides handling the hundreds of details connected with the opening. She truly was grateful to him, knowing all too well that she didn't have the patience for a job like this while Martin not only did them well but seemed to thrive on them.

When they finally arrived upstairs, Martin sat down in the waiting room.

"Come sit down, I'd like to talk to you for a minute. I think it's time for the next step," he said.

She sat down across from him, "and what is the next step?"

"I think we're ready to invite Brant into this operation," he said, "maybe take him out to a nice place for dinner then bring him back here, show him around in preparation of presenting him with my idea. What do you think?"

"When do you think? Opening night?" Dora asked.

"I thought at first that was a good time to do it, but then I thought better of it," Martin said. "There would be a lot of confusion and noise, which wouldn't exactly be the right environment for making decisions."

"Whatever you think, Martin." She reached out and patted his hand. "You've done a fantastic job and I'm proud to be your partner. So, whatever you set up, just let me know and I'll be there."

Martin smiled back at her. It would be so easy to fall under her spell when she was like this. Sitting there looking all soft and gorgeous, she had awakened the old urges once again, but he knew he could never make any moves in that direction without opening the door to pain and betrayal. He knew her too well and had seen her other side often enough to be extremely wary of tangling with her.

"I have to tell you, Dora, it's been a lot of work but fun too in a lot of ways to see something like this come together. As for Brant, I think I'd better call him and give him some dates to choose from and I'll let you know how it goes."

"Does Brant know about this place?" Dora asked.

"Only that we were considering a new business venture on the side. I haven't said much about it to him because I knew you wanted to get this baby deal settled before we put Brant in the mix."

The truth was that her sexual appearance was so engrained in her actions that she didn't think she could do business without it and being pregnant somehow lessened her capabilities, but now that the baby had been born, she had her power back.

"How are things going there at home?" Martin watched, fascinated, seeing the loathing creep into her expression with his question.

"Now, with Greg back in school, it's very difficult for me. The brat howls most of the day."

Watching the hostility on her face when she talked made Martin uncomfortable.

"If I had let him go earlier when I had the chance, it wouldn't have come to this," Dora continued. "Not only that, but Greg has gotten so attached to him," she said with such revulsion in her voice that it disgusted Martin to see the look on her face, "he acts as though the baby was some kind of special gift just for him and I know he's going to give me a lot of grief when the baby goes."

Martin could hardly believe this conversation, "Are you going to tell him you're going to sell the baby to the highest bidder?"

"Absolutely not!" She looked at Martin as though he had lost his mind, "That's all I'd need is to let Greg have something like that on me. No, the baby will just disappear and he'll get over it. After we get this deal through with Brant, maybe I'll get rid of Greg too. I won't need him anymore for pickups."

Martin could almost feel the viciousness in the air. "When are the people taking the baby?" Martin asked. Dora sighed in relief, "I've only a week and a half to wait and he'll be gone."

Martin was watching the expression on Dora's face. He could barely comprehend what he was seeing. How could a mother feel such blatant contempt for a child she had given birth to?

"And you?" Martin asked, fascinated, "What will you feel when the baby's gone."

"Peace." Dora said emphatically, "Peace and richer, that's what I'll feel. There are days I'd like to kill the howling bastard and I might have already if it hadn't been for the money I'll get for him. Even then, sometimes I wonder if it's worth it."

Martin, who had been studying her facial expressions, finally looked away. *This*, he thought, *is truly the face of evil* and too late, he wished he hadn't had any part in it.

Chapter Ten

Greg was glad his jobs took less time now that it was fall. It gave him more time to spend with Aaron after school. He was getting older and stayed awake for longer periods of time.

Greg had always enjoyed school, but now he dreaded leaving Aaron each day, not trusting his mother to get up and tend to him. Sometimes it made Greg nauseous just thinking about the things that could happen to a baby when no one was there to care. As far as Greg was concerned, Aaron might as well be alone when his mother was there.

Arriving home from school one afternoon the first week of October, he heard the baby screaming as he entered the house.

Frantically, Greg ran to the bedroom. His mother was standing by the crib with Aaron in her hands, shaking him fiercely, her face distorted with hatred.

"What are you doing?" he shrieked, grabbing the baby from her. "Are you trying to kill him? Get away from him, I'll take care of him. Just get away." His hands were shaking as he held the wet screaming baby to his chest.

Dora turned toward him, her eyes blazing with rage. "I can't stand it anymore," she yelled through clenched teeth, "all he does is scream all day. I can't take it anymore."

"Well, if you fed and changed him once in a while maybe he wouldn't cry so much," Greg yelled after her retreating figure. He heard the kitchen door slam and knew she wouldn't be back until after the pick-up.

Since she had brought the baby home, he knew she didn't like Aaron, but it hadn't occurred to him that she might hurt him. Now, he realized he should have known. Hadn't he received more than a few beatings from her? As far back as he could remember, he had been the target of her beatings. It was her system of teaching.

Laying Aaron back in the crib, he stripped the wet clothes from the little body and wrapped him in a dry blanket. Laying him on his own narrow bed, Greg placed a pillow on each side of him so he wouldn't roll off.

Running to the kitchen, he measured out the formula and set it to warm. Racing back to the bedroom, he grabbed the wet bedding from the crib and threw it on the floor. Hurrying to the bathroom, he wet a washcloth and wiped down the plastic covering on the crib mattress. All the time, the baby was crying.

"Don't cry anymore, brother's here, I'll take care of you." Greg repeated over and over as he hurried from one thing to the other. Back in the kitchen, he checked the temperature of the milk and poured it back into the bottle.

Returning to the bedroom, he wrapped the blanket closer around Aaron before picking him up. He walked to the rocking chair and sat down, holding the bottle while the baby drank almost ferociously while his tiny hands waved in the air.

Greg talked softly while holding him tightly in his arms, trying to quiet him so he wouldn't drink so fast. Much to Greg's relief, after a few seconds, Aaron was calmer and settling down to drink his milk more slowly. Greg continued to hold the baby in his arms long after he had gone to sleep.

Finally, Greg roused himself and gave Aaron a sponge bath instead of playing with him in the small tub. After making up the crib with fresh bedding and dressing him in his night clothes, Greg laid the sleeping baby down and covered him lightly. Bending, Greg kissed Aaron's flushed cheek as he swiped at the tears of frustration rolling down his own cheeks.

He had to think of some way to protect Aaron. During the activity of his chores, his mind was in turmoil. After a great deal of thought, he decided he would leave a note for his mother since he wouldn't see her tonight and she would be sleeping in the morning. She would be back around midnight because there was a pick-up tonight.

After he finished writing it in big print, he left it on the table where he knew she would see it. It read, 'I will be coming home each school day during my lunch hour to take care of Aaron. Since the school does not allow the students to leave the school during this time, you had better think of something to tell them, because I am going to do it. Greg.'

He knew this would only be a temporary solution. As Aaron grew older, he would need more attention than a few minutes now and then. A babysitter was the answer. He could still take care of him after school and weekends. He would have to talk to his mother about getting a babysitter for his daytime care. She would probably object because for some reason she hadn't wanted it known that a baby existed. She had warned him not to talk about Aaron to anyone and he didn't. Now, although it would seem that

80

his mother hated Aaron, she must realize that something had to be done.

Glancing at his watch, he saw it was time to make the pick-up. He strode quietly into his bedroom for a last check on Aaron before leaving. The baby was sleeping soundly.

The weather was as dark and gloomy as his thoughts. He felt for the plastic bag in his pocket as a light misty rain began to fall. Tonight, the forest noises did not penetrate his troubled mind. One idea after another emerged and was discarded because it was impractical. He felt so helpless to change the course of his life and now there was Aaron who was more important to him than his own life.

After the car bringing the package arrived, he immediately put it in the bag to keep it dry and headed for home.

As he ran, his mind once again reviewed his desperate situation. With his mind so preoccupied, he forgot the usual cautions as he ran. The leaves were wet and slippery beneath his feet and it wasn't long before he went sprawling into the darkness, the package flying in one direction and the flashlight in another. When the flashlight hit the ground, it went out, leaving him in murky darkness.

He knew the general direction the package had taken and lowering himself to the ground once again, he began to crawl to where he thought it had fallen, all the while moving his hand in wide circles among the dead leaves and broken branches, finally locating the plastic bag that contained the package.

Fear twisted his stomach as he turned the package slowly in his hands, feeling for a break in the outside covering. To his relief, he felt none; then went on feeling about the ground for the flashlight. Suddenly, he realized he had lost too much time and gave up the search. He would have to come back in the daylight and search for it.

His progress was slower now, without the light and it seemed a long time before he saw the lights of the house.

When he saw his mother's car in the driveway, his spirits sank. As he drew nearer the porch, he could see through the kitchen window that she was talking on the phone. He leaned his weary body against the wall next to the screen door.

At first, he paid no attention to what she was saying, but eventually her conversation began to penetrate his weary brain and he stood erect, listening intently.

"If it's possible, I'd rather it was when the boy is in school Monday and Mr. Becker, you will not be taking the baby out of this house unless I have my share of the money in my hands, is that understood?"

There was a pause while Dora was listening to the other person's reply. "Yes, I have all that information ready for you."

Greg became aware of her footsteps as she paced back and forth across the width of the kitchen. He began to shake with rage as he realized she was talking about Aaron. She was going to sell Aaron.

From his vantage point, Greg heard her hang up the phone, but he still stood where he was, trying to calm himself before going in. He couldn't let her know he had heard her conversation. She might be forced to do something sooner if she realized he knew. He needed time to think this through. He knew he would have to do something, if he was ever going to, before Monday. His mind was in turmoil.

When she heard the door open, she turned to him, "Where have you been young man?" she yelled, "You know what time you are supposed to have that here. I've been worried about you."

No longer afraid of his punishment, Greg threw the package on the table in front of her and walked past her toward his room. "Yeah, I just bet you have," he said flatly.

"You come back here, you've got some explaining to do."

Greg moved steadily down the hall to his room. Though he wanted to slam the door, he didn't because he knew it would awaken Aaron and frighten him.

He knew there would be trouble in the morning over this little episode, but since he was so late, he was fairly sure she would let it go for tonight. He heard the kitchen door slam shut, the car engine start and the tires crunching on the gravel as she sped away down the long driveway to the highway.

Greg walked over to the crib, his eyes brimming with tears. The night light allowed him to see the flushed cheeks of the sleeping child. He bent and kissed him before walking to the window; his mind was a mess of confusion.

The conversation he had with Mr. Dunn flashed into his mind.

"You know, son, some days when you come here you look like you're carrying the world on your shoulders. I'd like to help you if I could," Farrell Dunn said. "When I have what seem like insurmountable problems, I turn them over to the Good Lord." Farrell waited, watching Greg's reaction.

"But I don't know how to do that, Mr. Dunn."

Farrell Dunn smiled, "There's nothing fancy about it. You just talk to Him and tell Him what's on your mind, just the way I'm talking to you."

Greg nodded, thinking that must be what you call prayer, talking to God.

The thought came to him now because he couldn't figure a way out for Aaron, or himself either for that matter.

"Okay," he whispered, "if you're listening Mr. Dunn's God, I know you don't know me but if you could help me to figure out what to do about Aaron, I'd appreciate it very much because I love him." Thinking this was a little abrupt, after a few seconds he whispered, "Thank You and Amen."

He was wet and chilled from the drug run and suddenly realized he was shivering. With one last glance at Aaron, he grabbed his night clothes and headed for the shower.

As he stood warming his tired body beneath the spray, his mind was churning, searching for answers. He supposed if someone was willing to pay a lot of money for a baby, they must want a baby very much and would no doubt treat him good and love him. The drawback was he would never see Aaron again; how could he stand it? Aaron was the only beautiful thing to ever happen to him in his lonely life. How could he give him up? Even to his sad mind, this sounded selfish. He did want Aaron to have a good life. Maybe letting him go would mean people to love and care for him. That would be better than anything he could do. Greg sighed. It wouldn't be quite so bad if he knew the people and could go see him sometimes.

Greg stopped in the middle of toweling himself off. Like a flash, it came to him! He knew what he was going to do.

Let's see, he said to himself, *tomorrow is Friday, so I'll have to do it Saturday night.* He knew his mother would be busy with the opening of the new business so he'd be able to figure everything out tomorrow.

Greg smiled, "Thank you Mr. Dunn's God for helping me and Aaron."

Friday afternoon, when school was let out early, he had gone home, taken care of Aaron and put him down for the afternoon.

Glancing at the closed door to his mother's bedroom, he knew she was still sleeping but would soon be getting ready to leave and he'd rather not be there to listen to her complaints.

By stopping at Mr. Dunn's house so often to check on him while he was on crutches, they had formed a close friendship, enjoyable to them both. Even though Mr. Dunn was getting along nicely now and really didn't need him, Greg enjoyed talking to his friend.

Now, carrying the burden of what he was about to do, he wished he could ask his advice. Greg knew Mr. Dunn was very smart, but he knew in his heart this had to be his responsibility.

Farrell Dunn watched Greg approach the house. He saw the sadness on his face and recognized the burden he carried by the slump of his shoulders. He opened the door before Greg had a chance to knock.

"Come in and welcome. I'm glad to see you." He watched Greg closely as he entered. "Let's sit in the kitchen and have some of Marge's cookies, what do you say?"

Greg followed him to the kitchen, removed his jacket and sat down opposite Farrell at the table.

"Did you have lunch?"

"Yes, they let us out with half a day, teacher's conference."

"Now that would make most young people happy. How is it I'm looking at such a gloomy face?" Farrell put his hand on Greg's shoulder before setting down across the table from him.

"Oh, it's nothing; I guess it's just one of my moods."

"You're not having woman troubles, are you?"

"No," he said, but it did bring a smile to his face. When he thought about it, he guessed he could say he was having woman trouble all right.

"You know son, I'm joking with you a little because it's fairly easy to see that something is troubling you. I'd like to help you if I could. You've been a good friend to me and I want you to know I've appreciated it. Go ahead and help yourself to those cookies."

As Greg munched on his cookies, he considered telling him, but he knew it was impossible. In order to tell him a little, he'd have to tell it all and where would that get him? Aaron would be taken away somewhere. Some of the drug people would probably be put in jail, with him right along with them, if one of them didn't kill him first. No, he couldn't tell Mr. Dunn anything.

"Oh, don't worry, I'll be over my mood by tomorrow. As a matter of fact, these cookies have already done a pretty good job of it."

Greg realized now that he shouldn't have come. Mr. Dunn was a pretty sharp guy. He was more aware of things than most people.

"Well, I'd better get on home or I will have woman troubles with my mother if she notices that I haven't finished my chores." He tried to sound cheerful so Mr. Dunn wouldn't worry. Actually, he did feel somewhat better just knowing someone cared. "Don't look while I sneak out the door with another cookie," he said, as he slid one into his pocket.

Farrell smiled. "Before you go, I wanted to ask you if you talked to God about your problems yet?"

"Yes, I did." Greg looked down and scuffed his foot on the entry rug before raising his eyes to Farrell. "And I think He already did help me. But, I don't understand why your God would want to help me with my problems. He doesn't even know me."

"Come back and sit down for a second, could you? We have a couple of mistakes to correct." Greg returned to the chair across from Farrell.

"The first thing is," Farrell began, "he's not just my God, he's yours too. As a matter of fact, he's everyone's God and the second thing is, He has always known you since the day you were born. He has been waiting until you found him." Farrell waited a few seconds before continuing. "You know, life can get pretty rough sometimes and I asked Him to guide me through every day. As you know, left to my own devices, I can get myself into a peck of trouble and it sure is a comfort to have my beset friend by my side to help me. If you talk to Him every day, it won't be long before you'll know He's your best friend too." Greg nodded. Farrell hesitated a second and then he said, "I've kept you long enough. We'll talk some more another day."

Greg stood and looked at Farrell, "Are you a minister?"

"Yes, I'm a retired minister, but you don't have to be part of the clergy to talk to God. Anyone can, you know. Everyone has a soul. It's where God lives within us. We carry him in spirit everywhere we go. All you have to do is let Him be part of your everyday life." Farrell hesitated, "There's quite a lot more to tell you about this subject, but we better wait until another time. Right now, you better get on by."

Greg nodded, "Okay, I'm out of here. See you later." Farrell watched as he rode his bike out of the yard. He hadn't believed Greg's mood story. There had always been an underlying sadness about the boy for as long as he'd known him.

Farrell had discussed the boy with Marge a few days ago. She had told him, "I do worry about him, Farrell. There are times when he seems happy enough, but it seems as if underneath it all he is carrying a burden of some sort. I feel there is something definitely wrong. Does he talk much with you?"

Farrell told her he had initiated some religion into their visits and the boy seemed quite receptive. He asked her if he ever talked about his home life and she said there had been a vague reference now and then.

Thinking back, Farrell had to agree that Greg was quite evasive when it came to anything personal. He sighed. Maybe he would open up a little more as time went by. It might be just a matter of trust, depending on the people in his family. He guessed that the boy had been emotionally bruised somewhere along the line. *I'll have to be patient*, he thought, *most things have a way of surfacing eventually.*

Chapter Eleven

Steve Darnell stood in the doorway of the small room connected to their bedroom. He and his wife Tracy had spent long, happy hours transforming it into a nursery. He hadn't seen Tracy so happy and playful in such a long time; he had soaked it up like a dry sponge. Now, the room was finally ready for the baby. It seemed to reflect the joy they felt when they were working on it.

They had finally scraped together the extra money the woman had demanded and he had notified the lawyer. Now was the time for waiting and worrying. He had been uneasy about the transaction, but the fun he and Tracy had planning and fixing up the room had managed to keep his anxiety at bay. Now with everything ready and in place, his apprehension was in high gear. Suppose something went wrong? He didn't want to imagine what it would do to Tracy if, at the last minute, the woman changed her mind about giving the baby to them. When she had demanded more money, Tracy had gone into a deep depression until he had promised to get the money somehow. It had taken all their savings and now the house was heavily mortgaged too.

Steve shut the door quietly and went into the bedroom. Tracy was still sleeping. He bent and gently kissed her cheek without waking her. She was so beautiful and as he stood looking down at her, his love for her was almost overwhelming. He wanted desperately to protect her, but as each day went by, his uneasiness grew. Tracy must have picked up on it because one day she said, "You have to have faith, Honey. In just a few more days we'll have our beautiful baby." She did a little dance and kissed him. It was easier to believe it would happen.

On his way to work, he wondered how their lives had become so entangled with this baby obsession. It wasn't always so. Now it seemed to dominate their every thought and action.

He thought back to before they were married. They had worked in the same office, but there had never been an occasion to do more than say good morning to her. She was the boss' secretary and was seldom included in the general structure of the office staff. She never mingled socially with the outer office staff. However this did not mean she was unnoticed. After all, she was beautiful and efficient, but because she was in proximity to the boss, she wasn't allowed to interact with the water cooler griping club.

Steve too was intimidated, but for another reason. He thought of himself as ordinary. What would a beautiful girl like her see in someone like him? He thought of her often and wondered how he could manage to get to know her, or more to the point, for her to get to know him.

It may never have gone any further if fate hadn't stepped in and given him a hand.

The boss issued an invitation to all his employees to come to his estate for an informal picnic to show his gratitude to his loyal, hardworking employees who were responsible for the success of his company.

At this affair and with a great deal of forced nonchalance, Steve managed to introduce himself and start a conversation with her. He found her to be warm and interesting. There seemed to be no one with her, so he was in no hurry to move away. Seeing her drink was almost gone, he offered to get her another, but she refused, saying, "I'm afraid I'm a one drink person, but thank you anyway."

As they continued to chat, there was a disturbance at the bar.

"Oh dear," she said, "That's Chad Dawson. He's my cousin. Maybe I better go see if I can keep him out of trouble."

"I know Chad too," Steve said, "I'll go over with you."

They both set their glasses on the first empty table they passed on the way to the bar.

As Tracy approached Chad, she spoke to get his attention away from the argument while Steve drew the other man aside and advised him to move away from the disagreement. Turning back to Tracy, he could see that Chad was drunk and giving her a difficult time. Steve took a firm grip on Chad's arm, turning him away from Tracy.

"Hey, Chad," Steve said, "Maybe we had better help you get home; what do you think?"

"Why would I want to go home? It's a nice party," Chad said, thickly.

"Well, one reason might be this is your boss' house and maybe you'd like to keep your job." Tracy said dryly.

"Come on, Chad, no party is worth putting your job in jeopardy. I'll be glad to drive you home," Steve said.

"I've got my own car and I can drive myself home."

"No, you can't," Tracy said emphatically. "If Steve will drive you home, I'll drive your car. That way I'll know you're safe, along with everyone else on the road."

Steve and Chad followed Tracy and saw him safely into his own apartment and into bed before they left him.

On the way back to Tracy's car, she explained to Steve, "He's such a good guy ordinarily, but he should never drink; it changes his whole personality. Thank you so much for helping me out."

"Not a problem," Steve said, "Did you want to go back to the party?" Tracy hesitated, "No, I guess not. I imagine dinner has been served and besides, it would be awkward now."

"Well, I have an idea. Why can't we go out and get our own dinner? I don't know about you, but I'm hungry."

Tracy laughed, "Sure, why not? I'm hungry too."

It was the beginning. They dated for over a year and finally one night Tracy asked, "Would you say I'm a patient woman?"

"More than that, I'd say you are a wonderful woman."

"And on every date you tell me you love me. Do you think I love you too?"

"I'm hoping you do."

"Well then, why don't you ask me to marry you?"

Steve put his arms around her and brought her close to him.

"It's just that I've been afraid."

"Afraid! Afraid of what?"

"That you might say no; then everything would be a mess and I'd lose you."

"Oh, Steve, how could you think I'd say no? I love you with all my heart."

They had two glorious married years before the baby subject came up. One day she asked, "Steve honey, would you like children?"

"Sure, if you would, but I've been so happy as things are, I haven't given it any thought."

"Haven't you wondered why I haven't gotten pregnant?"

"Actually, I haven't. I just assumed you were using something."

"No, I haven't been."

Then it began; the doctors, the specialists, tests and more tests. As the results came in, she became sadder and sadder. They found no reason with either of them why she couldn't get pregnant.

Another year went by and still no baby.

As her spirits deteriorated, Steve had worked hard to assure her that as long as they had each other, it would be all right. But, it wasn't all right with her. As she felt more depressed, he felt more helpless. He didn't know what else to do.

One day in mid-July, she came home from work very excited. She had heard about a lawyer named George Becker. It seemed he knew how to get a baby for them.

They met with George Becker and discussed the particulars of this so-called adoption. Steve knew it for what it was; they were buying a baby. No matter how the lawyer sugar-coated the situation with fancy words and legal phrases, what they were discussing was illegal and Steve hated the idea. But there was no turning back now. Tracy had seen the picture of the beautiful baby boy. Even as Steve explained the risks in great detail, Tracy was ecstatic and their home was once more a joyous place.

Steve joined the festive activities and preparations, but beneath the laughter and love, he carried the burden of fear. There was nothing to do now but ride it out to the end and hope for the best.

Chapter Twelve

The dinner with Frank Brant went well, Martin thought. Dora had dressed elegantly, giving the impression of refined grace. While using the power of her natural beauty to do the early work, she estimated the range and margins of this operation of conquest. It didn't take her long to determine how to handle this situation.

As the evening wore on, Dora had played her usual game and had quietly set the bait, using her best moves.

When Dora excused herself to go to the powder room, Frank watched her retreating figure, "Is this an ongoing romantic partnership you have here Martin?" he asked.

"No, no, just a working partnership. I've worked with her for quite a few years. She was my connection for the west side when she lived in the city. She's very smart in the business and just as important, very careful," Martin smiled. "But, no romance."

"A very interesting woman," Frank mused, "I wanted to make sure I wouldn't be stepping into your private amusement park before I made any moves."

Martin laughed, "No, just business. She's been building us quite a customer base, as you probably know by the orders you've been delivering. I have been busy with the details of reconstructing the tavern, so she has done most of the night deliveries."

"Are you about ready to open?" Frank asked.

"Yes, we're going to open next week. It was one of the reasons I wanted you to see it in its pristine glory before we opened. It probably won't ever look quite as nice again and I wanted you to meet Dora. I consider myself lucky to have her for a partner in this. She's smart and ambitious."

When Dora returned, they left the restaurant and Frank followed them to the tavern in his car. "Well?" Dora asked when she and Martin were in the car, "How did I do with Frank?"

"Oh, don't worry," Martin laughed, "you've got him interested. Right now I'm anxious to see his reaction to the tavern, what we've accomplished and then on to the proposition."

"Are you worried about it?"

"No, I'm not worried, but maybe a little tense. I really think it would be to his advantage. For one thing, it would give him more free time and I know he has been wanting to open some new areas and the police might not lean on him quite so heavily if there was less activity around him."

They arrived and stood beside the car, waiting for Frank to pull in beside them.

Once inside, Frank surveyed his surroundings and nodded. "Very nice," his face reflected his approval. "Just right; not too fancy but neat and agreeably pleasant."

"Yes, that's exactly the impression we were after. We wouldn't want our customers to feel uncomfortable." Martin smiled, glad that Frank was shrewd enough to recognize his attempt to read the mind of the paying public. As they moved inside, Dora became more animated, discussing each room and how it had been reconstructed. Every move Dora made was meant to charm and inspire. She missed no opportunity to touch Frank's arm or hand whenever she was close to him. Each time Frank asked a question, Dora gazed into his eyes a second or two longer than necessary.

Martin was faintly amused at this superb performance. I should have brought my camera, he thought, I could have made a little side money selling this technique as a motivational film.

As they went through the door at the end of the bar, Dora said, "Now this door," she motioned to her left, "will be used by our drug customers. The door we just came through will be locked during business hours. The patrons will not see or mix with the drug people who will come up these stairs to our offices where we will do our business with them." As she ascended the stairs, Frank and Martin followed.

"This is a kind of waiting room," Martin said, waving his arm around the room to include the groupings of comfortable chairs, coffee tables and end tables with decorative lamps.

"And over here," Dora walked to the far side of the room, "is the door to the back stairs. If we have unwanted company coming up the front stairs, we can let our customers out down these stairs."

"Looks to me like you've thought of everything," Frank said.

"Over here are our offices," Martin said, "but I'll let Dora show them to you along with her special project, which, by the way, was entirely her idea," Martin said proudly. "In the meantime, I'll get us a drink."

"Keep mine light; I have to drive home," Frank said, "maybe a glass of wine would be best."

As they walked through the connecting door from Martin's office to hers, she explained about the two buttons that she called their 'heads up' buttons. "If either of us spot trouble, we can buzz the other." Walking across the room to the closet, she opened the door and said dramatically, "What you see here is a closet," and moving the few clothes on the hangers to one side, she pushed the panel open, revealing the narrow room between the two closets. "And now you see the preparation room." She smiled at the awed expression on Frank's face. In the room was a narrow table already set up with the mechanisms needed for weighing and measuring.

"Do your customers come here now to pick up their orders?" he asked as she closed the panel and turned off the light.

"No, no yet. I thought it would be better to wait until after we opened. I have made up some maps and set up a schedule of times and dates for them to start coming here to pick up their orders so they won't all be descending upon the place on one night. Of course, they'll never see this room under any circumstances."

"This is very clever," Frank remarked as he inspected the panel. "No one would know it's there," he said, rubbing his hands across the connecting line.

Martin was standing with the wine in his h and ready to pour, when he became aware of Dora's voice. He glanced in the direction of the open door to her office. She was leaning against the side of her desk with Frank standing close to her, his back to the door.

"Martin told me your dealers in the city and surrounding area come directly to you for their orders."

"Yes, most of them do," Frank said, but I still deliver some. We have three different locations right now. I have to keep changing them. As you probably know, you can't have the same location for too long."

"I've been thinking, when this place is open, why not give your dealers the option of coming here. You could bring the bulk material to me and I could do the packaging plus handle the sales. It wouldn't be much trouble to work them into my schedule. It's the same distance most of my customers will be coming. I have a geographical advantage with this town being in the center of all these towns around the lake. Of course, I would expect a larger cut because of the extra work. I'm sure you can think of a few advantages for you personally, too."

Martin, hearing this, was furious. She knew he had intended to approach Frank with this, but she couldn't wait to promote her status in the organization. All of it had been his idea; the towns around the lake, everything had been his idea. She was always looking out for number one, crawling through any crack to further her position. Besides, hadn't he been the one to foot most of the bills so far? Now, here was Dora with her "I," "My," "Me" language. He hadn't expected much from her, but maybe a little loyalty could have been in order. Well, it was too late now; she had put his proposition out for Frank's consideration. Martin was working hard to control his anger. They couldn't afford to show dissension at this point.

As Martin poured the wine, he called out, "Why don't you two come out here and we'll discuss it further." Martin hoped his voice sounded steady and calm without revealing the blazing rage he was feeling. He didn't mind too much that she had laid his idea out to Frank, but to stand there and repeatedly say 'my customers', 'my place', 'my business' was infuriating. When he was talking to Frank, he had given her a partner's credit for everything they had accomplished, which he felt was as it should be. He had consulted and secured every change and idea with her before moving ahead. Now, he wondered why he had been blind-sided by the betrayal. He should have expected as much from her.

As Frank and Dora came into the waiting room area, Martin was forced to push his fury back and get through the rest of the evening with Frank.

"Well," Frank said upon entering the room, "Dora has given me something to think about." Frank sensed a tenseness in Martin. "I imagine she has talked this over with you, hasn't she Martin?" he said, laying his hand on Martin's shoulder and taking the glass of wine being handed to him.

"Oh, yes," Martin said, glancing at Dora, "We discuss everything pertaining to the business."

"This certainly gives me something to think about," Frank said. "I have been worried about the city police. They've been leaning a little heavy lately. I have to do some fancy moving around with my deliveries, trying to steer clear of them and I do come out here anyway to deliver your goods." Frank was thoughtful, sipping his wine. "You two have a real good set-up here with this establishment; great cover, this tavern idea. Are the people working the bar going to be in on the drug business?"

"No," Martin spoke up before Dora could answer, "We thought it better they know nothing about this end of the business. Actually, there's no reason for them to know. The two businesses are totally separate. All transactions for the tavern will be legal in every way and hopefully it won't draw any adverse attention."

"Sounds good." Frank set his empty glass down. "Well, listen folks, I'd better be going. It's been a pleasure. You've shown me splendid hospitality and" glancing in Dora's direction, "beautiful company. I thank you and I wish you luck with this newest enterprise. I have some things to think about before I make a decision about this idea of Dora's, but I will tell you this much, it's very tempting." He shook hands with Martin and kissed Dora on the cheek. "I'll be in touch soon with my answer."

Dora poured herself another glass of wine before sitting down on the nearest chair and kicking her shoes off. Martin walked to the window and stood watching Frank leave. When he saw the car pull out onto the highway, he turned to Dora. "That was a neat backstabbing you gave me in there."

Dora leaned her head back and sipped her wine. "Oh, don't be ridiculous, Martin." Dora waved his words away as if she were too tired to be bothered.

"That's all you have to say?" Martin raged, his eyes blazing. "You think you can pass this off with a wave of your hand and a sigh?"

"Well, just exactly what did you want me to do Martin? The opportunity presented itself and I decided to jump in. I think he liked the idea, so what more do you want? What difference does it make who presented it to him?"

"You're right, it didn't matter who told him about it. What mattered is your all-consuming ambition for power; that you would leave me in your dust without a glance in my direction. Everything I've said to Frank about either business, I always included you because you're my partner and I had this foolish idea that we could build something good together, but I allowed myself to be deceived by your hypocrisy. Apparently, there is only room for you on your agenda," Martin seethed.

Dora stood, "Come on, Martin, calm down. It wasn't like that at all. I just didn't take the time to think it through. The main thing was you put the proposition out to Frank and when the opportunity came, I took it. I'm sure Frank realized you had input in the idea."

"Input? Input? Well, he sure didn't hear it from anything you said," Martin said sardonically. "I wish I could swallow this innocent act you're putting so much effort into for my benefit, but now I know what I should have known all along. You're a climber and it doesn't matter whose body you have to step over on your way to the top."

A surge of anger became obvious in Dora's expression, "Yes, Martin, you're right; I'm a climber and what's wrong with that? Do you think I want to be stuck here in this little backwater place all my life, pushing drugs with you? Well, no thanks, Martin. Someday I will take over where Frank leaves off and move right on past him. I'll be able to have everything the 'high and mighty' of this world enjoy. That's where I'll be while you're still here with your little two-bit organization."

Martin turned away, disgusted, "Well, I guess the cards are all on the table now. I can't say I haven't been warned, but since we are about to open this 'two-bit organization,' we better put this latest episode of 'True Confessions' behind us, at least temporarily. We will have to work together until you can figure out how to double-cross Frank, but let me tell you this, Dora, I won't forget this night of treachery ever. If I were you, I'd move very carefully with Frank. The two of you are a lot alike."

Once on the road, Frank Brant drove slowly, his mind going over the evening, almost word for word, looking for motives. He knew they were there; they were always there. Something had gone wrong between Martin and Dora toward the end and Frank couldn't quite get a hold on it. It had to have something to do with what Dora had told him. Things had been fine when Martin went to pour the wine. Maybe there were some romantic feelings on Martin's part, but he had believed Martin when he said there was no romance. Martin was pretty straight forward. He had known him for many years; almost from the beginning of his business. He knew Martin to be comfortable where he was in the organization. He had no big ideas or drive for advancement. Even this tavern enterprise surprised him a little. He hadn't figured him for that much initiative, but maybe Dora had given him a push. He liked Martin because he could trust him. If there was ever an honest criminal, Martin was it. Frank smiled to himself at this description, but it was true. If Martin gave you his word on something, you could depend on it.

But, Dora was a different breed of cat. Nothing went to waste on this woman. Everything put into action was aimed for a result. She was aware of her direction and she sure knew how to get there. There was no doubt in his mind that she wanted control and it wouldn't bother her a bit to step on some dead bodies to get it. She had the equipment to help her along the way. As for turning his customers over to her and Martin, he'd have to think a little more on the subject, although he was inclined to do it. It might loosen the watch the police had on him. Besides, it would give him more time to think about doing some expanding of his business. It was something he had wanted to look into for some time. He might even cultivate a little fun on the side with Dora. It might be amusing to watch this thing unfold. In any case, he reminded himself, *I had better watch my back around her.*

Chapter Thirteen

Greg's work schedule had eased some since summer. He had raked, dug up bulbs and transplanted shrubs. All the yards under his care were ready for the onslaught of winter and he was satisfied. He knew that his people were searching for things to keep him busy until snow shoveling time and he was grateful.

Saturday was his time to work for Mrs. Talbert during the morning and Mrs. Colby in the afternoon, but this week he had asked for time off. Mrs. Colby told him she was finishing moving out of her apartment and wouldn't be home until late afternoon, but there was no reason he couldn't work if he wanted to. She said that by now he knew what needed to be done as well as she did, but he explained to her that he was needed at home and would like to take the day off. Both she and Mrs. Talbert had graciously agreed and wished him well. He couldn't tell either of them the real reason; he wanted to spend the day with his brother because Aaron was going away and this day would be heavy with sadness.

Many times during the day his mind was flooded with doubts and fears. There were so many things that could go wrong, so many things to think about and remember. The only thing that kept him going was thinking about the alternative. During the completion of his chores, he repeated it like a litany; "if I don't do this, I'll never see him again." It was the fuel he needed to conquer his fear.

He thought about what Mr. Dunn had told him; "When things get rough, turn everything over to God. It's good to have your best friend beside you."

Greg stopped and whispered, "I know you don't know me very well yet, but I'm Greg Roberts and I could sure use your help in this thing that I am going to do. I don't know for sure if what I'm doing is right or wrong, but he's my baby brother and I love him, so if you could please keep him safe, I'd sure be grateful." Greg stood there for a moment longer, not knowing what else to say. Finally, he said, "If you're listening, thanks."

He waited until Dora was gone before he started getting things ready. He knew she wouldn't be back tonight since there was no delivery and no pick-ups. As soon as he heard her leave, he started gathering and sorting things that would go with Aaron and setting them in piles on his bed beside the diaper bag. There was no fear that Dora would miss any of the articles he was sending with him since she had nothing to do with anything concerning Aaron. Besides, most of the clothes Aaron had now he had bought himself. Greg set out two sets of clothing besides the ones he would be wearing, alongside two new cans of formula and two full bottles.

Greg played with Aaron in between the gathering of things, determined to keep him awake as long as possible so he would sleep during his journey tonight.

When it was dark, he wheeled the wagon into the hall. It had started to rain and the bottom of the wagon was wet. While he dried the wagon, it occurred to him that he would need something to keep the baby dry. He remembered the plastic covering over the crib mattress and brought it into the hall.

Aaron had been fed, changed and had a bottle. He should sleep until around ten, if Greg was lucky. This whole thing was off Aaron's schedule, but he had kept him awake all afternoon, so he ought to sleep through this sad journey.

He put the baby carrier in the wagon first, tucking the bags of clothing and formula in around it. He then carried the wagon out to the driveway before securing the sleeping baby. He laid the plastic loosely over the wagon, making sure no part of it was near the wheels and that one side was open.

Pulling the wagon across the bumpy field, Greg walked slowly since there had been no way to secure the carrier to the wagon. It was dark and he couldn't see well enough to avoid the uneven contour of the field.

I hope Aaron doesn't wake up, he thought. Maybe he shouldn't take the shortcut through the field, but by going this way it not only cut the distance in half, it also lessened the time on the open road. At this point, he didn't need a lot of people wondering why he was out wandering around pulling a wagon on a cold rainy night like this. It was the type of thing people were apt to remember. The way he had it figured out, most everyone was home from work by now and probably having their dinner. With any kind of luck, maybe he wouldn't see many cars while he was finishing his trip on the main road. By going this way, he'd be less than half a mile away from her house.

He hoped he hadn't forgotten anything. Again and again, he went over the list in his head. There wasn't very much room in the wagon to take many of Aaron's things and besides, Dora would be sure to notice if all of Aaron's clothes and blankets were gone.

As he trudged along toward the highway, the tears rolled down his cheeks again. He brushed them away impatiently. He just hadn't been able to think of any other way to do this. At least Aaron would be loved and taken care of properly. The people who had intended to buy him would love and take care of him too, but it was the idea that he wouldn't be able to see him or know for sure what was happening to him that bothered Greg. He knew in his heart he was being selfish, but he couldn't bear the thought of never seeing him again. Aaron was the nicest thing to ever happen to him and he couldn't give him up, at least not entirely.

If Dora had been a normal mother, she could have taken care of Aaron while he was at school and this wouldn't be happening. Had he ever once complained about taking care of the baby? Hadn't he willingly done everything for him that he could? But, of course, it wasn't about any of those things. It was all about money. It was the only thing she had ever cared anything about for as long as he could remember. It was her driving force; she cared little about who was trampled by its power.

Greg hated her for all the years of misuse he had suffered from her but most of all for what she was forcing him to do now.

A short distance from the main road he saw the diner lights flashing. As he walked steadily toward it, he saw her car pull into the parking lot.

Crouching down beside the wagon, he watched as she left the car and walked into the diner. He bent and kissed the baby's cool cheek as he rearranged the blankets and the plastic covering the wagon.

A new plan began to form. Now, he wouldn't have to take Aaron on the road at all and there would be less danger of being found out. If he walked farther up the field until he was away from the direct light of the diner, he could approach the car from behind and come out on the opposite side of the car. No one from the diner would be able to see what he was doing, although he would be exposed to traffic on the road, but who would think anything wrong with someone getting out of a car in the parking lot?

Before crossing the road, he watched carefully to see if she had locked the car. A jagged wave of fear ripped through his body.

Things had been going so well up until now. He calmed himself, thinking if the car was locked he could go back to his original plan and he wouldn't be any worse off, except he would have to worry about getting to the house ahead of her.

Bending low to the ground beside the car, he reached for the door handle. It opened, but before he had time to breathe a sigh of relief, he was startled by the dome light. He stood up, reached and turned the switch off and was in partial darkness again. He moved two of her smaller boxes, setting one on top of the other, to make room for the carrier seat. He was grateful that Aaron hadn't awakened. He searched around under her boxes and bags until he located the seatbelt.

After removing the plastic, he secured the carrier with the middle seatbelt and by moving the carrier as far to the right as he could, he was able to cross back over the carrier with the seatbelt from the right side. He covered the baby's small body with the blankets he had brought. Then, placing the heavy diaper bag on the floor beside some other bags, he tucked one of the bottles in beside him. Leaning down, he gave Aaron a whispering kiss on his cheek and gently closed the door. It latched but didn't close tightly. Pushing with both hands, he heard the door click shut. He reached for the handle to be sure it was locked. Satisfied, he glanced at the door of the diner to be sure no one was coming out before he grabbed the plastic cover and dashed into the darkness to the empty wagon.

Suddenly, his body felt so heavy he had to sit down on the empty wagon. A great wave of sadness poured over him. He wanted to lie down and die. What was there left for him now? Despite knowing he had done the best he could for Aaron, he was alone again. Because he loved Aaron, he felt the loneliness more sharply now than ever before.

He had no idea what was in store for him when he told Dora Aaron was gone. The one thing that he wouldn't have to worry about was the police. He knew Dora Roberts wouldn't involve the police in anything, ever. That being out of the equation, her next response would no doubt be to give him a sound beating; after all, he was the one responsible for him. It hardly mattered anymore, Aaron was safe. Tears rolled down his cheeks, mixed with the steady rain and dropped, unheeded, on his jacket.

Chapter Fourteen

Elaine Colby was tired, but at least this was the last time she would be going back to the apartment. It suddenly occurred to her that the apartment had never been home anyway.

Elaine's parents were killed in an automobile accident. She had moved to Carson Cove to live with her grandmother, which enabled her to finish out her last year of high school. When her grandmother had been alive, the only place where she felt comfortable was at her grandmother's house.

When she arrived with the remainder of her clothes and personal items, now stowed in the trunk and back seat of her small car, she would finally be home.

Upon entering college, she shared the rent of a house with five other college girls. Too late, she realized this was a bad idea. There was one party after another, with constant commotion, disorder and difficult confrontations with the other girls as well as their friends.

Elaine worked at the library two evenings a week and a half day on Saturday to help with her finances. It was difficult to avoid the conditions at the house and she spent most of her free time at the library where she could do her studying in peace.

It was uncomfortable to be around the other girls. Elaine knew they felt the same way about her, but it seemed the more often she left, the more infuriated they became. They assumed it implied criticism of their activities. Long before the end of the first year, she realized she wasn't part of the group, nor did she want to be. She had signed the lease for one year, so there was nothing to do but stick it out and make other arrangements for the next term.

Elaine had to work hard to keep her grades up to her satisfaction. She had little time to worry about their attitudes. She spent most of her happiest hours at the library and by the end of the school year she knew, beyond all doubt, she wanted to be a librarian. She changed her major to accommodate her plans.

The following years were less chaotic. With her grandmother's help financially, she found a small apartment off campus. Most weekends Elaine drove the forty miles from the college to Carson Cove to spend her free time with her grandmother. She thrived on the home-cooked meals and loving atmosphere. The long talks and small lessons on life brought new energy to her weekends away. Now, thinking back, she was grateful for the time she had been able to spend with her grandmother. All too soon, she was gone forever.

After college, there was Tom and the baby that would never be. She tried to push the thoughts away, but despite her resolve not to punish herself with this part of her life any longer, the events began to flash across her mind like a bad movie.

At the time, Tom was working for a large company in the city and they had met while he was doing research at the library. He was funny and flirtatious. Eventually, they had begun to date.

She smiled, thinking about how it all came about. One day as he was leaving, he stopped at her desk, as was his habit.

"Hey, pretty lady, do I have to find something else to research in order to see you or do you think we could have a normal date like regular people?" he asked, smiling.

Their dates were filled with laughter and romance and within a few months, she agreed to marry him. It wasn't too long after they were married that she realized how little they knew about each other's personality and character. They were totally opposite in their thinking and goals. She found herself yielding to his point of view, more often than she should have, in order to avoid conflict. There was no exchange of ideas or discussions leading to a compromise. All decisions were to suit him, but even with this being true, they were reasonably happy that first year.

Shortly after their first anniversary, two things happened almost simultaneously; she learned she was pregnant and Tom lost his job. The company was downsizing and with the internal structure change came the elimination of his division and his job. Since Tom was highly qualified, he wasn't worried about finding another job.

As time went by, he realized other companies were also in a bind and were not anxious to hire new people, especially at his pay level. Nevertheless, he wasn't' about to consider anything less.

He had always had a weakness for alcohol and now with circumstances beyond anything he could control, he made no effort to fight his weakness.

Elaine was working at the city library full time. When she arrived home each day, she found him in various stages of intoxication; either confused and senseless or mean and quarrelsome. As hard as she tried to avoid an angry dispute, it was almost a daily occurrence.

One day, she came home after feeling sick most of the day and announced that she wasn't feeling well and was going to lie down for a while.

"Why? What's the matter with you?" His words were slurred.

"I told you, I'm sick and I don't have the energy to play your stupid games tonight," she answered, as she started up the stairs to their bedroom.

"Stupid? Stupid?" he raved, moving up the stairs behind her.

She stopped halfway up the stairs, "Just leave me alone Tom, I told you I'm sick."

He grabbed her arm and yanked her around. She tried to pull away, reaching for the banister rail. When he loosened his grip, she lost her balance and plunged over the banister, down to the floor below. Tom stormed down the stairs and on into the hall without a backward glance.

Through her pain, she heard the car start and roar out of the driveway. As she tried to move, the pain became more intense, "Oh, Dear God," she moaned. "Not the baby."

Slowly she pulled herself up, dragged herself to the phone and called 9-1-1.

The same night she lost their baby, her husband drove his car into a tree and was killed.

After all this time, she still went over that fateful night, trying to find something she could have done, or not done, that would have changed the outcome, but she knew nothing was going to change the past. She had to move on.

Now there was a new job waiting for her and she was moving to Carson Cove. It would be a new beginning. Although it was difficult to imagine being happy ever again, she would be in the cottage where she would be surrounded by her grandmother'spirit of love, giving her comfort, peace and maybe healing. She could almost feel the soothing rhythm of the moving river in her soul as it whispered its way toward Lake Andrew.

Elaine had been coming out to the cottage every weekend, sorting through the remainder of her grandmother's life. Yesterday, the moving van had brought the furniture from her apartment. She would have plenty of time to settle in before beginning her new job at the school library in January.

Elaine thought about the beauty of her yard. Greg Roberts had worked hard through the summer months to bring it back to its original charm. Many adults lacked this kind of pride and dedication in their work.

Often, she stopped her own work to watch him. It troubled her to see the torment outlined so clearly on this face and wondered what he was thinking, at that moment, to look so burdened. She felt an odd kinship to the boy; not because of anything he said or the way he did his work, but because of the sadness he carried like a banner over his entire person.

There were times when sadness wasn't there. Quite often, midway through his work, she would stop him and they would share cookies and milk. Greg talked openly about school. They seemed to be kindred souls, as far as books were concerned. He gladly discussed the adventures in his reading. During these chats, Elaine realized he read far in advance of his age group.

She was more than a little curious about his home life, but even the most insignificant question in that area seemed to make him uncomfortable. His answers were vague and evasive. When

114

this happened, she didn't press him for further information, avoiding the subject thereafter.

Elaine sighed, *I had better pay attention to my driving*, she thought, *or I'll miss my exit.*

Originally, she had planned to arrive before dark, but it had taken a little longer than she had planned to clear out the apartment and she hadn't considered the shorter daylight hours. The skies were threatening and a misty rain had already begun to fall as she exited the thruway onto the main highway leading into Carson Cove.

When the flashing lights of the diner came into view, she decided to stop for dinner. Since she had skipped lunch, she was hungry as well as bone tired. She certainly didn't feel like facing the upheaval in her kitchen at the cottage tonight.

With dinner finished, Elaine lingered over her coffee until she began to feel some of her lost energy returning.

Opening the door to leave, she walked out into the parking lot and found a slushy mess beneath her feet. Shaking her head in disbelief and glancing at her watch, she calculated she had been in the diner for about an hour and a half at most. During that time, wet snow had fallen.

As she carefully picked her way to the car, she was aware of the cold wind penetrating her light jacket. Approaching the car, she pulled the sleeve of her jacket over her bare hand and cleared the snow from the tail lights, then the head lights. She hadn't even given a thought about a snow brush for the car since it was only mid-October. *I don't remember it snowing this early*, she thought, as she opened the door to get in. She waited for the defrosters to clear the windshield. Maybe being so close to Lake Andrew might influence the weather.

It wasn't too far now and she'd be home. As she pulled out of the parking lot, she felt warmer just thinking the word 'home.'

Elaine became aware of the sound of the tires as they threw slush to the sides of the road. When she broke over the brow of the hill leading into town, she realized she was moving too fast. As she applied the brake, the car began to fishtail down the hill. Removing her foot from the brake pedal, she tried to regain control. The car, well into the skid, accelerated as it continued to slide from one side of the road to the other and across the bridge at the bottom of the hill. It veered over the embankment, taking with it a portion of guardrail at the end of the bridge, finally coming to rest against the pilings.

Too late, Elaine remembered she had neglected to buckle her seatbelt before leaving the diner. She was thrown to the opposite side of the car, hitting her head against the window. The last thing she heard before she slipped into unconsciousness was the startled cry of a baby.

Chapter Fifteen

Marge Keller pushed the button on the remote control and the room grew quiet. She always listened to the early news since she could seldom stay awake long enough for the later version.

Moving toward the kitchen, she sighed. *Another boring meal coming up*, she thought. Marge knew she should plan for better choices and quite often she promised herself that she would. Too many of her meals became a bowl of soup and crackers. She leaned her head back and looked in the direction she assumed to be heaven and said aloud, "Oh Charlie, I really miss having you around you old billy goat. It's no fun eating alone."

Her husband had been gone for more than two years and since her son Jim had his own apartment now, she often felt the sting of loneliness.

She thought of the many years with the police department; typing reports, filing, making contact with police departments all over the country in search of information that would aid in apprehending and convicting criminals. It was interesting and sometimes exciting to see the results of her job. However, when

Charlie became ill there were two factors to consider; his illness and her department was about to bring in computers.

She knew it would take a great deal of extra time while she learned this new technology, plus getting the department organized and Charlie would require more of her time and attention. She decided it was time for her to retire.

Reaching into the cupboard, she took out the first can of soup that was close at hand without reading the label. It made no difference to her. After struggling with the can for a few seconds, trying to find the right position on the opener, it finally took hold and ran its course around the top of the can.

As she waited for the soup to heat, something caught her attention. She leaned over the sink closer to the window to get a better look. After a few seconds of peering out into the darkness, she walked to the phone and dialed.

"Jim Keller here," the deep voice said, answering the ring.

"Hi Jim, this is Mom."

"Hi Mom, what can I do for you?" Marge smiled; he always answered her calls with the same , "What can I do for you?"

"I hate to bother you but it looks like there might be a car off the road in the marsh this side of the bridge down below my house. There's a pair of headlights at an odd angle beamed in this direction. I thought if you weren't too busy maybe you could come check it out."

"Sure, I'll be right over," he said.

As Marge replaced the receiver, she heard hissing as the soup boiled over onto the burner, extinguishing the flame.

"Oh, what a mess," she groaned, grabbing a long strand of paper towel on her way by. After the cleanup, she went back to the window in time to see a patrol car arrive.

Jim Keller pulled the patrol car in close to the bridge, leaving all lights flashing. He was able to see the skid marks where the car had left the road and slid down the embankment into the marsh. The car was leaning against the pilings at the north end of the bridge with the two wheels on the driver's side about a foot off the ground. The motor was still running. Jim walked back to the patrol car and called the station.

After Jim explained the situation, the dispatcher said, "Jack Denver is on patrol, I'll send him right over. Where are you?"

"At the foot of the hill, just past the bridge on River Road."

"Got it. Do you think there's need for an ambulance?"

"I haven't looked the situation over yet, hang on."

With his flashlight in h and he slowly started down the embankment. As careful as he was, he had a difficult time keeping his footing on the wet slope. Approaching the car, he heard the piercing cry of a frightened baby. He tried the front door and it opened. After turning the ignition off, he moved the light around the front seat.

Speaking into his phone, he said, "Yes, send out the medics. There's a woman in the front and you probably can hear the baby."

The woman was sprawled awkwardly across the front seat. Taking hold of her outstretched arm, he carefully moved her jacket sleeve enough to feel a pulse and to his relief it was strong. *No doubt she had struck her head on the window on impact*, he thought. As he flashed the light around the front seat, he was relieved to see that there was no blood anywhere.

119

From the front seat, he unlocked the back door before carefully closing the front door. Boxes of clothing, beauty products and other personal items had spilled over the back seat area to such an extent that he didn't see the baby immediately, but following the noise and pushing a few items aside, he found the baby in a carry-on seat. He reached in and took hold of the handle, but it didn't budge. As he flashed the light around, he saw the seatbelts from both sides and the middle crossed the baby's body in such a way that it held the tiny child securely in place. Finally, he was able to loosen the straps and free the carrier holding the baby. As the seat began to move, the baby stopped crying momentarily startled by the movement, only to start again almost immediately.

Jim eased his way backward, propping the door open with his body until his feet were solidly on the ground. With the carrier in one h and he gently closed the door. Panning the light over the terrified baby, he noticed it was tightly wrapped in a blanket, but the small feet were fighting fiercely for their freedom.

Noticing a bottle of milk tucked in close to the body of the child, he held the nipple to the baby's mouth. The noise stopped abruptly as the frantic little hands took hold of the bottle. Jim had next to no experience with babies, but he was fairly sure it was too big to be a newborn.

"Poor little tyke, you're going to be all right," Jim said, setting the carrier on the seat of the patrol car.

A few minutes later, Jack Denver pulled his car up next to the railing and jumped out.

"What do we have here, Jim?" he asked.

"Looks like a loss of control and a slide down into the marsh. I took the baby out of the back seat of the car and put it in my car. I don't think it's hurt, just mad at the world would be my guess.

There's a woman in the front seat. She's unconscious, but her pulse is good. An ambulance is on the way."

"I'd better go check it out and get started on the report."

"I'll go with you. The baby will be okay here," Jim said. Glancing down at the sleeping baby, he closed the door softly.

When they arrived at the car, the woman was reaching up to the steering wheel to pull herself to a sitting position.

"Just sit still. Don't try to move around. The medics will arrive shortly," Jack said. "How do you feel?"

"Oh, my head," she groaned, closing her eyes.

"Lean your head back against the seat and take it easy. Can you tell us your name?" Jack pulled a pad out of his pocket.

"Elaine Colby," she groaned, her hand moving to her forehead.

"Where do you live?"

"I was just moving up at the end of the road," her left hand moved outward to indicate the direction.

"Can you remember what happened?" Jack asked.

"Yes," she sighed heavily, "I stopped to eat at the diner and when I came out it had snowed," she said softly, hesitating before going on. "There was slush on the road and I guess I was going too fast when I came over the hill. Trying to slow down, I went into a skid. I couldn't seem to get. . ." Suddenly she sat bolt upright. "Oh, my God," she screamed, "I hurt the baby. I remember now. I heard it crying." She tried to get out of the car. Jim gently placed his hand on her shoulder to hold her in the seat.

"No, no, stay quiet. The baby is fine, not a scratch on it," Jim said, trying to push her back on the seat. "Just stay still. The

121

medics are here now. Let them take a look at you. I've got your baby up there in my car all safe, so don't you worry about it. Everything is okay."

"But you don't understand it's not. . . "

But it was too late, Jim had turned away. The medics took over. Jim stepped away and Jack followed him up the embankment. Jim turned the sleeping baby over to one of the attendants.

They watched as the medics did a short examination, checking the Colby woman's vitals before strapping her onto the stretcher and into the ambulance.

"Is there anyone you would want us to notify, Mrs. Colby?" Jack asked as they carried her past where they were standing on the way to the ambulance.

"No, there's no one." Elaine said.

The woman attendant, with the baby still in the carrier, pulled herself into the ambulance behind the stretcher as the driver shut the door.

"I don't think it's anything too serious," the medic said as he passed Jim on the way to the driver's side, "but with a head injury it's best to have it checked out to be sure. There doesn't seem to be anything broken and that's good news."

"Where are you taking her?" Jim asked.

"Memorial," he said, starting the motor and closing the door.

"Thanks for giving me a hand here tonight, Jim," Jack said as they watched the ambulance drive away.

"Hey, no problem. I'll call a tow truck and have them tow the car in. I'll wait for them to get here so you can get back on your route. After I'm finished, I thought I might take a run out to the hospital and see if I can help the woman in any way since she's new to the community. It's good PR for our department to show a little kindness."

"Especially so, since there's a young, pretty woman involved," Jack taunted.

"Pretty doesn't hurt, but I'm just naturally kind and thoughtful," Jim laughed.

"Yeah, me too," Jack replied, "but my wife prefers me to show my kindness to the old and infirm."

Jim laughed again.

"I'll see you tomorrow morning. You're in on that drug meeting tomorrow morning, aren't' you?" Jack asked.

"Yeah, but I wouldn't have thought we had a drug problem out here. I haven't seen any evidence of it, have you?"

"No, but apparently the problem is already present."

After Jack pulled away, Jim dialed the number for the garage and gave directions to the accident site. Turning, he went back down the embankment to the car. He shone the light around the back seat, noticing the boxes had tipped over, spilling the contents onto the seat and the floor.

Checking his pocket to be sure he had the keys, he pushed the button that locked all the doors at once before he shut the front door.

Back at the patrol car, he called his mother, knowing she had watched what was happening from the kitchen window.

"Hi Mom, this is Jim. The excitement's over."

"So I noticed. Was anyone hurt?"

"They didn't seem to think she was hurt badly, but they took her to the hospital to have her checked over. There was a baby in the back seat. I don't think it was hurt at all. It was buckled in pretty solid. That baby sure has a set of hardy lungs though."

"I take it then that it was a woman involved. Anybody we know?"

"I didn't, but maybe you will. Her name is Elaine Colby and she's moving into the house at the end of the road."

"Oh, it must be Martha Kincade's house. It's probably her granddaughter. Now that you mention it, it seems as though I did hear something about her going to move out here. There has been quite a lot of action up there on the weekends lately."

"I was thinking I might take a run out to the hospital and see if there's anything else I can do for her; besides, I have her car keys and she might want to know where her car is. Do you want to come with me?"

"I'd love to if you would consider stopping somewhere to feed me."

"I guess that could be arranged, I haven't eaten yet either. You make a good date since you're such good company, but I guess I will have to face the fact that you're always hungry." He chuckled. "I'll be up after the tow truck leaves."

Chapter Sixteen

At the hospital, Elaine Colby was trying to clear her thoughts in between being hooked up to machines and various other tests the nurses were doing. It was difficult for her to think clearly with the throbbing headache, but she had to tell someone about the baby. She tried again to focus. How could a baby be in her car? Was she losing her mind? She could remember all the other events of the day and if there was a baby anywhere in the mix, why couldn't she remember it?

Down in the emergency room she had tried more than once to tell them but when it came to the word 'baby', no one would let her complete the sentence before reassuring her that the baby was just fine and she must stop worrying about it. They assured her so often that she began to wonder if the child really was all right.

If her headaches would let up, she could think more clearly. The doctor had said someone would be in soon with something for the pain. Elaine wondered about the definition of "soon" since it seemed to her that "soon" had come and gone long ago. Maybe if she reviewed the day it would take her mind off the pain.

Where had the baby come from? Obviously, someone had put it in the car, but when?

It couldn't have been at the apartment because she remembered bringing all the suitcases and boxes down before loading anything into the car. She had put all the biggest cartons and suitcases in the trunk, squeezing in a few small sacks and boxes. The rest went into the back seat of the car. The landlord had come out to wish her well and say goodbye. She returned his keys and started on her way. At no time had she been away from the car, so it had not happened at the apartment. The only other time she had stopped was at the diner. It had to have been there that someone put the baby into the car; there was no other time it could have happened.

Elaine searched her memory, trying to remember the people who had occupied the booths in the diner. She couldn't remember anything about the other people who came in or left. At the time, she was tired and too preoccupied to pay any attention to her surroundings. Nothing curious had happened to rouse her from her thoughts. She was almost sure none of them had a baby with them. She would have surely noticed a baby.

She looked up to see a nurse come in with two pills in a small cup.

"This will help your headache," she said, handing the cup to Elaine and pouring a glass of water from the pitcher on the nearby stand.

After taking Elaine's blood pressure and temperature, the nurse said, "The people who assisted with your rescue are here. Do you feel up to seeing them?"

"Yes, I would like to see them," Elaine said. Now that her mind was clearer, she would try to explain to these people about the baby.

Marge Keller led the way into the room and came directly to Elaine's bed, extending her hand.

"I'm Marge Keller," she said softly and turning back toward Jim, she said, "This is my son, Jim."

"Hi," Elaine extended her h and "I'm Elaine Colby."

"It's nice to see you in spite of the circumstances. Jim tells me you're moving into the house at the end of the road. Would that be Martha Kincade's house?" Marge asked.

"Yes. She was my grandmother. Did you know her?"

"Oh, my goodness, yes. She was such a dear lady. She was my neighbor. I sure will miss her. I live a few houses down on the opposite side of the road."

"Well, then you will be my neighbor too. I would have been all moved in by now if this hadn't happened."

"I'm so glad you weren't badly hurt, although you do have a rather large bump. I suppose you have a headache twice the size of New Jersey."

"Yes, but the nurse brought me something for it and it has lightened up some."

"And the baby, is it all right?" Marge continued.

"According to the nurse, it's fine, not a scratch." Elaine said, using the nurse's words. Then, looking past Marge to Jim, she asked, "Were you the one I talked to after the accident?" Elaine sounded puzzled.

"No, it was a friend of mine, Jack Denver. Mom saw the headlights shining off the side of the bridge and called me to check it out. I called the ambulance and the police station. Jack was sent over and he's the one who talked to you. I took the baby out of the back seat. Except for being mad at the world, it seemed to be okay."

This was the opening Elaine had been waiting for to tell them the baby wasn't hers. "Actually, the baby," she began, but at the same time, Jim was still speaking. "Excuse me, what did you say?" she asked.

"I was just saying you had the baby tucked in there good and snug. It wasn't about to get loose, that's for sure." Jim smiled down at her.

Tell them now, Elaine thought, but before she could begin, Marge picked up the conversation.

"How long will you have to stay? Do you know?"

"The doctor said I'd better stay overnight and if there are no further developments, I will be good to go in the morning." She turned slightly toward Jim, "Were you able to see how much damage there was to the car?"

"Not really, it was too dark to see very much, but I locked it and had it towed over to Morton's Garage." Reaching into his pocket, he handed her the keys.

"You'll need a ride home tomorrow," Marge pointed out, "I'll be glad to pick you up if you want me to."

"Oh, how thoughtful of you to offer. I'm in something of a bind without my car, I'm afraid, so if it wouldn't be too much of an imposition I'll gratefully accept."

"It's no problem at all and I'm glad to help out. I'll give you my phone number then you can call when you're ready."

"I can't thank both of you enough for all you've done for me."

After they left, Elaine's mind went back to the baby. *I have to report this to someone*, she thought, *but who?* The Kellers might have known someone to call about the situation. What on earth was she thinking not to have told them?

With a sigh, she leaned back on her pillow and closed her eyes. Her headache was almost gone and she was tired, but she wanted to see the baby. She pushed the call button to summon the nurse.

When the nurse appeared, she asked, "I know it's late but would I be able to see the baby for a few minutes?"

The nurse nodded her head, "Sure, but let me check and I'll be right back with one of our stylish wraps. Then we can be on our way."

When the nurse arrived at the nursery door, pushing Elaine in a wheelchair, she pushed a button to summon the nurse. When the door opened, she said, "We've come to see the Colby baby," and continued into the first room.

"You can stay here and I'll bring him right out to you," the nurse said, patting Elaine's hand.

Well, now at least I know it's a boy, Elaine thought.

The nurse brought the baby in and laid him in her arms. Elaine touched his cheek with her finger. His big blue eyes were studying her face, but he didn't seem to be afraid.

Tears formed in her eyes and rolled down her cheeks. If only this were truly her own baby; he was so beautiful. She hugged him closer to her chest.

"What's his name?" the nurse asked softly.

The first thing that came to her mind was the beautiful blue eyes of her grandfather Colby. "Matthew," Elaine said, "his name is Matthew."

"How old is he, about three months?"

Elaine nodded, "Yes, three months." Elaine was willing to accept the nurse's judgment since she had no experience in this area. Elaine continued to look at the baby as though she couldn't take it all in.

How could anyone give this baby away to someone they didn't know, she thought and *not know what would happen to him or maybe never see him again*? She couldn't even imagine a circumstance bad enough to cause anyone to give him up. There were so many places a mother could go for help. She must have truly been desperate.

By the time she was settled back in her bed, she was tired, but she couldn't help thinking about the baby.

What if she didn't tell anyone the baby wasn't hers? No one knew her in Carson Cove, so how would anyone know? It was pretty obvious that the person the baby belonged to, for whatever reason, didn't want him. So, who would it hurt to keep him? Maybe God wanted her to have him. Yes, that was what she would do. She'd keep him and tomorrow she and baby Matthew would go home. "Thank you, God, for such a beautiful gift," she whispered as she drifted off to sleep.

Chapter Seventeen

When Greg arrived home, he looked at the kitchen clock. He could hardly believe his eyes. The way he felt, it should have been much later. He had experienced the entire range of feverish emotions; love, hate, fear, anger, sadness, worry, relief and now, drained of all emotions, he felt numb. As he stood gazing up at the clock, he began to shiver. He looked down at his wet clothes as if he were seeing them for the first time. He walked to the back entrance hall where the washer and dryer stood and removing all his wet clothes, he threw them into the dryer and pushed the start button. He stood motionless in front of the dryer as if he couldn't think what to do next. It was as if his entire body had shut down. Finally, he stirred and walked to his bedroom. He opened the closet door and removed his robe and pajamas. Sliding his feet into his slippers, he walked across the room to Aaron's crib and looked in, almost as if he expected him to be there. Reaching down, he patted the pillow, "Good night Aaron," he whispered, "I love you." The tears flowed again.

He retrieved the plastic covering, still wet from the rain and snow and carried the wagon back to its place on the back porch. Taking the kitchen towel, he wiped the plastic dry before making up

Aaron's crib. As he started to walk away, he realized it should not look that neat. Reaching down, he rumpled the blanket and made a dent in the pillow.

He rambled aimlessly around doing his chores. He knew things had to look normal if this thing was going to come out right. Finally, exhausted, he went to his bedroom, threw himself across the bed and slept.

Greg awakened at dawn. There was only a faint glow in the sky where the sun would be showing over the edge of the horizon. He dreaded starting this day in motion. Not only would he have to deal with the loss of his brother, but he would have to suffer through whatever his mother would do. Tears filled his eyes at the thought of Aaron in a strange place, with a stranger doing all the things he usually did for him.

"Don't be afraid, Aaron," he whispered, "she'll be good to you and she will love you too, just like I do."

There wasn't any use in postponing it any longer. He walked quietly into Dora's bedroom and stood beside her bed, looking down at her. No doubt she hadn't been sleeping very long since she seldom came home before three. Being awakened after so little sleep wouldn't improve her disposition either.

She lay with her long dark hair spread over the white pillow. Her long fingers lay against the silky blanket covering her. The form of her slim body, her source of pride, was outlined and although her knees were slightly bent, her feet came close to the foot of the bed.

As Greg watched her sleep, he realized she was beautiful, but how he hated her; not only for the way she treated him, but more for the way she had treated Aaron.

"You've got to get up," he had spoken too softly, he realized. It was awkward for him to break into the silent morning.

Dora groaned and pulled the blanket closer around her. He knew the most effective way to rouse her would be to take hold of her arm and shake her, but he couldn't bring himself to touch her.

"Do you hear me? You have to get up. Aaron is gone; I can't find him anywhere." This time he spoke louder.

Finally, he had her attention. She sat up, squinting in his direction. "What are you saying? Have you lost your mind?"

"I'm telling you Aaron is gone from his crib. He couldn't get out by himself. What did you do with him?" just saying the words brought tears streaming down his cheeks. He brushed them off on the sleeve of his robe. It was important to present a dramatic portrayal of the situation and tears would reinforce his story. Considering the crushing burden of his sadness, it was not a problem.

"Let me get this straight. The baby is gone from his crib?" She was out of bed and struggling into her bathrobe. Greg nodded, again wiping tears from his face.

"So, where were you that you're just now noticing that he's gone?"

"I was sleeping," Greg answered weakly. "What are you going to do?" he asked as she pushed by him. She didn't answer as she moved in the direction of the crib.

"Did someone break in or did you leave the door unlocked?"

He heard the familiar sarcasm in her voice. Fear rippled through his body; he had forgotten about the locked door.

"I don't know, I didn't look, but you were the last one in." She would have remembered if it wasn't locked when she came home. He stayed out of her reach now, expecting her anger to move in his direction momentarily.

She moved down the hall, expressing her rage with every step. She entered the bathroom and slammed the door.

"What are you going to do?" he yelled through the closed door. "Aren't you going to call the police?"

She yanked the door open, staring at him with anger blazing from her eyes, "What, do you think I'm crazy? No, I'm not calling the police. Now, get your lazy butt out to the kitchen and get my coffee perking. I've heard just about enough of your screaming at me. Get out of my sight," she said, slamming the bathroom door shut again.

When he heard the shower running, he walked directly to the kitchen door and unlocked it. Then, moving to the counter, he plugged the cord into the outlet. He started to turn away, then turning back, he lifted the top to see if he had put in the filter and the coffee when he had set it up the night before. It was done, but he had no recollection of his actions the night before.

Walking slowly to his room, Greg made his bed and laid out his school clothes. He didn't feel like going to school, but if he didn't go, what would he do all day?

When Dora appeared in the kitchen, Greg, still in his pajamas and bathrobe, was sitting listlessly at the table, his hands supporting his head.

"Well, don't just sit there! Go get ready for school," she said, pouring herself a cup of coffee.

"Aaron's gone and you don't even care," he lashed out at her.

"Oh, I care about it all right and don't you worry, I'll take care of it. Now, get going."

After Greg left the room, she walked over and tried the unlocked door. She shook her head in astonishment. It was hard to believe she had forgotten to lock it. It was even harder to believe that someone would choose this one night to walk in and take the baby. First of all, it had to be someone who knew about the baby. Not many people knew one existed. Second, it would have to be someone who had an interest in the baby. Who else would that be except George Becker? He must have come sometime after the bar had closed. She knew it couldn't have been before, because the door was locked when she got home. The lock certainly wasn't a sophisticated mechanism by any means and could have been easily broken, but it showed no sign that anyone had tampered with it.

She walked to the phone and dialed the number for the Becker home. She counted six, seven, eight and finally heard, "Yeah?"

"This is Dora. Why did you take the baby last night?"

"Take the baby? What are you talking about?"

"The baby is gone, that's what I'm talking about."

"What kind of bull is this, Dora?"

"All I know is that the baby is gone," Dora said, anger rising in her voice. "Maybe it's just your way of cheating me out of my share of the money."

"Yeah, well just maybe it's your way of backing out of the deal. I've worked the better part of three months getting this deal set up to suit you; now you're pulling this on me? " His voice was low and mean. "This better not be some kind of game you're playing or you'll live to regret it."

"No George, this isn't a game; the baby is gone. If you didn't take it, then who did? You didn't by any chance tell these people where the baby was coming from, did you?"

"No. I didn't tell them. I'm not totally stupid. What about your other kid? Where is he?"

"He has been walking around here crying his eyes out and yelling at me. He's in taking a shower right now."

"If I were you, I'd take a real close look at him. Maybe he did something with him."

"No, he wouldn't hurt Aaron, he loves him."

"I didn't mean that he'd hurt him, but maybe he found out about our little scheme and has him hidden away somewhere."

"Now how could he know about it? You and Martin are the only ones that I have ever talked to about it; besides, if he took Aaron some place, he would be there with him. He wouldn't just leave him some place."

"I don't know about that, but I think you ought to let me come out and work him over. It might surprise you what I could get out of him."

"If there's any working over to be done, I'll do it."

"I'll tell you this, Dora. If I ever find out that this is another one of your schemes, I'm warning you right now, you're a dead woman."

"Oh, come on George, if it will make you feel any better, when I get this drug business up and going, I'll pay you your share." Dora slammed down the receiver. She was seething. Was George right? Did Greg have something to do with Aaron's disappearance? It just wasn't plausible.

When Greg came out of his room fully dressed, she watched him as he sat down to the table.

"Well, what are you waiting for? Get your breakfast. It's almost time to leave for school."

"I can't eat." He looked up at her. "I know you did something with Aaron because you hated him, just like you have always hated me," he said, his voice low and full of malice. Tears again streamed down his cheeks.

"Well, you're wrong; I didn't do anything with the brat."

"Then why won't you call the police?"

"I can't do that with this drug business, it's too dangerous and you know it. I can't have them snooping around here."

"I don't see that looking for Aaron has anything to do with the drug business," he said.

"It's not your business to see anything. Just get out of my sight," she screamed.

Chapter Eighteen

The night shift for Carson Cove's police force was ending. Each morning before the day shift took over, the officers met with the chief to give him their reports of the night's happenings, along with the reports of the day shift from the day before. If there had been any urgent events on either shift, he would have been contacted as they happened.

They gathered in the small room beyond the chief's office, which they referred to as the "glory room."

On the left, as they entered, they gathered around the large coffee urn and helped themselves to the refreshments and each other's company.

Most mornings, the room was filled with voices and laughter as the men entertained each other with parts of their private lives and happenings during their shift. But this morning everyone was somewhat subdued since the off-duty men had been summoned to attend the meeting. M uch of the talk involved speculation about what was coming.

Within a few minutes, they began seating themselves around the long table in anticipation of the chief's arrival.

As John Redding entered, he said, "Good morning," and the men returned his greeting. He stood six foot four inches with a sturdy athletic build, which if for no other reason, would have commanded their attention.

At age forty-four, he had taken the job of chief of police at the medium-sized police department of Carson Cove. He had earned the respect of the men under his command. They knew him to be intelligent, stern when it was called for, but always fair. When he took over as chief, he laid out the rules of conduct and expected them to be observed. Since the restrictions were reasonable, the men had no objections.

Today, he didn't sit at the table, as was his usual procedure.

"I have something to discuss with you, so we will not discuss the reports today. You can hand them to me on your way out after I've finished. I want to thank all of you who were off duty for coming in." Glancing around the table, he saw he had their full attention.

"I have been contacted by special agents from the Drug Enforcement Agency. They are asking for our cooperation in their fight against the drug operations in the area. The DEA have been collecting evidence for a sting. They are after the head of drug operations in this county. They know who he is, but they need evidence to put him and his group of peddlers away. They seem to think there may have been a change of venue recently and there's a good chance that Carson Cove may have been the lucky winner."

He hesitated, "This is very important so pay close attention. What they are asking is this. I've been given a list of license plate numbers for you to watch for. If you spot one, you are not to stop them, do a search, or question them unless they have broken the law in some way. If it is possible to follow them without creating suspicion, do so. Otherwise, write down the plate number, time and location. If you see anything even vaguely suspicious that might pertain to drug dealing, you are to report it to me and I will contact the DEA. This is, at least for now, only a heads up. They believe the drug lords are setting up a new place of business. Be aware of new businesses or new owners of old businesses or just more activity than usual in any area. Make note of it and we'll discuss the response, if any. Unless they are causing a disturbance, don't shake them up. Are there any questions?" He looked around at the alert faces, waiting. "All right, its' time to hit the road. Stay alert and stay safe."

Jack Denver opened the locked door of the patrol car and seated himself behind the wheel while his partner, Jim Keller, walked to the passenger side. Jim settled into his seat and picked up the sheet with the list of license plate numbers they were to watch for.

"Well, that meeting was enough to shake up our comfort zone," Jack said.

"No doubt about it," Jim replied as he glanced over the numbers on the sheet. "It's going to be difficult to memorize these plate numbers, there's nothing to grab onto with these numbers."

"What's that supposed to mean, 'grab onto?'" Jack challenged.

"Oh, you know, something to help you remember them, like a sequence; something like 294 PAL, or something similar."

"Do any of them have letters?" Jack asked, glancing toward the list in Jim's hands.

"Yes, most of them have at least one and some two."

"Well, we could memorize the number before and after the letter, which would draw our attention and that would give us time to get at least the first few numbers. Maybe it would be enough for the DMV to identify the vehicle and the owner. What are the chances that more than one vehicle would have the same sequence?"

"Hey, good idea. In fact, an excellent idea." Jim said. After a brief pause, he added, "You know Jack, anyone would have to be deaf, dumb and blind not to realize the drug operation has invaded the country, but somehow living here in the Cove has lulled me into a false sense of paradise."

"Yeah, I guess it's easy to get complacent, but don't forget, it wasn't so long ago that a high school teenager died of an overdose, so it's no doubt here, count on it."

Chapter Nineteen

Elaine Colby awoke at dawn with only a pink smudge showing on the eastern sky where the sun would soon slide over the edge of the horizon. The hospital was still quiet with the lingering night watch.

Sliding her legs over the side of the bed, she sat up and looked out over the roof tops with the smoke stacks of factories clustered in the distance. Thin streams of smoke floated aimlessly into the early morning sky as furnaces were pushed into service to quell the autumn chill.

Elaine sighed, thinking of the tiny child in the nursery, wondering if there was a mother somewhere worrying about what might be happening to him. Would she miss him, wishing she hadn't given him away?

Doubts about her own decision to keep him crept into her mind. She had no knowledge of the laws concerning such situations, but she assumed the child should be turned over to the authorities. She had little confidence in the so-called authorities when it involved the welfare of a child. It could be lost in the tangled web of law and edicts, being forced to grow up in an institution while waiting for them to find their way through the paper maze of reality.

Of course, there are other things to be considered too, she thought. Suppose she didn't know how to take proper care of a baby? There was no question in her mind about her ability to learn, but this was a three-month-old baby. If the baby had been hers from the beginning, there would have been a doctor to advise her about proper care along the way. It would have been a gradual learning process within the natural progression of time. Now, it would be like jumping into the middle of the pool before you learned to swim. Some people advocated this method of learning, but given a choice, she would have preferred a more orderly procedure. Since this wasn't an option, she would deal with it.

Her mind moved on into what lay ahead. There wasn't a crib for the baby, but a phone call could remedy that problem. She would ask Mrs. Keller to stop by the store to buy diapers and baby food. Now, here was another thought; what does a three-month-old baby eat? She was beginning to worry. It seemed like she heard somewhere that doctors these days wanted babies to have formula fortified with vitamins and other nutritional things until they were six months old.

She pictured herself in a store with twenty varieties of formula on the shelf. Maybe it would say on the carton in big red letters 'for babies three months old.' The manufacturers alerts people with children's toys about age-appropriate things, so why not formula? She sighed. The mother might have included some instructions. If she had, they would probably still be in the car.

That was another thing, the car. Hopefully, Mrs. Keller wouldn't mind stopping at the garage on the way home to get some information on the condition of the car. She would need the personal things she had loaded in the trunk and the back seat. If it couldn't be driven, she'd have to arrange to rent a car until the damage was fixed. She wondered if it could be taken care of before the insurance company looked at it and estimated the damage. She'd have to ask Marge; she might know.

It certainly would be a busy day, she thought, smiling to herself. A new chapter in her life was starting and what a beginning. The title of this chapter might be called 'Confusion.'

It was after eleven before patients were discharged from the hospital. Marge helped Elaine buckle the baby in his carrier in the back seat of her car.

"Do you have grandchildren?" Elaine asked.

"No, Jim is an only child and he's not married." There was a short pause, "It's a good thing Jim's not here to hear me say that. Whenever I tell people he's not married, he always says, 'there goes Mom, advertising again'." Marge laughed, "But you know, it would be kind of nice to have grandchildren before I'm too old to enjoy them. I have kind of adopted Greg Roberts as a substitute. He's such a great young lad. I enjoy him so much. I see him go by quite often. He does some work for you too, doesn't he?"

"Yes, he sure does. I love having him around too. What a smart child he is and you should see how he has cleaned up my yard. I don't know where I could have found anyone any better to do the job."

"Speaking of work, are you settled into your new home?" Marge asked.

"Just about. I have a few cartons left to unpack in the kitchen and of course, the stuff I was bringing in the car. I was going to ask if you would mind taking me around to the garage I need to pay them for the tow job and see if the car is safe to be driven. I don't want to be without a car for very long now that I have the baby." The word "safe" triggered a long look at the sleeping baby in the back seat. She cringed slightly at having said, 'now that I have the baby,' but immediately realized this particular phrase could apply to his short past as well as the present, but even so, she had better be careful how she worded things in the future.

"It's no problem at all," Marge said. "Also, if you need anything at the supermarket, now would be a good time to get it while you have a babysitter and a car handy."

Elaine hesitated, "Well, if you're sure it wouldn't be too much of an imposition, I really do need a few things."

"Don't you think twice about it. You've got enough to worry about as it is. One supermarket coming up."

When Elaine returned to the car with her baby supplies, she said, "I can't thank you enough; you are so thoughtful to do this for me. I'm truly grateful."

"It has been a long time, but I still remember what it's like to drag a baby around every place you go."

When they arrived at the garage, Marge sat in the car with the baby while Elaine talked to the mechanic.

He told her he found no reason why she couldn't drive the car home. "You will no doubt have a problem opening the front door on the passenger side; it took the most punishment. Other than that, I saw nothing that would interfere with driving it."

When Elaine told Marge she could drive it home, Marge said, "Now you go ahead of me and I'll follow you just in case something goes wrong."

Elaine nodded, starting toward her car when Marge called after her, "and now don't be going too fast until you're sure how the wounded beast is going to act."

Elaine waved, signaling she had heard. She smiled, thinking it felt kind of good to have someone worry about her.

Marge pulled into the driveway behind Elaine.

"It handled just fine," she said. "I'll just get these things into the house and I'll be right back to get the baby."

"No, no, you go ahead and take the bags in. I'll bring sleeping beauty in; I haven't had a chance to hold him yet. He's been such a good baby through this whole thing. He probably will be awake all night, having slept so much now," Marge said, unbuckling the straps from the car seat.

Arriving in the kitchen, Elaine sat her parcels down on the counter, then turning, she took the baby from Marge.

"Now, if I could use your bathroom, then I'll be on my way," Marge said.

"Sure, down the hall, first door on the left."

"I'm getting to an age that no matter where I go, the first thing I have to do is find out where the bathroom is located," Marge said, disappearing down the hall.

When Marge returned to the kitchen, Elaine was sitting at the table, cuddling the baby.

"This is such a pretty little cottage. I like what you've done with it," Marge said.

"Thank you," Elaine smiled. "I feel so comfortable here. It's so cozy, it makes me feel loved almost as much as when my grandmother was here."

"I think the warmth of her spirit is still here. Well, say, I better get on down the road. His Highness," she nodded toward the baby, "will be looking for some attention pretty soon. If there's anything you need help with, just let me know. You have my number." She turned toward the door.

"Thanks so much for all you and your son have done for me. I really do appreciate it," Elaine said.

"I'm glad to have been useful. I'll be up to visit soon."

Chapter Twenty

Greg put a slicker on over his winter coat as he walked out the door. Since the snow from the night before was gone, he would be able to ride his bike. The clouds were dark over the lake, threatening heavier rain, but as he rode down the long driveway, he was met with only a foggy mist.

It was Sunday afternoon and Greg knew Dora wouldn't be getting up for a while since it had been almost dawn when she came home.

He had long ago come to terms with the fact that she had very little regard for him except for his role in the drug business and he hesitated to cause any problems. He learned the conditions of survival early on; keep your marks up, don't do anything to cause the school officials to come nosing around, don't have friends to the house and keep out of her way as much as possible. Every lesson had been taught with pain from her hands. As he pedaled his way up the hill toward the Colby house, he thought about how he would approach the subject of Aaron. He had never talked to any of his friends about his home life, even before it included Aaron. As far as he knew, no one knew he had a brother. He had sometimes been tempted to tell Mrs. Colby since she was such a gentle, loving person. For reasons he couldn't quite define, he felt some kind of connection with her. There was an undercurrent of sadness about her, even when she seemed happy, quite similar to what he felt most of the time. Still, he hadn't dared tell anyone about the baby and now he was glad that he hadn't. He knew now why his mother had been so adamant on the subject. She intended to sell Aaron right from the beginning and didn't want people wondering what happened to him.

Greg knocked on the door and stood waiting. When Elaine came to the door, she had Aaron in her arms.

"Oh, Greg, it's you. Am I glad to see you! Can you help me out for a little while?"

"Sure, that's why I came up. I thought you might need some help since you just finished moving in."

Aaron was kicking and squirming, his arms reaching out to Greg. Elaine looked down at the baby in her arms, surprised.

"My goodness, will you look at how excited he is; I think he likes you. This is Matthew."

"Hi, Matthew," Greg smiled, taking the two outstretched hands in his. He wasn't prepared for Aaron's reaction to him. "Little kids usually do like me. I do some babysitting when I have time."

"Really? Well, that's good to know. Come on in."

"What happened to your head?" he asked, looking at the bruise on the side of her face. It had turned a greenish-yellow over night, with purple overtones seeping down beneath her eye.

"Come on into the kitchen. We'll have a little snack before we get to work and I'll tell you all about our little adventure," she said, kissing the top of Aaron's head.

"I didn't know you had a baby," Greg said, taking off his rain slicker and draping it over the back of the chair.

"Oh, didn't I mention it? Come, sit down; you can hold him while I get milk and cookies out for us."

While Elaine moved around the kitchen, Greg held his baby brother close to him as Aaron made happy noises, waving his hands around. Greg bent and kissed his cheek, "I love you, Aaron," he whispered into the tiny ear.

Coming back to the table, Elaine set the glasses and milk beside the plate of cookies. "I guess we'll have to do without homemade today. Go ahead and pour us each a glass of milk and help yourself to the cookies," she said, taking Aaron from him before seating herself across the table from him.

"Now, about the bruise."

While she related the early part of her day, Greg's thoughts were occupied with watching Aaron play happily on Elaine's lap, but as she came to the end of the story about the accident, fear rippled through him. Aaron could have been hurt.

As she finished, she said, "Just before I lost consciousness, I heard Matthew's startled cry and I was afraid he'd been hurt."

She saw the alarm on Greg's face.

"But, don't worry, everything turned out great; he wasn't hurt at all, not even a scratch, thank God." Once again, she hugged the baby to her and kissed his forehead.

"We were taken to the hospital to be checked over, just to be sure everything was okay, so we had to spend the night there. We didn't get home until about an hour ago. Mrs. Keller was kind enough to help us until I picked up my car. What a super nice lady she is."

"Yes, I work for her on Wednesday afternoons. She is a very nice lady." Greg smiled, thinking about her.

"Anyway, it sure made a mess out of the car. Did you notice?"

"No," Greg said, "guess I wasn't paying much attention to the car."

"Well, now that I think of it, you wouldn't have noticed. The damage is on the passenger side," she paused for a second then continued, "I pawed through the back seat to find a few of Matthew's things. It sure is in a terrible uproar out there, so if you would please, you could bring in the rest of the stuff from the back seat and the trunk. Things are scattered all over, so just gather them up and put them back in the boxes. When you bring them in, I can sort them out later. Here are the keys; the round one is for the trunk."

As Greg loaded the small boxes with the articles lying around on the back seat and the floor, he noticed the absence of the cans of formula and the bag of Aaron's clothes. He was glad she had found them.

He knew his days would be long and lonely without Aaron, but it was comforting to know his baby brother would be loved and safe.

"That's everything," he said, setting the last box down inside the door. As he looked around the kitchen, he saw Aaron asleep in his carrier.

As Elaine paid him, she asked, "Would it be possible for you to come after school tomorrow?"

"I think I can, unless my mother has something extra for me to do." He wondered as he said it what people would think if they knew how little his mother cared about what he was doing.

"It would be really great if you could. Matthew's new crib will be delivered tomorrow. If I remember correctly, it doesn't come assembled. Maybe you could help me with it." As an afterthought, she added, "He's growing so fast he outgrew the bassinet so I didn't bother to bring it." She smiled as she glanced in Aaron's direction. "It will be fun to cuddle him in my bed for one night."

Greg thought of the empty crib in his room. It was too bad she had to buy a new one. "Sure, I'll be glad to," he said, "I'll see you tomorrow." As he mounted his bike, he turned back to see Elaine standing at the door. "Tell Matthew I said goodbye." He had almost said Aaron. He decided he had better do some practicing on saying Matthew before he made a dangerous mistake.

Riding his bike down the hill, he felt like singing or doing somersaults. He was so happy with the way things turned out.

Looking skyward, he said, "Thank you God."

As he glided down the hill, he removed both hands from the handlebars. Holding them out to his side gave him the feeling of flying.

As he passed Mrs. Talbert's house, he thought he heard someone call. Glancing back, he saw Mrs. Talbert waving to him from the porch. Turning back, he rode into her driveway. "Did you call to me, Mrs. Talbert?"

"Yes, do you have an extra few minutes? I need to talk to you."

"Sure," he said. Pushing the kickstand in place, he approached the steps.

"Come in a minute if you would please." She held the door open for him to pass. "I saw you go up and I've been watching for you to come back by. You were going so fast I almost missed you.

Please sit down," motioning as she lowered herself into the opposite chair.

"As you probably know, I go south for a couple of months during the winter. Usually my son comes in once a week to check the house and see if everything is all right. There could be much damage if, for some reason, the furnace quit, don't cha know. Then, of course someone might break in, although nothing like that has ever happened before, but you never know. You know, I've always been so fond of this house. My husband and I bought it when we were first married. The early years were pretty hard back then. Sometimes the payments were due before we were ready for them." She stared out the window, reflecting.

Greg waited.

Suddenly, she turned her eyes back to him, almost as if she had forgotten he was there. "Oh my, will you listen to me, carrying on like that? What I'm trying to say is my son is retired now. He and his wife are going down with me. Of course, I would pay you if you would check through the house each day until I get back," she finished and watching his face, waited for his answer.

"Sure, I could do that and you wouldn't have to pay me. I would be glad to do that for you," he said.

"Oh, no, no, I'll pay you. It will be such a relief to me, you can't imagine. I know you to be a good and steady young man. I trust you. I talked to Marge Keller about it. She agrees that you would be reliable. It would make me feel so much better about leaving just to know you're looking in once each day. You know, just walk through and make sure everything is okay."

"When will you be leaving?" he asked.

"Not for two weeks. If you would stop by the first part of next week, I'll give you the key and the phone number where I can be reached in case something does go wrong. I'm so pleased you will do this for me." She stood and walked to her desk where she kept her purse. Following her lead, he stood, preparing to leave, cap in hand.

"Here," she said, handing him four fifty-dollar bills.

"Oh, no, Mrs. Talbert, that's way too much," he said, shocked.

"Now you listen to me, young man. It's worth it to me. If you want good trustworthy people to work for you, then you certainly should expect to pay them what they're worth." She smiled at him. "Now, you go along, I'll see you next week."

As he started to leave, he said, "Thank you so much, Mrs. Talbert, for trusting me and for the money. I'll take good care of your house, I promise." He glanced down at the bills in his hand.

"I have one word of caution though. I wouldn't mention our little transaction to your friends if I were you. Everyone isn't as honest as you. I did tell Marge Keller though. If she sees you coming and going, she might think bad of you. We can't have that, now can we?" she stood at the window, smiling as he rode away.

Marge stood by her mailbox as Greg rode up. "Well, hi there good looking. I see you have been up to see Mrs. Talbert. "

"Yes, I just left. I'm going to look after her house while she's gone," he said proudly. "She said you knew about it."

"Yes, I know. She told me she was going to ask you. Just because we're old doesn't mean we don't recognize a good thing when we see it." She winked at Greg. "Say, speaking of good things, have you been up to see Elaine Colby's baby?"

"Yes, I was coming from there when Mrs. Talbert stopped me."

"He sure is a beautiful baby and so cheerful. You can tell he's had great care and been loved," Marge nodded, smiling.

Greg smiled too, not knowing what to say. After a moment's pause, he said, "I think he liked me."

Marge laughed, "Well, of course he did, what's not to like?"

Chapter Twenty-One

Steve Darnell awoke early as he always did, but today was more than just an acquired habit. It was because his mind was whirling through seemingly endless anxieties.

He glanced at the sleeping form of his wife, Tracy. She had been so happy all these weeks; just as they were before this baby obsession had taken over their lives.

It had been a nightmare getting the money together, but it had been worth it to see Tracy's transformation. He loved her so deeply; she was his world. Whatever it took to see the happiness glowing on her face again made it all worthwhile.

The savings account was completely gone and now the newly paid-off mortgage on their house was back where they had started so many years before, fully mortgaged once again. These things wouldn't matter if this deal finally went the way it should.

He couldn't deny that it made him uneasy, after all these years, to be starting over with nothing in reserve in case of an emergency, but it couldn't be helped. He certainly couldn't put a price tag on Tracy's health; mental or physical. He wished the thing was over with once and for all.

Steve rubbed the back of his neck to ease the tension he was feeling. He wished he felt more confident about the outcome. He hadn't liked the lawyer from the beginning. Just knowing a lawyer who would deal in selling a baby said a lot about his ethics. He smiled sardonically. *I'm a good one to sneer at someone else when it comes to their character*, he thought, *I'm buying a baby.*

Well, he sighed, *it will be over soon, one way or the other.*

Mid morning at his office he received a call from George Becker's secretary asking if he and his wife could come to the office early in the afternoon.

"Why? What's this about?" Steve, who was already waiting for the axe to fall, was suspicious.

"I don't know sir," she said stiffly, "I'm sure he'll tell you when you get here."

Steve sat at his desk for some time, his anxiety growing with every passing minute. Finally, he picked up the phone and dialed his home phone number. When Tracy answered, he said, "Good morning, honey. How are you this morning?"

"Great! Oh, Steve, just one more day; can you believe it?"

"Listen, honey, I just had a call from Becker's office. He wants us to come in about one o'clock, can you make it?"

"Sure, but what does he want?"

"I only talked to his secretary and she didn't seem to know."

"Oh, Steve, maybe we'll be able to get the baby a day early." He heard the excitement in her voice.

"Now, stay calm, honey. It may be just some last minute loose ends to clear up, so don't cross any bridges prematurely."

"Oh, Steve, I'm so excited. I can't wait to hold him. I'm going to bring the car seat, just in case."

Steve groaned silently, "Why don't you come down about eleven-thirty. We can go to lunch before we head out to he city."

"Okay, but I don't think I'll be able to eat anything."

When Steve hung up the phone, he went to the safe and dialed the combination. Back at his desk, he counted the money again before arranging it in his wallet. His anxiety had increased. He was fairly sure he wouldn't need the money today. He tried to blame his feelings on his sense of integrity; although it did bother him to have to deal with such a sleaze bag, that wasn't exactly it. The feeling bordered on fear. He felt as if something dreadful was about to happen. It was just a matter of when. If this deal fell through, what would it do to Tracy? He didn't dare think about it.

True to her word, Tracy ate very little of her lunch. She had chattered almost continually while pushing the food around on her plate.

As they neared the city, she grew quiet. Steve glanced at her face, trying to discern if he had transmitted his own troubling thoughts to her or if she was just quietly anticipating what she hoped was about to happen.

Upon arriving, they walked down the short hall to the office door. As they entered the reception area, the secretary picked up the phone and announced, "Mr. and Mrs. Darnell are here." The secretary made no comment, but within seconds George Becker opened the office door. "Please, come in and have a seat." Turning back to the receptionist, he said, "No calls."

Closing the door silently behind him, George walked slowly behind his desk and sat down heavily. Sighing, he said, "There's no easy way to say this. I'm afraid I have bad news for you. I can't tell you how sorry I am." He glanced at Tracy's stricken face and quickly looked away. "She has decided to keep the baby and there's nothing I can do about it."

Steve was immediately on his feet, his face flushed with anger.

"How can you do this to us?" Steve growled, striding the few steps to the desk, his fists clenched.

"Believe me, Mr. Darnell, it's not any of my doing. I don't feel any better about this than you do," George said. "There isn't anything I can do." He handed Steve the money he had paid down at the beginning of the arrangement.

"You can tell me her name and believe me I'll do something about it," Steve yelled, pounding the desk with both fists.

George stood behind his desk, "You know I can't do that. This operation had to be strictly confidential for both our sakes. Surely you knew that from the start."

"I'll tell you what I knew right from the start; that if this happened what it would do to my wife." Steve turned to look at Tracy, but she was not in the chair.

Steve ran through the office door, which now stood open and into the reception area.

"She just ran out," the receptionist said.

Steve ran across the room into the hall. Tracy was going through the door into the street.

"Wait, Tracy!" Steve yelled, "Tracy…"

Tracy walked deliberately through the outside door without looking back. Crossing the sidewalk, she stepped out into the busy street.

Steve tore open the door, realizing what she was about to do.

"No, Tracy, no!" His anguished scream hanging on the air as he heard the screeching of tires, screams from the watching pedestrians and the thunder of automobiles slamming into one another.

He watched as Tracy's body flew through the air, landing almost at his feet.

Steve knelt to the sidewalk and lifted her small broken body into his arms. Anguished tears rolled down his cheeks, falling onto her beautiful face.

"Why, Tracy, why?" he moaned.

People crowded around him as he rocked the beautiful woman in his arms.

All traffic stopped and the entire area was in total chaos; people were running around in all directions, police cars came with howling sirens, an ambulance whooped its arrival and people were crying or staring in disbelief.

Steve Darnell was only vaguely aware of any of it. As the tears streamed down his face, he knew that if she were gone, his reason for living would go with her.

George Becker stood in the window of his outer office beside his secretary, observing the pandemonium. Neither one spoke.

Chapter Twenty-Two

Tonight was the grand opening of the tavern and in spite of his strained relationship with Dora, he was excited. A large ad had been placed in the local paper and they were ready.

During the renovations, many of the town business owners had stopped by to wish them well. Dora, of course, doing what she did best, had charmed them almost out of their shoes. At the same time, she had attempted to mend the breach in her relationship with Martin by giving him all the credit for the planning and details connected with getting the business up and running. She praised Martin highly and affectionately.

In mid-afternoon, before the opening, the mayor of Carson Cove stopped by to congratulate them and welcome their new business to the community. Martin was holding a meeting with the bartenders and waitresses, reinforcing his instructions and rules. Dora met the mayor outside as he was surveying the pleasant surrounding.

"Hello, I'm Dora Roberts, part owner," she said, extending her hand. "Welcome to the D and M Tavern," she smiled.

"I'm Verl Wiley, the mayor of Carson Cove. I wanted to welcome you to our town and wish you success," he said, shaking her hand.

"How nice of you to come," Dora said warmly. "You'll have to excuse Martin, he's giving the help a little brush-up on the rules and regulations, but he'll be finished in a few minutes. I know he'll want to meet you."

"It must have taken a great deal of foresight to turn this place around." The mayor waved his arm to include the surrounding area of the yard and parking lot.

"Well, I'll tell you," Dora shook her head for emphasis, "I'm so lucky to have a partner like Martin Delmont. He's the one with the business sense in this venture. I've learned a great deal from his adventuresome spirit."

As she finished, Martin stepped out into the yard. Dora motioned him over. "Martin, come meet the mayor of Carson Cove."

Martin walked over to stand next to Dora, extending his hand to the mayor.

"Martin, this is Verl Wiley," she smiled and turning back to the mayor, she said, "and this is my partner, Martin Delmont. I'm sure he'll be glad to show you around and if you'll excuse me, I have some work to do. I'll be up in my office, Martin, if you need me." Laying her hand on the mayor's arm, she said, "It was a pleasure to meet you Mayor and thanks again for coming."

"A very charming lady you have there," the mayor said, his eyes following her departure toward the door of the tavern.

"Yes, indeed," Martin smiled, "she is all that, to be sure."

Dora always had that effect on people.

"She says you're the brains behind this enterprise. Quite some job you've done on this old place."

As they walked through the downstairs, Martin described the work and challenges that had been accomplished. He was debating the idea of taking him upstairs to see the office area when the mayor looked at his watch and announced that he had an appointment and suggested, laughingly, that it might be in poor taste to miss one of his own meetings. He told Martin that he and his wife would be there for a short time during the evening.

As Martin watched the mayor drive away, his thoughts went back to Dora. Since their quarrel last week, she had apologized extravagantly for her conduct and retracted most of the things she had said at the time. She used the many changes, the heavy workload and upsets in her personal life as excuses for her thoughtless behavior. Martin wanted to believe her superb act of contrition, but considering all the years of infidelity to every cause except her own agenda, he had to assume this too must be an act to further her own interests.

After Martin had received a phone call from George Becker about the failure of the baby transaction, he wondered, *was this another of Dora's treacherous schemes?* George had been as angry as Martin had ever known him to be. If Dora was playing her usual tricks, she should realize she was playing with dynamite. George Becker was not one to take a double-cross kindly. Dora should watch her back.

Martin had an interest in this transaction because the money from the baby had been promised to pay Dora's share in the renovation of the tavern. Although her investment thus far had been minimal, it had not hurt him financially, but he felt since her name was on everything as a partner, an investment on her part would indicate commitment.

The drug business was strong and profitable for both of them, but they had not heard from Frank Brant as of yet. Martin wasn't too concerned because he realized there was a great deal to be considered with transferring the operation.

Martin stood facing the huge neon sign announcing the D & M Tavern and the smaller one below that said OPEN. Neither sign had been turned on yet.

Dora walked the short distance and joined him.

"It's beautiful, isn't it?" she said quietly.

Martin looked at her face, almost in disbelief. For once she actually sounded sincere. He noticed the fine lines beginning to appear at the corners of her eyes. Not that they altered her beauty because there was no question she was still an attractive woman.

"You look tired," Martin said.

"Yes, I am tired." She rubbed the back of her neck, "It's more about the baby business, I guess, than anything."

"What happened?" Martin had no intention of telling her about his conversation with George Becker.

Martin followed Dora to the white bench which was in front of the landscaped area near the front door. Dora sighed as they sat down next to each other.

"The deal was set for Monday of this week, but as it turned out, Sunday morning Greg woke me up telling me the baby was gone and accused me of taking him away. Greg was throwing a gigantic fit, yelling and screaming at me to do something. Topping his list was to call the police. Of course, that was out of the question with this drug business about to take off big time. All we'd need is to have the police nosing around asking questions. I called George, thinking he had somehow double-crossed me and taken the baby ahead of time so he wouldn't have to pay me my share of the money. We ranted, raved and threatened to kill each other for a while and that solved nothing."

"Of course, I still have to put up with Greg's long face and accusations. I'll tell you one thing, after we find out what Brant is going to do and we get things organized, we won't need him anymore. That's when I'll get rid of his whining mouth for good."

"Get rid of him? Are you insane?" What do you mean, get rid of him?" Martin was instantly angry.

"Oh relax Martin, there are ways." Dora's voice was calm and matter of fact. "I think he would try to run away eventually anyway. We can't have that; he knows too much." Once again, Dora sighed, "I thought about hiring someone to do the job, but I can't leave myself open to blackmail. Nothing says I can't do the job myself."

Martin thought about the gun she always carried with her. "You told me you promised his mother on her death bed you would take care of him. Doesn't that mean anything to you?" Martin was angry.

"You don't see her around anymore, do you?" Dora smirked.

"That's it. You took the money and the property besides the life insurance money, gave your word and you don't think you have any responsibility to her or the boy?" Martin shook his head in disbelief. "You don't think he has earned his way with all these years of running drugs for you?"

Martin watched the anger rise on her face. "I think I have earned all of it and more, just by having him around. When his mother came back to live at the house, I thought she could join me in my line of work. She was beautiful and small. A lot of men would go for a woman like that, but she didn't approve of what I was doing and didn't want any part of it. Besides, she was pregnant with Greg. About the only good part of the whole thing was that she owned the house and I never had to pay rent. She didn't have anything else to do except preach to me and disapprove of what I was doing. After Greg was born, she was sick most of the time. I'm here to tell you, it wasn't easy for me trying to carry on my business with her and the brat hanging around." Dora sighed heavily, thinking about those years.

"As she saw me getting increasingly irritated, she took the brat and went places. She gave me her will, which was drawn up to make me the legal beneficiary of all her properties, money and legal guardian of Greg. Toward the end, I had to make outside arrangements for him to be taken care of because he was only four years old when his mother died. So yes, Martin, I think I earned everything I got out of that transaction."

Martin was stunned at such a cold-blooded account. He felt slightly sick to his stomach listening to her. Questions filled his mind. Something didn't make sense about the whole story. He had loved Judy Collins as he had never loved any other woman before or after she was gone. They had planned to be married, but when he told her about his drug business, she had walked out of his life. He was hurt and angry. He wasn't in contact with her, nor did he know where she had gone until some years later when Dora had contacted him, telling him that Judy was dying she asked if he could come because Judy said she needed to talk with him. He had gone to the hospital immediately, but it was too late, she had slipped into a coma and never regained consciousness. Martin asked Dora if she knew what Judy had wanted, but Dora said no. Judy had said it was between her and Martin.

Dora had asked him at that time how he knew Judy and he had only told her that he had known her a number of years earlier.

That's how he had met Dora, which eventually resulted in Dora's involvement with the drug distribution of his customers in the city, along with her own lucrative business.

Because Judy was Greg's mother, Martin had been interested in the boy's development over the years and felt sorry for the way Dora had treated him.

Dora sighed heavily, "How did we get on this subject anyway? We have tonight to get through and besides, I'm sick of thinking about the whole mess. Do you want me down and mingling with the people tonight?"

"Yes, if you would, at least for a couple of hours. I'm sure there will be a sizeable crowd and they will expect to see both partners." Martins' voice had lost all the excitement and was almost expressionless.

"Well, then I better go home and rest a while before I get ready. I'll see you later."

Martin stood, his hands in his pockets, watching her drive away. His mind was spinning as he began picking her statements apart. First, the missing baby. He had never before known anyone with such a cold-blooded attitude. Not only that, but she made it sound as though she had no responsibility in the matter. However, he had been down a road paved with her lies too many times to trust anything she said. The way George had sounded on the phone, Martin had to believe his rage was authentic, which would mean he had nothing to do with the disappearance. This left Greg to be considered. He couldn't believe it was Greg. There was no duplicity in the boy. True, he openly hated the drug business and anyone connected with it. This included Martin, but he loved the baby. As far as anything he had heard or seen, the boy had gladly taken full care and responsibility for him. Now, if Greg had disappeared along with the baby, it would be a different story. But as it stood, he marked Greg off the list of suspects.

It was just as difficult to think that someone walked in off the street and took the child. What were the odds of that happening? In the first place, very few people knew about the baby and secondly, the few who did, were told it had died at birth. There was a small chance that the people who were buying the baby had somehow found out who was selling it and had stolen it. However, George told him with previous sales of this kind, he kept no records of the buyers. So this brought him back to Dora. Judging from past performances, he had to conclude Dora was behind this shady transaction, no matter how convincing she sounded.

Her announcement came to the forefront of his mind. She planned to get rid of Greg permanently, at her convenience, with no more emotion or feeling involved than pouring the remains of a cup of coffee down the drain. She had indicated thoughts of this nature at different times before, but this time Martin knew she meant it.

Something about it had stuck in his mind. Dora had said Greg was almost four years old when Judy died. Martin had seen Greg during that time. He would not have guessed he was more than two or three at the most. Something about that didn't add up, or did it? He didn't know how old Greg was now, but he could find out easily enough. This would take some serious thinking and a little investigation.

Martin shook his head. Why had Judy gone to Dora for help? She should have known he would help her. He supposed the answer to that was the same reason she had left him in the first place. She didn't want her son to be around the drug business. There was no way she could have known how Greg would be treated by Dora and unknowingly forced him into the drug business anyway.

Even though the boy hated him for the same reason Judy did, Martin admired the boy's character, forged despite his difficulties with Dora. Greg must have inherited his strong will from Judy.

Martin's mind was churning. He'd have to think more on this subject when things calmed down. He was suddenly very weary. Glancing at his watch, he knew he had to get going too. It was going to be a very long night.

Chapter Twenty-Three

When Greg left school, he went directly to Elaine's house. He hoped she hadn't already put the new crib together. When he rang the bell, Elaine called from the living room to come in.

Greg found her kneeling on the living room floor with the crib parts lying in a pile before her. She was studying the pamphlet that came with the boxes. Matthew lay in the carrier nearby, happily kicking and waving his arms. Greg went to him and kissed his cheek.

"Oh, Greg, I am truly happy to see you, but I don't know if we're going to be able to do this." She held up two different bags of screws and bolts of various sizes, looking doubtful.

"Well, let's not give up before we even start," he said. He took the bags from her and looked at the different sizes.

"I'll go out to the garage and bring in some tools. I'll be right back."

When he returned, he picked up the booklet. "Can I look at the instructions for a minute?"

"Sure, help yourself."

"First, we have to identify each piece because the book tells what piece goes where in a kind of sequence."

Elaine sat on the floor Indian style, watching.

He began separating the pieces and arranging them on the floor in front of them.

When the doorbell rang, they were both startled. Elaine pushed herself to her feet and went to answer the door.

"Well, hi there." Elaine hesitated as she tried to recall his name. "Jim, isn't it? Would you like to come in?"

"Maybe for a minute or two. I just came by to see how you were doing since the accident."

Greg took the opportunity to go to the baby and play with him while listening to the exchange in the next room.

"I see by the bike out front that you already have company."

"Yes, I bought a new crib for Matthew and Greg was nice enough to stop by and help me put it together. Do you know Greg Roberts?"

"I've not met him in person, but I sure have heard about him from my mother."

"Come on in then and you can meet him."

"I thought I might be able to meet your husband as well, is he here?" Jim hadn't heard anything in her conversation at the hospital to indicate there was a spouse, but he wanted to be sure before he stepped into another man's territory. She was a beautiful young lady and he was drawn to her warm and friendly nature.

She hesitated only for a second. "My husband died eight months ago in an automobile accident," she said quietly, but before he could say anything, she continued, "but come in and meet Greg. Of course, you have met Matthew before." Elaine smiled.

As Jim entered the room, he extended his hand to Greg. "I've heard many good things about you from my mother. I'm Jim Keller."

Greg took his h and smiling, remembering some of the things Mrs. Keller had said about her son.

"I was getting started on the crib, sorting out the parts," Greg extended his hand toward the pieces of crib lying on the floor.

"Maybe I'll be able to help with that some, if Elaine wouldn't mind."

"I'd be grateful, thank you," she smiled.

Jim removed his jacket. "It's my night off, so I've got some extra time on my hands. Now, this handsome young man over here," Jim looked over at Matthew, "I supposed he's supervising the operation."

In less than an hour, the crib began to take shape. Jim picked up a piece lying on the floor. He looked puzzled, "Where do you suppose this goes?"

"I don't know. It looks like it should have gone over there," Greg pointed.

"Yeah, looks like you might be right. You know what I think, don't you?" He made an exaggerated motion over his shoulder toward Elaine, who was holding the instruction booklet. "I think our instruction reader skipped a line or two." Greg laughed.

"Oh, sure," Elaine smiled down at the two kneeling on the floor, her eyes sparkling, "incompetence always has to find someone to blame." They all laughed.

When the crib was finished, Elaine remarked, "Looks like I'm going to lose my bed partner."

At this, Jim stood erect and rolled his eyes in Greg's direction, raising his eyebrows.

Greg laughed as Elaine frowned in Jim's direction.

"Behave yourselves," she said sternly, but she smiled. "Now, if you two could get this into Matthew's bedroom I'd be 'evah' so grateful," she feigned an excessive southern drawl as she pointed to the open door across the room from them.

Jim winked at Greg and bending toward the baby, he lowered his voice, "You better watch out for those southern girls, they'll keep you jumping every minute."

"Don't you listen to his jaded remarks, Matthew." She lifted him out of the carrier. "I imagine it's time for a little change and then you can try out your new bed."

Greg and Jim positioned the crib in the baby's bedroom as Elaine came back through the connecting door from her bedroom carrying Matthew. The baby stretched out his arms toward Greg.

"If you wouldn't mind holding him for a few minutes Greg, I'll get the bedding and make up the crib."

Greg held his baby brother tight in his arms and kissed his cheek. The baby took hold of his finger; much the same as he had the first day he came home from the hospital. Greg felt an overwhelming sadness, instantly bringing tears to his eyes. He quickly turned and walked to the window with Matthew in his arms, worrying that Elaine or Jim might notice.

"It's kind of a shame to cover up all those goofy-looking ducks," Jim said as he helped Elaine slide the fitted sheet over the corner nearest him.

Elaine laughed, "I doubt he'll miss them, but you'll notice the same little ducks are floating around on the bumper pads."

"You should have bought sheets with footballs and baseballs instead of ducks." Jim pouted.

"I think I'll let him be a baby for a while before he has to live up to all that macho stuff. He can chase balls around after he learns to walk."

She turned to take the baby who was sleeping soundly on Greg's shoulders. She took him quietly into her arms, kissed him and laid him in the crib and covered him gently.

"It's too bad we can't remember being a baby." Jim's voice was soft, "All that kissing and hugging along with goofy little ducks and soft blankets. Just feel how soft that blanket is, Greg."

Greg smiled to himself. He'd already had a great deal of experience feeling Aaron's blankets, but he walked over to the crib and touched the blanket anyway. All three walked quietly out of the room.

"Oh, wait a second, I almost forgot." Elaine went back to her bedroom and came out with a little box in her hand.

"What's that?" Greg and Jim asked almost in unison.

"This, gentlemen, is a baby monitor. I put this in whatever room I'm in and I'll hear Matthew's every move or whimper," Elaine said smugly.

"Well, Greg," Jim said, "I guess we can rest assured that Master Matthew is being well cared for, although the poor little thing won't have much privacy." He turned a serious face to Elaine. "We men do need a little privacy."

Elaine rolled her eyes heavenward. "Get out of here, talk about goofy!"

Greg gathered the tools and started toward the door.

"Greg, when you have the tools put away, come back in and I'll pay you."

"No, you won't." Greg was emphatic, "I only get paid for outdoor work. I was glad to help out."

"Me too," smiled Jim.

"Without your help, I might have been trying to figure the thing out until day after tomorrow. I'm ever so grateful, thank you. I think we should order a big ol' pizza and celebrate. What do you say to that?"

"I love pizza," Greg grinned.

"Me too," Jim agreed.

Chapter Twenty-Four

The grand opening of the D & M Tavern was very successful, Martin thought, as he looked around the noisy bar room. People had been coming and going all evening. He enjoyed getting acquainted with the town's other proprietors and discussing the various aspects of running a business. At one point it crossed his mind how pleasant it might be to operate this place without the undercurrent of drug. Of course there wasn't any money in a tavern operation, at least not close to what could be made handling the drug trade. He had plans for his future retirement and they would take money, a lot of it. He already had a good start on his investments and now, hopefully, he would be able to increase them, bringing his retirement into reality sooner.

As the crowd thinned out, he glanced in Dora's direction. She stood with a small group of women. She had dressed extremely conservative for tonight's party, knowing there would be women present. She had the innate ability to recognize what was called for in every imaginable situation. Tonight she wore an understated black evening dress with no adornment except for a pearl necklace and matching earrings. She wanted the spouses of these men to think that she was of no threat to them. Martin knew she was successful by the smiles and laughter coming from the group of women. As always, the world was her stage. When she did have occasion to welcome the lone male, she gave him her usual charm, meant for men only. The fact that she was a beautiful woman did nothing to sideline her mission.

As closing time neared, he instructed the waitresses to start clearing the empty tables. Only a few people were at the bar. Dora had gone upstairs.

Although he had the full staff on hand tonight, they would not be on duty during the regular working hours. He had made out the schedules a month in advance.

As the last customer left, he walked over and shook hands with the bartenders. "You did a great job tonight and I want to thank you."

Turning to the waitresses, he smiled. "Everything went well, thank you. I look forward to a long and happy relationship here with all of you. If I can help you in any way, don't hesitate to come and talk to me."

Turning to the older bartender, he said, "I'm going up to my office now. When you leave, would you please lock up and turn off the lights?"

The bartender smiled, "I sure will, Mr. Delmont."

Martin sighed as he ascended the stairs. He was tired but happy the evening had gone so well.

Dora was sitting at her computer studying the screen in front of her. She looked up and smiled, "Is the opening night over, Mr. Tavern-man?"

"It sure is, how about a real drink to celebrate? I've had enough ginger ale to last me a while."

She laughed, "Me too, now that you mention it."

"I think I'll have a good old martini, how about you?" Martin walked across the room to the small bar.

"Just a glass of wine for me, Martin." She left the large sitting room and with a sigh, seated herself in a comfortable chair.

Martin handed her the glass of wine and sat down heavily across from her. *I must be getting old*, he thought, everything was aching.

"Tired?" she asked.

"Yes, aren't' you?" He was surprised because she didn't look tired at all. She looked excited.

"Frank Brant called a while ago to say he was on his way out to talk to us. I think he's going to let us take over his customers, don't you?"

"Maybe, but I don't want to get my hopes up." Martin got up and walked over to the window facing the front. The lights were off and the parking lot was empty.

"The hired help is gone and we're all closed up," Martin observed.

"Good, I'm sure Frank wouldn't care to be seen." Dora looked over at Martin, "It must be a relief to have this project up and running. Now you can relax and let go of all those many details that have been on your mind for so many months. I'm sorry that I haven't been much help to you."

"Well, no, not in the tavern enterprise, but you had most of the drug work to keep up. Now, I'll be able to jump back in since our cover is in place. I've already discussed the manager's job with Benny Krim. He's the head bartender and he'll take over all the functions of the place except bookkeeping and the ordering."

"I met him earlier; he seems to know his job. I've been working on the schedules for our customer pickups. Once we get it set, it's going to save us so much time. We won't have to be running all over creation trying to deliver their orders.

I've already talked to them individually about it and they seem to be agreeable. The next pickup time we will bring them here and show them the setup and what to do."

"Sounds like you have this part of the program well underway," Martin said.

"Yes, it will be busy until we get it organized. Then, I think it will settle down. If Frank does give us his customers, we can do the same for his customers as we have with ours; different times, different nights. You did plan to have the pickups at night, didn't you?"

"Yes, I did, but it might be something we should think about. I don't think the law is quite as vigilant with drug trafficking in the daytime as they are after dark," Martin said thoughtfully, "but maybe it wouldn't hurt to put some feelers out on the subject."

"A lot depends on what Frank has decided. No use worrying about it until we know. I think that's him coming in now," she said, observing the car lights reflecting off the front windows. "He knows to come to the side door and use the identifying button, which I showed him the last time he was here."

When she heard the buzz, she went to the intercom, "Yes?"

"Frank," came the answer. She smiled, pushed the button to unlock the door and waited at the top of the stairs to greet him.

When he was seated next to Martin with a drink in his h and he turned to Martin, "Tell me, how did your grand opening go?"

Martin smiled. "Almost better than we had planned. What a crowd! It sure exceeded our expectations. I actually enjoyed the small talk and good will."

"What gave me the greatest pleasure of all was knowing we were successfully deceiving a roomful of people," Dora beamed with her triumph. "They lapped it up like a litter of starving kittens."

Frank laughed. *Leave it to Dora to cut to the core of the rotten apple*, he thought.

"Now that our cover is in place, we can devote our time to our real business. Dora has already started to organize our customers," Martin said, giving Frank his opening, if there was a need for one.

"Well," Frank said, "that's why I came tonight. I'm turning my customers over to you if you agree on the profit sharing. Since you two will be doing most of the work, I figure sixty percent to you and forty to me. What do you think?"

Martin looked at Dora, who was smiling and nodding her head.

Martin nodded, "Sounds fair to us."

"All right then." Frank reached into his pocket and drew out a list of names that covered the entire page. Dora's face showed surprise and pleasure.

"It's too late tonight to set up the schedules, plus no time to bring them out here to teach them the routine, but I'll be back early Monday and we can get it organized. How does that sound?"

"Fine with me. How about you, Dora?" Martin asked.

"Fine with me too," Dora glowed.

Frank stood and shook Martin's hand and gave Dora a hug.

"I won't keep you any longer tonight. I know you must both be tired, but I think this will work out well. I'll see you about nine Monday morning and we'll figure on spending most of the day getting it organized."

Martin and Dora stood at the window watching until they saw Frank drive away.

"Wow, we're off and running." Dora rubbed her hands together gleefully.

"Yes, so we are," Martin sighed. "Now, let's go home."

Chapter Twenty-Five

Marge Keller took the cinnamon buns from the oven and drizzled icing on top, then placed them on the cooling rack before heading to Elaine's house.

As Marge cleared away the remains of her baking efforts in the kitchen, she marveled at how close their relationship had become in such a short time. Marge had been up to visit twice since Elaine had moved in. With the baby in the stroller, Elaine had invited Marge to go for walks with them on some of the beautiful autumn days. Since they had the first snowfall in early October, she supposed this could be called Indian Summer, but whatever it was called, it certainly was enjoyable.

After the walks, they always stopped at Marge's house for refreshments, extending their visits. Marge liked the girl very much and admired her cheerful outlook on life in general.

Marge was hoping Jim would take Elaine on a date and get to know her. Of course, she had no way of knowing if Elaine would be interested.

Marge sighed. She could only hope and wait for things to happen, if they were ever going to. Despite losing her husband and a baby to bring up alone, Elaine seemed capable of handling the situation.

For reasons she didn't clearly comprehend, it was comforting to Marge to realize the similarity of their viewpoints on subjects they discussed.

She supposed it might come from her old habit of measuring every woman's nature to see if she were fit to be Jim's wife.

Marge was happy to see Jim had shown considerable interest in Elaine, although she knew better than to try to initiate any motherly talks on the subject. She had made it as clear as possible to Elaine, without getting downright pushy, that she would be glad to babysit if she ever wanted to get away now and then for an evening or shopping during the day. So far Elaine hadn't taken her up on the offer.

Marge had called Elaine earlier and asked if she wanted drop-in company bearing cinnamon rolls. Elaine replied that the coffee would be perked and ready.

Marge had noticed Greg ride by earlier and since there was no other house at the end of the road, she assumed he was going to Elaine's. She thought that by the time she arrived, it would be time for him to take a break. Although there wasn't much yard work left for him to do, he stopped to visit Marge fairly often. She was grateful and told him so.

As she walked the short distance with the buns in her tote bag, she felt the absence of the bird songs she loved so much. Most of the songbirds had gone south and the trees were bare. She enjoyed the crisp sunny days Mother Nature was giving them before winter began.

Marge enjoyed the quieter winter months at the Cove. The people who owned the property along the lakeshore had long since closed their camps and headed back to their homes in the city or wherever. Some of the older retired people who had lived here most of their lives also went south in search of warmth and sunshine. Once there, may of these people had moved into trailers or rented camp-like places. It seemed to Marge as if they were continually uprooting their lives.

She couldn't see herself abandoning her comfortable home for five or six months for anything the south had to offer. Probably it had a lot to do with her laziness. It seemed like too much work to her.

As she approached the Colby yard, she saw Greg kneeling near the flower beds, cutting the dead stems, pulling dead leaves away from the fall flowers and then throwing them near the wheelbarrow. She walked over to where he was working.

"Am I ever glad to see you. Now I can take a break. Mrs. Colby said you were bringing refreshments." His shoulders sagged and he dropped his head in exaggerated weariness. "I'm not sure I can make it all the way to the house," he said weakly.

Marge smiled at his theatrical performance. "Well, it sounds like I made it in the nick of time. So, what's new in your big old world, Greg?"

"I'll bet you can't guess what," Greg said excitedly.

"Probably not, so you better tell me," she advised.

"Okay, I'll tell you, I am growing!" he yelled and then, lowering his voice, he added, "My jeans got real short and I had to buy new ones. My shirts were tight too and the sleeves were halfway to my elbows. I've grown a whole size. Even my feet got bigger." She watched him as he did a cart-wheel and smiled at his antics. It had never occurred to her that he was conscious of his smaller than average size, but now realized she should have known.

"You know, now that you mention it, when I saw you go by the other day I thought you looked taller. Of course, it's only natural that you'd grow up eventually," she sighed loudly. "I suppose I'll love you no matter what size you get to be." Greg laughed.

As they stepped onto the front porch, Elaine opened the door.

"Hi, Marge. I see you found my right-hand man. Come on in, you two."

Greg held out his hands, "I've got to wash up first."

"We'll try to wait for you," Elaine said, "But I'd hurry if I were you."

As Greg disappeared down the hall, Marge whispered, "Did you notice how much he's grown lately?"

"You're kidding, right? You don't think I missed hearing about it, do you?" they both laughed as they entered the kitchen.

"To tell the truth, he's around so much I honestly hadn't noticed. Another thing I found out is that his birthday was in May and he is now thirteen."

"Oh, I wish I had known. I could have had a little party for him," Marge groaned.

By the time the coffee was poured, along with a glass of milk, Greg was back. Elaine pulled the buns apart and set one on each plate, leaving the rest on the serving platter beside the butter.

"These are fantastic," Elaine said. Greg nodded, his mouth was full.

"Thank you," Marge took a little bow. "I suppose the man of the family is sleeping."

"Yes, his morning nap. He should be waking up any time now." Elaine glanced toward the bedroom. "He's the best baby anyone could ask for."

Greg glanced toward Elaine's happy face as scenes from the past with Aaron's real mother flashed into his memory. "These are very good; do you mind if I have another one?"

"Of course not, just help yourself." Elaine moved the platter toward him. Finally, Greg stood, pushing his chair back.

"I'd better get out and finish up. I told Mr. Dunn I'd help him with some things before I go home, but before I go I'll check to see if Matthew is up."

"You haven't met Farrell Dunn, have you?" Marge asked Elaine.

"No, I've been too busy to be very neighborly."

"Someday we'll have to walk down and I'll introduce him. He's such a charming man, isn't he Greg?"

"Oh yes, charming would be the word I'd use to describe him all right," Greg smirked, rolling his eyes, "I'm outta here." Before he shut the door, he stuck his head back in, "Thanks for sharing."

Elaine and Marge laughed as the door closed behind him. "Maybe the word charming was a little too feminine to suit Greg."

"That would be my guess," Elaine agreed. After a few seconds, Elaine said, "Before you called, I was going to call you. I need to discuss a couple things with you. Tomorrow night I have a date, on the condition that I can get a babysitter. You have offered different times but I don't want you to feel obligated if you have something else planned."

"I don't have a thing planned and I'd love to babysit." Happiness glowed on Marge's face.

"Oh, thank you so much and of course, I'll pay you."

"Oh no, you will not pay me. It will be my pleasure. You know, Elaine, I sit down there most evenings watching television, knitting and feeling useless. Sometimes I go to town activities just to be around people, more than being interested, although I usually do enjoy myself. I know this will be fun. Not having any grandchildren to play with, except Greg, whom I've kind of adopted. What time would you like me to be here?"

"Well, your son is taking me out to dinner and he said he'd pick me up about five, so maybe about four-thirty. That will give me time to explain a few things before I leave."

Marge nodded, "That sounds like a good idea."

Elaine refilled their cups. "You probably know that Jim has been stopping by quite often since the accident. He's a lot of fun to be around. It really seems quite odd, to me at least, to feel so comfortable with someone I hardly know. Having been out of the dating world quite a long time you might expect there would be awkward moments, but it's never happened. I feel like I have always known him on some level." Elaine smiled, "I guess we're just kindred spirits." Shaking her head, she said, "Well, enough of the dissection of personalities. There is something else I want to discuss. I've been hired to be the high school librarian so I'm planning to start back to work in January and I'll need a babysitter. I don't want to assume that you would want to take on a full-time job, but maybe you know of someone."

Marge was thoughtful for a few seconds, "If you wouldn't mind if I brought him to my house sometimes and trusted me to take him with me occasionally to run an err and I'd be glad to take on that job too. If I remember correctly, schools have quite a few days off, so I don't imagine it would be a burden at all."

Elaine was ecstatic. "I hope you know you were my first choice, but I didn't want to impose on our friendship in any way by asking for too much. Are you sure Marge? After all, this is your retirement and you should be free to come and go as you choose."

"I do belong to a bowling group. And my friends and I get together each month to play cards, which is centered more on eating than playing cards. I sometimes think, but both are at night, so there's no problem."

"Well, all right, if you're sure. I'm not going to put much effort into talking you out of it," Elaine smiled. " and" she added, "you will take money for the job."

"All right," Marge conceded, "but we'll discuss it later. I have to get going right now as I have a few errands to run."

"Are you taking any of these buns home with you?"

"Oh no," Marge said, "I made them for you and Greg."

"In that case, I think I'll wrap a few of them for Greg to take down to share with his friends, if you don't mind."

"I don't mind at all. That's an excellent idea."

As Greg pedaled slowly toward Farrell Dunn's house, his mind lingered with Mrs. Keller and Mrs. Colby. He was glad that they were friends now. When he first met Mrs. Colby, she seemed sad and kind of lonely, but now with Aaron and her new friends, she seemed totally different.

As he neared Mr. Dunn's house, his thoughts turned to him. He had grown fond of Mr. Dunn in the short time he had know him and enjoyed his company, although Greg thought it sometimes seemed as though Farrell could read his mind, judging by some of the questions he asked.

The situation with Aaron was settled now and that was one worry off his mind. He marveled at how it had come about. Being at a dead-end and not knowing what to do. As a last straw he had asked Mr. Dunn's God to help him. The answer had come into his mind so fast, it had almost been scary. Mr. Dunn had said Greg should think of Him as his God too, because He knew him before he was born and knew what was in his heart and soul. Now, that was something to think about. He was going to talk to Mr. Dunn a lot more about the subject in the future, if he even had a future, that is.

There were many things Greg would like to talk with Mr. Dunn about, but he couldn't scrape up the courage to do it. He didn't dare for fear Mr. Dunn would hate him if he knew he was running drugs. Greg even thought about making it sound as if it were someone else and he was just curious about the end result. But he knew Mr. Dunn was pretty smart and he'd see through that game in about ten seconds. Now, he might have another problem to worry about. For two weeks, there hadn't been any pickups. This seemed more than a little ironic since he looked forward to a time when he could get away from the drugs and now he was worried because there hadn't been any pickups. When his mother was pregnant, there were no drugs involved, but somehow this was different. Somewhere in the back of his mind, even though he pretended not to, he knew she would go back to it. He supposed it could be they were out of the drug trade since they had the new tavern, but he really couldn't buy into that. Knowing how greedy his mother was when it came to money; it seemed unlikely. He had to think the business was probably going through the tavern and that they didn't need him to deliver drugs any longer. If this were true, why hadn't his mother told him there wouldn't be anymore drug deliveries? Now she seemed to be ignoring him completely, almost as if he were invisible. Of course, he had to acknowledge he had treated her pretty harshly and accused her of every kind of criminal act he could think of in order to cover himself when Aaron had disappeared, but somehow he had a bad feeling about how she was acting now. He feared the drug dealers too. If he was no longer useful to them, they would want to get rid of him because he knew too much.

He had always thought he'd run away. He had enough money hidden away to be able to go, but now there was Aaron. Greg knew Aaron was being loved and taken care of, but he couldn't bring himself to leave him. He loved the baby so much and Aaron loved him too. It was the first time in his life he had ever loved anybody or felt loved in return. He looked forward to the times when Aaron reached out to him and he could hold him in his arms. As if that wasn't enough, there were all his friends; Mr. Dunn, Jim, Mrs. Keller, Mrs. Colby and Mrs. Talbert. They acted as though they really cared about him. He had never known kindness and caring from anyone until now. How could he leave?

Arriving at Mr. Dunn's house, he tried to push these thoughts away. Mr. Dunn seemed to be able to pick up on his moods all too easily.

Greg opened the door and called, "Mr. Dunn, it's me. Wait until you see what I've brought for you."

"Come in, my boy, come in," Farrell said, coming to greet him. "What have you got here?" he asked, taking the package from Greg's outstretched hand.

"Mrs. Keller made them for Mrs. Colby and she said I could bring some to you. Wait until you taste them, they're really good!"

"Well, if Marge Keller made them, I know that's the truth, I've had her baking many times."

Greg hung his jacket on the rack and followed Farrell into the kitchen.

"I'm glad to see you Greg. I was about to get started on some house cleaning, but it won't hurt my feelings if we wait until we do some sampling." Setting the buns on the table, he went to the cupboard, removed two glasses, then went to the refrigerator for the milk.

"Well, actually," Greg hesitated, "I had some up at Mrs. Colby's, so these are yours."

"If my memory is accurate, when I was your age, I could have eaten a dozen or so without much of a problem," Farrell said, "but if you're too full, then that's another matter."

"Well, I might be able to eat one more," Greg said, "just to keep you company."

Farrell laughed, "Help yourself."

As they ate, Farrell said, "You look a bit happier today. Can I assume the problem you were worrying about has been solved?"

"Yes, I took care of it by doing what you said. I asked God for His help and the answer came right into my head."

"It happens that way sometimes, but not always. More often than not, you have to wait. The main thing is to talk things over with Him every day and trust Him to keep you moving in the right direction. It's a great comfort to know He's always beside me to help with my decisions. It can be that way with you too."

Greg frowned, "How can He be with you all the time and be with me too?"

Farrell smiled, "God is like the air; He's everywhere in spirit. We just have to trust Him. He doesn't give you everything you want, mind you, but He does give you what you need to cope with the problems of life, although He does expect you to do the work. Speaking of work, I think we better get started on this old house, what do you think?"

Chapter Twenty-Six

Steve sat holding Tracy's h and talking low, hoping on some level she could hear his voice. She lay motionless in the hospital bed, in a coma. Her head was bandaged from the operation performed to relieve the pressure on her brain and the purple bruises from her cheek bones had seeped below her eyes. The doctor had told him that the scan of her spine indicated another operation, but a specialist was being brought in to make the decision. It was too early to tell if there was any permanent damage or if she would come out of the coma, but they were hopeful. Steve came every day after work trying to find something encouraging in her situation, but so far there had been no change.

The doctor told him she could come out of the coma at any time, but Steve had heard of cases where a person didn't want to wake up. The circumstances being what they were, he thought this could certainly be the case with Tracy since her accident was obviously an attempt at suicide.

Steve stood, laying her limp hand on the light blanket beside her still body and walked to the window.

He looked out over the rooftops across the city with its lights shining through the early darkness. He watched the slow-moving cars making their way along the street; on their way home from work, he imagined.

A powerful wave of rage and loneliness swept over his tall, thin body. How could everyone be so unaffected, coming and going as usual, when his life was in such turmoil? He wanted to scream them into attention and have them feel his violent rage.

Sometimes, he hated Tracy as much as he loved her. How could she claim to have loved him and do this horrible thing to him? It was as if their life together was of no significance and his feelings counted for nothing.

Once she decided to have a baby, nothing else was of any consequence. It became an obsession which dominated her every thought and action.

He turned away from the window, looking once again at her expressionless face and was consumed with frustrated rage. He wanted to kill the people responsible for this horrific situation. He couldn't stand around this room any longer. He knew what he had to do. His whole body demanded action.

He had to find the woman responsible for selling her baby. The only way to do that was to get into the lawyer's office.

Steve had, more or less, forgiven the lawyer his part in this barbaric scheme since the lawyer had given him back all the money he had paid. Steve had paid off the latest mortgage on the house and placed the rest in a savings account in his name only, since Tracy's future was in question. The lawyer seemed to be angrier than Steve, although he still wouldn't reveal the woman's name.

When he left the hospital, he drove to the location of the lawyer's office. He was aware that it faced a fairly busy street, but as he drove, he thought about how the inner office was laid out. If he remembered correctly, it was a long narrow building with only the reception area facing the street.

As he drove slowly by, he noticed there was some sort of business on either side, but neither of the buildings were connected to the lawyer's building and there was walking space between them. The entire block appeared to be just off a business district since there were no homes.

Now it was totally dark and traffic was sparse. All the businesses were closed for the night, with the exception of a small café on the corner. He noticed their large parking lot. As he came around the back side of the block, he tried to estimate the distance where the back end of the law office would be. After parking the car, he walked between the buildings, but the street lights didn't convey enough light to the area for him to identify the back side of the law office. He turned back.

Sitting in the car for a moment before starting the motor, he thought about what he would need if he came back later in the night to try and find a back door to the place. He considered breaking in the front door, but even with little or no traffic at that time of night, it would be too dangerous. There was always a possibility that there might be an alarm system, although the rundown condition of the building didn't indicate anything too sophisticated.

It was shortly after one o'clock in the morning when he returned to the street where the law office was located. After parking his car in the café parking lot, which was now empty and the café closed, he walked quickly down the block to the front of the law office. He had a flashlight in one hand and his small bag of tools in the other as he hurried down the alley toward the back. As he had surmised, it was fairly easy to gain entry. With his screwdriver, he removed both sides of the clasp holding the lock in place and he entered the building. Walking down the long hall, he opened one door after the other looking for filing cabinets. Finally, opening the door to Becker's office, he noticed an extension to the left of the desk where there were four filing cabinets. He hadn't noticed the small alcove when he and Tracy had been there.

Pulling open the first drawer, he started moving each file toward him. He had no idea how he would recognize it since he didn't know her name, but he smiled as he saw an added tab beside each name, such as house closing and a date or court case, etc. After two hours of slowly going through each file and all four cabinets, he found nothing pertaining to the sale of a baby. He sat down in the chair at the desk and began going through the drawers. There was nothing. He examined the big calendar lying on the desk with notes about Becker's schedule.

Discouraged, he leaned his tired head on his hands and as he did, his elbows moved the calendar. He saw a scrap of paper sticking out from beneath the heavy cardboard. Lifting the calendar, he found many scraps of paper with reminder notes hand written on them. Carefully moving the calendar aside, he began reading the notations on each one. As he neared the end of the scraps, his heart sank. He wasn't going to find anything. He was discouraged and tired. Then, he saw it. It read, 'Dora Roberts – turn over baby.' Right behind it was the same date that was permanently etched in his memory.

"Dora Roberts, you're as good as dead. Wherever you are, I'll find you," Steve whispered.

As Steve walked to his car, he felt more tired than he had ever been in his entire life.

Chapter Twenty-Seven

Farrell Dunn walked out of his house into the early morning sunshine. Even though he was an early riser, he waited until after the early morning commuters were well on their way into the working world before he started out for his morning walks.

His leg was completely healed, but his doctors advised walking as good therapy; not only for his leg, but for the rest of his body as well. His stride was shorter and his pace somewhat slower than it once was, but he noticed a dramatic improvement in the way he felt during these last few weeks and he was encouraged.

Most days when he walked, he felt a lifting of his spirit and a sense of nearness to the creator, but today he was preoccupied. He had a problem. When he considered the amount of time he has spent on it lately, he knew it was time to move on it. Even though he was worried about the outcome, he decided he would go to Marge and lay the whole thing out so they could discuss it, for better or worse. He couldn't just keep dragging it around in his mind and getting nowhere. He had, in the past, discussed a great many things with her because of her clear thinking and remarkable understanding of human nature. But he was a little worried about how this would go because she was involved. He couldn't seem to get around this wall of guilt he carried.

Marge Keller answered his knock with a welcoming smile.

"Come in, come in," she said, motioning him inside, "It's just the right morning to have company for breakfast."

A wave of emotion went through Farrell at her cheery greeting. " and just what makes this the right morning, if I may ask?"

"It's always a good morning when I find you on my doorstep."

He watched her walk to the cabinet and remove two cups. Maybe this wasn't going to be too difficult after all.

"The cream and sugar are already on the table," she announced, as she set a steaming cup of coffee in front of him before returning to the stove. "Breakfast is on the way."

Farrell sipped his coffee. "Do you have anything planned for a short time after breakfast?"

"Nothing that can't wait. Why?"

"There's something heavy on my mind and I wanted to talk it over with you to see what you thought about it."

"Now you've got me curious, but let's have breakfast first and we can get to it over a second cup of coffee."

During the small talk at breakfast, Greg's name came up. They were both concerned about him.

"I've been giving him books to read and had some discussions about prayer. I don't think anyone else has ever discussed the subject with him."

"Maybe not," Marge said. "He talks about some books he reads and some about his school work. I find him to be very intelligent for his age, but I haven't been able to get anything about his home life out of him, have you?"

"No, I feel as though I've made significant progress in some areas, but not about anything personal. I'm hoping he will confide in me more in time. I've found his knowledge of God to be sadly lacking. I have been instructing him, but I try not to be too excessive at any one time. It's been my experience that young people have a tendency to shy away if they think you're getting pushy, but so far, he seems receptive. He asks a lot of questions." Farrell glanced at Marge, "From the first time I met him, I sensed an undercurrent of sadness about the boy."

Marge nodded, "Yes, I noticed it too. It's as if something is dogging him no matter what he's doing." Farrell smiled at her choice of words. "It does seem to me, though, that the last few weeks he has been somewhat happier."

"I ran into the principal of the school the other day. We've been friends for a good many years and I brought Greg's name into the conversation," Farrell said. "I thought she could give me some insight on the subject. She praised him highly, saying he was a straight A student. He never gives his teachers any trouble. The only thing she mentioned was that he didn't socialize with the other students except in the classroom, although he is well liked. She said he doesn't participate in any after-school activities. I told her about his after-school jobs and she thought he might be lonely. I've tried to fit lonely into my thinking, but I can't accept it. He seems to enjoy the company of the people he works for without any problem. He met your son and told me about the good time they had one afternoon. He beams when he talks about the baby up at the end of the road, so I can't settle on loneliness because underneath it all, the burden he carries is still there. I've given it a lot of thought and took it apart in my mind to see if I could find a reason. What I came up with was fear." Farrell sipped his coffee.

Marge was startled, "Fear? You think it's fear?"

Farrell set his cup down, "I don't mean the ordinary kind of fear. I'm thinking of something more obscure; something private. For example, suppose a child did something wrong and he knew he'd be punished if he was found out. Maybe fear isn't the right word. Let's call it apprehension, it fits better."

Marge was pensive. "Yes, now I see where you're going. It does seem to fit Greg's situation better than loneliness." After a moment's thought, she added, "Of course, a great many things fit that category. For instance, if he did something he considered to be wrong, he wouldn't want to discuss it with you because he would think he might lose your friendship. There are any number of things it could be," Marge said, moving her cup in half circles on her napkin.

"Exactly," Farrell smiled, "Maybe he saw something he knew was wrong and feels guilty about not reporting to the authorities because he feels threatened or was threatened." There are dozens of similar scenarios, once you get thinking along those lines," Farrell said, almost triumphantly, but then immediately added sadly, "It could also mean he's in danger."

Marge heard the change in his voice. "Of course, we shouldn't' be too fast to jump to conclusions, Farrell. Remember young people are apt to feel an exaggerated importance of their plight in life because they feel so helpless to change it."

"Yes, I know that's true, but now, since I have all these troubling thoughts in my mind, I won't be able to put them to rest," Farrell glanced out the window in thought, "at least I have a direction and I'll keep trying to get him to talk to me."

He flashed a faint smile in her direction, "Of course, it might just be an old codger with too much time on his hands."

Marge laughed, "Come on Farrell, codger doesn't apply until you're seventy-five, so you have quite a few years before "codger" comes into play. Besides, I see all those pretty widows eyeing you up at church every Sunday, trying to get your attention. They think you're the catch of the season. However, I do think you probably have more time to brood now that you're retired. I know I do too. Some days it gets pretty lonely, although I do manage to keep quite busy. But, I don't seem to have a purpose anymore without Charlie. It's been two years now since he's gone and Jim is out on his own too. I imagine you must feel it too, sometimes, since you took early retirement. I know you lost Beverly some time ago. How long has it been?"

"Close to six years now," Farrell sighed. "Yes, it's lonely. As a matter of fact, this is one of the subjects I wanted to talk to you about. I occupy some of my time volunteering at the hospital and I fill in for the pastor when he needs to get away. I still write the column for the church newspaper, but at the end of the day I go home to an empty house. There's no one to share the everyday events of my life. I'm thankful that you fill in many of my empty spaces. I know I haven't told you, but you must know that I love you very much."

Marge saw the worried look on his face and wondered what was wrong. What was there to be concerned about? Marge reached across the small table, taking his hands in hers. She moved her thumbs over his long fingers as if to smooth away his problem.

"Farrell?" Her voice was softened as she searched his face. "Don't you know that I love you too?"

Relief flooded through his body. He wanted to go take her in his arms, but he stopped himself because he had to tell her his real problem. Now that they had come this far, he had to get it out in the open and talk about it. He was too emotionally involved to think clearly about it. Maybe Marge could help him.

"Oh, Marge, "I'm so grateful to hear you say you love me too. I know it's your nature to be kind and loving to everybody and I wasn't sure that it was more than just kindness toward me. I could only hope, but that's not the whole problem. It's that I feel so guilty." He watched her face as her beautiful eyes widened.

"Guilty?" she questioned.

"Yes. Let me explain." I don't really understand it myself. I thought I had loved her, but when I met you it was like I had been living a lie my whole life. Like I had been under a cloud and all at once the sun came out! I felt alive and joyful. I don't ever remember feeling that kind of love for my wife when she was with me. My love for her was ordinary, as if I deprived her of my best. I didn't know about this kind of love or that I could feel this stronger emotion until after she was gone. I never felt this way before for anyone until I got to know you. Now, I'm carrying this terrible guilt because she deserved better than I was able to give her."

Marge listened to him, thinking the situation was close to being funny, if it wasn't for the despair in his voice and the sadness on his face. Here was a man, highly educated, with strong Godly beliefs and yet he knew so little about human nature.

"Farrell," she said softly, "would it bother you to tell me about your wife and maybe some about your marriage?"

"No, not at all." Marge noticed the hard lines soften in his face.

"We met when I was in seminary school. She was one of the secretaries in the office. She was attractive and had a gentle voice. There was an air of dignity about her; a self-assurance that was very calming, like a cool breeze on a hot day. She was gentle and efficient. I was having a hard time with some of my subjects and there was a restfulness about her that would bring me down from my peeks of frustration. I fell in love with her."

"What a nice memory," Marge smiled.

"We were married right after my schooling ended. She had great faith. Truth be told, I often wondered if she wasn't a better minister than I was. She sure made a great minister's wife. She got along so well with the sometimes-quarrelsome ladies groups, acting as a mediator with her quiet common sense. Sometimes, when I would get to hooting and hollering about worldly affairs, she'd tell me, 'You go give the world a good beating, Honey. I'll be here waiting to smooth out your wounded ego,' and she did too." Marge smiled knowingly.

"Over the years," Farrell continued, "my faith grew and I lost some of my bluster and I learned there was a better way of handling my affairs more efficiently. She was terribly disappointed when she learned we weren't able to have children, but she seemed to accept the Lord's decision. Money was never a problem with us, as it is sometimes with other ministers. I had a steady income from the investments I had made with inheritances. To add to it, her family was well-to-do and were very generous with her. I set up an account for her early on and added to it monthly if it was needed. She seldom used it. During the early months of our marriage, we did have some problems. She did very little housework and no cooking. When I arrived home to a messy house and nothing for dinner, it would, to say the least, upset me. After much loud discussion, I was informed she had no intention of being a housekeeper or a cook. We ate out most of the time or ordered in from places that delivered. It took a while, but I finally decided to hire a housekeeper and she cooked too. It cost quite a sum, but it was worth it to me. I appreciated that she did a great job with the church members. The women loved her, so what more did I want? After we got past that hurdle, peace reigned again. As we moved to bigger churches, I thanked God that we had solved the problem."

"The last two years that we were at the Centerville Church, she began complaining of being very tired and not feeling up to par. At my insistence, she began turning some of her leadership duties over to the other ladies in the group. I finally persuaded her to go to a doctor. After many tests, they found cancer. We were very hopeful at first and after the radiation treatments, she did seem to feel much better. Meanwhile, I applied for a smaller church, which brought us here to the Cove. It gave me more time to be with her and much less pressure. She seemed better for about a year and again connected with some of the groups out here, but before long, it was back. I resigned as pastor and did what I could for her. She had many doctor appointments and hospital stays. I continued with the column that I wrote for the four-county church newspaper and I filled in for the pastor now and then. Eventually, they couldn't do anything more for her and they sent her home to die. I hired a nurse to care for her until she was gone. That's about it," he said, looking at Marge.

Marge nodded, "Do you think the years before she was sick were happy for her?"

He hesitated, "I'd like to think so. It was during my busy times, but when we were home together we shared little bits and pieces of our day; you know, some of the funny little things that happen when you're dealing with church people. We would discuss some different ways to solve problems. I'd say yes, I think she was happy."

"I don't remember thinking about it too much. I do remember being grateful for her understanding ways." He smiled, "When I was tired of meetings and people in general, I looked forward to coming home where it was peaceful and refreshing. I guess I was happy enough, except now and then when there was a ruckus with my church people."

"Farrell, dear, do you want my opinion?"

"Yes, I do; that's why I brought it to you."

"I understand from what you have told me it was a difficult time in your life, with diverse demands on your mind and body. I think Beverly was just the right type of lady you needed to share it with you. She seemed to have an inherent ability to know what was needed for a minister's lifestyle. I don't think it was anything she learned, I think it was just part of her nature. Nor do I think it was something she hated doing. She certainly made it clear to you, in a hurry, what she wasn't going to do and had no intention of doing. Shouldn't we think then that she was happy with what she was doing or she wouldn't have been doing it?"

"I guess you're right, she didn't do anything she didn't want to do," Farrell mused.

"In my way of thinking, you were blessed to have someone like her who could willingly take on some of the work of your vocation. Not only that, I believe it gave her some form of importance. From everything I heard, she sure didn't lack for admiration for the way she handled difficult situations and difficult people. Have you ever thought that maybe, along with what love you were able to give her, it was all she expected and all she needed to make her happy?"

Farrell sighed, smiling, "No, I've never thought of it that way, but when you take it apart and look at it, it does sound reasonable."

"Early on," Marge continued, "before it occurred to you how to solve your problem, you came home to a messy house and no meals in progress, although your wife was there half of every day. This had to be difficult for a neat and orderly person like yourself.

You know Farrell, it's not unheard of for a husband to expect a certain amount of comfort upon arriving home from work. Didn't you say for a while you took on the things you felt were her duties as a wife?"

"Yes, I did what little cleaning I could and all the cooking, unless we ate out. I was willing to help her with any of the housework but she made no moves in that direction, which led to angry words many times. After I figured out a solution, it put an end to the conflict. Almost every day was smooth and cheerful. In her defense, I have to say, she came from a well-to-do- family who, no doubt, had continual hired help, consequently she probably had minimal experience with housework or cooking."

Marge nodded, "If you stop to think, Farrell, it was a busy time in your career. Your duties at that time involved energizing a lagging church. You were young and I know you put your heart and soul into it. You must have done a great job since you moved, fairly quickly, to the bigger churches."

"You look back now, using your more leisurely days as a standard and you think you should have given her more attention. But really there was no indication that she felt a lack on your part. Not only that, but you're assuming some of the guilt that belongs to her. I know it's not nice to speak ill of the dead, but if you really think about it, she had things pretty much her way. She gave little thought about how it was affecting you." Marge hesitated, thinking maybe she had gone too far, but she decided to go on. "Now you want to move on with your lonely life and love someone else and you feel guilty because you didn't love her with the same intensity you love someone else. There are many forms of love and all are different depending on where you are in your life. Do you feel guilty that you didn't love your wife the way you loved your mom and dad, or the way you loved the little pony-tailed girl next door when you were ten? Of course not. We love a lot of people in a lifetime and all in different ways. I don't believe, with the exception of idiots or maniacs, that there is a wrong way to love."

She watched for a change in his thoughtful face as he turned his empty cup around on the saucer.

As Marge reached for the coffee pot to refill his cup, she said, "Hey, Mister Minister, aren't there a few things in the Bible that have something to say about love?"

Farrell laughed, "Now that you mention it, yes, there are. For one, Galatians, chapter five, says:"

'The fruit of the spirit is love, peace, long suffering, kindness, faithfulness, gentleness and self control. Against such there is no law.'

"Thank you for reminding me. I should have come to you a long time ago. It would have given me so much peace, but I've been working so hard at being guilty that I just haven't had time."

They laughed together and Marge was happy to see the sadness had left his handsome face, followed by a gentle smile in her direction.

"I hope you don't mind if we have a slight change of subject."

"Not at all," Marge said, amused.

"I was wondering if you had ever considered marrying again?" he said, hopefully scanning her facial expression.

"Of course, a lot would have to do with who I was considering, but yes, I've given it some thought." She waited, watching him.

"I didn't know your husband too well, only to speak to really with a few added comments about the weather and such things. I saw the two of you together, not only in church most Sundays but around town in other places too. When you were together, I could almost feel the tenderness and kindness between the two of you. It was like a loving friendship. It was just there for everyone to see. After having that kind of relationship in your marriage, I was afraid you might consider it would be some sort of betrayal of Charles if you were to think about marrying again."

The way Farrell had said it, it sounded to Marge almost like a question. She took a few moments to think about it. She supposed the outward appearance of their marriage could give that impression to people.

"There's no question, Farrell, that Charlie and I had a good marriage. As a matter of fact, we had a great marriage and there's no question that we loved each other. But it doesn't take anything away from my love for him to now love you and I do, dear man. I love you in a different way than I loved Charlie, probably because you are such different people with totally different personalities and temperaments. We are in a different time and place in our lives now. Can you underst and Farrell? One doesn't take anything away from the other."

Farrell nodded. He stood and walked to where Marge was sitting, pulled a chair close and sat down, taking her hand in his. "I want to ask you to marry me right this minute, but there is something nagging at me and I might as well get it out right now. I have tried to avoid thinking about it because it's difficult for a man to face," Farrell sighed heavily.

"I've wondered if my wife's lack of sexual interest was maybe due to my inept behavior. If it was, I wouldn't want to make those same mistakes again."

Marge could hardly keep from laughing, "There are people who have very low sexual drive and she may have been one of them. In any case, if it was due to your inept performance, you shouldn't worry about it." Marge smiled, "If there's any lack in your behavior, I'll teach you."

She watched the change in his eyes as he pulled her up and into his arms.

"I've waited such a long, lonely time to do this," he moaned.

Marge pulled away enough to see the tears fill his eyes and roll down his cheeks. Marge reached up and brushed them away. He kissed her gently and pulled her back into his arms.

"Will you marry me, Marge? Please say yes, before I turn into a pile of mush at your feet."

"Oh, yes, my dear, I will marry you." She leaned away slightly with his arms still around her.

"We do have something else to consider," she said.

"And what would that be?" Farrell asked.

"I'm much older than you."

"Oh, I see," he said, relief showing in his voice. "I'll tell you this, lady, I don't care if you're Methuselah's older sister."

He pulled her close in his arms again. After a few seconds passed, he asked, "Just how old are you?"

She whispered in his ear, "fifty-three."

He laughed, "Three years older. Somehow I think I'll figure out a way to cope."

Chapter Twenty-Eight

When Jim drove into Elaine's driveway, his mother's car was already there. It didn't surprise him. Elaine had called to say the date was on, if he was still interested and said his mother had consented to babysit Matthew. Jim had smiled at the word consented. Knowing his mother, she was probably flying higher than a helium balloon right now. Not only had her only child decided to have a date with a proper young lady with marriage potential, but she would have the pleasure of a baby to keep her company.

Jim had to give his mother credit; she hadn't once given even one obscure hint on the subject of Elaine. He smiled to himself. It must have been difficult for his mother to restrain her zealous attitude when it came to his lack-luster performance in the love and marriage department, especially with a likely candidate as conspicuously choice-worthy as Elaine.

From the first day he had stopped by Elaine's house, there had been an easy connection between them. It was hard to describe, even to himself, but there was no mistaking the feeling of emotional communication between them. There had been no pretense or stiff formalities that first day, only a comfortable kinship and a strong desire for a closer look.

She was slim and attractive and he did appreciate these qualities, but somehow, he knew it wouldn't have mattered if some of those things were lacking. It was her internal spirit that had somehow connected with him. He had, over the years, dated a fair number of girls, but none had affected him quite the way Elaine had.

He definitely wanted to examine this relationship in depth. Maybe her magnetic draw would wear off under close inspection, but he intended to find out.

When he stepped up on the porch, Elaine opened the door.

"Whoa, lady, you're looking mighty fine."

"Why thank you, kind sir." She motioned with her h and "Come on in for a minute. I'll get my sweater. I think it might get colder after the sun sets."

"Oh, ye of little faith. I think I could keep you warm, but maybe you had better have it." Jim walked over to where his mother was sitting with Matthew on her lap, "Hi little one. Hi Mom." He bent and kissed the baby's forehead and his mothers' cheek. "You look happy; does it feel good to be back in the harness again?"

"You certainly have a remarkable way of expressing yourself. Harness indeed!" That put a smile in her sarcasm. "But to answer your question, yes it does feel good to be around a baby again, especially this one." She kissed the top of Matthew's head as Elaine re-entered the room carrying her sweater. "You two go along now and have a good time and Jim, you try to behave yourself, you hear me?"

"You really know how to take the fun out of an evening," Jim grumbled, as he smiled. "We'll be back around ten, so don't start worrying too early."

Elaine walked over and kissed Matthew, "You be a good boy for Marge. We'll be back soon."

"He'll be just fine," Marge said.

When they were settled in the car, Jim asked, "Where would you like to eat? Anywhere special on your mind?"

"No, not really. What are the options? I haven't been around town enough to know what's available except for the diner outside of town."

"Well, the diner has good food, but I was thinking a little more upscale. Donahue's, which serves a fairly good steak, is not too far up the road and then there's Bellemos, if you like Italian and Dick Knapp's Seafood Parlor down on the waterfront. They are all good eating places."

"I love seafood. Let's go there." Elaine sighed, "This is really a treat for me. It's been a long time since I've been out for dinner."

"Then seafood it is. It's an excellent choice. I like seafood too and the view from the restaurant is incredible. A special attraction for your dining pleasure," he added, giving her his best imitation of an advertisement.

Elaine smiled. "It sounds like you might own stock in the company."

"Don't I wish," Jim laughed. "It sure draws the tourist trade in the summer and it's plenty strong the rest of the year too. I'm afraid I'm more in the category of eater than investor though."

"If that's true, you sure keep yourself trim," Elaine observed.

"Well, I work out almost every day. I have to with Mom forever baking up delicious calories to encourage my weakness."

"Oh, I know exactly what you mean. I've had samplings of your mother's baking. It's so nice to have your mother stop by fairly often. Of course, she seldom comes empty-handed. I also put Matthew in the stroller now and again and trot down her way. I know so few people out here, it would be quite lonely without her friendship. She's so comfortable to be around."

Once they were settled in the restaurant and had placed their order, the conversation began again.

"Did you always live in the city?" he asked.

"No, only during my college and marriage years, but it seemed much longer. In my heart, I always longed for Carson Cove. I was here often while growing up and I loved it here." She seemed to withdraw into a quieter mood. "The company my father worked for sent him all over the country. When I had time off from school and during my summer vacations, I was sent to my grandmother's house. My mother would travel with him. After high school, I began college. During my second year, my parents were both killed in an automobile accident."

As she hesitated, Jim reached out and took her h and "It's okay if you'd rather not talk about it. I'm sorry to make you sad."

"Thanks, but it's all right, I don't mind talking about it. Sometimes I feel as though I hardly knew them and I guess that's the odd part. They were so wrapped up in each other that it seemed almost like I was an intruder. It wasn't as if I was neglected or needed anything, but it was almost as if there was a barrier around them that I couldn't penetrate. But, it wasn't that way with my grandmother."

As she spoke the last few words, it was as though the sun had appeared from behind a cloud. "She always said I belonged to her and I felt that way too. Now that I'm living in her house, it feels like I have her spirit back with me."

She hesitated a moment and then added, "Your mom makes me think of her in many ways. She's so thoughtful and gentle and best of all, she seems to like Matthew and me. Add to that, she's such fun to be around," Elaine finished, smiling.

"You know, you're right," Jim nodded, "I never really thought of it quite that way, but she is a lot of fun. I wish you could have known my dad. The two of them were a class act, for sure. I was a very lucky kid. Every now and then Dad would tell me he was mighty glad when I came along because I gave Mom something to fuss over. She was always telling me to be careful. Every time he left the house, it was always, 'Be careful Charlie, I just got you decently broke in and I'd hate to start over again,' or some other goofy saying. She had dozens of those little phrases that she would throw at him along with her 'be careful Charlie.' I guess that's what I remember most from my childhood, the love and the laughter. I wish every kid could have the loving care I had."

When their food arrived, there was a temporary lull in the conversation and Elaine's attention was drawn to the beauty outside. "The view is spectacular, isn't it?" she observed.

Her statement interrupted his appreciation of her tranquil expression. "Yes, it is. They take excellent care of the grounds. Add the water as a backdrop and it certainly is something to behold."

The conversation was light while they enjoyed their meal.

"Are the fish caught locally?" Elaine asked.

"No, about the only fish here in the cove are for the sports-minded. The tourists enjoy going out now and then, but nothing commercial."

"It certainly is a delicious meal. Thank you so much."

"Definitely my pleasure, ma'am."

Elaine set her nearly empty plate aside and sipped her coffee.

"Do you think it's time to look over the dessert menu?"

"I'm sorry to say I'll have to pass on dessert. I don't think I could eat another bite."

"Well then, I think we should take a walk outside and get a closer view of this fantastic sunset, what do you say?"

"Sounds like a great idea."

Jim picked up the check and they walked to the cash register. After the bill was settled, Jim took Elaine's hand as they walked out to the garden walkway and onto the beach. The wind coming in over the water had an edge. Elaine hunched her shoulders against it.

"Maybe you should put your sweater on," Jim suggested.

"Yes, I think I'd better. The wind is a little chilly out here by the water."

Jim held the sweater while she put it on, then with his hands on her shoulders, he turned her around to face him. He bent and kissed the end of her nose. "You are a very tempting woman," he said, noting the surprise in her eyes.

He took her hand again as they walked down the beach. It was deserted as they made their way along.

After a short distance, Jim stopped. "I'm thinking our choices of shoes is not compatible with sand walking.

Elaine laughed, "I'm not sure there are any shoes made for sand walking."

Jim pointed toward the walkway. "Let's head for the bench up there."

When they arrived, the sun was setting, casting long shimmering streaks of gold, red and orange across the ever-moving water. The changing view was breathtaking as the sun slowly sank below the horizon.

Jim put his arm around her, pulling her closer. She nestled into the warmth of his body, laying her head on his chest. She felt secure in his embrace. A feeling of intense longing flowed through her body. She could not remember a time she had ever felt such comfort.

Eventually, Jim roused. "Maybe we should go. The sun is almost down." Rising, he took her hands and pulled her to her feet and into his arms. As she raised her eyes to meet his steady gaze, he gave her a gentle kiss on her lips.

As they walked slowly back toward the car, he said, "It felt good to hold you. I hated to let you go. Not only that, but I hoped you noticed my aim is getting better."

Elaine laughed. "Oh, yes, I noticed."

When they were seated in the car, Jim turned in her direction, "I want to talk seriously to you for a few minutes."

Elaine studied his expression, trying to discern if there was a problem as apprehension crept into her mind.

"First, I want you to know," Jim began, reaching for her h and "what I'm about to say isn't a line I use. I have to admit, I've dated quite a bit, but with you, it's a whole new ballgame. I've been to your house almost every day since you moved in, trying to figure out this strange feeling I have when I am with you. From the very beginning, I felt a powerful bond between us." His voice was gentle as he searched her face.

"I felt it too," Elaine's voice was almost a whisper.

Jim nodded, "It's so easy between us, I hoped you felt it because I want to be with you often. I want to recognize your moods and the way you feel about things. I want to talk to you about important things as well as nonsense. I want to hold you in my arms a lot more, to comfort you if you're sad or laugh with you when you're happy." He sighed. "Maybe you might think it's too soon for me to feel the way I do after such a short time, but it's like I've been waiting for you forever. I guess what I'm saying is, can we take it real slow and easy and get to know each other better? I want to be a part of your life and Matthew's too. Are you willing to give me a chance?"

"Oh, Jim, yes," she said softly, turning to him. "It's odd to hear you say what you did because I felt drawn to you from the beginning too. You can't imagine how happy I am to have you near, or the comfort and caring I feel in your arms. But, you're right, we should move slowly and examine our emotions with caution. Its' too easy to make big mistakes. It's all new right now and maybe time will change the way we feel. It's better to find out before we get in too deep. It's not a matter of giving you a chance. It will be giving *us* a chance."

Jim pulled her into his arms and kissed her with all the pent-up passion he was feeling.

When he moved away, he said, "Well, I think we should get moving before we get thrown out of the parking lot for indecent behavior, but I wanted to give you a sample of what may be in your future."

Elaine laughed. "You sure know how to give a girl something to look forward to."

As Jim inserted the key, he turned to Elaine, "Would you like to go over to the D and M Tavern and have a drink?"

Elaine shrugged. "Sure, if you want to, but I'm not much of a drinker."

"I'm not either, but I'm curious. At one time the place was a home. The people who lived there raised a large family, but it has been empty for a lot of years and it was pretty run down. I've heard that the new owners have put a small fortune into the renovations. I'd just like to see what they've done to the place."

As they drove away, Elaine observed, "It's starting to get dark so much earlier now."

"True. We might not be able to see many of the improvements on the outside if it's too dark."

"Where is it located?"

"Not very far, just on the edge of the village. At least I think it's within the village limits."

The parking lot was fairly crowded when they arrived, but they found an empty space along the hedge of flowers. The front was bright with light flooding the area.

"It seems to be fairly popular," Jim remarked. "Let's take a walk around and look at the landscaping before it gets any darker."

He took her hand again as they walked around the left side of the building. Elaine admired the beautiful fall flowers and the neatly trimmed shrubs. As she named the different flowers, Jim stopped, looking at her. "Wow, beauty and gardening expertise too."

"Oh, I learned most of it from Greg," she laughed. "He's an absolute encyclopedia of information when it comes to plants."

They turned to walk back to the front of the building. Entering, they found a table toward the end of the bar. The room was moderately noisy with voices and laughter. After they ordered, Jim asked the waitress if the owners were in the building.

"Yes, they have offices upstairs. If you want to speak with them, I could call them down."

"Oh no," Jim said, it's not necessary to interrupt them. You can tell them we admire their great renovation job. It's nice to see the old place come to life again."

"Thank you, I'll tell them." The waitress walked back toward the bar.

"Everyone seems to be enjoying themselves," Elaine observed, scanning the tables around the room.

"They do, don't they? It's nice to see people who can have a few drinks without becoming disagreeable. Of course, it's early yet," he added.

After a moment, he said, "Well look who's here." Jim stood and motioned to the couple walking in the door. As they approached, Jim invited them to sit at their table.

"What a nice surprise," Jack Denver smiled. "It's been all of three hours since I saw you last."

"Hello Ann, it's always nice to see you. I'd like you to meet Elaine Colby." Looking at Elaine, he added, "And this is Ann Denver. The funny-looking specimen with her is her husband and my partner, Jack Denver."

Ann smiled, nodding to Elaine, "Don't pay any attention to the two of them; they're mentally deficient."

"I think my feelings have been bruised," Jim moaned.

"To say nothing about mine," Jack said, placing his hand over his heart while seating himself.

"This is quite a nice place," Ann said, looking around the room, appreciating the tasteful décor. "Have you been here before?"

"No, we had dinner at Dick Knapps seafood place and Jim was curious as to how the new owners had renovated it. He tells me it was once a home."

Jack nodded, "Yes, that's true, but looking at it now, you'd never guess it's origin. What a difference money can make."

Ann gave him a poke, "Oh, don't be so cynical."

"I'm not being cynical, it's the truth."

"I have to agree. They must have spent a fortune in order to turn this poor old house around," Jim said.

Ann turned to Elaine. "I hear from Jim you have an adorable baby."

Elaine was surprised. "Really? Jim told you about Mathew?"

"He certainly did." Ann leaned toward her and lowering her voice to a stage whisper, she added, "Not only that, but your name comes up quite often too."

Jim turned to Jack, "It must be difficult living with such a gossip." Both women laughed.

"Do you have children?" Elaine asked Ann.

"Yes, we have a set of twins; a boy and a girl, they're four. My mother takes them for a visit once a week so I can get caught up with my errands and shopping. God bless her merciful soul. They sure are a handful at times."

"I'm sure it would be very difficult to handle two of them when you're out and about," Elaine said.

After the waitress brought Jack and Ann's order, Elaine asked, "Did I hear you say that you and Jack work together? What kind of business are you in?"

Jack raised his eyebrows, glancing at Jim and Jim's eyes grew big with disbelief.

"You're kidding me, right? I thought you knew."

Elaine looked up in time to see the expression on Jim's face. Had she missed something? She shook her head, "No, I don't know."

"Jack and I work for the local police department. We're partners most of the time."

Jack was thoughtful. "I'll bet you didn't realize I was there the night of your accident. I was in uniform, but it was dark and you were pretty well out of it."

"You're right, I didn't know. I knew Jim was there because he came to the hospital later that night and his mother said she had seen the headlights and called him." Elaine said.

Jim took over, "And it was my night off so I wasn't in uniform, so how could you have known? Now that I think of it, the times I've been to your house, it's been during my free time and you wouldn't have known unless I told you. I guess the subject just never came up."

"Jim and I ride patrol together most of the time and usually our off time coincides, but not always. Thus, the partner thing that led you astray," Jack finished, smiling at Elaine.

"There sits Carson Cove's finest," Ann announced with exaggerated hand motion toward the two men.

Jim extended his hand to Jack. "I commend you for your teaching abilities. Ann seems to have finally grasped the true significance of our rare qualities."

Jack shook his h and nodding slightly in acknowledgement. Elaine laughed as Ann rolled her eyes.

Jim shook his head in wonder, "The most surprising little item in all of this is my mother's silence. She's been around Elaine quite often. The fact that I'm with the police department is usually one of her biggest selling points when she's talking to eligible young ladies." Jim sighed heavily, hanging his head in mock sorrow, "I guess she's given up on me."

"Oh, quit your whining. Your mother is no quitter. She's not going to let you off the hook that easily," Jack scoffed.

Ann laughed, pushing herself away from the table, "Come on Elaine, I think we deserve a ladies room break, don't you?"

"Great idea," Elaine agreed.

As the two sat watching Elaine and Ann walk away, Jack smiled, "I like your friend. It's about time you regained your sanity with regard to women."

"Yeah, I'm thinking she might be a keeper if I can get her to ignore a few of my faults."

Jack sipped his drink. "Not to change such a lovely subject, but were you able to look around the outside before you came in?"

Although the noise in the room was sufficient to cover his voice, Jack had spoken quietly.

"Not too thoroughly, no, but we did walk around to the left side for a short distance. It was pretty dark by the time we arrived. However, I did notice a side door and could make out a staircase leading up to the second floor. There are two windows on that side. The upstairs seemed to be well lit. When we walked back around the front, I noticed two big windows facing toward the road and they were well lit too. The waitress said the owners had their offices up there. That's about it," Jim said.

"Well, that's something. I figure the next time we're on the night patrol, we could take a run over here during the wee hours and take a good look around the back. There ought not to be anyone around then. I don't know why, but I have a weird feeling about this place."

"I think after the meeting and the outline we were given of what to look for, your mind is set up for a whole new agenda and I think you became more aware of details you would hardly notice any other time," Jim reminded him.

"You're probably right, but consider this; on the way in I noticed what an ideal spot this is. It sits back away from the highway surrounded by trees for great cover and no close neighbors. What more could anyone in the drug business want?" Jack hesitated momentarily, "And to top it off, it is a new business."

"I hadn't put it all together, but you're right. We should definitely give it some attention." Jim hesitated a moment and added, "I have another little item too. It probably has nothing to do with any of this, but I ran into old man Harris at the gas station. He lives down on the north side of the waterfront and he says we ought to do some checking down there. According to him, there's some activity on the water about two in the morning. He thinks it's an odd time of year for that kind of action. Usually by the middle of September it's pretty quiet on the water. He said even during the tourist season there's no one on the water that time of night. Have you heard anything along that line?"

"No, but we can mention it to the chief in the morning and unless he's got something urgent going on, we can run over there and ask a few questions and see what we come up with. Maybe other people have noticed too."

When the ladies arrived back at the table, they each had another drink.

"We have arranged our future social life," Ann told them.

"What a concept! As if you didn't always, so let's hear it," Jack said, smiling fondly at his beautiful wife.

"I have your schedule and neither of you are on duty next Thursday, so unless either of you have other plans, we will have a cookout then. Of course, you and Jim will do the cooking."

"Well, of course. Why wouldn't we? Our picture is on the cover of "Skill and Grill" this month, isn't it Jim?"

"Well, if it isn't, it ought to be."

"I was thinking about asking your mother and Farrell Dunn too. What do you think?" Ann asked.

"I don't think they need my permission." Jim said.

"What I mean is, do you think it is presumptuous to invite them both to our little get together, smart mouth?"

Jim laughed. "I think it's a great idea, Ann. I was just teasing. I really think they were meant to be together and I'm fairly certain the day will come when they will admit it. It's the best thing that could happen to both of them, I think. Of course, they haven't asked for my opinion."

"Then that's settled. Someday next week I'm going over to Elaine's house for mid-morning refreshments and get to know Master Matthew. We'll invite Marge too. That's about as far as we got with our social calendar. You will be informed with further developments as they occur," Ann said.

"Well, I don't know about you, Jack, but I feel cheated. We don't have a social director in the men's bathroom."

Jack laughed, "It doesn't appear as if we need one."

"This has been fun running into you two, but I think we better get on home now," Ann said to Jack.

"Yes and I better get this lady home, too. I don't want Matthew to worry. I'll see you tomorrow morning, Jack and it's always nice to see you Ann."

Elaine turned toward Ann. "I'm so glad we ran into each other. I'll be looking forward to your visit."

On the drive home, Jim noticed Elaine was quiet.

"Is everything all right?" he asked, "you're very quiet."

"I was just doing a little forward thinking. Your friends seem really nice and a lot of fun. How long have you known them?"

"Jack and I have been friends and competitors all through school and police academy. He's like my alter-ego. Since he married Ann, we haven't done quite as much frolicking around town as we once did, except in the patrol car, but I suppose we had to grow up eventually. Jack sure picked a winner with Ann. He thinks even I might be on the right track, finally, with you."

"Really?" Elaine was amused. "Does he always critique your friends?"

"Most of them weren't around long enough for him to meet them. You and Ann seemed to hit it off."

"Oh, yes, we did. I'm looking forward to her visit next week."

When they arrived at her house, he walked her to the door and gave her a gentle kiss. "I won't come in tonight, but I'll be around."

She watched him back down the driveway as her thoughts moved on to Mathew. If this relationship progresses, she knew she'd have to tell him how she came to have him. She couldn't imagine how she could love Matthew more than she did, even if she had given birth to him. How could it be wrong? But, if she truly thought it wasn't wrong, why had she kept it a secret? She had assumed that Matthew's mother had given him to her because she wanted her to have him, although she could not imagine any circumstances bad enough that his mother would have willingly given him up.

If she told Jim and there was some sort of law involved in a case like this, being a policeman, wouldn't he feel obligated to report it? Suppose it meant that Matthew would be taken away from her? Fear rippled through her body.

Chapter Twenty-Nine

It was an unusually beautiful day for November. After Greg had finished with the raking at Mrs. Colby's, she had asked him if he could watch Matthew for a few minutes while she ran down to the drugstore. He had baby-sat a few other times while she ran quick errands. It always pleased him since it gave him time alone with Aaron to love and cuddle him, openly. He still had a difficult time remembering the name change. In his mind and heart, his brother would always be Aaron.

Elaine always insisted on paying him for the time she was gone, although he tried to refuse it. Aaron was growing so fast and was so much fun to play with now. He was within a few days of being five months old and each time Greg was around him, he said: "thank you God for telling me where to take him." It was certainly obvious that Aaron was happy and was being given loving care. Greg would always be grateful.

When Elaine came back, Greg rode down the road to Mrs. Talberts house and finding everything in proper order, rode on down to visit Mr. Dunn. Farrell was sitting on the porch when Greg rode into the yard.

"Well hello my good friend. Come on up and sit awhile."

Farrell motioned, as Greg engaged the kick stand to keep his bike erect.

"What have you been up to this fine day?" Farrell asked.

"Just checking out the neighborhood. There's not much left to do now until snow comes. I did a twenty-minute babysitting job for Mrs. Colby." Greg smiled, remembering the fun with Aaron.

"You get along pretty well with that baby I hear," Farrell said, watching the happiness on the boy's face.

Greg laughed. "It's not too hard to get along with him."

Farrell scanned the sky. "What's on your calendar for the rest of the day?"

"Nothing in particular, but I can usually find something to do."

"I've been sitting here thinking about taking a ride around the lake. Do you think you'd like to come with me?"

"Oh yeah, I'd like that. I've never been all the way around the lake," he said with enthusiasm and then lowering his voice he said, "Yes sir, I'd like that very much."

Farrell grinned, patting the boy's shoulder. "I'll just lock up the house and we'll be off."

Traffic was light and Farrell drove at a moderate speed, enjoying the view. Many of the trees still had most of their leaves and their colors flashed as the gentle breeze moved across the water. Farrell noticed the boy's attention was glued to the passing scenery.

"At different times in my life, when I'd hit a low spot, I'd come out here and drive around the lake. No matter what the season, it always gives me spiritual lift."

"Did you have a low spot today?" Greg asked

"Oh no, todays trip is just to enjoy the day and the company, but I'll share with you something that has to be a little bit of a secret for a short time. Marge Keller and I are going to be married very soon and I'm happier than I've been in many years."

"Wow, that's great! Mrs. Keller is a very nice lady. How come it's a secret?"

"It's just a temporary secret until we can discuss some of the details and tell her son. We've been invited to a barbeque at Jack and Anne's place and Jim will be there. We thought we'd announce it then."

"Are you going to her house to live or is she coming to yours?"

"That's one of the little items we haven't discussed yet. We won't be making any changes before we get married. We have a lot to talk about before that happens. I'm going over for dinner and to spend the evening. I'm sure we'll have many plans before the day ends. Of course, she's had all day to think about it."

Greg frowned. "Suppose you don't like the things she has thought about all day?"

"Well, here's the way it is; I already won the prize when she agreed to marry me, so I don't really care how the gift is wrapped. Do you understand my meaning? "

Greg wrinkled his nose, "I guess so. You plan to let her do everything and you'll just stand there and get married."

Farrell laughed. "Oh no, that's not the way it is at all. What I meant was any way she wants it done is fine with me and I'll help her in any way I can. All I want is to make her as happy as she has made me by loving me enough to marry me. That's the way it is when two people love each other. "

As they entered the outskirts of Scofield, Farrell slowed to accommodate the thirty-mile speed zone.

"My stomach tells me it's almost lunch time. There are at least three places we could stop. What would you like? My treat."

Greg didn't hesitate, "Hamburger, fries and a Coke, but I can eat about anything. I'm not fussy."

"That sounds pretty good to me too," Farrell said, "Let's see what we can find."

As they rode slowly on, they saw a group of teenagers standing on the corner, playfully pushing an shoving each other around.

"I hate them." Greg said, his voice low.

Farrell shot a quick surprised glance at Greg, "You know those boys?" he asked his mind organizing a little sermon on the evils of hatred. This was a new side of Greg and Farrell picked up on it immediately.

"No, but they're all alike," Greg mumbled.

"Really, in what way?"

"They stand around in groups like that as if they own the sidewalk and wait for someone smaller than they are to come along so they can shove them around and beat them up. They think it's some kind of fun game."

"So, you hate all of them in general, rather than some one person, is that right?"

"Yeah, I guess," he paused, his head down. "When I was living in the city, I sometimes had to go blocks out of my way just to avoid going near them. I took some beatings from them when I was little, but it didn't take me long to figure out what to do."

Farrell was astounded, "Tell me, son, did you tell your parents or the police about this?"

"Yeah, I told my mother once when it first happened, but it didn't mean anything to her. She beat me before the street gangs ever thought of doing it. She had warned me to stay away from the police from the first day I was on the street. She hated the police. Every lesson she ever taught me was with a beating. I hate her too."

"And your father?" Farrell already guessed the answer to that question.

Greg's voice was barely audible. "I never had a father." He knew he had said too much and seemed to shrink into himself.

Farrell pulled into the first fast food place he came to. "I'll tell you what. Why don't you go over and get each of us an order and I'll stake out that table over there. It's such a beautiful day and we can enjoy the view while we eat," he said, handing Greg a twenty-dollar bill. "And after we eat we can get us a big old ice cream cone to finish up, what do you say?"

"Sounds pretty good," Greg smiled, but as the boy walked away, Farrell saw the burden heavy once more on his shoulders.

While Greg was gone, it gave him time to think of the best way to proceed. The boy had opened up but was obviously sorry for doing it. He could hardly ignore what Greg had said without saying something about it. Somehow, he felt there was much more to it than what had been said, but what could it be?

When Greg came back with lunch, he set it on the table and handed Farrell the change. He seemed fairly cheerful.

"I think I'll sit on your side of the table with you," Greg said. "I wouldn't want to have to wait for you to describe the view to me with your mouth full."

Farrell laughed, "Good thinking," he said as he moved farther down the bench.

They ate in silence for a few moments.

"You know, Greg, sometimes it's a comfort to share a part of your life with your friends and I'm sure you realize I'm in a position where I could do a great many things to alleviate the situation you're in. Probably something should have been done when you were younger, but now you're old enough to make these decisions yourself. What you told me was in confidence and will not go any further without your permission. I do want you to know if you ever want me to step in and help you, you know where to find me. Deal?"

"Deal," Greg said.

They continued to eat and after a few moments he turned to Farrell. "It's not so bad now that I'm older. My mother's either sleeping or gone most of the time. She and Martin Delmont have opened a tavern over on the other side of town. As long as I do my chores and keep my school work done, I'm free to do what I want as long as I don't get into trouble."

"When we lived in the city, just as it is here, I wasn't allowed to have friends, except at school. I could never ask them over to my house and I couldn't go to theirs, so I kept pretty much to myself, never going out of my way to act friendly. I was lonely sometimes, but I buried myself in every book I could find. The last few years we were in the city, I found jobs similar to what I do around here, but it wasn't the same. With the people out there, it was do your job, here's your money, see you next week or whatever. Out here everyone visits with me and feeds me good stuff and makes me feel like I'm really somebody. They seem glad to see me anytime, not just when I'm working. You know, like they're my friends. Sometimes I just go talk to them 'cause I like them, just like I do with you. They always act like they're glad to see me."

Farrell put his arm around Greg's shoulder and gave him a quick hug.

"We don't act as if we're glad to see you, we are glad to see you. "

After disposing of the paper cartons, they walked over to the window for their ice cream cones, then on to the car. They sat a short time to bring their cones down to manageable size before continuing on their way.

At one point, Farrell pulled the car to the side of the road and they walked slowly through a lightly wooded area to the edge of the water. They sat down on the slope and enjoyed the afternoon breeze as they listened to the waves lapping the shore.

"It's peaceful here," Farrell said, "It's hard to believe the world is in such turmoil most of the time." After a short pause, he continued, "I know there's a lot more to your story than what you've told me and I want you to know I'm willing and ready to help you in any way I can. All you have to do is ask. We're friends and that means a lot to me. Will you remember that?"

Greg nodded, "Yes I will. Thank you."

Farrell sighed, "Well now, my boy, I think we'd better finish our little trip and get on home since I have a date with a pretty lady tonight and I better clean up a little, just in case I'm able to get in a little snuggling."

Chapter Thirty

Martin Delmont sat staring at the phone, after talking to the detective. Finally, he leaned back in his chair stunned. So many years had passed. It hadn't occurred to him to investigate until recently. Now it seemed so obvious. Why had it taken him so long? All he had to do was think back to those early days to know the answer. He wasn't about to give up the chance of big money or excitement of outsmarting the law. Nothing else mattered to him, at least not long enough to derail his grasping desire for more. There was never enough.

He has thrown away the only decent emotion he had ever felt, for what? A great deal of money and years of empty, lonely greed. Now he knew the truth without a doubt. He had proof and it was too late.

He heard Dora come into her office. He looked at his watch. It was quite early for her, since she had been practically living out at Frank's house recently.

He supposed she had brought the goods as always, which meant it was time to get to work filling the orders for the week. Leaving his desk, he walked across the room and opened the closet door. Pulling the key ring from his pocket, he unlocked the sliding panel. Pushing it open, it revealed the long narrow table with the boxes of resealable bags, tags and the two scales. He reached out and pushed the light switch on, which also turned on the air conditioner.

Dora had not joined him as she usually did. He reclosed the panel and moved to her office door.

"Are you in there, Dora?" he asked. "I'm ready if you are."

"Could you come in for a minute please?"

Now what's going on, he wondered. Dora was sitting at her desk when he walked in. A large bundle was sitting on the table next to her desk.

"What's up?" he asked, observing the expression on her face.

"Frank and I have broken up. We had a little disagreement. He said to tell you he'd call you later and set up some different arrangements."

Martin felt a surge of anger, "I hope you haven't screwed anything up. I have worked with Frank ever since I started in this business, long before you were around and never had any problems."

"Oh, just relax Martin. There's no problem now either. He will probably want to deal with just you since he's upset with me."

"So, what's the disagreement about?" Martin's voice was sharp with anger.

"Calm down. I had been nosing around on his computer, trying to get some answers, when I remembered he had told me once, he didn't do any drug business on his computer because the Feds have a way of breaking into anyone's files. He had gone to the airport to pick up one of his orders, but apparently he had forgotten something and came back. He caught me going through his desk. I tried to convince him I was just being nosey, poking around but he didn't buy it. He said I wasn't to come near the house anymore, which is fine with me. It happened just ahead of me breaking it off anyway. I'm sick of his high and mighty attitude." Dora shrugged, "No big loss there."

"Did you find what you were looking for?" Martin asked.

"Let's just say we won't need Greg much longer anyway." Pushing away from her desk, she added, "Come on, let's get to work."

They seldom talked as they weighed, sealed and tagged the orders. Truthfully, Martin was relieved that the relationship was over as long as it didn't interfere with the connection between him and Frank. They had been friends a long time and he was always uncomfortable with Dora putting the moves on Frank. He knew her for the double dealing bitch she was. He had been continually worried, although he had warned Frank. He was well aware that she was capable of every kind of treachery. It would make no difference to her whose body she had to step over to get where she wanted to go.

They finished the last of the bags and were stacking them in the order of their pickup times.

Dora sighed tiredly, "If it's all right with you, I think I'll go on home and catch up on things there."

"There's not much going on here, so go ahead. I plan on getting the tavern records caught up to date. I can't believe how well that's going. Benny Krim is a great manager and he's doing a terrific job." She nodded.

Even though he knew she had little interest in the tavern business, she never dialed to irk him with her no comment brush off when he mentioned it.

As he locked the panel door, she said, "The changeover of our customers has gone surprisingly well, don't you think?"

"It sure did; no problems at all."

As she pulled her coat off the hanger, Martin asked, "How's Greg been doing since he doesn't have to run drugs for us anymore?"

I don't know. I haven't been around too much when he's there. His departure is one of those things I want to get organized in my mind." Dora said with an odd tone in her voice.

"What are you thinking about, a private school or some place like that?"

She laughed, "No, I was thinking of something a little more permanent than a costly school."

She had referred to killing him before, but he hadn't thought she really meant to kill him. After all, he had heard people say such things about their kids before, but it was assumed that they were upset by something they had done. Everyone knew they didn't really mean to kill them.

"You certainly can't be actually thinking of killing him."

Martin was aghast. How could she make such a cold-blooded statement without any noticeable emotion?

"I certainly am. I can't believe you can be so shocked. You must realize he knows way too much about our operation to let him live. I've done quite a lot of thinking about it. I don't see any way around it. What I'll have to do is report him missing and fix up a note saying he's run away from home. The police are used to that with teens. They'll ask a lot of questions, make a big deal out of it for a while and when nothing turns up they'll forget it. I've got to think it through a little more, but it would be the least suspicious was to go," she said putting her coat on. "I'll be back before the first pick up is due."

After Dora left, he sat down at his desk. Pulling the pile of bills and receipts over in front of him, he sat staring at them. He could not seem to focus on what lay in front of him. His mind was whirling, spinning from one thing to the next, a mingling of feelings and thoughts, mixed with anger.

Martin realized he had to settle his mind and think this whole mess through. He had to make some decisions before it was too late. He was so deep in his mental maneuvering, he was startled when the phone rang.

Picking up the phone, he said, "Martin Delmont."

"Hi Martin, this is George Becker. Are you busy for a few minutes?"

"Not too busy to talk to you. What can I do for you?"

"I just wanted to ask you something. Does Dora ever talk to you about what she's doing about finding the baby?"

"Actually no. She was upset with the loss of the money when it first happened, but she hasn't said anything about it since. I don't think she's doing anything about finding it."

"Doesn't that seem a little strange to you? It gives me all the more reason to believe she knows where the baby went. I think she sold it to someone else, so she didn't have to give me my share of the money."

Martin was sick of hearing the squabble over money.

"Otherwise," George continued "why wouldn't she be looking for the baby?" The anger was beginning to rise in his voice.

"She did say, at the time, she didn't want to alert the police not only because of the business we're in, but also because selling a baby in itself is a crime."

"It just seems a little odd to me that she wouldn't be making a few waves about losing that much money, to say nothing about a mother not knowing if her baby was dead or alive, or how it was being treated. It's one thing to sell your baby and know it's being taken care of. But it's another to not care what became of it. I don't believe it for one minute."

Martin cut in. "You have to consider the cold blooded heartless person you're talking about." Martin was thinking about Dora's plans for Greg.

"Not only that," George continued, ignoring Martin's statement, "but a few weeks ago, Steve Darnell came here asking for the name of the baby's mother. He said he would kill her if he ever found out her name, even though I had given him his money back. Later my office was broken into and he may have found her name. But if he doesn't get to her first, you can tell her if I find out she double-crossed me, she's as good as dead."

Martin, anticipating what would happen next, held the phone away from his ear. When Becker's phone slammed into the cradle, he gave a long low whistle. Martin had hardly hung up the phone, before it rang again. It was Frank Brant. "Well did she tell you what happened?" he asked without preamble.

"Yes, but I suppose what I heard was her version. Along with a few other things, she indicated she has your list of contacts."

"She might think she has, but you can't believe I'd be so foolish as to leave something like that where she could find it do you?"

Martin couldn't believe, after listening to George Becker's ravings, how calm Frank was.

"The fact that she would try a stunt like that, just about says it all. I know you had alerted me to her nature, so I wasn't totally surprised, but that ended it. You can believe I'll take real good care of her in the very near future. I hope you don't depend on her too much, because you're going to be without her very soon. I'll call you a little later in the week when I figure out a schedule. Don't worry I'll take care of her." Frank said, hanging up the phone.

"Apparently, you'll have to stand in line," Martin said to the dial tone.

Chapter Thirty-One

Elaine had given Matthew a bath. She bent down to kiss his little bare belly while making a growling sound. Giggling, he raised his hands and grabbed the hair on each side of her face.

"Ok you little ruffian." She took his hands out of her hair and nuzzled under his neck. Matthew screeched with laughter.

"Well," she said, "I think I better get you dressed. We've got to go to a barbeque."

She accented each syllable as she moved her head up and down in rhythm to her words, each spurring an explosive giggle. She repeated the word twice, just to enjoy his laughter. "Say, my little ray of sunshine," she said, "we really do have to get down to business here."

As she dressed him, she continued to talk to him. "You will be the most handsome dude there and you will show them all how a real gentleman acts. This is your first social event, but I know I can trust you to show your best side. Well, now don't you look grand?"

Matthew smiled and wiggled his way upward, as she brought him into her arms. She sat in the rocking chair and fed him his bottle before laying him in the crib. It was his routine to nap about two hours and then he would be awake for most of the evening hours.

As Elaine stood looking down at the sleeping child, she was troubled. Until Jim came into her life, she hadn't thought about it at any great length. Now as time went on their relationship was growing closer almost by the day. She knew the time was coming when she would have to tell Jim about Matthew. She couldn't understand why she was feeling so guilty. Had she done something wrong? Maybe she should have notified someone, but who? It wasn't as though he was running around on the street and she picked him up, brought him home and hid him away. Someone had put him in her car, with almost everything he needed. She had thought of him as a wonderful gift from God. Then why has she kept it a guilty secret from everyone, including Jim? Thinking about revealing it now, she wondered if it was possible for some agency to step in and take Matthew from her. Just the thought of it filled her with fear. The only other alternative she could think of was to break off her relationship with Jim and then what? In spite of the slower pace idea of getting to know each other better, she knew it was too late. She loved Jim and she knew deep within her heart that they were right for each other. She could not imagine how empty her life would be without him. They would have to work this thing out together.

She picked up her robe and walked slowly to the bathroom to take her shower. Her spirit lightened some thinking that Jim would be here to pick them up soon.

Jim took her into his arms and held her close. Sighing, he said, "I miss you when I can't see you every day. This slow thing we're doing isn't working out too well, at least not for me. I know right now that I'll love you to my last breath and I know in my heart that we are right for each other."

242

"Yes, I know," she said quietly and smiling to herself, having thought almost the same thing such a short time ago. "I don't know how I could love you more than I do right now. I do have a problem we should talk about sometime soon, but I don't think it's urgent. I'm hoping we can fix it together, but right now we're going to a little party. Matthew is ready. I'll just give him a quick diaper change and we can be off." She knew this was right. A burden had been lifted from her heart.

When they arrived, she was surprised to spot Greg standing with Jack and Farrell.

"Oh, I didn't know Greg would be here. How nice."

"Of course, I cleared it with Ann and Jack first, but I didn't see how we could not invite him. He's practically part of all our families. He's a great young man; I like him," Jim said.

"Oh yes, I do too and Matthew loves him."

As they got out of the car, Jack, Farrell and Greg came forward to greet them.

"How's things going, Jim?" Farrell asked shaking his hand.

"Couldn't be better, sir," Jim said, "I don't think you've met Elaine Colby and Matthew."

"it's good to meet you both," Farrell nodded to Elaine, "but I sure have heard about this baby from Marge and Greg."

Elaine smiled. "This is Matthew's first venture out in society, I hope he'll behave himself."

"You probably have more to worry about with Jim than the baby." Jack nodded in Jim's direction. "He gets pretty wild around people of culture, but he does come in handy now and then, so we put up with him," Jack smiled at Elaine.

"In that case, I'll try to keep a tight rein on him." Elaine said. As she turned back to the car, she saw Greg talking to Matthew in the back seat.

"Hi Greg," she said. "I'll take Matthew out of the car seat and carry him over to the table. If you would, please, could you bring his carrier and his bag over? I'll get him settled in. After that, if you could watch him for a minute, I'll go see if I can help the ladies in the kitchen."

"Sure, I'd be glad to."

"Now that everyone is here, Jim, we better get the grill up and running. The ladies will be prancing out here with their offerings before long. You're welcome to tag along Farrell, if you'd like."

"Thanks anyway, but I'll go on up and get acquainted with Matthew." Farrell said.

"Well in that case, you could give me a hand with the ice chest," Jim said. "We'll set it right there at the end of the table."

Later, the women arrived carrying trays of food and arranged the filled dishes along the center of the picnic table, before finding a seat to wait for the men to bring their offering from the grill.

Ann and Jack's twins came out of the house behind the women and went directly to the baby.

"My name is Amy. What's your name?" Amy asked the baby as she climbed onto the bench to see better.

Greg smiled, "He's too young to talk yet, but his name is Matthew."

"Oh," Amy said, not taking her eyes off the gurgling baby whose hands and feet were in almost constant motion. She reached her hand out toward the baby.

"No, Amy. You know Mama said we couldn't touch him, just look," her brother said climbing up beside her.

"I'm not going to hurt the baby , Andy, besides, Mama isn't looking," Amy said, but she withdrew her hand. "He's pretty," she sighed.

Listening to the two little ones, Farrell was amused by the exchange. "Boys are usually referred to as handsome," he said. "Only girls like you are pretty."

Amy seemed perplexed and looked across the table at Farrell. Putting her hands on her hips, she said, "I think all babies can be pretty. When he gets big like him," she pointed at Greg, "then he can be handsome."

Farrell laughed, "Say, I think you might have something there."

Ann called the twins, "Come sit down; I'll fix your plates. Dad and Uncle Jim are bringing the meat over now."

When they were all seated, Jack nodded at Farrell, "Since we have clergy with us, we'll ask him to lead us in our prayer." Jack said, grabbing Amy's hand as she reached for a pickle from her plate.

Following Jack's lead, everyone joined hands around the table, and bowed their heads.

Farrell stood taking Marge's hand on one side and Greg's on the other. "Father," he began, "we ask your blessing on all our friends and loved ones gathered here today. We thank you for the young people in our lives, who keep us alert and give light to our spirit. We thank you for your guiding hand in our daily lives and ask You now to bless this food offered by our gracious loved ones. We ask all things through your Son and our Savior, Jesus, Amen."

"Amen," came the chorus of voices around the table

Ann stood and announced, "The plates and utensils are down at this end; so everyone can start here and go around to help themselves. The soft drinks are in the ice chest at the end of the table. Amy stay put. I've already fixed plates for you and Andy."

"Yeah, but you forgot dessert."

"Well," Ann said, "we'll see how your plate looks before we consider dessert."

"It will all be gone by then," Amy said sadly.

Jack put his hands on his twin's shoulders, bent his head between them and whispered, "I'll be sure to save you some, okay?" The twins smiled up at him.

Elaine waited until Jim had filled his plate before handing Matthew over to him and made her way around the table.

As everyone began to eat, the compliments began for the tasty variety of food. When things quieted down, Farrell asked, "How are things down at the police department?"

"Fairly calm," Jim answered, since he was sitting across from Farrell. "Things will be slowing down even more with people closing down their camps for the season."

"We have a great chief," Jack added. "Do you know John Redding?" he asked Farrell.

"I know who he is, but I've never met him."

"He encourages all of us to take part in community events and make ourselves available to help with activities for young people. It's his belief that the more involved we are with the kids, the less apt they are to look for trouble."

Jim nodded. "He certainly sets a great example with his community service when he's able. He attends most of the school programs. His plan is for us to have a more personal relationship with young people."

"While we're on the subject," Jack said, "I have to mention my wife and the small group of mothers who do much work for our youth groups in spite of their work load at home. I admire her and all of them. We seldom get a chance to tell them how much they are appreciated." Jack smiled across the table at his wife.

"I love you too Jack." She smiled at her husband. "The kids today have so many difficult choices to make and it's very satisfying to be able to help them, even in a small way."

When Ann finished her meal, she asked Elaine if she could hold Matthew for a few minutes.

"Oh, oh Jack," Jim leaned his head closer to Jack, I think that means somebody's wife would like another baby."

"No, you're wrong. It means, I've already got my hands full, but it's fun to hold someone else's baby," right Ann?

"What it means is, would two slow witted apes get me a soda, please?"

Later, as most everyone was finished eating, Ann pulled the cake closer to her, getting ready to slice. Before she made the first cut, she said, "We can thank Marge for this beautiful cake."

In the meantime, Jack made a quick trip to the house to bring out the ice cream and as Ann placed each slice on the small plate, he added a large scoop of ice cream.

Marge stood, "I have an announcement to make," she said. When she had everyone's attention she added, "I have received a proposal of marriage and I have accepted."

She watched Jim's face to see his reaction, since he and his father had been so close.

Jim smiled. "I guess you finally got some young handsome dude to fall for your baking bribes!" He turned to Greg, "I thought you'd hold out little longer, Greg."

Everyone laughed, along with Marge who quickly added, "You're absolutely right, Jim, except my young handsome dude is a bit older than Greg."

Farrell stood and taking Marge's hand in his, he bent and kissed her cheek.

"Just to clear up misconceptions, I am the winner of this fair lady's hand in marriage," Farrell said with pride.

Jim looked at Farrell, extending his h and "Congratulations sir, I got two out of three right. That's pretty good for me."

Jack chimed in next with his wishes for future happiness. Meanwhile Elaine and Ann were hugging Marge.

"Okay, you ladies," Jim said, "It's my turn to give mother a hug. You deserve the best, Mom and I know you've found him. I love you, Mom."

"I love you too, Son," Marge said, wiping the tears from her eyes. She turned and looked at Greg. "I need another hug from my adopted grandson."

Greg moved into her arms as she said, "I love you, Greg."

He smiled, "I love you and Mr. Dunn too," he said.

Marge looked at Farrell, shocked, because he had never said it to them before.

"Well, I think we better get on with dessert, don't you?" Marge glanced at the twins who had been watching the events patiently.

"Do you have any plans yet, such as the date?" Ann asked, while distributing the plates.

"Only loosely. Farrell has already contacted his Bishop to set a day when he's free to do the job. After that we'll be able to pull the whole thing together. We hope it will be soon. Farrell will be moving in with me and he'll rent his house until he decides whether to sell it or keep it. We both agree it should be a small affair. We won't be going away for a honeymoon. We decided to wait until summer and take a trip to the New England states. Maybe by that time we'll be used to each other's little quirks." She glanced at Farrell who nodded and took over, "That's about all for now, but I would add a couple of things. I won't be moving in until after the wedding and I would appreciate a little muscle at that time." Turning to face Jim, he asked, "Will you be my best man?"

"It would be my pleasure!" Jim said, nodding.

Farrell gave Marge another kiss on the cheek before sitting down beside her. She was still holding his hand.

Farrell sat looking at his dessert, "I don't think I can do a proper job of this with my left hand."

Marge was amused, "Oh, I suppose I can turn you lose for a few minutes, if you behave."

On the way home, Jim asked Elaine, "You're quiet, are you tired?" "Yes, but I was thinking about your Mom and Farrell. I'm so happy for them."

I've been hoping they would get around to realizing what they meant to each other. I'm happy for them too."

Elaine turned to look in the back seat, "I can't believe how good Matthew was. Of course, Greg hardly left his side the whole time. Matthew sure loves him. They took to each other right from day one."

Matthew began to whimper as they neared the house.

"It's getting near his supper time, bath and bed," Elaine said.

"I don't wonder. The poor little guy had to sit watching all that food disappear and he hardly got a smell." Jim said glancing in the mirror.

He helped Elaine carrying her bag and the baby carrier into the house, while Elaine carried Matthew.

"With all you have ahead of you, getting Matthew ready for bed and all, I think we had better call it a day. What do you think?"

"That's probably a good idea, even though I hate to end our day."

After a gentle kiss for her and one for Matthew, he said, "I'll stop tomorrow night and we'll see what's to be done about your problem."

Chapter Thirty-Two

Police Chief John Redding looked at his watch; it was still early. He was waiting for Dan Newlan, the special agent from the Drug Enforcement Agency. He had known Dan for many years and before he transferred to the DEA, he had worked for him.

John had been receiving a steady flow of information from the reports being turned in. Carson Cove, it would appear, had a drug problem.

Pushing away from his desk, he walked to the window. It had been another beautiful fall, at the lake. He loved living in Carson Cove. After his wife died, he had taken a job out here so he could live a quieter life and spend more time with his two boys.

Many of the trees had already lost most of their foliage and the temperatures were beginning to drop. Usually the winter months, after the tourists left, ushered in a quieter time for the police department. Although he had to admit, even with the extra people flocking to the beaches and camps along the waterways in the summer months the department had very few problems. They sure did give a large boost to the local economy.

He hated to think that his town had drawn the attention of the big-time drug dealers. *When had this happened*? he wondered. He was aware of small operations here and there; it had been like that for years, but now it seemed there were some big deals going down. The DEA had tracked them from the city to Carson Cove.

John sighed and turned away from the window, thinking about his two teen-age sons. The temptations they faced every day were daunting. He hoped and prayed they were strong enough to resist. They were fairly sensible kids, but you never know. He remembered the heartbreak of the parents of the young boy who had died from an overdose a few months ago. He couldn't imagine their lives or how their family could ever be the same again after such a tragedy. They would always feel the guilt of having left something undone or unsaid hat could have turned him away from drugs before it was too late. His men also felt the guilt, thinking they had somehow let their community down. He could only hope that some good would come from the youngster's death. Maybe some other teens his age would think twice before starting down the same destructive road.

Turning, he walked the short distance down the hall to the meeting area. His men were standing around the coffee machine talking.

"Good morning," he smiled. "I'm glad to see you are all here." They nodded and returned his greeting.

Jim Keller was closest to the coffee machine. He poured Chief Redding a cup of coffee and handed it to him.

"Thanks," he said, accepting the cup. "Be seated now if you would please. We're going to have a guest speaker this morning." He waited while the men settled. Turning toward the door, he saw the officer coming in and stepped toward him. The chief shook his hand before they walked to the head of the table together.

Chief Redding remained standing beside Dan Newlan. Looking around at the men seated at the table, he said "I want to thank all of you for coming this morning. I know some of you are just coming off the night shift. I wanted you to meet Dan Newlan and hear what he had to say. He is from the DEA assigned to the City of Crawford. He nodded toward Dan, indicating he had the floor and sat down.

"I asked your Chief if I could have a few minutes of your time this morning to thank you personally for your tremendous efforts. It has confirmed what we had only suspected. I can't tell you too many details at this time, but I will tell you this much; we have been working for over a year gathering evidence. We finally thought we had enough to make an arrest, when the operation shifted out here to Carson Cove. We didn't want to tip our hand by following them and that's where you came in. Your night shift spotted the car belonging to our person of interest out here three times this month, along with plates from four of the towns around the lake. One of you reported a business in this area that matched all the requirements which we gave you."

Jim flashed a smile and glanced at Jack Denver, knowing it had been in his report, as they had discussed it.

"It may please you to know," Dan continued, "we have had four shifts of special agents on the identified business. We are sure now that the newly opened tavern is the drug unit here in the Cove doing his work for him. We're planning to take that outfit down with him. We have no reason, as yet, to think the employes at the tavern have any connection with the drug trade. You will also probably be glad to know Operation License Plate has been suspended temporarily. Thank you again for your cooperation and diligence."

He walked around the table and shook hands with each man. Chief Redding dismissed his men. Since Dan had requested extra time, John nodded toward his office. He stopped at his secretary's desk and asked that there be no interruptions except emergencies. John held the door open for him to enter. Dan walked to the window and stood looking out; as John had a few minutes earlier.

"You have such a beautiful town here by the lake. The drug business is like a creeping disease; always moving, seeping into every crack and crevice of our nation. This group we're after stretches across this whole area and Frank Brant is the leader of the pack. We'll be thrilled to take this jackal down, but there's no cure for the disease. There's always another waiting in the wings to take its place." Dan came over to John's desk and sat across from him.

"What drugs are we talking about?" John asked.

"There are two types of heroin fairly common on the streets now; White China, from the poppy fields of Asia and Black Tar coming in from Mexico. Of course added to the list are others that have been around forever. Brant has connections for all of them, so I would imagine the variety is out here as well as in Crawford."

After a short pause, Dan asked, "Do you know Dora Roberts and Martin Delmont?"

John hesitated; "Not really. I met them both the night they had an open house for the D&M Tavern when they opened for business. Apparently, they are partners in the business. They did a tremendous overhaul on that old house. It exhibits good taste and a lot of money."

"With the help of your men, we have positive proof that it's the new headquarters for Brant's local enterprise. Recently, Dora Roberts spent a lot of time with Brant at his house. She appears to be bringing the goods back to the Tavern for redistribution. I have four men reporting on her movements and the activities around the tavern. There has been no evidence that the tavern itself, or any of the people who work there are involved in the drug business. However, we will close it down when we make the arrests and question them. Of course, the one exception is Martin Delmont. The dealers from the towns around the lake go to the side door and up the stairs to where the offices are located for their pickups. We have a tap on both Delmont's and Robert's phone. We have gathered a great deal of information, not only for their drug trade but other things that will interest you. I'll get that information to you as soon as I can." After a short pause, Dan asked, "How much time do you need to reschedule your men?"

"This time of year it's pretty quiet here in town; anytime you're ready we'll be ready," Chief Redding replied.

"Good, because we'd like to do it tomorrow if it's possible. Here's the plan. Tomorrow, starting at 8:00 am, we hope to arrest Frank Brant and three of his main henchmen in Crawford. By noon, we'll be out here. Our men will be arresting the dealers in the towns around the lake who have been traveling to the tavern for their supplies. At the same time, we hope to grab Delmont here in the Cove. And last but certainly not least, we'll go after Roberts. She doesn't usually come to the tavern until around 2:00 in the afternoon, so we figure we'll pick her up at her house. Now for your men. According to the area map, there are three main routes out of Carson Cove and two of them lead to towns around the lake. Do you still have the lists of license plate numbers?"

The Chief nodded.

"Have your men stop all cars coming or going, but any with the listed license plate numbers are to be arrested and cuffed on the spot. Any other cars can go on their way. Hopefully this won't take more than a couple hours." Dan sighed, "I guess that's about it, except I would ask you to be here in the office where I can be in constant contact with you. As we progress if there are any problems I will need you here."

"I'll be here," John said.

"And here's my number in case you have to reach me."

As Dan stood to leave, John stood and extended his h and "Good luck my friend. I hope this comes off without a hitch."

Newlan smiled, shaking the Chief's h and "Thank you."

Chapter Thirty-Three

After excusing his night duty men and taking their written reports, he laid out the specifics of the road block duty to his remaining unit.

Experience told John Redding there were many things that could go wrong with an operation of this scope. He was nervous. Even knowing the project was well planned did not alter the fact his men had little or no experience with something of this magnitude.

Since there was time before he expected to hear from Dan, he pulled the small stack of reports from yesterday in front of him. As he glanced through them, he noticed the longer report from Jack Denver and Jim Keller. They had discussed the complaint about the late-night activity on the lake and they were going to look into it.

According to the report, Denver and Keller had questioned many of the occupants who lived there year 'round. They found a number who had noticed late night activity. Further questioning had narrowed the problem down to a centrally located small cottage. The people who lived next door said they didn't know the people nor had they ever seen anyone there in the daytime. Next, they went to see Richard Alstein, who owned most of the property along the water front. He told them the property was privately owned, but he didn't know who owned it. Their next step was to go to the town records. They discovered the name of the owner was Dora Roberts.

The chief let out a low whistle. It wasn't too difficult to put this situation together now that Dan Newlan had connected Dora Roberts and Martin Delmont to the drug enterprise in Carson Cove. The dealers across the lake were no doubt taking a short cut across the lake to pick up their goods. Who knows? Maybe Dora Roberts had a little private business going on that didn't include her partner. Whatever the case, he knew Dan Newlan needed to have this information. John made a copy of the report for Dan before filing it. The first call from Newlan came at Ten fifteen, which was about the time he had predicted. He told the chief they had Frank Brant and three of his associates in custody. They were processing them now.

"I've sent most of my men out to the towns around the lake. We figure they'll be in place and start the arrests at eleven-thirty."

"My men will establish their car inspection checks at 11:15." The chief said. "It sounds like everything went well in Crawford."

"Couldn't have been smoother. Now if we do as well out your way, I'll be a happy man. We've had seventeen under surveillance for the better part of a year and I hope we can get at least half of them. If they have figured out something might be coming down, they'll head out of town or go into hiding."

"My men are ready and waiting, so I'll say good luck, but I know there hasn't been much luck involved here. I know it has taken months of planning and hard work to bring you this far. God be with you my friend."

"Thanks John, we need all the help we can get. I've got four men with me and we'll go after Delmont next. We don't have a lot of evidence on him, but after the arrest is made, we'll be able to search the place thoroughly and hopefully find what we need. My surveillance crew tells me that Roberts doesn't come to the tavern until around three each day. So, when we have secured Delmont, we'll try to grab her at her house around one-thirty or two. There's a lot that could go wrong, so tell your men to be especially alert for Roberts and Delmont, along with any of the lake gang."

Greg Roberts hated it when school let out early. He could only hope his mother was still asleep. Maybe he could sneak in quietly, change his clothes and be gone without her even knowing he had been there. He could take a run down to see Mr. Dunn or Aaron or maybe he'd run over to Mrs. Keller's first. She always had something good baked. Anything was better than being around where his mother was. She'd been acting so weird lately. He hadn't been able to figure out what was going on with her. Now that he wasn't delivering drugs anymore, he had no way of knowing what was happening. The one thing he did know from past experience, it was best to stay out of her reach whenever possible.

Leaning his bike on the side of the porch, he walked quietly up the steps and into the hall. He could see her purse sitting on the kitchen table, which meant she was up. He stood for a moment listening, but he couldn't hear any movements.

As he started toward the hall, he froze and he looked at the floor. He bent to pick up a small hand gun laying on the floor just beyond the table. After looking it over he turned and laid it on the table beside her purse.

When he entered the hall leading to his bedroom, he saw her. She was sprawled out on the floor and there was blood splattered everywhere. He stood staring for a few seconds before turning back to the kitchen where he picked up the phone and dialed. When a voice answered he said, "Can you send an ambulance please? Something awful has happened. I think my Mother is dead. My name is Greg Roberts."

"Can you tell me the address?" the operator asked.

Greg told her and she said, "The ambulance will be there in a few minutes. Are you alright?"

"Yes," Greg said. He stood holding the phone a few seconds and then dialed Farrell Dunn's number. When he answered, Greg said, "Mr. Dunn can you come up? I think my mother is dead. I already called the ambulance."

"Greg, are you home?"

"Yes."

"Don't go anywhere; I'll be right there."

Farrell grabbed his keys and raced to the car.

Greg was sitting on the porch steps when Farrell arrived. He took the young boy into his arms and held him. His whole body was shaking.

"Can you tell me what happened?"

"I came home from school and found her lying on the floor in the hall."

"You left school early?"

"Yes, half a day."

Farrell heard the ambulance coming before he was able to see it.

It was past noon and Chief Redding was beginning to worry about Dan and what was going on at the tavern. So many things could have gone wrong. When the phone rang, he grabbed it on the first ring.

"Hi John, we've got Delmont and we've closed the tavern down. I've got a list of the employees and I told them we'd be in touch later. In the meantime, my men have been searching the upstairs offices but so far haven't found anything incriminating. We must be missing something. How's everything on your end going?"

"My men have only been on the job for about an hour. I haven't had any word from them as of yet."

"Things seem to be going so fast with us; I forgot the time sequence," Dan said, "in any case, we still plan on going up to the Roberts place about 1:00. I haven't heard from my lake crew either, but I'm sure I will soon. I'll keep in touch."

When the chief hung up the phone, his radio crackled almost immediately. The 911 dispatcher was calling all officers in the vicinity to Dora Roberts' address for a possible gunshot fatality. Chief Redding's mind was reeling.

As the chief arrived at the Roberts' place, he saw a member of the ambulance crew standing outside. The chief approached him at a quick pace and asked if he was first on the scene. The paramedic responded, "Yes, upon arrival we found the dead body of a woman identified by her son to be Dora Roberts. It would appear that she has been dead for at least a couple of hours. I instructed the crew not to touch anything more than necessary. I figured you could take it the rest of the way, since it's a gunshot to the head and this is a crime scene."

"Thank you for your careful handling of the crime scene, paramedic."

Redding immediately dispatched two of his men to take over the check point on Larkin Road to relieve Denver and Keller. He then radioed Denver and Keller to meet him at the Roberts' residence as soon as they were relieved.

When Jim heard the radio message, he was startled. "Whoa," he said, pulling his cell phone from his pocket. "Jack, can you catch that car coming through? I'm calling the chief. The address he gave us is Greg Roberts' home."

The chief wasn't surprised to see Jim's name on his cell phone.

"Hi Chief, what's going on? That's the Roberts address isn't it? Is Greg alright?"

"Well, he hasn't been hurt. Farrell Dunn is here with him. His mother, Dora Roberts, was killed with a gunshot wound to the head. When Greg came home from school, he found her. I'm getting ready to question him now."

Jim was relieved, but he realized the boy must be badly shaken. "Thanks Chief. See you up there as soon as our replacements arrive."

Chief Redding called Dan Newlan. "Dan, I am at the Dora Roberts residence; looks like she's been murdered."

Dan asked, "Ok, is it okay with you if I come there anyway and look the place over for drug evidence?"

"Sure," the chief said, "I'm here if you need anything."

"Actually, it doesn't surprise me much from what I have heard from their phone taps," Dan added. Give your men another half hour and you can call them off the road blocks. I expect my men to be calling in anytime now."

When Chief John Redding approached the Roberts house, Farrell Dunn and Greg were still sitting on the porch.

He shook hands with them and introduced himself.

"I've talked with the ambulance personnel and sent them on their way. I'd appreciate it if you stay so I can ask a few questions later," he said as he disappeared into the house. Both men nodded in agreement.

A middle-aged man from the crime scene investigation unit stepped away from the group.

"The paramedics examined her to see if there was any use in resuscitation. There wasn't, so they went no further. It's a pretty messy scene," he warned the chief as they walked to the hall.

"Gunshot to the head was the cause of death?" John asked.

"Yes, it looks like that, but as I say, we didn't do much of an examination. The blood around the wound has started to dry and that says she's been dead at least two hours, maybe more."

"When I came in," Redding said, "I noticed a gun on the table along with a purse. Were they there when you arrived?"

"Yes, they were there. I warned my people not to touch them."

"Good. Thank you for waiting until I got here. I don't see any reason for you to delay your examination any longer. If I need to question you further, I know where to contact you."

He walked to the door and as they left he asked Farrell and Greg to come in. He indicated they should sit at the table and he sat down opposite Greg.

"First of all, I want to thank you, Mr. Dunn, for being here for Greg," the chief said.

"Greg called me and told me what had happened. We're close friends so I came right over."

John turned to Greg. "It's sad, Greg, that you would have to be the one to find your mother under these circumstances. I know you're upset, but I have to ask you if it would be possible to tell me about your morning?"

Greg nodded, "Do you mean since I came home from school?"

"Actually, I meant from the time you got up this morning until now."

"Well, most days are about the same. I get up, shower, get dressed, eat breakfast and go to school. I remember to plug in the coffee pot so it will be ready when she gets up."

"You saw that your mother was still in bed so you plugged in the coffee pot?"

"No, I didn't see her, but I knew she was there because the door was shut. She always shuts the door when she goes to bed."

"So, you plug in the coffee pot every day, right?"

"Well, not on Sundays because she sleeps late on Sundays; it's her day off."

"I see. On Sundays you spend time with her?"

"Not any more than I have to. I make myself pretty scarce on that day."

John didn't miss the sarcasm in his tone. "Really? You and your mother didn't get along too well?"

Greg hesitated before answering. "I think she hated me, so I guess she thought of me as a nuisance, except when I was useful to her." Greg knew immediately he had said too much.

"Useful to her? In what way?" John had picked up on the phrasing as soon as it was out, along with the change in his facial expressions.

"From the time I was quite little, she taught me how to do the housework, take care of my clothes and get my own meals."

John frowned. There was no doubt in his mind that the boy was telling the truth, but maybe there was more to it than what he said. He would go after more later. "You came home from school early today?"

"Yes, school let out at noon. When I came in, I saw her purse on the table, so I thought she must be up early. She usually doesn't get up until around two and leaves before I get home."

"You haven't mentioned the gun. Was it there on the table when you came in?" John asked, pointing at it lying by the purse.

"No, it was lying there on the floor. I was going to my bedroom to change my clothes when I saw it lying there on the floor. I picked it up and put it on the table. Then, when I started down the hall, I saw her lying there and I came back and called 911."

"Was it her gun?" John asked.

Greg shrugged, "I don't know."

"Did you walk down the hall to see her?"

"No, her eyes were open and there was blood all over the place, so I thought she was dead. I came back out here and called 911, just in case she was still alive. After that, I called Mr. Dunn and came out and sat on the porch. That's about it." Greg said, looking down at his hands.

"You did a good job," the chief said, "thank you." I'm sorry to put you through that, but it had to be done."

Greg nodded slowly, as though living a dream.

"Do you have grandparents or aunts or uncles that we could notify for you?" John asked.

Greg shook his head, "None that I know of."

John looked at Farrell, "Then I guess you two aren't related. The next step would normally be to notify Social Services."

Farrell held up his hand. "If you wouldn't have any objections, I'd be more than glad to take him home with me until this thing gets settled and for that matter, indefinitely."

"If it's agreeable to you, Greg, I see no reason you couldn't go with him." He looked back at Farrell, "Just give me your address and phone number so we can reach you later."

Farrell reached into his wallet and handed him his card. John was pleased to see the title of Rev. before his name and the church with which he was affiliated. You couldn't be too careful where kids were concerned.

The chief looked back at Greg, "Why don't you pack a couple changes of clothes. There's a great deal more we have to talk about and I'll be in touch with you sometime tomorrow. You're better off out of here right now. Pretty soon this place is going to be crawling with police and county officials."

When Farrell saw Greg hesitate to go down the hall to his room, he put his hand on his shoulder and said quietly, "I'll come with you."

They had only been gone a few minutes when Jim Keller and Jack Denver arrived with the DEA agent, Dan Newlan, pulling in behind them. The chief greeted them, then they followed him down the hall to look at the dead body of Dora Roberts. Jim gave a low whistle, but no one said anything as they walked back to the kitchen.

"You know, John, this could be drug related since she was knee-deep in the drug business," Dan said.

"Yes, I've been thinking the same thing, but for now we will have to treat it as we would any other murder. We'll just start digging until we gather the clues to know what we're dealing with here."

"Well, I can report that we have Frank Brant and his three buddies from Crawford in custody and Delmont as well. My men picked up eleven from around the lake and your roadblock nabbed another two. In anyone's book, that's quite an accomplishment. Right now, I've got to go back to the tavern. We haven't found any evidence there that we were looking for. Glancing at Jim and Jack, he asked, "Would either of you happen to know who did the reconstruction on the tavern?"

"I know who owns the construction company, if that would help."

"It sure would. Could you write the name down for me?" Dan said as he handed him his notebook.

"I'll be on my way and thanks so much for your help. I'll be in touch tomorrow. I have some information from our phone taps that I'm sure will help in your investigation."

"Okay, thanks and I think I might have something that might interest you too." John said, thinking of the traffic across the lake.

After Dan left, the chief said, "Jim, run out to my car and get a couple of evidence bags and we'll get these things taken care of before our company arrives." He gestured toward the table where the purse and gun sat.

After the items were deposited in the chief's car, the two men sat down at the table across from their chief.

"For the next few days, you two will be assigned exclusively to this case. I'm going to call in Hale Cooper to take over for me when I'm out of the office. The remaining crime scene people and the coroner from the county offices are on their way. There's going to be a lot of confusion here shortly and before they get here I want you two to give the house a quick look. Just take note of anything unusual and since Dan thinks she was into the drug business, watch for anything drug related in particular. After they get here, you're free to go. I want you to start digging into Dora Roberts' background. I understand she lived in Crawford before moving out here. I'll be in contact with Mr. Dunn later to check on Greg. There are a lot more questions I have for him, but I imagine it will be late before we're finished here today, so it will be tomorrow before I get to it."

As they started down the hall, Jack turned into the first doorway while Jim edged around the body to the bigger room at the end of the hall. It didn't take long to realize this had to be Dora Roberts' room.

At his immediate right was a small but well-appointed bathroom. When he stepped through the door, the lights around the large mirror automatically came on. The counter held a multitude of creams, lotions and makeup. On the right, a section of the mirror opened to shelves meant to be a medicine cabinet, but it was empty.

Once back inside the bedroom, he stood still, his eyes moving slowly around the room, taking in the surroundings, which were lavish compared to the other rooms he had walked through.

The furniture was gleaming mahogany and at the windows hung graceful cream-colored velvet drapes hanging in folds part way down the sides with a swag crossing the top. The walls were painted a few shades darker than the drapes, while the carpet was a rich brown and soft under his feet.

268

To his left stood a dresser that filled the rest of the wall. A number of colorful bottles and boxes were spaced along the top with an ornate lamp at each end. All were reflected in a full-length mirror.

As his eyes continued around the room, there in the middle of the windowless wall stood a medium-sized bed with delicately carved designs on the headboard. A frilly top coverlet hid whatever was underneath, as well as the pillows.

The wall to his right was obviously a closet. He walked over and pushed the sliding door, revealing a full line of well-organized clothing. Beneath the clothing was a shoe rack the total length of the closet containing dozens of pairs of shoes of every color and heel size and design.

Everything in the room shouted money. While he stood there, slightly awestruck, his mind reviewed the bare bones of the other rooms he had seen; no curtains at the windows or rugs of any kind, two cheap-looking chairs, a st and a lamp and a small television set in the small open area off the kitchen, which must have been considered a living room.

The kitchen had all the basics; a stove, refrigerator, sink and cupboards. A small table stood in the middle with four chairs and again, only a shade at the one window. He had noticed the washer and dryer in the entryway as he entered. There were no decorations in any of the rooms, although he had to admit, every room was neat and clean with no clutter anywhere.

His mind wandered to his mother's living room where you could always find a newspaper and a pile of unread magazines near her chair. On a stand beside the lamp, you could see a dish with whatever fruit was in season a small dish of candy and a piece of clothing on the footstool needing a button, along with a spool of thread.

In this house there was nothing to suggest anyone lived here. He guessed that was what was bothering him; except for this room, the house didn't look as if it were occupied.

While he stood contemplating, Jack's voice came from the other room.

"Chief, Jim, can you come in here for a minute? There's something here you should see."

When they entered the room, they saw the small neatly made up bed with two stacks of books. The other window had only a shade, just like most of the windows in the house. On the wall opposite Greg's small bed they saw what Jack had called them in to see. Opposite the bare window stood a crib.

The chief looked at Jim, "You knew the boy fairly well, did he ever mention a baby?"

"No sir, he never did. Of course, it could be his crib from when he was a baby."

The chief shrugged. "It seems a little odd that they would go to all the trouble of moving it out and setting it up if it wasn't going to be used."

"Not only that," Jack said, "but take a look at this." He pulled open a drawer full of neatly folded baby clothes.

"Okay, I guess you better check this out when you start on Roberts' background. Check the county birth records and let me know what you find. I think I hear the county officials arriving now."

Chapter 34

Farrell Dunn glanced across the seat at Greg's sober face. The boy didn't look sad or in mourning. It was as if he was perplexed or worried about something. Thinking back on some of the guarded remarks the boy had made, Farrell concluded that there had been little love between Greg and his mother.

"How are you holding up, son?" he asked.

"I'm all right. It's just that it was a shock, that's all."

Farrell nodded, thinking what an odd statement it was for a boy who had just seen his mother lying dead on the floor.

"I shouldn't have called you and got you mixed up in this mess," Greg said, rubbing the palms of his hands together nervously.

"I'll always be grateful you did. You know don't you that Social Services would probably have been called if I hadn't been there. Before this is over, it may still happen since you're under age they will assume you need supervision."

"Why?" Greg sat up straight and alert in his seat, looking at Farrell. "I can take care of myself. I've been doing all right practically ever since I could walk.

Hearing the anger in the boy's voice, Farrell reached out and touched Greg's arm. "Listen to me a minute, Greg. The officials don't know anything about your life and most young people your age would need their help. Would you mind staying with me, if I could arrange it, at least until things get straightened out?"

"No, I wouldn't mind, but Mr. Dunn, there's no need. I've mostly been alone for years. I cook my own meals, keep myself and the house clean, do my own washing and get to school on time. About the only thing she did was leave me money to buy groceries. Even in the city before coming out here, I had my jobs and saved a lot of money. Before we moved out here, I had planned on running away to get away from her beatings, but I was younger and could never figure out how to get away with it."

"Greg, I have to say, you are an outstanding young man. I've never known anyone like you, but I know *this* for a fact, the officials wouldn't allow you to live there alone. I want you to know you're welcome to stay with me as long as it takes and for that matter, after Marge and I are married, if it comes to that. I know Marge would be delighted."

Greg sighed. "Thank you Mr. Dunn, but you don't really know me and what my life has been like.

 I'm worried that maybe if I stay with you, I'm putting you in danger. I know quite a few people who might want me dead now that she's gone. I have information about a lot of people."

Farrell was shocked. "No son, I won't change my mind, not ever as far as that's concerned, but I do want to tell you some things about this situation. The police will be around now and will be asking you many more questions as this investigation goes on. I would advise you to tell them everything you have on your mind. Here's your chance to get out from under the burden you've been carrying. It's time to put your trust in their ability to do the right

272

thing by you and everyone concerned. They have ways and means to handle it. Please think about it son. It's time." Farrell patted Greg's knee for reassurance. He couldn't judge the reception his advice was getting by Greg's silence. He could only hope for the best as he pulled into his driveway.

Early the next morning, while the sun was still struggling to make an appearance above the clouds gathered on the horizon, Farrell walked out to get his daily newspaper. It was his habit to skim the news with his first cup of coffee. This morning, he had added incentive to see what was reported about Dora Roberts' death.

As Farrell sat down to his coffee, he picked up the paper. After he glanced at the headlines of the world news, he noticed the column on the left side. It read: "DEA and local police cooperate in significant drug bust in Crawford and Carson Cove. Story on page three." Directly below it was "Dora Roberts, murder victim in Carson Cove. Story on page four."

Farrell quickly turned the page to four and read, '*Authorities report Dora Roberts was found dead at approximately twelve o'clock Wednesday afternoon by her son, Greg Roberts, when he arrived home from school. Police Chief of Carson Cove, John Redding, said it apparently was a gunshot wound to the head, but there was little else to report this early in the investigation. She and her son had moved to Carson Cove over a year ago and she was part owner of the newly opened D & M Tavern on the outskirts of Carson Cove.*'

Farrell read it twice, although it didn't tell him anything he didn't already know. He refilled his cup and returned to the paper to read about the drug bust.

The newspaper article went on to say, '*The DEA, in conjunction with the police in Crawford and Carson Cove, made eighteen arrests on Wednesday. DEA surveillance teams had been gathering evidence for over a year in preparation. Arrested in Crawford was Frank Brank, suspected of being high in command of the North Eastern branch of the drug cartel and two of his subordinates. Brant joined forces with one of his smaller units in Carson Cove, led by Martin Delmont and Dora Roberts, who had opened the D & M Tavern, thought by officials to be a cover for illegal drug trade. However, the DEA has found no evidence that the tavern itself was involved in any way with the drug trafficking.'*

The reporter continued, *'Delmont was arrested in Carson Cove along with twelve of his cohorts in the small towns around Lake Andrew. It had been the intention of the DEA to arrest Dora Roberts along with Delmont, but she was found dead in her home. In an ongoing investigation during the last twenty-two months, the Crawford Police, in cooperation with the DEA, have confiscated more than nine hundred thousand dollars' worth of drugs, cash, guns and vehicles.'*

Farrell stopped, let out a big sigh and continued reading.

'The investigation revealed a major drug pipeline from New Jersey to Crawford. Many came to this city to set up shop and deal in large quantities of drugs. The United States Attorney for the Northeastern District was quoted as saying, "Drug trafficking crimes are a never-ending battle in large cities, as well as small towns, across America today."

Farrell leaned back in his chair, considering what this had meant in the life of young Greg Roberts, when he spotted Greg coming down the stairs.

As he called out his good morning to Greg, the phone rang. It was Marge.

"Farrell, have you seen the paper this morning? I'm worried about Greg."

"Oh Marge honey, I'm sorry, I should have called you. Greg is here with me. He called me yesterday right after he found his mother. I went right up and stayed with him. The police came and after asking some questions, the chief said he could come home with me and he'd be in touch with us sometime today."

"Oh, thank God for that, Farrell, but did you read the report about the drug bust?"

"Yes, I did." He glanced at Greg in the kitchen, reading the newspaper. "It answers a great many questions and brings up a great many more, wouldn't you think?"

"Yes, it sure does," Marge said, "I'm so glad he's with you." She sighed.

"Listen Honey, can I call you back later? Greg just got up and I want to get our breakfast started. He's reading the account in the paper now. After I know what the chief plans on doing, maybe you could drop by. I'll let you know when things have cleared away. I love you Honey."

"And I love you, my dear. Talk with you later," she said as she hung up.

Farrell watched the boy's face as he finished reading the articles. When he looked up at Farrell, he said, "Now you know." His voice was sad and low.

"Yes, now I know what the paper says, but by your reaction, I'm guessing you were somehow involved, right?"

Greg nodded.

"I'm going to ask you one questions and then we'll get breakfast started. Was anything you did with the drug business done voluntarily?"

"No Sir, I hated everything about it and I hated everyone who was mixed up in it. Believe me, I took a lot of beatings because I told them how I felt."

"Thank you. That's all I need to know. Now, let's get on with breakfast. I'm not too prepared for a young man's taste in cereals, but we could have some waffles and bacon this morning. We'll go shopping for food more to your liking later."

"Waffles and bacon sounds great to me!"

"You could set the table while I fry up the bacon. The waffles are the kind that go in the toaster. The butter and syrup are in the fridge."

While they were cleaning up, Farrell said, "You do know this drug thing may possibly change the direction of the questioning and may even involve the Drug Enforcement Agency."

"Yes, I know and I've thought about what you said. I will tell them anything they want to know."

"I don't think you'll be sorry if you do and you know you have friends now who will stand with you to face anything that's ahead of you."

"You don't think they will all hate me now, do you?"

"No, Greg, I can tell you without any doubt in my mind, they won't hate you. That isn't how it works when you have friends who love you."

Chapter Thirty-Five

Thursday morning, Jim Keller and Jack Denver arrived in the chief's office early, well ahead of the regular time allotted for the morning reports. Since they were off their regular beat with special duty, they knew they were to report directly to John Redding.

By way of greeting, John said, "Help yourselves to a cup of coffee and come sit down." They were two of his most reliable men. They were alert, thorough and seemed to know instinctively how to handle people, which was advantageous to getting them to talk freely.

"I know you didn't have much time yesterday after you left here, but how did you make out?"

Jim made a motion with his free h and indicating that he would start. "Jack and I decided that we were more or less on a fishing expedition to find out all we could about who Dora Roberts was."

The chief nodded.

"Jack left me off at the Wilton Street Hospital to talk with the staff to see if I could get any information, in case she had been there. As it turned out, she did have her baby there. After I told them that I was investigating the Roberts murder, they spoke freely, although they had nothing much of interest to say. I was about to give it up when another nurse came into the area. After I explained why I was there, she told me she had assisted Dr. Ridgeway with the delivery. She said she remembered the birth because the doctor had said he had expected Mrs. Roberts might have problems since she was quite a lot older than most having her first pregnancy. I told her I was under the impression that Roberts had an older child. She said, "No, the doctor would know." So, I left it at that.

"I wouldn't have thought it was very professional for her to be casually talking about a patient," the chief observed.

"Well, I told her I was investigating the woman's murder, so maybe that covered it."

"Borderline." The chief smiled and glanced in Jack's direction.

"While my other half was playing up to the pretty nurses," Jack nodded in Jim's direction, "I went and dug around in the county records. I had no difficulty finding my information. Dora Roberts gave birth to a seven pound, eight ounce boy on June 28th of this year. The attending physician was Dr. Edward Ridgeway. While I was there, I dug around the records and found Roberts' old address. After I picked up Jim, we went and had something to eat. By the time we found the street where the house was located and looked the territory over, it was getting late. We could see that it was a large attractive house in a neighborhood of other well-kept houses. There is a for sale sign in the yard with the agent's name and phone number. I thought we'd see what you thought about it and maybe go back today to talk with some of her old neighbors. It's been by experience that neighbors know more of your business than your mother-in-law."

John and Jim both laughed. "Good idea," John said. "I've got Hale Cooper coming in to cover the office this morning while I go with Dan over to Farrell Dunn's place to talk to the Roberts boy."

"Have you talked to him to see how he's doing?" Jim asked.

"No, but I did talk to Dunn just before you arrived. He said the youngster was calm and seemed to be doing well. I talked with the boy before he left with Dunn yesterday. I tell you, I was surprised at how calm he seemed after seeing his mother and the mess in the hall. He told me about his morning and he was clear and open with everything. Of course, I didn't ask anything about the drug operation. We just touched on the surface. There's plenty more to find out yet, I'm sure."

The chief was silent for a moment, sipping his coffee, thinking. "Depending on what you find out this morning, I may want you to take a little trip over to see Martin Delmont. He ought to have known her better than anyone. Of course, the next hurdle will be if he will talk without his lawyer present. It's time to hear from the rest of the men and give them some information about the murder and the drug bust. Actually, they probably know as much as we do if they read the morning paper."

After the half-hour meeting and collection of reports, the chief returned to his office to find Dan Newlan waiting.

"I hope you don't mind, I helped myself to your coffee," he said.

"Not at all. So, how did you make out getting evidence against Delmont and Roberts? I know it was a concern when we last talked."

Dan smiled, "You know John, sometimes it happens this way, something just keeps gnawing at you, but you can't seem to get a grasp on it. Then, all of a sudden last night it came to me;

Delmont's and Roberts' offices are back to back and between them each has a closet. What I had missed was the space allotted for each closet. There was barely enough room in each of them for the width of a hanger and yet there was quite a bit more room left over between them. So, this morning I did a more thorough search and close to the floor I found a button that slid the panel open to a long narrow room with a table loaded with measuring devices, plastic packets and a sealer, along with a large amount of material waiting to be measured. Not only that, but there was a stack of packets with names and times for pickup. You, John, are looking at a happy man. We got them good."

"That's great news. I thought I had a piece of news that might have been of interest to you. I'll tell you anyway, but with Roberts dead, I don't know that it will help your case any. We had some complaints from some of our waterfront people about middle of the night activity on the lake. With a little investigation, my men found a small cottage belonging to Dora Roberts. It doesn't take much imagination to figure some of the dealers were taking a shortcut across the lake for their pickups."

"You never know, John. With the drug business, sometimes it's an unlikely piece of information that might tie in and make a big difference. It might just be the thing that will help those small-town dealers to squeal loud and clear." Dan reached into his pocket and handed a tape to John. "This is a copy of the tape we took off Delmont's phone tape. I think you will find it quite interesting. It's a little difficult to believe one woman could anger so many people to the point of wanting to kill her."

"Thanks Dan, I won't take the time to listen to it until we get back," he said, locking it in his desk drawer.

"I'll be turning everything we have over to the Attorney General for the prosecution, but it's been great working with you again."

"Same here, Dan," John said. "Well, what do you say we go down and talk to the Roberts boy. They are expecting us."

After arriving at Farrell Dunn's house and the introductions made, they all settled around the table. Farrell asked if it was permissible for him to stay. "I've heard bits and pieces about this drug situation from him already, but I'd like to be here to give him a little loving support."

Dan looked at John, "It's fine with me, what do you think?"

"It's fine with me too, but I wouldn't want to read anything said here today in tomorrow's newspaper. If it's at all possible, I would prefer that the boy's name never be mentioned again in connection with any reports given out about the murder or the drug business, understood?"

Farrell nodded, "You have nothing to worry about with me."

Dan reached across the table and lightly patted Greg's hand to get his attention since he was looking down at his folded hands.

"The chief and I agreed," Dan said, "that I would ask questions first."

Greg nodded, now sitting straight in his chair and looking at Dan.

"I want you, Greg, to go as far back in your memory as possible and tell us everything you remember about your mother's drug business and the names of any connections she had with anyone, all right?"

Greg glanced at Farrell, who smiled and nodded.

"I guess the first thing was before I started school. She bought me a vest to wear under my jacket. I've never seen one in a store that was rigged quite like that one, but this one had a zipper across the whole bottom of it." Greg motioned with his hands. "Then, she walked me to three different houses on different streets and told me what I was to do. I was to go to the doors of these houses and knock and the person answering the door would do the rest."

"Do you remember the names of these people and the addresses?" Dan interrupted.

Greg frowned. "I didn't know all of their names, but I'll tell you the ones I know and all of their addresses."

Dan wrote them in his notebook as Greg responded. "Go on."

"That was just the beginning. She told me all kinds of horror stories of what would happen to me if the police caught me or if things didn't go quite right with the dealers. The dealers knocked me around quite a lot, but I suppose I asked for it in a way because I hated them so much and told them so. In time though, I learned my biggest problem was the street gangs. They hung around on the corners and slammed me around and sometimes beat me half to death. It took a while, but I learned the corners where they hung around and I avoided them. Sometimes the police were my best protection. If they saw me walking they would drive kind of slow behind me until I got past the corner. As I got older, my route was longer and longer until I had a many as ten pickups divided up on different days after school."

"Hang on a minute before you give me the names and street numbers. Let's go back to the vest. Am I to understand you carried the drugs and money in the lining of that zippered vest?" Dan asked.

"Yes, my mother put the money in there for me to take to the dealers and bring back the drugs the same way."

"Were you ever tempted to try some of the drugs you were carrying?"

"No Sir, not ever! I had taken so much punishment because of the drugs, from all of them and I hated every one of them but most of all my mother. There isn't hardly an inch of my body that hasn't carried a bruise at one time or another and my mother was the worst. Everything she ever taught me, she pounded into my body. From the time I can remember, I knew how to take care of myself. I did my own washing, got my own meals and kept the house clean. I was to always 'look presentable.' She didn't want the school officials or the social people snooping around. I had to keep my marks up or she was right on me. Everything about my life was for the benefit of the drugs. Martin Delmont was coming around pretty regular back then. He always acted as if he liked me."

"What do you mean, he acted as if he liked you?" Dan asked.

"When she would be knocking me around, he stopped her and said nice things to me, but he was mixed up in his own drug business and as far as I was concerned, he was no better than any of the rest of them." Greg's voice was low and bitter.

"So, when you moved out here to Carson Cove, was that the end of the drug business?"

"Only for a couple of weeks. Then, it was business as usual. Pregnant and all, Martin brought my mother back into the drug business full force."

Greg then told Dan about clearing the path to the side road and the late-night pickups.

"After the tavern opened, that ended my job with the drugs. I was kinda worried about it."

"Worried?" Dan asked.

"Yeah, well I figured if they didn't need me anymore, they'd kill me off like they did with the two guys in Crawford when they wanted to get out of the business. They said they knew too much, so that was that, at least so they said."

Dan frowned. "We have most of the ones you named in jail and we'll go after the rest of them now. Like the chief said, we'll keep your name out of it, if at all possible and hopefully they are going to have bigger things to worry about than chasing after you."

Turning toward the chief, he said, "That's about it for me and looking at Greg, he said, "thanks for your information."

John Redding looked thoughtfully at Greg. How was he going to approach him about the murder of his mother? John realized from listening to what he had told Dan, that there was little or no love lost between mother and son. Here was someone who knew little else other than abuse his entire young life and yet managed to be a respectable and fairly intelligent young adult.

Finally, he said, "You know Greg, it has been my experience that such a deep-seated hatred as you feel for these people and your mother will affect you more than it ever will any of them. I hope it doesn't."

This statement drew a faint smile from Greg and a quick glance at Farrell Dunn.

"You sound like Mr. Dunn, but it's really hard for me not to hate them. Until we moved out here and I got to know Mr. Dunn and all the people I work for, I never knew there were people like them. They really care about me and talk to me like I'm intelligent; like I'm somebody worth knowing." He hesitated and then continued, "Mr. Dunn says if I must hate, I should hate the drugs, what they do to people and the greed that has rule over their weakness. I'll try."

Farrell Dunn smiled; the boy had been listening after all.

"You, son, are an amazing young man," John said, shaking his head. "Now I want to ask you a few questions. Do you know anyone who would want to kill your mother?"

"No, not really, but knowing her and the way she was, I'd think there might be quite a few. Actually, except to see her coming and going now and then, I didn't know much about what she was doing. She left the money to buy groceries and as long as I did my chores, that was about it. Except for Martin Delmont and Frank Brant, I never had any contact with anyone else out here."

John nodded, "When we went through your house, after she was killed, we found a baby crib and baby clothes in what we assumed to be your room. Is that correct?"

Greg sighed. "Yes," he nodded. "The same day she got home with him, she more or less gave him to me. We moved the crib into my room and I made room in my dresser for his clothes. The rest of that day she showed me how to take care of him. I was scared I might hurt him, but she didn't care. The next afternoon she was out of there and from then on I did everything for him. I rearranged my schedule so I could be home in time for his feedings. Even though she was in her bedroom until three in the afternoon, she never looked at him as far as I could see. I was never to mention that there was a baby or to take him anywhere. I did everything around his schedule and during the evenings I washed his clothes and did chores and homework. It worked out pretty good during lunch hour. I felt bad for Aaron because I knew how she treated me and I wasn't about to let her hurt him because I loved him so much."

"Where is the baby now?"

"We had a big fight about her getting a babysitter if she wasn't going to take care of him and the next morning when I got up the baby was gone."

"The baby was gone?" Greg had John and Farrell's full attention.

Greg nodded. "She was still asleep and when I woke her and asked her where he was, then all hell broke loose. She acted as if she didn't know he was gone. She raved and stomped around and finally went to the phone and called someone named Becker and accused him of stealing the baby so he wouldn't have to pay her the money. From listening to what she said, I figured she must have been going to sell him. I tried to get her to call the police, but she wouldn't because of the drug business. When I kept at her about calling the police, she said don't worry, she would take care of it."

Tears came to Greg's eyes just thinking about having to give up his brother, even though he knew it was the right thing to do. His brother was being loved and given good care.

"That was it? The baby just disappeared and nobody did anything about it?"

"I loved him, but there wasn't much I could have done," Greg said defensively.

Dan Newlan, who had been leaning against the cupboard across from the table, interrupted, "Excuse me, John, could I speak to you for a minute?" he asked, stepping into the hall.

"I think I'll be on my way now, but I think you should wait and listen to the tapes before you go any further with the boy. I'll be in touch later."

"Sure and thanks again."

"Oh by the way, I'm thinking the boy knows more about the baby business than what he's telling you. Think about it."

As he watched Dan leave, he wondered if it was true. Greg did seem to hesitate before he answered. Well, he better wait until he hears the tapes.

"It's getting near lunch time," John said as he reentered the room, "I think we'll quit for today, but I'll be in touch as soon as this investigation progresses."

Farrell stood, "Before you go, I'd like to ask you a couple of things, if you have a minute."

"Of course," John nodded to Farrell.

"Is it possible for Greg and I to go up to the house and pick up some of his belongings?"

"Sure, I'll call the guard at the house and tell him to expect you. Am I right in thinking Greg is going to be staying here for the duration, at least?"

"Yes, if it can be arranged."

"No problem, as things stand right now."

"And what about school?"

"I'd hold off on that. The weekend is coming up and I think they may be releasing Roberts' body later today. I'm sending two of my men over to the county jail to talk to Delmont and see if he knows if she had a will or some arrangements. It's possible he would be able to tell us what to plan for her burial. As far as we know, he was the person closest to her."

Farrell nodded, "Is there any chance I could pay a cleaning service to come in and clean up the hall.?"

"Not yet, maybe in a week or so. We haven't had a chance to go over the place thoroughly as of yet, but I'll let you know when we are finished. After we're through, I'll be removing the guard, but

I want the place locked up." Looking at Greg, he asked, "Do you have a key?"

"Yes, she had one too, probably in her purse. Since we've been there, we've never unlocked the windows, so they're all locked."

"Good," he said, shaking Farrell's hand and then Greg's. "Thank you for your cooperation."

After the chief was gone, Farrell looked at his watch. He wanted to talk to Greg a little more about the missing baby, but it could wait. "It's almost lunch time, but I think I'll call Marge first before we get started. She wanted to come over to see you after everyone left."

"I didn't know she knew I was here."

"She sure does and she's concerned about how you are. She doesn't trust me to know how to take care of you properly."

"Does she know about the drug stuff I told them about today?"

"I don't know how she could. Even I didn't know about the things you told the officers today. I imagine she read about your mother's death and is worried about how you are taking it. She probably wants to see for herself that you're alright."

"It's okay if you tell her sometime. It's just that it would feel kind of weird for me to tell her. Do you think if you tell her I was involved that she'll hate me?"

Farrell put his hand on Greg's shoulder. "I can personally guarantee you, she will never hate you."

"Okay," Greg smiled, "I've got to run up to the bathroom."

When Greg came back down the stairs, Farrell said into the receiver, "Hang on a second and I'll ask him. Marge has homemade soup and warm buns along with a cake for dessert. She's going to bring them down and she wants to know if it's okay to bring Elaine and the baby too?"

Greg put both fists in the air over his head and brought them down with a hop and a loud whoop.

Marge laughed into the phone.

"I take it you heard the answer," Farrell said, "so hit the road. We'll set the table."

Chapter Thirty-Six

Chief Redding sat at his desk thinking. He had listened to the telephone tape again and taken notes. He had made a list of suspects and had begun filling in the facts pertaining to each one. Brant and Delmont were already in jail and the other two, George Becker, the lawyer and Steve Darnell, would have to be found and questioned. Brant had been arrested by the DEA about the same time as the murder, but it didn't automatically eliminate him as a suspect. He certainly was in contact with enough nefarious people who could have done the job for him.

He picked up his notebook and flipped back through the previous pages until he came to the name Benny Krim. He said the name aloud and picking up the phone, he dialed the number.

When the phone was picked up, he heard, "Benny Krim here."

"Ben, this is Chief of Police, John Redding. I'd like to ask you a question."

"Sure, go ahead."

I understand that you were at the tavern working when the DEA agents arrested Delmont. Do you know what time Delmont arrived that morning?"

"Yeah, he usually came in about the same time as I do, but that morning he was already there, which would have been sometime before 8:00. I had only been there a short time when he came down the stairs and told me he had forgotten something and he'd be back in a few minutes."

"And was he?" John asked.

"Well, I'm trying to think," Ben said, "I don't think he was gone much more than an hour, if it was that long."

"Thanks, Ben, I'll be back in touch."

That puts Delmont back in the game, John thought.

When Jack Denver and Jim Keller came back from their search for information in Dora Roberts' old neighborhood, John said, "It's almost lunch time, so before we begin, let's order a pizza. I have a variety of soft drinks in the fridge and while we eat I can hear how you made out and tell you what I've learned. What do you think?"

"Sounds great," they agreed.

After John called in the order, he told them about the threats on Dora Roberts' life, revealed from listening to the tape. He also explained about the additional names and added his conversation with Ben Krim.

About that time, the pizza arrived and as they were eating, John told them about the information Dan Newlan had obtained from Greg about his life while living with Roberts both in Crawford and Carson Cove. He also told them about the decision to keep Greg's name out of all reports for the boy's protection.

"It's hard to imagine," Jim observed, "how the poor kid could have managed to turn out so well, considering those conditions. It's like he has a dark cloud over his head, like the kid in the funny paper. The only time I've seen him really happy is when he's around Elaine's baby and that baby sure loves him too."

"I think you'll see a big difference in his demeanor," John said, "now that he's finally rid of all that guilt and seeing the end of his entanglement with the drug dealing. I personally don't think he could be in a better place than right here where he is. Farrell Dunn is a force to be reckoned with and the boy not only respects him, but he listens to him. One thing is certain, he isn't mourning the loss of his mother."

Jack smiled at Jim, knowing the new information they were going to reveal on that subject.

The chief nodded toward Jack, as he reached for a piece of pizza. "Your turn."

"Well," Jack began, "we didn't do too well until the very last one, then we hit pay dirt. All the neighbors we talked to agreed that she must have been a rather high-class prostitute since she seemed to be such "good friends" with so many of Crawford's highly placed officials and Crawford's mayor was mentioned by most of them. However some did concede that they supposed it was his business since he wasn't married."

"The house Roberts lived in is situated at the end of a cul-de-sac, which made it fairly easy for the people on both sides of the road to track the action. I'll let the ladies' man here tell you about Sadie Prior's story. She fell for his line right from the start."

"Jealousy," Jim said, nodding in Jack's direction.

The chief smiled, being aware of their verbal banter.

"Sadie Prior," Jim stated, "also agreed with the others about Dora's chosen profession. Mrs. Prior is a widow and she spent quite a lot of time sitting in the park, which was a short walk from her house. Dora apparently hadn't started her second profession with the drugs as of yet; at least none of her neighbors mentioned it."

"During her trips to the park, Mrs. Prior met Judy Collins, who was there with her little baby boy. They became close friends. Little by little, Judy told her about her life in the orphanage and how Dora had been her champion; defending her against all comers. Although Judy didn't approve of the way Dora made her living, she didn't feel she could desert her. She even hoped she could change her mind about it, eventually. Dora's job was the reason Judy had to leave the house whenever Dora "entertained," even though the house belonged to Judy. It seems that Judy had an old eccentric uncle who came to see her a few times at the orphanage. Judy said he was weird. Just before she and Dora were old enough to leave the orphanage, he died leaving Judy the house, a large bank account and a lot of properties.

"When they left the orphanage, they moved into the house, which she considered to be high class. She used it to meet her elite clients and so began her new profession. Judy started school and became a legal secretary. Soon after, she met and fell in love with Martin Delmont. She lived with him for over a year, planning their marriage. When she found out about his connection with the drug operation, they had a big argument and she left him. She moved back home and almost immediately found out she was pregnant. She never told Delmont because she wasn't about to have her baby anywhere near Delmont or his drugs. Once back in her home, she began planning her future with the baby. At this point, I interrupted Mrs. Prior and asked if she knew the baby's name. she said it was Greg, Greg Collins."

The chief gave a low whistle.

Jim continued. "At this time, Judy began selling off the properties with plans to buy a bed and breakfast so she could be with her baby. Judy invited Dora to come in as a full partner. Dora refused, since she was making big money at what she was doing and Dora was all about money. When the weather started turning cold, Mrs. Prior invited Judy to come to her house instead of the park and they became closer friends. By this time, Greg had turned two and Judy became ill. Finally, after much urging on Mrs. Prior's part, Judy went to the doctor. Up to that time, she hadn't found her bed and breakfast or property that could be converted. There were many tests and specialists involved before they found she had an inoperable cancer and had a year, at most, to live. As time went by, the disease worsened and she had to face the fact that she would die soon. She went to a lawyer and willed her large bank account and house to Dora, with the condition that she would take care of her baby and change her profession.

Toward the end, Mrs. Prior saw Judy in the hospital. Judy told her she had asked Dora to contact Martin so she could tell him about Greg. About a week later, she lapsed into a coma and soon after, died. Mrs. Prior didn't know if Judy had told Delmont or not, but she said she saw the big black Cadillac in their driveway quite often after Judy died. She knew it was Delmont's because his initials were on the plates, so she assumed Dora probably told him about Greg." Jim looked up from his report, "Well, there you have it. We have a lot of background, but I don't know if it will help to solve the murder," Jim finished.

You never know. It's like a big puzzle. You put the pieces together and hopefully you will have a picture of a killer," John said. He had been taking notes and as he closed his notebook, he exhaled slowly. "This afternoon I want you to go over to the county jail and talk to Delmont. The warden is expecting you. Find out if he knows if Roberts had a will or if she and Delmont had discussed anything about her wishes in the event of her death. Stop back here and let me know what you find out. I expect to hear from the county examiner sometime today. I sent Hale Cooper out to pick up Steve Darnell for questioning. They'll be here any time now. I don't know how long it will take, but I'll see you when you get back."

They were hardly out the door when Forensics called. They told the chief that the gun he had turned in was a Smith and Wesson thirty-eight caliber revolver. The chief had assumed it was the gun used to kill Dora Roberts, but according to Forensics, it was not. The gun that killed her was a Lugar twenty-two caliber pistol. Then whey, John wondered, was the Smith and Wesson lying on the floor a few feet from the body where Greg found it. While he was still pondering the fact, the county medical examiner called to tell him the time of her death was between seven and ten Wednesday morning.

The chief went to the computer and started a double page chart with names and gathered data, with questions yet to be answered, beside each name he added information and quotes from the tape Dan had given him.

As he compiled the known facts about Frank Brant, Steve Darnell, George Becker and Martin Delmont, his mind lingered on Martin. Since he had met him personally at the tavern opening, he was inclined to try to find evidence that would take him off the suspect list. He had liked the man. Since he had arrived later than most of the guests during the opening night at the tavern, things had quieted down and Martin had given him an unhurried tour of the place, explaining some of the more difficult renovations. Martin had been excited and proud of what had been accomplished. The place certainly indicated thoughtful consideration every step of the way. John remembered Martin laughing when he told him, "I wanted the place to be just under being elegant enough to scare off what might be my regular customers, but nice enough to encourage good behavior." He had to admit, Martin had what he would describe as quiet class. It was hard to think of the man mixed up with the drug cartel, let alone a murder.

He was still thinking about Delmont when Hale Cooper arrived with Steve Darnell.

After Cooper introduced the chief to Darnell, John said, "The reason I had you come in is I understand that you made a threat to kill Dora Roberts. Is that right?"

"Yes, I did," Steve admitted, "but at the time I didn't know her name. It wasn't until later that I found out her name. I think I should go back and start at the beginning."

"After Tracy and I had been married for about two years, we decided to have a baby, but nothing happened. Tracy became more and more depressed and then obsessed. She made appointments and more appointments and finally we had to accept that we couldn't have a baby. As it turned out, it was my fault."

"As time went on, the situation became more and more bitter and she became more depressed. Then one day she came home from work very excited. She had heard from one of her coworkers about this lawyer who had a baby for sale. At first, I refused to go and talk to him, but I was afraid I'd lose Tracy if I didn't go. After all, it was my fault she couldn't have a baby. Finally, I agreed to at least talk to him."

This, John thought, is how law-abiding citizens get involved in criminal acts.

"The lawyer told us about the baby and even showed us a picture, which just about clinched the deal, until he revealed the amount of money involved. When we returned home, I did my best to change her mind, but to no avail. We're not rich by any means and this would mean years of debt. In the end, I gave in."

"You did know that selling a baby is a crime," John interrupted.

"I'd like to pretend I didn't, but yes, I knew and I hated myself almost as much as I hated the lawyer for getting us into this mess. Then, one day the lawyer called for us to come in early to his office. It would have been two days before we were scheduled to pick up the baby. Tracy was sure we were going to get the baby early, but I had a bad feeling about it."

"When we arrived at the lawyer's office, he told us that the baby had disappeared, or some such story and we wouldn't be getting the baby. He gave us back the money we had paid up front. While I was having my tantrum with the lawyer, my wife walked out to the front of the building into heavy traffic. I'm pretty sure she intended to kill herself. You probably heard about it since it was in all the papers."

John nodded, remembering the headlines from the city paper; 'Emotionally Disturbed Woman Hit By A Car' with a small paragraph below explaining she had been taken by ambulance to the hospital in critical condition.

"She was in a coma for three weeks," Steve continued. During that time, I broke into the lawyer's office and found the name of the woman, with every intention of killing her if my wife died. I wasn't worried about my break-in ever being reported, but it didn't matter to me at the time. In the meantime, apparently someone got there ahead of me and killed her. I don't expect you to believe me, but I didn't kill Dora Roberts."

John had been watching his face as he declared his innocence. "How is your wife doing?"

"She's recovering slowly with all kinds of medical people working on her mind and broken body. You know Chief, the hardest thing for me to handle was that my wife cared so little about leaving me, that she could try to kill herself with no thought about anything but the baby. Right after that came the thought that I could have taken another person's life. I think now, neither of us, at that time, were our normal selves. Now we talk about adopting a baby sometime in the future and about the fact that it will take longer but we seem to have come back to a place where we're happy with each other again. We both seem to be more content."

"Buying a baby is, of course, a crime, but I'm not going to charge you since the deal wasn't complete. I will notify the police in Crawford and let them decide what to do about the lawyer. He's out of my jurisdiction." The chief took a long speculative look at the young man in front of him.

"I do believe you when you say you didn't kill Dora Roberts. It sounds to me as if you and your wife have already come to terms with what your future might hold."

John smiled, "I do want you to be available in case we need to talk again. Other than that, I think you can go."

John stood, smiling and extended his hand to Steve Darnell. "Now, get out of here. I've got a murder to solve."

As Steve left, John made a note to call the chief of police in Crawford and tell him about George Becker's baby business. He had no intention of mentioning Darnell's name as things stand right now. He figured the Darnell's had learned a hard and lasting lesson and it made no sense to involve them. Actually it wouldn't surprise him if the Crawford Police already knew. In many cases such as this, concerning lawyers, the police lacked enough evidence to put them out of business.

As he was contemplating his notes, he received a call from the county coroner's office telling him they could arrange to have the body taken to the morgue any time they were ready. They were now in the process of faxing their report to him.

Soon after, Jim and Jack were back.

"Well, that didn't take long," he said.

"No, it didn't. Delmont said we should check with Ben Krim. Delmont said he had set it up with Krim that if anything happened to him or Dora he would have the instructions to do what was necessary since neither of them had any close relatives."

"Really? That's interesting. I wonder when that happened. When I talked with Ben, he didn't mention it."

After checking his notebook for the number, he picked up the phone and dialed.

"Benny Krim here."

"Hi Ben, this is John Redding. My men have just come back from talking to Delmont and he said you have been informed of the steps to take if he or Roberts were to die. Is that right?"

There was a long hesitation before he answered. "not that I know of," Ben said. After another few seconds he said, "Oh wait a second, maybe he did. The same day the DEA arrested him, he gave me an envelope when he came back. Do you remember I told you he left that morning shortly after eight and was gone about an hour? When he came back, he handed me an envelope and said when I had time I could read it, but there was no hurry. I was in the middle of my book work so I stuck the envelope in the back of the ledger and kept on working. With all the commotion later on, I forgot all about it. I supposed it had to do with the running of the business. Unless someone has taken the book, I guess it would still be there. It's the only thing I can remember him giving me and that was the same day he was arrested," Ben finished, thoughtfully.

"Ben, is there any chance you could meet us at the tavern and we'll take a look at it to see what it has to say?"

"Sure, I could do that, but the agent took my key."

"Yes, I know, he gave it to me. Can you be there in about twenty minutes?"

"Sure, see you there," Ben said.

"We'll meet you there and thanks Ben."

Arriving from opposite directions, they met at the mouth of the long driveway leading to the tavern. As they stepped into the tavern, Ben looked around at the big bar room, almost longingly, before continuing toward the back.

"The ledger is back here in my office." Ben said.

The chief looked around the orderly room, enjoying Ben's neat desk with his family photos occupying one corner. How long had it been since he had seen the top of his desk, he wondered? As Ben unlocked the filing cabinet, removing the ledger, he began turning the pages toward the back.

"Is there any chance they made a mistake when they arrested Mr. Delmont?" he asked.

"I'm afraid not." John answered.

"He is such a good man, I like him very much. It is hard for me to believe he was mixed up with drugs." Ben added sadly.

John nodded, reaching out to take the long envelope Ben was handing him.

"Here Chief, sit down. You boys can sit there on the bench. I'm afraid I don't usually have much company in here, so I haven't asked for better accommodations."

The chief glanced over the message on the paper and then at Ben.

"I'm going to read this aloud to save time. I hope you don't mind," he said, as he began to read the letter.

> *Hi Ben,*
>
> *I'm afraid I have neglected you and the business these last few days, but I have just found out that I have a son. This fact has changed my outlook on life considerably. I went to my lawyer and made out my will to insure the boy's future and then took steps to insure he had a future as best as I was able.*
>
> *Now, about the business. I have deposited a hundred thousand dollars in your business account. I would hope you would be able to continue to keep the tavern running until the lawyer reveals the provisions of my will and the plans for the future. I know you to be an honest and trustworthy man and I admire you greatly for the man you are. In case Dora Roberts or I should die, you are to use what is needed from this account for our cremation and a cemetery plot for each of us. Since she has no known relatives and I have no one close, there will be no services.*
>
> *Thank you, Ben, for your meticulous bookkeeping and for being one of the few people I can fully trust.*
>
> *Martin Delmont*

When John finished reading, there was total silence.

Finally, John spoke, "It certainly gives us something to think about, wouldn't you say?" John watched the frown on Ben's face.

"Of course, I'm flattered he thought so highly of me. I imagine if he was into the drug business, there weren't too many people he could trust, but what really puzzles me is why the letter? I was available to talk to him almost any day of the week. Another thing, I get the impression from the way he wrote he seemed to be expecting trouble of some kind; possibly even death. Once he found out he had a son, he acted as though he should be in a big hurry to get things done." Ben shrugged. "Maybe he somehow found out he was about to be arrested, but it seems to me, with the kind of money he had available, if that were the case he'd have been long gone out of here," Ben sighed and shrugged again.

"Yes, I think the way the letter is worded has given us all a lot of think about. Right now it would be guess work with no evidence to back it up. We do know that Dora Roberts is dead, so if you would go ahead with that and let me know as soon as you have the particulars, then I'll let the coroner's office know who will be making the arrangements. They notified me this morning that she could be picked up any time. Also, I'd like to have a copy of this letter, if possible."

"Sure," Ben said, "just give me a couple minutes to warm the machine up."

When they headed back to the station from the tavern, John Redding took the back seat in the patrol car so he could go over the letter again. Jack Denver took the driver's seat with Jim Keller beside him. Breaking the silence, Jim said, "You have to think Dora Roberts hadn't told Delmont about Greg or it wouldn't have been recent news to him."

"You're right," the chief responded, "I would have guessed Delmont calculated it from the dates the detectives gave him on the phone. It would account for what Delmont said after talking to the detective; *'the bitch knew all along and she never told me.'* I thought at first, remembering what Greg told Dan, that Delmont did know. Greg said Martin always acted as though he liked him and stopped Roberts from beating him when he was around, but now I think Delmont's reaction to Greg may have been because he knew

Greg was Judy Collins' son and out of his fond memories of her, he wouldn't let Roberts misuse him."

"Yes," Jack added, putting his turn signal on as he approached mainstream traffic, "according to what Sadie Prior told us, there was a large bank account, besides a considerable number of properties involved. If she was willing to care for Greg, it would all be hers. Roberts might have figured if Delmont knew that Greg was his son he would try to take him away from her and she might lose everything."

"I'm back where Ben was," Jim said, "why the big hurry? It sounded like everything Delmont did was within a week's span of finding out that Greg was his son."

"That brings me back to something else Greg told Dan," the chief said. "He told Dan he was relieved when he didn't have to be running drugs anymore after the tavern opened, but he was worried. When Dan questioned him further, he said, *'when they don't need you anymore, they get rid of you.'*

"Well, there's enough evidence to prove that's true on the city streets," Jack said.

"So, you think maybe Delmont heard of some kind of scheme to get rid of Greg?" Jim half turned, directing his question to John in the back seat.

The chief was thoughtful. "Let's play Ben's game of guessing for a few minutes and see where it leads us."

"Let's suppose Roberts told Delmont she intended to get rid of Greg. She wouldn't think twice about talking about it because, according to Greg, it was done all the time. Since he was fond of Greg, maybe he tried to talk her out of doing it. She would no doubt say something like, *'Don't be foolish, he knows too much,'* which he does since he gave a lot of names and addresses to Dan. Delmont knew he hadn't convinced her and assumed she would go through with it. Now, let's suppose Roberts told him the school was letting out early on Wednesday and that it would be a good day to take care of the unfinished business. I haven't had a chance to tell you, I was informed by the coroner's report this morning that the Smith and Wesson we turned in wasn't the gun that killed her, so why was it lying on the floor near her body? Let's suppose it was her gun and she had it ready to use on Greg when he got home. This would answer the question of why Delmont was in a hurry to get things arranged before Wednesday. He had a deadline, so to speak. He had to include himself in the plans in case something went wrong and she got him before he got her. He planned to kill her, which would explain the statement, '*I went to the lawyer and made out my will to insure the boy's future and took steps to insure he'd have a future as best as I was able.*'

"When you put all the pieces of information together, it sure makes sense," Jack said. "The problem is, there's a whole lot of 'supposes' hanging all over it."

"It's true. We don't have any evidence, unless you count this letter and a good lawyer could rip it apart in about five minutes," the chief added.

When they arrived back at the station, the chief said, "Since our best suspect is already behind bars and the two of you aren't back on your regular schedule, you can go home. I'm going to do a few things here then I'll do the same thing."

"Is there anything we can do to help before we go?" Jim asked

"No, but thank you. It will only take a few minutes I just want to jot down some things for Monday. I want to talk to the mayor of Crawford about this relationship with Dora Roberts. It may have something to do with Greg's brother being missing. Then I'd like to notify Farrell Dunn about Greg's new freedom from the Robert's family tree so he can tell Greg."

The chief hesitated, thinking, "Will you be seeing Mrs. Colby this weekend Jim?"

"I sure am if she doesn't have other plans."

"If you do, I've been thinking it might be a good idea to tell her about Greg having a baby brother and observe her reaction. She would have no way of knowing about it, since Greg told us he was forbidden to tell anyone about it, but he may have confided in her. Farrell told me Greg goes up to her house almost every day. He hasn't been in school since Robert's death. If he told her about the baby, maybe he told her about its disappearance too. Dan seemed to think Greg knew more about it than what he was telling."

Jim nodded. "You might be right. Greg has grown very close to Elaine and the baby so it's possible he did confide in her."

"Well that having been said, I guess I'll make my notes, then go home and see what my boys have been up to. These last few days I've been so preoccupied, I've hardly talked with them. You have a good weekend and I'll see you on Monday, unless you hear from me sooner."

Chapter Thirty-Seven

Jim was inclined to go directly to Elaine's house, but he heard his mother's voice, "Don't you think that would be more than a little presumptuous?"

"Yeah, yeah, yeah."

"Sassy brat," his mother retorted.

Jim laughed at his imagined dialogue with his mother, but the truth was, he had missed Elaine and the baby fiercely these last few days. How long had it been? Five days altogether, between his regular shift and the three days since Roberts' death. Of course, he had talked to her briefly on the phone when he had a few minutes but it wasn't the same as holding her in his arms, or hearing her gentle voice close to his ear and the kisses that aroused feelings too long dormant.

This weekend he wanted to discuss their future together, if she was willing. He longed for a home like he had known growing up and the easy companionship Jack and Ann had with their family. Now he had finally found the one who could make it all happen.

He made up his mind. He'd go home, shower, then check to see if she had plans. If not, he would ask if he could come over and if she wanted to, they could go out to dinner somewhere and proceed from there.

He remembered she had mentioned some sort of problem she wanted to discuss with him. He hoped whatever it was, it wouldn't be a stumbling block to their future together. He didn't want to ever think of a life without her.

Arriving home, he called her. She was pleased and excited to hear he was free tonight and tomorrow too, although she declined eating out since Matthew was having a bad day. She offered dinner at her house instead and they could discuss plans for tomorrow, while spending the evening together.

"I'd just as soon save the outing for some other night, if you wouldn't be too disappointed," she said.

Disappointed? It was exactly what he wanted. "Sounds great to me," he said calmly.

After the initial show of affection, they settled on the sofa, content for the moment, while loving the closeness of being in each other's arms.

"How's the man of the house doing?" Jim asked, chuckling.

"Not so well. He's working hard at cutting himself a few teeth and drooling about a quart an hour. We do a lot of changing clothes but he's reasonably good natured, even with what's going on."

"Isn't it early for cutting teeth?" Jim wondered.

"I don't really know. It's my first go around with teeth cutting. The doctor hasn't commented on the subject one way or the other, so I guess it's probably normal."

Elaine glanced at her watch. "I think it's time to get dinner out of the oven while it's still edible."

"Can I help?" Jim said.

"Sure, come on, you can set the table while I toss the salad. Are you hungry?"

"Hungry is such a tame little word. Good old Webster must have a more fitting word for this occasion. Jack and I have been doing the grab and run thing from drive-by places for the last three days. When I get home, I'm too tired to cook so something gets thrown into the microwave and I call it good enough. I guess you might say I'm more than hungry."

Elaine brought the food to the table and poured their coffee. They ate in silence for a few minutes.

"What a treat Honey," Jim said. "I appreciate you going to all this trouble."

"I don't mind cooking, but more often than I'd like to admit, I do the same as you do; stick a one dish meal in the oven. It's no fun fixing for one. Your mom tells me the same thing. Now there's a real cook! I'll bet she'll be right in her glory when she's cooking regular meals again after she's married to Farrell."

"There's no doubt in my mind that you're right," Jim said. "And speaking of such things as marriage, it's one of the topics I'd like to discuss with you a little later tonight."

As they finished eating dessert, Jim reached over and took Elaine's hand. "This week I've been miserable not being able to see you. I've spent every moment thinking about you. I love you so much." He stood and walked around the end of the table to her chair. She stood and moved into his waiting arms.

"Oh Jim, I love you so much and I missed you too. I'm so grateful we found each other."

"Elaine, Honey, will you marry me?"

"Yes, my dear one, I will marry you."

He kissed her with all the pent-up energy of the past few days and she responded eagerly, matching his passion. "I will always thank the Good Lord for bringing you to me," she whispered.

"Amen," he said.

"Matthew is being extremely good right now, so I think we should clear things away while we get the chance," Elaine said, moving away.

While Elaine put the remainder of the food in smaller containers, getting them ready to refrigerate, Jim started to rinse the dishes and load the dishwasher.

"I hear that Greg has been spending quite a lot of time up here on his days away from school?"

Elaine nodded. "Yes and I love the company. He reads a lot and we discuss authors and their methods. He's such an outgoing and friendly young boy. Not only that, but he keeps Matthew occupied too. Matthew has become so attached to him and so have I."

"I know it's a little early in our relationship, but after we're married, what do you think about adopting Greg," Jim asked.

"I think it's a fantastic idea," she smiled. "It occurred to me to talk to you about it at a later time if our relationship worked out. I wasn't sure how you'd feel about adding yet another child to this little family." Elaine turned and gave Jim a joyful hug. "If it were possible for me to love you more than I already do, this would do it," she said. "Enough of this mushy stuff, now get back to work," she said pointing to the open door of the dishwasher.

Jim sighed, "I'll have to remember to add bossy to the long list of your charms."

Elaine laughed.

"The chief was talking about Greg this afternoon and he told me to ask you if Greg had given you any information about his baby brother."

Elaine stopped with her hand on the open door of the refrigerator. "Baby brother?" She was shocked. "Greg has a baby brother?"

"Well, I guess that answers the chief's question. Apparently, he would be about four months old. He disappeared awhile back before Dora Roberts was killed. The chief thinks Greg might know more about the disappearance than what he's telling. I think the chief is baffled and he's trying to find a clue as to where to start looking for him."

Elaine's mind was racing through the events. After a few moments trying to digest this new information, she asked, "The chief doesn't suspect that Greg did something harmful to the baby does he?"

"I think he wondered at first, but after he talked to Greg, it was pretty obvious how much Greg loved his brother. He told the c hief he took full care of the baby from the first day she brought him home from the hospital. Not only that, but Greg found evidence that Roberts was going to sell the baby."

Jim finished filling the dishwasher while Elaine put the remainder of the food away, her mind churning. The time element when she found Matthew in her car, the condition of the baby, the care with which he had been strapped in and most of all remembering Matthew's reaction to Greg that first day and every day since. It all fit in, right up to Greg's loving attentive attention to Matthew. Oh Dear God, the baby Jim is talking about has to be Matthew. All of her early worries came flooding back. She had to have some time to think this thing through.

"I guess, by your reaction, Greg hasn't said anything to you about it."

"No," she hesitated, "No, he hasn't said anything at all."

She hoped her voice was steady. She had to pull her thoughts away from this new information until she was alone.

Jim sighed. "The chief will be disappointed. I suppose we'll have to question Greg more thoroughly and see what we can find."

"What makes your chief think Greg might know more than what he's telling him?"

"Well, I wasn't there, but I would guess it was his actions when he was questioning him. He didn't seem as worried or upset as everyone might have expected, considering the entire scenario." Jim stepped up to Elaine and put his arms around her, once again pulling her close. "Well, don't be concerned. We were just looking for an easy answer. It will mean we'll have to work a little harder now. So, let's get back to the topic at hand. Do you think it's too late for us to get married tonight?"

It was difficult for Elaine to push aside the turmoil going on in her mind, but she smiled. "I think it might be a little late to ask your mom to bake a wedding cake tonight."

Jim laughed. "Oh, I suppose you're right, but let's make it very soon. Do you want a big wedding?"

"No, I really don't, if it's all right with you. As for myself, I'd invite my closest friends and relatives. About the only relatives I have are a few cousins, that I hardly know and some friends that I worked with in Crawford. Most of my real friends are right here in the Cove now."

"That's fine with me. Whatever you want my darling, as long as you're my wife at the end of it."

He kissed her then, releasing his long controlled desires. She responded with intense emotions.

"Well," Jim sighed, pulling away, "I think we should postpone our future fun and games and get to what it is that you were going to tell me. What do you think?"

Elaine hesitated, needing a few moments to refocus her thoughts about the baby situation. She was convinced by the information that Jim had given her that she should wait and give herself time to rethink the subject in depth and talk to Greg before she told Jim about how she acquired Matthew. She was positive Jim would connect the facts of the disappearance of the baby with the appearance of Matthew in her life, just as quickly as she had.

"The more I think about it Jim," Elaine said, trying to think of a plausible reason that would give herself some time, "I think I should wait a few days. There are a couple things I'd like to do first and Matthew will be stirring in a few minutes wanting some attention. If it's all right with you, I'll set a time when we can discuss it more thoroughly without interruption."

"Sure Honey. It's just that I hate to have something bothering you if I can help with it."

"Oh, don't worry about it Jim, it's nothing urgent," she said, knowing it had to be taken care of as soon as possible.

Later that evening, after Matthew was fed, bathed and they had enjoyed their play time with him, Elaine hoped, he was down for the night.

Jim said, "I guess I had better get going. I've got some chores to do at the apartment." He reached out and took her back into his arms. After a lengthy kiss he said, "You know we skipped right over the engagement period and jumped right to the main event. Why don't you ask mom if she could babysit tomorrow afternoon from about two o'clock on, then we could go ring shopping and dinner afterward to celebrate? I'll call mom tonight and invite myself to breakfast tomorrow morning and tell her our breaking news. What do you think of that?

"Sounds like a plan to me," Elaine laughed. "I'll call your mom tomorrow morning to see about the babysitting. I'll tell her I have some shopping to do, but I'll let you do the 'news breaking' thing, but don't get your heart set on her babysitting. Now that Farrell is more prominent in her life, she might have plans herself. If she can't babysit we can do our shopping a different time."

After Jim left, Elaine poured herself another cup of coffee and sat down at the table. She went back through the previous months to where Matthew came into her life, but this time she included Greg's story of his baby brother's disappearance. The more she thought about it the more convinced she was that they were talking about the same baby. She looked at her watch and went to the phone and dialed Farrell Dunn's number. "Hello Mr. Dunn, this is Elaine Colby. I'm sorry to be calling so late," she apologized.

"Oh, that's no problem. Since Greg hasn't started back to school yet, we've gotten into the habit of staying up later and catching a movie now and then. Is anything wrong?"

"No, nothing like that, but something has come up that needs taking care of and I was wondering if I could borrow Greg for a couple hours tomorrow morning?"

"I'm sure it will be fine, but hang on and I'll let you ask him."

Greg came to the phone. "Hi Mrs. Colby. Sure, I can come up, what time?"

"How about nine thirty, is that okay?"

"Sure is, I'll be there." Greg's voice was happy.

Elaine groaned silently, thinking of what was ahead of her.

Chapter Thirty-Eight

At the same time Jim was working on his future with Elaine, John Redding was enjoying himself with his young boys Don and Bill. He had released his housekeeper early and taken over the preparations for dinner.

Late that evening as he prepared for bed, he was preoccupied with the new information he had received from his boys.

He sat on the end of his bed in his robe, after he had showered, holding the blanket that always laid across the foot of his bed, in his arms.

He reviewed the conversation the boys had while they were clearing away the dinner table.

He enjoyed their good-natured banter. They were only a few months over a year apart in age and he was grateful they got along so well. Don had become a teenager last week and now and then he gave Billy a few verbal jabs about his new exalted status.

John had not been looking forward to their teen years, not knowing what to expect from them. He could only hope that his influence and the early training from their gentle mother would get them through their monster years.

While doing the dinner chores, Don had asked about his classmate, Greg Roberts.

"How's Greg doing, Dad? He hasn't been in school."

"Very well, considering the circumstances."

"Will he be back Monday?" Bill asked

"No, probably not until the middle of the week." John was thinking about the funeral arrangements and whether it was advisable to send him back to school before that segment was completed.

Bill laughed "We were thinking that maybe the mad man got him."

John had glanced away from his dish washing duty to the direction where the boys were standing. Don saw his father's inquisitive look. "Oh, don't pay any attention to the nutcase over here. He's talking about the license plate."

John turned away from the sink and wiped his hands. Hadn't something about a license plate come up before? Now the boys had his full attention. "Okay you two, come clean." He smiled, waiting to hear about one of their silly jokes.

Don sighed, indicating he was the long-suffering brother. "Well, the other day," he began, "the bus was having a hot flash or something and Mr. Ennis, our bus driver, stopped to talk on the phone to the bus garage people, which made us late getting to school. We were sort of limping on toward school, going slowly, when this big black Caddy pulled out around us. When we went by Greg's house, it was just going up Greg's driveway.

At first John thought it might have been some kind of joke between the boys, but now he was interested, "and the mad man?"

"Oh that was just the license plate. It had the initials MAD and a bunch of light weight brains picked up on it saying, a mad man was after Greg." He gave his brother a quick glance over his shoulder.

"You wouldn't remember what day that was would you?" John asked.

"Sure, it was Wednesday. I thought we'd be too late for the test, but we had to take it the next day anyway."

John laid the extra blanket on the chair with his bathrobe and climbed into bed. He moaned as his bones complained. He was tired. I must be getting old, he thought, but his mind was still churning. He ought to get right on this new development, but he and the boys had made plans. He'd wait and call the bus driver sometime tomorrow and ask him to stop by his office on Monday. If remembered correctly, the lady Jim had talked to had mentioned something about a license plate too. He'd check it out when he got back to the office Monday.

Following his nightly ritual, he said, "Good Night Marie," and patted the pillow next to him, "I love you."

Chapter Thirty-Nine

When Greg arrived Saturday morning a few minutes before the designated time, he asked Elaine, "Do you have any work for me Mrs. Colby?"

"No, Greg, but come in and sit down. I need to talk to you."

Greg walked over to the table, pulled out a chair and sat down. He studied her face while she sat down across from him. "Is something wrong?" he asked.

"No, not exactly wrong. It's just, well I don't know where to start, but here goes. I knew you quite a few months before I actually moved here to the Cove. We talked about many things but never about my past and you never asked. You seemed hesitant to talk about your home life so we could hardly describe our relationship as being up close and personal. I knew you only as the person you were while you were here. I learned about your personality and character by your excellent work habits and the talks we had. It was enough at the time, but now something new has come up. Jim Keller was here last night and he told me about the disappearance of your baby brother. Of course, you probably know I wasn't aware that you had a baby brother, let alone know about his disappearance."

"My mother forbid me ever to mention him to anyone. I guess she had other plans for him right from the beginning." Greg stated.

Elaine nodded, "Well I was shocked, to say the least. Jim went on to say that the chief thinks you know more about where this baby is than what you have told them and wanted Jim to ask me if you had confided anything about it to me. As you may know, Jim and I have become very close and we have now made plans to be married. Early on I told him that I have something on my mind that I have to tell him, but Jim has been very busy with the investigation of the drug bust and the death of your mother, so it has been put aside temporarily. I had intended to tell him last night about how I came to have Matthew, but when he told me about your brother, I put it off again. I have let everyone think he was my natural born son. The reason I changed my mind about telling Jim the truth last night was that it only took me a few minutes to realize that the circumstances surrounding Matthew's appearance in my life closely matched your brother's disappearance. I couldn't believe it was a coincidence. I knew Jim would pick up on it just as fast as I had. Greg, I'm going to ask you now, is Matthew your missing brother?" She waited, watching him closely. His eyes filled with tears.

Looking across the table at her he said, "Yes, he's my brother and his name Aaron."

Elaine sighed in relief. "Thank you, Greg, for telling me." She said softly. "I know this has been very difficult for you, but could you please tell me what happened that made you give him to me?"

Greg frowned, but he nodded, "One day when I came home from school, my mother was standing beside Aaron's crib holding him at arm's length screaming at him and shaking him really hard. It scared me because I had read something might happened if you did that to a baby. Poor Aaron was very wet from top to bottom and I knew he was probably hungry too. I was sure she hadn't done anything for him all day. I grabbed him away from her and took care of him. I knew then I had to do something before she hurt him anymore. I figured she must hate him just as she always has me. I should have known. She practically gave him to me the first day she brought him home from the hospital. After that as far as anything I ever saw, she never even looked at him, let alone do anything for him. All during the years when she was beating me, I had thought about running away but I couldn't figure out how I could get away with it, being so young. Now if I tried to run away with Aaron, I knew I couldn't take care of him and I sure wasn't about to go without him."

Now Greg hesitated, wondering if he should go on. He decided he might as well tell it all now that he had gone this far.

"Later that night, I heard my mother on the phone talking to someone about money. At first I didn't pay much attention, but a little farther on, I heard her ask if the people who were taking the baby had come up with the money for him. She said he could pick him up Monday morning at nine and she would be waiting and he better have all the money or he wouldn't get the baby. I knew she was talking about Aaron. That was on a Friday night and she was always busy Saturday night, so if I was going to do something, I had to do it then." Once again he hesitated, then went on, "I've been going to Mr. Dunn's house quite a bit and he's been talking some about his God. One day he told me that he was my God too and I should talk to Him like I would a friend and share any troubles I had so he could help me with them. I was worried that I'd never see Aaron again. I didn't know what to do, but then I remembered what Mr. Dunn told me, so that's what I did. I told God the whole story and asked him to please help me. While I was still standing there at the window thinking, it came right into my mind. I didn't have much time to think it through. Mostly I was thinking you'd take good care of him, be kind to him and maybe after you got to know him you might love him like I did. I figured too he'd be where I could at least see him sometimes."

By the time he finished, tears were rolling unchecked down his cheeks as well as Elaine's. She went around the table and took Greg into her arms and held him for a long time.

Soon, Elaine began searching her pockets for tissues for herself and Greg.

"The next morning, after I put him in your car," Greg said wiping his eyes and blowing his nose, "I got to wondering if you might have turned him over to the police or maybe one of those agencies and that's why I showed up at your house. When you didn't say anything about finding him in your car, I knew you were going to keep him and not say anything. I was so happy I could just about have flown around the house a few times."

They both laughed through their tears.

"Well, we better get back to business here before Matthew wakes up from his morning nap. I think the first thing we should do is settle his name. Aaron is a beautiful biblical name, as is Matthew. Did you know that?" Elaine asked.

Greg shook his head. "No," he said, looking at her frowning.

"I find it hard to believe that your mother, being the kind of person she was, would have given him a name from the Bible."

"Oh, about that," Greg said. "She told me one of the nurses named him."

"Oh, well that explains it. In the Bible, Aaron was brother to Moses and they led the Israelites out of Egypt, but I'll let Mr. Dunn tell you the details about it. I'm sure he'll be able to do a better job than I can. What I want to tell you right now is that from now on Matthew will be Aaron Matthew. It will take me a little while to practice, but I'll get it eventually. Now, I think the next step would be telling Jim about what went on here this morning."

"I don't see why we have to tell him about all this stuff," Greg said.

"Yes, I suppose it does seem that way, but there are some good reasons we have to go through the proper channels. The biggest reason is, I can't marry Jim with this big secret between us. It wouldn't be fair or honest. You know, sometimes silence is the biggest lie of all. Another reason is, the police are already looking for clues to the baby's disappearance and with all the available methods at their disposal, it's only a matter of time before they find out. What you probably don't know is, I was married before coming here to Carson Cove. My husband was killed in an auto accident and the same night he died I gave birth to a baby who didn't live after it was born. The facts pertaining to the situation here are such that I could not have a four-month old baby within this time frame. I think it would be better if we volunteered the information rather than letting their investigation eventually find out about it. I think the longer we wait, the more apt it is to be considered a crime."

"Yes, but suppose they come and take Aaron away from you. What will we do?"

"I've given thought about that too, but I think we have to face it and see it through. Don't forget, we have some strong friends who will do everything in their power to help us once they know and let's not forget our loving God. He has brought us this far and I've already put the whole thing in His hands to finish the job for us. We have to do our part the right way and trust Him to do the rest."

"I guess you're right, but how do we go about it?"

"Good question," Elaine said. "We could tell Jim about what we have talked about here today. I'm sure he would have to tell Chief Redding. There's no doubt that he'd have to know this."

"I'd like for us to tell Mr. Dunn first, before the police get into it," Greg said. "He's been so good to me and he's been asking questions about my brother. I didn't tell him as I didn't want to get you into trouble for keeping Aaron a secret."

"Alright, now let me think a second. Jim and I have a tentative date this afternoon to do some shopping, if Marge will babysit. Then, after, we are going out to dinner. On the way home, we'll pick up…" she hesitated, smiling, "Aaron. How about I ask Mr. Dunn when he comes to pick you up this morning? If you and he could come here about 7:00 tonight, we could tell Mr. Dunn and Jim at the same time. We may as well see if the chief could come as well. It would save having to repeat it again and we could be fairly sure we wouldn't be interrupted."

"I hate to even think about it."

Elaine shrugged, "Can you think of a better way?"

"No." Greg sighed, "It's not going to be easy no matter how we do it, but it has to be done so let's do it and get it over with."

"Alright then, I'll go first with my story about life in Crawford, then you can tell them what happened with you and your mother after the baby came home; adding what you heard from your mother's phone conversation and then you could say you knew you had to do something to protect him. I could then tell them about all the excuses for not telling anyone he wasn't my baby. Then, I would turn it over to you to finish." She watched as Greg nodded.

"After Jim and I are married, we'll find out what we have to do to adopt Aaron and you too, if you wouldn't mind."

"Oh wow, really? You want to adopt me too?"

"Yes Greg, you too. That's one of the reasons we have to do this thing right. Then, we can go ahead and start the legal process."

Greg's joy suddenly turned to sadness. "Mrs. Colby, I have to tell you something. I don't know if Jim knows or not, but I'm pretty sure you don't. Maybe you and Jim won't want to adopt me once you both know."

"I was mixed up in my mother's drug business. I was what they call a drug runner. I didn't like doing it. Once I was old enough to understand what it was all about, I really hated it. My mother and the drug dealers knocked me around and beat me, so I didn't have much choice. I did what they told me to do. I carried money to the dealers and brought the drugs home to my mother. She sold them to her regular customers. It was my mother's idea that the police wouldn't notice a little kid running around the streets. Of course, my mother threatened me with every kind of punishment if I did anything to draw the attention of the police. There were gangs that would hang around on the street corners and they would push me around, trip me up, or slap me just for the fun they had doing it. They never suspected what I was carrying or I probably would never have lived this long. I was so happy when we moved out here, until she got back into the drug business with Martin Delmont. Then it was business as usual."

"Oh Greg," Elaine said, "I'm so sorry and don't you worry about the adoption. This doesn't change my mind and I know it won't Jim's either. I'm just sorry for all that you have suffered in your short life."

"You know Mrs. Colby, sometimes I kind of asked for what I got. I didn't really understand it myself because it doesn't make sense, but I said some pretty nasty things to my mother and the dealers. I knew what their reaction would be. It was almost like their punishment made me feel a little less guilty. Does that make sense?"

"Yes, in a kind of abstract way it does," Elaine said. "Are you going to include the part about the drugs when you tell Mr. Dunn and Jim?"

"Mr. Dunn already knows some of it because he and Chief Redding were there when I told the Drug Enforcement agents the names I delivered to. Jim probably knows too because he and Jack have been working with the chief on the drug arrests, so I would think they would have been told everything that was going on. They all know that I have a brother and that he's missing, even Mr. Dunn. I think they may as well hear the whole thing from start to finish."

"I guess we're ready then. When was Mr. Dunn going to pick you up?"

"I'm supposed to call him when I'm ready." Greg looked worried.

Elaine stepped over and hugged him. "We can do this Honey. Don't be worried. I'll be right there beside you. Are you all right?"

"Yeah, I'm okay, but I sure will be glad when it's over with."

"Yes, I'm sure you will and so will I," she nodded, even though she knew this would only be the beginning.

When Farrell came to get Greg, Elaine invited them both to come back at seven o'clock.

"Is this some kind of a party?" Farrell asked, smiling.

"Well no, not exactly. Greg and I have some things we want to discuss with you, Jim and the chief."

Farrell nodded, accepting her explanation, although he was curious.

After they were gone, Elaine laid out Matthew's clothes and packed the diaper bag with extras for his trip to Marge's and made a fresh batch of formula for the day.

She decided she would take a chance on her shower since Mathew had not roused as yet. She remembered his habit of a short play period after he awoke before he alerted her with his fretful whimper.

She laid out her black slacks and although she knew the sun was bright, she added a fairly heavy sweater, thinking of the chilling winds coming off the lake this time of year.

As she stepped into the shower, her mind and body warmed, thinking of being with Jim. They were to shop today for her engagement and wedding rings. Her memory went back to her failed marriage and problems that had caused the trouble. She realized now that the excitement and love had died long before the accident. Had she misjudged him? Had she expected more from the marriage than he was capable of giving? Would the marriage to Jim be the same? She was older now, but was she any wiser? What did she want from a relationship? Love, tenderness, understanding, companionship and fun of course. Was that asking too much?

Thinking back, she seemed to have had that with Tom before their marriage. It was after the vows were spoken that the trouble started. It hadn't taken her long to realize that he wanted the same thing after the marriage as he had during the courtship; go out every night to bars or clubs and laugh and drink with his friends, with her beside him. When she tried to initiate a new set of conduct rules, he balked, sulked and then began going alone. When she tried to talk to him about a home life and children, he hadn't indicated directly that he didn't like her ideas, but he put her off indefinitely every time the subject came up. She was bored and angry with his type of fun, which meant he ended every outing by coming home in various degrees of intoxication. When she told him she was pregnant, he was furious and accused her of purposely ignoring his wishes, which of course she had. She had thought that once it was a fact, he'd be willing to settle down. It didn't happen. Now, here she was, ready to marry Jim. Could this turn out the same way? Did she really know Jim after such a short time?

As she stepped out of the shower and began to dry herself, she knew that Jim was totally different than the self-serving Toms of the world. Jim had the same ideas about home and children as she did, which was fairly obvious when he broached the subject of adopting Greg and the way he had accepted and loved Aaron Matthew with no questions asked. She smiled at her reflection in the mirror. She knew in her heart and soul that her love for Jim was not a mistake.

After delivering Aaron, who had to be Matthew for a little longer, to Marge, they drove on toward Crawford.

On the way, Jim said, "There're some things we ought to talk about Honey. The first is, do you think you could put a little less distance between where you're sitting and where I'm sitting?"

Elaine laughed and loosening her seatbelt, moved over next to him. Giving his arm a squeeze, she asked, does that make you happier?"

"Yes, it does and just for the record, after we've been married for forty or fifty years, it's where I'll want you sitting. Next is, we haven't discussed living arrangements. Do you want to live in an apartment, buy a house, or buy some land and build a house here in the Cove or somewhere else? There are many options."

"Oh Jim, I wouldn't want to leave Carson Cove, would you? I love it here."

"No, I wouldn't want to leave here, but I want you to know ahead of any decisions you make, I don't care where we live as long as you and the kids are waiting when I get there."

"Oh Jim," she frowned, I can't make a decision like that alone."

"Yes, my darling, you can. Most decisions we will discuss and decide, but this one has to be yours."

"Alright then, would it be possible we could live in my house, would you mind?"

"Not at all. If you want to, it's fine with me. The only problem I can see with it is that it's quite small, but it's easy enough to take care of that with some additions here and there, how's that?"

"Great! I love the cottage so much." She gave his arm another squeeze.

Jim smiled, patting her h and "I hate all this bickering over every little thing, don't you?" Elaine laughed.

At the jewelers, they spent a long time looking and trying ring after ring on her finger, some more than once. Finally, she held up her hand so the diamond sparkled in the light.

"This is the one, I think." She smiled at Jim.

He returned her smile, looking at her long fingers and well-manicured nails.

After the measurements and other details were taken care of, they returned to the car.

"I hope I didn't bankrupt you with my choice." Elaine said.

"As a matter of fact, your taste in diamonds is very conservative. You chose the one you liked?

"Oh yes, it's beautiful. You might have noticed, I'm not into jewelry too much. I do like earrings, but that's about it."

Jim made a mental note to call the store later and order a pair of diamond earrings to give her the night before the wedding.

"Well, if you behave yourself, I might consider getting you a pair of diamond earrings for our 50th wedding anniversary."

"What a deal," Elaine laughed. "It gives me great incentive."

Meanwhile, Greg and Farrell had spent the rest of the day finishing the Saturday house cleaning. When Greg finished cleaning his room, he called down to Farrell that he was going to finish what was left of his homework. Farrell told him he was going to run to the store. When Farrell returned, Greg hurried out to help carry the bags into the house.

"Did they have a big sale on fresh vegetables today?" Greg asked, glancing into the bags.

Farrell smiled. One of his more persistent goals was trying to get Greg more interested in eating vegetables and often pointed out the benefits.

"No, but they just looked so delicious I couldn't resist." Farrell accented the word delicious and Greg laughed.

Farrell was glad to see Greg more cheerful. When he came home from Mrs. Colby's he seemed a little subdued.

"You know Greg, I think we have earned an eat-out dinner."

"It's fine with me." After setting the bags on the counter, he turned to Farrell. "You know, a pizza has delicious vegetables all over the top of it if you stop to think about it. There's tomatoes, peppers, onions, mushrooms and probably some you can't even see under all that cheese."

Farrell frowned as though he were giving it some serious consideration. "I did think about having a pizza, but I wouldn't want to force something like that on you if you were getting sick of it."

"Me, get sick of pizza? I don't think so, not in this lifetime," Greg said.

Farrell laughed. The boy was such fun to have around. He had brightened his daily dull routine and he loved him.

Later that evening as they approached the Colby house, Farrell noticed the return of Greg's tension and although he wondered about it, he didn't say anything.

Greg went directly to Matthew while Elaine led Farrell into the living room where Jim and the chief were watching the sports news on TV.

"If you'll excuse me for a few minutes," Elaine said, "I'll get Matthew settled down for the night. Greg, you can come and help if you'd like and Jim, you could get Mr. Dunn and Chief Redding some refreshments, if you would please."

"You know young lady, I think it might be time you and I were on a first name basis, what do you think?" Farrell asked.

"I think it's a great deal, so Farrell it is and you can call me Elaine. It does sound more friendly."

After Matthew was changed and in bed, Elaine asked, "I'm ready, are you?"

Greg nodded, "About as ready as I'll ever get, I guess."

As they went into the living room, Elaine said, "Thank you for being patient with us. Now, Greg and I have things to tell all of you, which is the reason we invited you here tonight. I'm going to start my story first and then I'll turn it over to Greg."

Elaine took a deep breath and began. "When I first came here to the Cove, I didn't know anyone and I didn't think it mattered if anyone knew about my previous life, but now in these few short months I have met some very good and dear people who have helped me a great deal and I wanted you, Jim, especially, to know." She hesitated and looked at Jim. "For the past few weeks I've been trying to find a good time to tell you and now it's time."

"I met Tom in college. Through those years, we had a sort of off and on type of relationship; nothing too serious. He had a part-time job and I was working some evenings and every Saturday at the library. Toward the end of our college years, there were many parties and fun things to do and eventually we found ourselves getting serious. We were married after we graduated," Elain sighed, looking down at her folded hands.

"The first year seemed to be one party after another. He seemed to thrive, while I was getting no home or private life. The parties were repetitious and boring. His drinking increased to a point where I was driving home more often from these outings. We were quarrelling almost daily and I began refusing to go with him anymore. We discussed beginning a family. I thought maybe he would settle down if he were responsible for a real family. He was less than lukewarm about the idea. When I told him I was pregnant, he was outraged and accused me of purposely going against his wishes and of course I had." She gave another deep sigh but continued.

"One night I wasn't feeling well and was going to lie down. On my way up the stairs, he was coming down to go to yet another one of his parties and he was angry that I wasn't going with him. As he pushed by me, I lost my balance and fell down the stairs. He continued on down and out of the house. The long and short of it was that I lost my baby and my husband before the night was over."

The tears were sliding down her cheeks as he made a motion to Greg. "I'm going to stop temporarily now and let Greg bring you up to date about his life," she said, motioning to Greg.

"I think all of you know some of what I'm going to tell you," Greg began, "but not all of it."

He told them in detail about his early life in the city and his problems with his mother running drugs and what had occurred after she brought Aaron home. When he came to the part of the story about his mother's treatment of Aaron and the phone call he overheard, he said, "I knew then that she was going to sell him and I had to do something and do it fast. Mr. Dunn and I had been talking about some praying and about sharing our problems with God and asking for His help. So, before I went to bed that night I told God the whole story and what I had to do and asked Him if He could help me. That's when it came right into my mind, just as clear as if He had spoken to me." Greg glanced at Farrell, who in turn nodded and smiled.

Elaine stopped him with a motion of her hand and took up where she had left off.

"When I was released from the hospital, my grandmother came out and stayed with me for two weeks. During the time she was there, she invited me to come out here and live with her. I put her off, telling her I'd think about it after I figured out the financial mess we were in and see about finding a job out this way. As it turned out, things weren't as bad as I had imagined, but I dreaded the daily commute to the city. However, I did spend most weekends with her. She had such a peaceful spirit and together we healed my aching soul. After she died, I wished I had spent more time with her, but if she taught me anything, it was not to spend my life looking back. she said, 'Put your hand in the Lord's and He will give you the courage you need to go on with your life,' and she was right."

"She had left her house to me in her will. After she was gone, I started applying for jobs in this area in earnest and I will begin working at the high school library in January. Little by little, I started moving things out here on weekends and gave my notice on my apartment and job. It was during the summer months that I became acquainted with Greg through his hard work bringing my yard back to the beauty it was this past summer. It wasn't until October that I finally packed the last of my belongings into the car and started for Carson Cove. I was tired and hungry, so I decided to stop just outside of town for dinner."

Once again, Elaine stopped and turned to Greg, "Your turn."

Elaine glanced at the three men. Chief Redding was nodding with a half-smile and Farrell and Jim were frowning. She knew they were all beginning to figure it out.

"After my mother left to go to the tavern, I began piling things on my bed and I made a fresh batch of formula. All the time I kept playing with my little brother to keep him awake as long as possible so he would sleep during our little trip. I brought the wagon into the back hall to dry off. I rigged up a sort of roof over the wagon with plastic bags, to keep him dry. I put a few clothes and blankets into plastic garbage bags so I could carry them since there wouldn't be much room in the wagon after putting Aaron and his carrier in. When it was dark enough, we started out across the field. By going that way, I figured it would cut out about half the distance on the road. I thought a kid pulling a wagon might be something people in passing cars would remember. It had turned colder and started to snow quite hard by then. When I came out to the road, the diner was right there and I saw her car in the parking lot along with several other cars, I tried the door and it was unlocked. The dome light came on, so I reached up and turned it off. I shoved the boxes she had on the seat over on both sides and made room in the middle for the carrier with Aaron in it and set the bag of his stuff on her bags. I kept watching the door of the diner, afraid someone would catch me, but no one did. I closed the back door carefully trying not to awaken Aaron, but it didn't close tight so I had to push real hard until it clicked shut. I grabbed my wagon, ran back across the road and waited until I saw her come out. It was snowing quite hard by then. After she cleaned the snow off the car, she drove away and I went back home." The tears were streaming unchecked down his cheeks, remembering how he felt as his baby brother went out of sight.

Elaine took over again. She bent down and gave Greg a hug and whispered "You did very well." She looked at each of the faces before she started and knew they were all aware of the ending.

"I did try to tell the people involved that night that the baby wasn't mine and I even tried to tell your mom, Jim, later at the hospital, but somehow it never did happen. After you and Marge left, the nurse took me down to the nursery and I held the baby in my arms for the first time. He was so beautiful. His big blue eyes were searching my face. It felt so right. At that moment I knew I wasn't going to turn him over to anyone, I'd just keep him. After all, no one really knew me and they would just assume he was my baby. I wouldn't have to say anything. I said a prayer for his poor mother who must have been in some terrible situation to feel she had to give this beautiful baby to a stranger. I wanted to think that maybe this was God's way of making up for the loss of my own baby. I knew it was irrational to believe this, but it gave me the excuse I needed at the time. When you and I, Jim, began to get serious, I knew I had to tell you. I didn't know anything about Greg having a brother or of his disappearance until last night when you told me. That's why I postponed telling you again, until I had a chance to talk with Greg this morning."

Jim was on his feet now, moving toward Elaine and taking her in his arms, held her close.

Greg looked up at Farrell. "I couldn't tell you because I didn't want to get Mrs. Colby in trouble and I was afraid somebody might come and take Aaron away from us."

"You did just fine, my boy. We'll all stand together and do whatever needs to be done," Farrell said, patting Greg's shoulder. "I do believe the good Lord had a hand in all of this. With Him leading the way, I believe it will turn out right."

The chief nodded. "This information does change a few things, but I'll do everything I can to help. I have worked with the people from the agencies many times over the years. Their main concern has always been the welfare of the children involved. After listening to what you have had to say, I don't imagine there will be a problem in that area, although we will have to notify these people. I know from past experiences they have financial problems just as most government agencies. It's not at the top of their list to snatch children out of their homes, unless they find the most appalling or dangerous conditions. Most of the time they work with the people and encourage them to improve the conditions before they take action."

John was now speaking directly to Elaine. "Your circumstances have created an entirely unique situation but in spite of that, I do think you can lay to rest your fears of losing the baby. As things stand the child is an orphan. I do think they will give your home and the baby a close inspection and possibly you may have to go back to the beginning and take foster parenting classes, as a protocol, to cover their regulations." The chief revealed a half smile as he continued. "Although you experienced an unusual journey into motherhood, I'd say Greg chose the best person to give his brother to." Everyone nodded, smiling.

"I'm assuming you want to adopt the baby eventually."

"Yes, definitely," Elaine said.

"I don't know much about the rules of adoption," the chief said, "especially to a single person, but I'm sure it won't be hard to find that information. Possibly Social Services can help you with that."

Jim roused, "That won't be a problem long because Elaine and I are going to be married as soon as we can arrange it. We also would like to adopt Greg too, if we can wrestle him out of Farrell and Mom's grasp," Jim smiled in Farrell's direction.

"Greg is welcome to stay at my house as long as he wants to," Farrell said, "and even after I marry Marge. I know she would love to have him but as far as adoption, I think we would have a hard go of it because of our age. Besides, I'm sure he'd love to be with his brother along with a family life with Jim and Elaine."

Greg looked up and smiled at him. "God sure knows how to take care of business, doesn't he Mr. Dunn."

"He sure does, son," Farrell smiled, "He sure does!"

There was a ripple of laughter at Greg's statement with everyone nodding in agreement.

There was a pause, "What we have here are three different situations," the chief mused, "With each segment strangely connected. We have the drug crimes which Greg has been helpful with and we have many of the people involved in prison waiting for prosecution and no doubt jail time. Then we have the murder and Greg's decision to move the baby out of harm's way; and I want you to know Greg, that it is a great relief to me personally to know the baby is safe and cared for. As far as I'm concerned, when you couldn't take care of him any longer, you took him to a responsible person and that's all the law requires. One more thing I'll tell you as long as you 're here, Dora Roberts was not your mother. I'll let Jim tell you about it."

"The chief wanted Jack and I to find more information about Dora Roberts after she was killed," Jim began. "While you were very young your mother, Judy Collins, became sick and made provisions for her friend, Dora Roberts, to take care of you. Shortly thereafter, it became known that she had only a short time to live. At that time she turned the rest of her properties and a large sum of money over to Dora Roberts with the promise that she would take good care of you. Your real mother was a good lady and I know she had no idea of how you would be treated. Jack and I talked to a lady who knew your mom very well. Someday, when things get a little less hectic, we'll call her and make an appointment for you to talk with her. She was very close to your mom and I know she would be glad to tell you all about her. She would be glad to see you too."

Jim wondered if he ought to mention who his father was at this time, but thought better of it, since he hadn't talked to the chief.

"Thanks Jim," Chief Redding said and turning to Elaine he told her he would set up a time for them to go talk with the people at Social Services. I'll be glad to help in any way that I can."

Elaine nodded. "Thank you," she said.

"Now," he said standing, "I better be going. I've got to pick my sons up at the movie theatre. I thank you for bringing me in for this meeting. It will save the department a lot of time and money. I know it has been difficult for both of you." He included Greg with a nod in his directions. "Thank you all again and I'll see you Monday morning Jim. Good night all."

After the chief left, it was quiet for a few moments." Elaine sighed. "Even though I'm still a little worried about losing Aaron Matthew, I have to admit it's a relief to get it out in the open. How about you, Greg?"

"Yeah, me too kind of, but I'm still worried that those people might take Aaron away. I guess I will ask God to help Aaron again, or maybe Mr. Dunn can do it. God has known him longer than me."

"I think," Farrell said smiling, "maybe we could all do some talking to Him about it."

Nodding in agreement they all stood in a circle, joining hands, while Farrell led them in prayer.

Chapter Forty

Monday morning dawned bright and clear. Carson Cove, situated in the southern part of the state, seldom experienced harsh winters but occasionally, as the 'locals' worded it, they did get buried. Even the weathermen could seldom agree on the unexpected turns.

It was Chief Redding's opinion that he should enjoy each day as it came along and this Monday morning made it easy to comply, with its bright sun and clear skies. As he unlocked his office door, his mind was already busy with the day's agenda.

Taking notes from Friday out, he began reviewing what needed to be accomplished and first on the list was Martin Delmont. He would leave Jim at the office and have him register the meeting with Elaine and Greg in the file on the computer. Shortly after nine, he would call Harold West to see if he could talk him into coming out to the station to talk to him this afternoon. This morning he would take Jack with him to charge Delmont with murder and if he was cooperative, answer some questions. There was a possibility Martin wouldn't talk to him without his lawyer, which is what most often happened.

When Jim Keller and Jack Denver arrived, the chief informed them of his agenda.

"While Jack and I are on our way down to the county jail. I'll bring him up to date on what went on Saturday night," the chief told Jim.

"I imagine before the day is over, Elaine will do the same for my mother and Ann," Jim said.

When John called Mayor West for an appointment, West was agreeable to meet with as soon as Roberts name was mentioned. John outlined what his men would be doing for the afternoon. He wanted them out of the office during the interview. It was a possibility that West had no connection with the baby case and if so, there would be no reason for them to know. A man in his position politically had to be very careful.

Once settled, the chief called and received permission to come in and talk to Delmont and charge him with murder. When they arrived, they were shown into a small reception area where there was a small table and four chairs. Almost immediately the guard brought the shackled Delmont in and left the room to stand guard outside the window.

After Martin Delmont had heard his rights and was charged, he asked if John could spare a few more minutes. He needed to talk to him alone. Redding smiled and nodded for Jack to leave the room.

"Please sit down chief," Martin said indicating the seat across the table from where he sat.

John smiled. It seemed a little odd with Martin playing the role of host under the circumstances.

"You know, chief," Martin began, "When you came to the tavern opening night, we talked quite a long time and I felt like I had made a friend. I like you and I still do."

Despite the situation, the chief liked Martin too.

Martin shook his head in sadness. I was proud of fixing up that old place and Dora took no interest in what I was doing. All she cared about was that it was going to be a great cover, but for me it was an accomplishment. For the first time in my life I enjoyed myself, even though it was a lot of work. I took that old run down house and made it into something beautiful. Standing there looking at it, I suddenly realized how alone I was; how lonely. I thought how great it would be if I had a wife or a child like Greg, to give me a purpose in my life. It hurt worse when I had to admit it was my own fault. I was the one who made the choice. Greg couldn't be my son or could he. I knew he was Judy's son but he wasn't old enough to be my son. I always liked Greg. I thought about the times I was there when Dora beat him. I always stopped her. I asked her once, how she could punish the boy like that when he was so small. Her reply was that it was the only way she could control him. I had no idea who his father was, but I wondered if he knew how his son was being treated. At the time of Judy's death, I supposed Dora had Greg, but I never saw him until some years later. Once the question was on my mind, I couldn't rest until I knew. Finally, about a month ago I hired a detective. He was just finishing up some details from another job, but he assured me he would get right on it the following week. About two weeks later he told me the date of Greg's birth. When I learned that, it confirmed I had a son and I went on to find out his grade in school, which was hard to believe because of his size. This meant that Dora knew he was my son and now she was going to kill him. It was then that I made plans to kill Dora Roberts."

"You might want to stop right there," John interrupted. "You've been charged with murder and you will be prosecuted."

"Yes I know chief," Martin smiled, "I knew you'd figure it out without much of a problem. I didn't have too much time to cover my tracks. I'm telling you this because I'm going to ask you a favor. Don't you see, Chief, I couldn't let her kill my son. He's all I have to show for my whole, foolish, lonely life. I had a chance at something good but lost that when I let Judy go. I've never loved anyone like I loved her. She wanted me out of the drugs and I could have done it back then without any consequences."

John knew what he meant. It was no secret to law enforcement that drug dealers had ways of handling deserters.

"I refused because of the money." Martin continued. "I traded the most loving and generous person out of my life, along with a son, because of my greed." He sighed, "And then here was Dora saying she was going to get rid of him once and for all. She had said it other times, but this time I knew she meant it. All our customers were now coming to the tavern for their pickups. We didn't need Greg any longer. He knew too much. She inadvertently told me the day and time. She told me classes on Wednesday would be dismissed at eleven o'clock and I should not worry if she didn't show up for work that day because there would be lots of work to do at home and she laughed. I wondered as I had many times before, how could I have gotten mixed up with this heartless, insane bitch. I knew I had only a few days to get everything done. There was one thing I couldn't figure out how to change. Greg would be the one to find her." Martin looked across at John, frowning, "Is he alright? What's happened to him?"

"He's fine. He's living with Farrell Dunn. Do you know him?"

"I know who he is, not much else. He's a minister, isn't he?"

"Yes, Greg worked for him at different times and they are close friends. The day Greg found Roberts, he called an ambulance first then called Farrell, who came right up to be with him through most of what followed. After the initial questioning, Dunn took Greg with him and he's been there since. Dunn is a good man. Greg is happy there. Tell me something, would you have any objections if he was adopted by members of this family?"

"None at all, as long as the boy is happy with the arrangements. Once things have settled down, my lawyer will be in touch to tell Greg what I have set up for his future. The next thing will be to persuade him to take it. Do you know he refused to take an allowance from Dora because it was drug money?" Shaking his head, Martin said, "I have to admire the kid. Maybe someday when you feel the time is right, you could tell him I'm his father which is the main reason I had to stop her. I'd like to talk to him sometime, if he'd consent to it."

"Yeah, well maybe. I'll have Farrell do a little work on him first about forgiveness. You mentioned something about a favor?"

"Yes, my lawyer is thinking I should plead self-defense in this murder charge. That's the reason I've told you all this."

"Self-defense? We have no evidence to suggest self-defense." the chief said.

"I know there's no proof of it, but it is the truth, she fired the first shot."

"How could that be? There were no fingerprints on her gun but Greg's because he picked it up off the floor. We know he didn't do the shooting since he wasn't let out of school until more than an hour later than the shooting. Her finger prints weren't on the gun."

Martin nodded. "Let me tell you how it happened. When I came in she was coming down the hall with the gun in her hand. I had my gun ready too. She must have guessed what I was there to do. When she raised her gun, I dropped to the floor and her shot went wild, but mine didn't. Her gun dropped out of her hand to the floor. I reached down and picked it up without thinking of my finger prints, I wiped the gun clean. I was very nervous. It wasn't until much later that I realized I should have put her finger prints back on the gun." Martin sighed heavily. "The stray bullet will be found in the hall."

The chief nodded. "I'll have my men up at the house tomorrow to do the search."

"I would ask you too, if my lawyer could get in touch with you when you find the bullet to get the details."

"Sure." John said.

After a few more questions about Martin's comfort and if he needed anything, he stood ready to leave.

"Thank you chief for giving me the extra time. I'm grateful."

On their way back to the station, John told Jack a condensed version of what had been said, including the self-defense plea.

"Do you think he was telling the truth about her firing the first shot, or for that matter, any shot fired," Jack asked.

"I do and I'll tell you why," the chief said. "The report from the coroner said the shot that killed her was from a very low position with a sharp upward angle. Finding the bullet won't prove that she fired the first shot, but it might give him reasonable doubt. If his lawyer chooses the right jury, the fact that he was there to save his son's life might make quite a difference in his prison term."

After a short pause, Jack asked, "Did he mention where his car was?"

"I don't think he had thought anything about it until I asked him. He said it had been arranged for Baker's garage to pick it up for a yearly checkup and it might still be there, or possibly they may have taken it back to the tavern by now. Except for a few details, I guess that's about the end of our murder investigation. This afternoon I'll have you track down the car and get some pictures of the plates. The prosecuting Attorney will need them for evidence. Delmont said his lawyer will see about closing down the house and since the DEA didn't confiscate the car, it will be locked in his garage until he decides what to do with it. He also mentioned if he ever finds out who has Dora's baby, we should advise them that Dora's bank accounts and the house would go to the baby, since he is her only relative. I didn't tell him that the DEA already put a lock on her money and probably his too. I asked if he knew where the baby is. He said no, but to just ask Greg. Now the bitch is dead, he'll tell you and laughed. He said, "She hated that baby from day one. All she saw in him was dollar signs. It was Greg who loved and cared for him and I give him credit for getting the poor little kid out of her reach."

"That's kinda strange, in a way," Jack mused. "Delmont knew and didn't tell Roberts. I wonder how he knew."

"It probably had something to do with the process of elimination," the chief said. "He was well aquainted with the people who were involved. Remember, Delmont had been burned by Roberts fairly often through the years, so why tell her something that would hasten Greg's murder. When she told him she intended to kill Greg, it locked in her own death sentence."

John paused, "Well we're one step ahead of Delmont. We already know where the baby is, but he was right. Greg did know where the baby was. If Dunn and Greg are home this afternoon, I think I'll have Jim let him know all of this. I think from different things Greg has said, he's going to be very upset when he finds out that Delmont is his father."

As they neared the Cove, Jack's cell phone rang. "Would you get that chief?"

It was Jim calling from the station. "Where are you?" he asked.

"We're about ten minutes away, why, what's going on?"

"If you haven't stopped for lunch, I'll run out and get us each a sub sandwich so we can eat while we discuss what's next."

"Sounds good to me." The chief said. "We'll be there in a few minutes."

After they left, John sat at his desk thinking of Martin's testimony about the bullet. They would go up to the house tomorrow and see if they could find it. There was no doubt in his mind that Martin had a good lawyer. Money wasn't part of his worry, based on how smart he had been with other things he had taken care of. He was so deep in thought that he was startled when Mayor Harold West knocked on his office door.

"John Redding, Police Chief of Carson Cove," he announced, extending his hand.

"How do you do. I understand you asked for a meeting out here."

"Yes, please have a seat mayor. I presume you have heard about the Roberts murder?"

The mayor nodded.

"While my men were doing background check on Roberts, your name came up a few times," the chief said.

"Yes, Dora and I were friends," West said. His voice was steady and calm. He waited.

John looked for signs of uneasiness in the man and found what bordered on arrogance.

"From the information we have," John said, "she became pregnant and in the early months of her pregnancy moved out here. She gave birth to a baby boy June of this year. I wanted to talk to you privately to learn what you know about this situation. The child is now in a foster home and will, if no close relative comes forward, be considered an orphan." John paid attention to his reaction to the announcement.

"And you think there is a possibility that I am the father"

It was a statement rather than a question.

"It did cross my mind, yes."

There was a long pause. Finally, West got up and walked to the window. John waited.

"I knew Dora for about two years. I asked her to marry me but she wanted nothing to do with marriage. I felt she would be a great asset to someone in my position. She knew all the right moves when it came to handling people."

John remembered Martin had made a similar statement about her and his business.

"She wasn't someone you could love. She was cold and difficult by times, but I felt she would have been useful to me. At the time, I didn't think her profession was that lucrative, although, she sure wasn't a cheap companion."

John was beginning to wonder what this had to do with the baby, but he waited.

"Then one day she came to me and said she didn't know how it happened, she had taken every precaution. She had dropped all her other customers so she knew it was mine. I let her get away with it although I knew she was lying. Once again I offered to marry her but she refused. She told me an abortion was necessary and I would be paying for it. She wanted two thousand dollars to get the job done. Again I agreed and now you're telling me she had the baby?"

"Can I ask you how you knew she was lying?"

"I knew because I'm sterile. It was the reason my wife left me, among other things." He flashed the chief a slight smile. "We were married for five years and we had been trying to have children right from the beginning. Well the long and short of it is, we finally gave up and were tested. That's when we found out I was sterile. If you need proof of the tests, I have them at my office. I can make copies of them and fax them over to you."

"Thank you, but that won't be necessary. With that kind of proof, why did you pay for the abortion?"

"Because I knew who I was dealing with. She could have ruined my political career if she took notion to. Do you know why she didn't have an abortion? Having a baby wasn't her style. It did occur to me that she may have used that method to rob me."

"Oh yes, she was pregnant. We have a baby to prove it. The reason she didn't have an abortion was she apparently planned to sell the child to the highest bidder."

"Well, now I feel better about the money I spent getting rid of her. It was worth every penny."

John stood and the mayor followed suit.

The chief extended his h and "Thank you for coming out. It saved me a trip."

Chapter Forty-One

Farrell Dunn looked at the boy sitting across from him, studying the contentment in his expression. Greg looked up from his bowl of cereal.

"What?" he asked, as though Farrell had asked him a question.

"Oh, I guess you caught me appreciating the view. You are a different boy now that you have unloaded your heavy burden of guilt."

"Yeah, I feel different too."

"Thank you God!" Farrell smiled heavenward. "But Greg, there is something I have been meaning to ask you. A couple times I've heard you mention the money you saved in order to run away. Is it still at your house?"

"Oh no, I always keep it with me."

"You do? It's here in this house?"

Greg nodded, "Sure, do you need some?"

Farrell laughed, "No, but I'm not comfortable having a large amount of money here at the house. How much are we talking about?"

"I'm not sure, but I've been putting it in my bag whenever I earn money from my jobs. Maybe there might be five or six hundred. I've been saving since I was about seven years old. I'll go get it and we can count it."

Farrell shook his head as he watched him leave the room. When he descended the stairs, he was carrying a duffel bag over his shoulder. Entering the dining room, he set the bag on one of the chairs and unzipped it. The bag looked empty to Farrell, but he said nothing as Greg reached in and removed a heavy piece of cardboard. The money was in the bottom of the bag. Greg began piling the money on the table. The bills had been carefully concealed beneath the cardboard bottom.

As the piles of bills began to mount, Farrell asked, "Didn't you spend any of the money you earned?"

"Once in a while, but not too often. When we were in the city, my mother had this thing about how I should look so she bought all my clothes. She didn't want any authorities nosing around. Even my clothes were connected to her damn drugs."

Farrell gave him a quick look followed by the inclination to correct his language, but he realized the word was not in his regular vocabulary and it was a fairly apt description of the drug business.

"I did buy a few things that Aaron needed. She never seemed to notice that he was growing out of some of his clothes. I didn't care because I didn't want her anywhere near him."

Farrell nodded and they began to count the money. Farrell was astounded as the total climbed to over a thousand dollars.

"Is this the same bag you carry back and forth to school every day?" he asked.

"Sure," Greg said, "why? It's what I carry my gym clothes and books in."

Farrell glanced at the boy. "You sure are full of surprises. I have a suggestion for you. I think it would be a good idea if this money was in a bank. It would be in a safer place. I'll teach you how to manage an account at a bank. You can get the hang of it all. Maybe you could start saving for your education, what do you think?"

"Sure, why not, if you think I ought to. Since I'm not going to run away anymore, now I don't really need it, except maybe I ought to be paying some to you for my rent and food. I'd be glad to pay my way."

"Just looking at your happy face is worth more to me than any money you could pay me. Besides, I enjoy your company too." Farrell gave him a little poke in the ribs and added, "Most of the time." Greg laughed. "Right now we better get these breakfast dishes done," Farrell finished, enjoying the boys laughter.

Greg was finishing his homework when Farrell called up the stairs. "Greg, do you have anything going on this afternoon.?"

"Nothing special, why?"

The Chief wants to know if it's all right if he sends Jim Keller down to talk with us, what do you think?"

"Sure, why not?"

"No reason I can think of," Farrell smiled.

When Greg came down the stairs, he asked, "what's he want to talk about?"

Farrell shrugged his shoulders slightly, "He didn't say but I'm sure we'll find out."

When Jim arrived, they sat down around the dining room table and waited until Farrell brought in cold drinks and sat down.

"The chief wanted me to come down and talk to you Greg, since you're a good friend of mine."

"What about?" Greg asked. Apprehension creeping into his voice.

"Well, it's about your father."

"My father? You know who my father is?"

"Yes, we do." Jim hesitated, trying to think of a good way to soften the information that was coming, wondering what Greg's reaction would be, but finding none, he said, "His name is Martin Delmont."

Farrell looked as surprised as Greg.

Greg was on his feet. "No!" he shouted. "That can't be right."

"I'm sorry Greg, but it's true," Jim said.

Farrell stood and put his hand on Greg's shoulder. "Easy son, easy. Sit back down," Farrell said, pulling the chair back in position. Greg leaned his elbows on the table and laid his head on his hands.

Jim knelt in front of Greg. "Listen to me Greg, please. Judy Collins was your mom. She fell in love with Martin and she planned to marry him until she found out he was involved with the sale of drugs. When he wouldn't promise to give up what he called his business, she left him without telling him she was pregnant with you. He never knew that you were his son until a few weeks ago."

"How did you find out?" Greg asked, his voice calmer.

"Do you remember me telling you about the nice lady who was your mom's friend?"

Greg nodded.

"Well, Judy herself told her about it and the reason why. Martin just found out about it lately. He knew you were Judy's child but he didn't know who your father was because you were small for your age. He didn't connect the time sequence with the year Judy lived with him. Dora knew but didn't tell him."

Greg nodded, looking defeated.

"You probably didn't know this," Jim continued, "but he has admitted that he shot Dora Roberts."

"He did?" this time both Greg and Farrell questioned in unison.

Jim smiled. "Yes, he did and do you know why?" Jim didn't wait for an answer. "He told the chief, 'I couldn't let her kill my son. He's the only good and decent person in my life.' You see, Greg, Dora Roberts intended to kill you that day when you came home from school early and she told Martin about it."

Tears rolled down Greg's cheeks once more, Farrell handed him his handkerchief and held him in his arms.

"Why couldn't you have been my Dad, Mr. Dunn? Why did it have to be him?"

This comment brought Farrells eyebrows up, along with a slight smile and a glance in Jim's direction. Jim was already smiling at Greg's innocent comment.

"According to what the chief told me, it sounds as if the man had finally realized what is truly important in his life," Jim said.

"Yes," Farrell said, "judging by his actions I think that's true and here's something else to think about, he recognized and admired the kind of boy you have become. You did it without any parental guidance and little adult supervision. Try to remember too, Greg, it's never too late to change. You and I will be going to visit your father soon. I plan to go often. I want to try to help him turn his life over to our merciful God. As I said, it's never too late to change. God's waiting for him."

Greg looked incredulous. "You think God is waiting for my father?" His words were disdainful.

"Yeah, Greg I do. He's waiting for a lot of people. God made an incredible beautiful world and then he made us to share it with Him. He gave us eyes, ears, feeling and a soul. He also gave us free will. Many of us tend to blunder through life without ever reaching out for His daily guidance and comforting friendship. Without it we tend to be a mean and quarrelsome people trying to find satisfaction in all the wrong ways, while moving farther away from His love and friendship. So many people never realize how empty life is without God."

Jim listened just as attentive as Greg to Farrell's words. He was thinking that he had never heard any better sermon than this from the pulpit where he and his mom went to church.

"You expect me to go and see him?" Greg asked quietly.

"Yes son, I do. At least once and I'll insist that you go with me and talk with him and listen to what he has to say. You owe him that much. After that, I'll leave it up to your own judgement whether you want to go. I will be talking to you on the subject of forgiveness. We are all sinners and we can't ask God to forgive us if we aren't willing to forgive others. Forgiveness is a bit complicated, so we will talk more about that later."

Jim stood and picked up his jacket preparing to leave. "I understand you have been asked to do the graveside service for Dora Roberts. When is it?" he asked Farrell.

Farrell nodded. "Yes, it's at ten tomorrow morning."

"Well," Jim said, "I guess I'd better be getting back to the station." Then turning to Greg, he put his hand on his shoulder, he added, "Pay attention to Mr. Dunn Greg. He's a very smart man."

"Yes I know. I always listen to him."

The day was overcast with a chilling wind. Farrell drove to the cemetery early to see if Benny Krim had followed his instructions. He pulled his coat up around his neck and hunched his shoulders as he walked toward the tent and the open grave. The men were laying the artificial grass over the area. His pulpit still stood outside with half a dozen men and folding chairs leaning against it.

Farrell greeted the men and asked if they needed anything.

"Well we could have used a little sun and a little less wind," one of the men answered, smiling, "but you'll have some protection with the tent anyway."

"Yes," Farrell said, "and I'm grateful for that. I guess we've become a little spoiled with the warm fall we've been having." Farrell stood looking around a few more seconds. "I'm going to go for now but I'll be back soon. I have to go home and dress a little warmer, I'm thinking."

"Sounds like a good idea," one of the men said.

When Farrell and Greg returned, they saw the police car and some others parked partially off the road near the tent with a small group of people huddled together.

"I wonder why they're here," Greg said.

"Do you think it might be because of you?" Farrell recognized everyone. "I think it's called friendship or maybe love," Farrell said smiling. "It's what friends do. They stand by the people they love and give them support during difficult times."

As they approached, the chief turned to greet them with a handshake, followed by Jim, Jack and Ben. Elaine, Marge and Ann each gave Greg a hug before entering the shelter of the tent. As they entered, Marge asked if she could sit next to Greg. He nodded, smiling.

The closed casket was suspended over the grave with an oblong pillow of flowers laying across the top.

Farrell walked to the pulpit. "Please be seated," he said.

"Our soul," he began, "is how our body connects with our loving God. Our heart, our mind and our body long for that connection. All too often we are distracted from His gentle voice with the temptations the world has to offer. The voice of our Lord cannot be heard. No matter what we have substituted for His voice, it is never satisfying, never enough. The Lord gives us a life and eventually, most of us have choices to make. These choices are our life. It saddens me that a people of God didn't affect Dora's choices. I'm sure the Lord is sad too. Only He can rescue us and continue to love us because we are His children. I have a book entitled, 'Grace for The Moment', written by Max Lucado. It reminds us that the only Son of our Father obeyed him even unto death and I quote, "On the eve of crucifixion on the cross, Jesus made his decision. Better to go through hell for you, than to go to heaven without you." Farrell hesitated a moment looking at everyone sitting around the casket.

"We don't have to know," he continued, "what made Dora Roberts the way she was, before we ask the Lord to have mercy on her troubled soul. It's not for us to judge her, because even though she spent some time in our midst, she belongs to God now. We ask for his mercy and forgiveness as we lay her earthly body to eternal rest."

Farrell walked to the casket and extended his hands. "Please bow your head in prayer. Lord, please receive the soul of Dora Roberts. I quote from 2 Peter: The Lord is not slack concerning his promise... but is long suffering to us..not willing that any should perish but that all should come to repentance. Now join hands while I read the 23rd Psalm.

'The Lord is my Shepard: There is nothing I shall want: He maketh me to lie down in green pastures: He leadeth me beside the still waters: He restoreth my soul: He leadeth me in the paths of righteousness for His name's sake: Yea, though I walk through the valley of the shadow of death, I will fear no evil for though art with me: Thy rod and thy staff they comfort me: Thou preparest a table before me in the presence of mine enemies: Thou anointest my head with oil: My cup runneth over: Surely goodness and mercy shall follow me all the days of my life: and I will dwell in the house of the Lord forever. Amen"

With a nod to the two men standing by, the casket was lowered into the earth and Farrell walked back to the pulpit.

"I want to thank you all for coming. I understand the ladies have a luncheon waiting for us at Mrs. Keller's house and we are all invited. Thank You." Farrell walked over to Greg and took his hand. The two walked out of the tent to stand and shake hands, thanking everyone as they left the tent.

Chapter Forty-Two

Shortly after lunch Farrell called up the stairs to Greg. "Chief Redding wants to know if you have more belongings up at the house?"

"Yes, not a lot, but I have some clothes in the hamper and a few in my dresser. I also have some library books that are probably overdue by now. Why?"

"He said he and his men are checking the place over and we could pick up the rest of your things before it is locked up for good."

"Sure, okay. What do you think will happen to the house now?"

"I don't know but if she was renting I suppose it would be turned over to the owner and that would be that. If she owned it, I suppose eventually it would be sold. If Aaron Matthew is her closest relative and it looks as though he is, I would think the money might go to him. I don't know how the law works with the DEA involved. In any case it's not anything we have to worry about."

As Greg descended the stairs, Farrell handed him a large suitcase. "Do you think that will do the job?" Greg nodded yes.

"The place hasn't been cleaned yet. Is that going to bother you?" Farrell asked.

Greg hesitated for a couple of seconds. "I guess not that much."

Arriving at the house, they walked into the kitchen area.

"Hello?" Farrell called out.

Jack Denver stepped out of the hall. "Well , here's a couple of friendly faces. How are things going?"

"Fine thanks," Greg answered, "but I don't know about Mr. Dunn. He's probably ready for the nut house by now, having me around all the time."

"If I remember correctly he always liked nuts," Jim chimed in, leaning his head around the corner and into the kitchen, smiling.

"Never you mind about my taste in life's little delicacies. Greg and I are getting along just fine," Farrell smiled.

"Hey you two, don't be harassing my guests. How are you Farrell? And you Greg?" John said stepping into the kitchen.

"Excellent,ccouldn't be better," Farrell said.

John quickly went on, "Good. We're giving the place a thorough once over before the clean-up crew comes in. We're looking for anything connected with either case. The boys here in the hall are looking for a stray bullet. They haven't been too successful as yet, but we'll keep looking. You go ahead and gather up Greg's belongings."

"It won't take too long. We already have taken some of his things and he doesn't think there's too much left," Farrell said.

Jim stood aside as Greg folded back the first panel of the closet door and took out his winter coat and two heavy shirts.

As Greg reached up to close the panel, Jim frowned. "Wait a second, Greg. Leave it open. I think I'll take a look in there. Maybe the panel was open when the shot was fired. It's possible, during all the confusion, it may have been closed after that. Sometimes people do things like that automatically without thinking about it."

Jack joined Jim with his light and they began to examine the inside wall of the closet while Farrell and Greg continued into the bedroom and began emptying the drawers. As they were finishing they heard Jim shout.

"Hey chief, I think we've found it." Greg and Farrell went to the open door and peered out into the hall.

"Looks like it might be," the chief said, "but if it is, the bullet must have gone through and hopefully lodged in the wall behind the paneling. Go out and get your tools and remove that one side. We'll see what's behind it."

When the last nail was out and the panel removed, it revealed the bullet partially embedded in the stud.

"Don't touch it," the chief warned, examining the angle the bullet had entered the stud. "I think we better call the crime lab to come up and take over at this point."

"Well, I think we're all set," Farrell said, "so we'll be off. I think Greg and I will run up to Mrs. Talbert's and look her place over now. We usually walk up after supper but the wind seems to be picking up and the temperature is supposed to drop."

"Yes," the chief agreed and his two men pulled out chairs and sat down to wait for the crime lab people to arrive.

"You know chief," Jack said, "I can't say as I understand why Martin thinks finding the bullet is going to prove anything that will help him."

"You never know," Redding said. " If he dropped to the floor as he claims, it would explain the angle of his bullet. The angle of her bullet in the stud might help his story of her taking the first shot.

Farrell Dunn had been working diligently, but carefully trying to change Greg's attitude about going to see his father. Farrell had insisted the boy go at least once. The coming week ahead, Greg would be going back to school which would be upsetting enough, considering the circumstances. Farrell would like to have this behind the boy before he had to take on another emotional problem. With Greg it was difficult to tell if he was making any progress, although it seemed that Greg was listening.

"What you're saying is that people can do anything they want to me and as long as they say they're sorry, I'm supposed to forgive them and forget all about it, right?" Farrell noticed a tinge of sarcasm in Greg's voice.

"No, that's not what I'm saying," Farrell said softly, "There's a lot more to it than that. It does sound as though if someone says they're sorry it turns the situation around and somehow it's you who is guilty if you don't forgive them. And they are free to go back to chewing their gum and doing whatever they always do." Farrell noticed a hint of a smile on Greg's face.

"It's not that way at all. In the first place, forgiveness does not have anything to do with forgetting. God gave us memories so we wouldn't forget. Without memory how would we learn to behave in a manner pleasing to Him? There are many places in the

Bible that tell us about the times God remembers His people's wrongs. When He says he won't remember our sins, He means He won't use them against us, if we are truly sorry for them and are trying to change. Nor does it necessarily mean we don't have to pay for our sins. God forgave Adam and Eve, but turned them out of the garden. He forgave Moses but wouldn't let him enter the promised land. The person who is doing the forgiving has a right to ask for restitution. Our Father gave us Jesus, His only Son, who willingly became human in order to pay the debt we all owe for our daily sins. All He asks of us is to keep trying to follow His example."

Farrell sighed, before continuing. "Martin Delmont will pay dearly for his crimes against society and against God. Only God can know his heart and soul. Only God will know if he has changed and only God can decide whether to have mercy on him or not. It's not our place to punish him, it's our place to forgive him as God in His mercy forgives us." Farrell stopped and waited.

"Will you think about what I have said, Greg?"

"Yes I will."

Chapter Forty-Three

Farrell Dun and Greg were on their way to see Martin Delmont. It was visitor's day. Greg's face registered his feelings of hostility clearly.

Farrell tried to think of ways he could change the boys' mood as he drove, but nothing had worked. As they entered the prison gates, they were thoroughly searched before being escorted into what appeared to be a dining hall with long tables and chairs.

Other men were situated in different parts of the room with their company. The guard brought them to a table well away from any of the other groups.

"We'll bring Delmont right out," the guard said and left. There was a guard standing on each end watching the prisoners, and their visitors. Greg was noticeably nervous and Farrell laid his hand on his shoulder to reassure him. He was slightly apprehensive himself about how it would go, but he felt it was the last barrier to Greg's peace of mind. He could only hope that Martin would be able to minimize or even nullify the hatred Greg had harbored for him. Farrell hoped he would show Greg there was another side of Martin that Greg had not been aware of. Farrell knew it would not be an easy task for Greg to separate the drug business and its motives from his father. It was a lot to ask of a boy his age, considering what he had been through in his short life.

Martin nodded to Farrell as he sat down beside Greg.

"I want to thank you for coming, Greg. I know how you feel about me but I'm glad you came because I want to talk to you about your mom. And I don't mean Dora Roberts. I mean your real mother, Judy Collins. There isn't anyone around you that knew her any better than I did, except Dora and I don't imagine you ever heard your mother's name mentioned from her."

Martin had Greg's full attention and Farrell was mildly relieved to see the look on Greg's face had changed to curious. Greg turned slightly in his chair to study his father's face, waiting.

"I'll start at the beginning," Martin began. "I met Judy right after she graduated from secretarial school. She was applying for a job at the company I was working for. At the time, I wasn't too deep into the drug business. It was sort of a side line with me then. When she came into the firm, she was the most beautiful little lady I had ever seen. I fell in love with her at first sight. She was fun, funny and always a lady. After what seemed like a long time to me, I finally convinced her to go on dates with me. She was not only beautiful on the outside, she was the gentlest, kind and loving person I had ever known. After a very long time I asked her to marry me. She must have found something to love about me, because she said yes. I convinced her to move in with me while we planned our wedding." Martin sighed and glanced toward the barred window, remembering.

"It was shortly after that when the trouble started. I was making good money, not only from my job but with the sale of drugs too. I started buying her expensive jewelry. To say she was less than impressed would be an understatement. I was hurt. I'd never known a woman who didn't like expensive gifts. She wanted a simple wedding, I wanted a big splash. She wanted a small cottage in the suburbs, I wanted a large show-off house with all the trimmings. We were arguing all too often. I didn't appreciate what I had. Finally the day came when she found out about the drugs and it was the beginning of the end. She gave me an ultimatum; give up the drug business or she was done. She said she could compromise with everything else because she loved me, but the drugs were a deal breaker. I told her she didn't have the right to tell me what I could or could not do and she was gone. Like a fool I let her go. More than once I wanted to go after her but my pride wouldn't let me. I could have given up the drug business back then, without any problems, but I was greedy. I wanted it all." Martin sighed again. "Your mother, Greg, was the best and most loving person in my whole life and I threw it all away for money. I've never loved anyone like I did her. It took me a long time, but finally, when it was too late, I understood what your mother wanted from me. I wanted the same thing by then." Martin had tears in his eyes as he finished. There was no doubt in Farrell's mind that he had been hearing the truth.

After a long pause, Greg asked, "What do you think my mother wanted?"

Now Martin turned and faced Greg. "She was satisfied with me loving her. She wanted to go for walks, holding hands, sitting by the fireplace, holding her in my arms. Just being and doing things together and loving each other. I found out too late, Greg, that without love, nothing else you are able to scrape out of this life, is worth anything. Your mother knew it from the beginning but it took me too many years to realize it."

After another heavy sigh, Martin took a deep breath and began again. "And now, Greg, about you. I knew from the start you were Judy's child but there was such a time span before I got to know you, I didn't figure out that you were my son. It wasn't until just recently when Dora mentioned what school grade you were in that I did the math. Then I had someone go look up the record in the county clerk's office and I realized that Judy was pregnant when she left me."

The guard motioned to Martin that his visiting time was up. Martin stood, shook hands with Farrell and thanked him. Then he turned to Greg and extended his hand to him. "I hope you will come again." Greg said nothing and Martin turned away to go.

Finally, Greg called, "Mr. Delmont." Martin turned, "I'll come again," Greg said.

Chapter Forty-Four

Martha Benson shoved her chair away from her desk and sat looking out the window. She knew she would miss her job, but as she grew older, it had seemed that her work load had grown more burdensome with every passing year. She knew it was time to retire. She would miss the contact with so many of, what she termed, her people. Today she had lunch with Chief Redding to introduce him to her replacement. Martha had worked with John on many cases and they seemed to think alike when it came to procedure. She had tried, while turning over her people to Rhyma Vale, to discuss some of her decisions on the more difficult cases. It was hard to explain to someone new that sometimes you had to bend, even the most relentless rules to fit the people you were dealing with, without endangering the children. Of course it was the same mind set. They never had a problem coming to an agreement when it came to the welfare of the children.

While she was discussing some of her past cases, Rhyma hadn't expressed her thoughts about any of Martha's past decisions, which left her wondering if Rhyma had approved of the way they had been handled.

She supposed everyone brings their own ideas to a new job, but she was a little worried about how Rhyma might do things. She was a very personable young woman and certainly friendly. She was in her late thirties, dressed neatly, seemed very observant and efficient.

Suddenly Martha smiled. She had just described herself some thirty years ago when she had started this job. She would stop worrying about Rhyma's work ethics.

When John Redding walked to their table at the restaurant and greeted Martha, both women stood while Martha introduced Rhyma. She was amused at their surprised expressions and wondered what they had expected.

John was a handsome man, slightly over six feet tall, plenty of dark hair with a little gray showing at the temples. He was always trim and well dressed.

John's expression told Martha he too was pleased with what he saw. Rhyma Vale was about six inches shorter than John and even Martha was a little jealous of her figure. Her long dark hair accented her sparkling dark eyes. Her natural beauty needed very little makeup.

"Well," Martha said, "Let's sit down and maybe we can get the attention of the waitress."

After they placed their order, John sighed looking at Martha. "I guess it's now official, you're really going to retire."

Martha smiled. "It's about time, I think. I'm tired and worn out. There comes a time when every job needs new blood."

"From what I've seen so far," Rhyma spoke up, "I don't think your job has suffered any ill effects under your jurisdiction, whatever your age."

John's attention turned to Rhyma Vale. "I've worked with this lady many times during the past few years and I couldn't have asked for anyone more considerate or helpful to work with."

"Oh, will you two stop. You are trying to make me blush, but thank you both."

"When will you be officially retired?" John asked.

"By the end of this week." Martha said. "I'll be glad to be out of the continual turmoil but I'll be sad too. I know I'll miss the satisfaction of helping so many people, especially the younger ones. In the past few years there has been an increasing number of disturbed people and somehow it seems the children always pay the price."

Both listeners nodded and there was silence for a few moments. Rhyma leaned slightly forward across the table with toward John. "Were you the one who taught Martha about her theory of bending rules or did she teach you?"

Martha and John both laughed. "I'm not sure," he answered, "but you know most rules and laws give you a little wiggle room if you look hard enough for it. Ask any lawyer." John smiled at Martha. "I figured right from the beginning I wasn't hired just for my good looks, so I let my intelligence lead the way around the rules."

Martha picked up on the subject where John left off. "I know the Good Lord warns us about judging people but in this business it's essential. You have to judge not only people, but situations carefully and I might add, you should allow yourself room to change your mind when it's necessary. If the circumstances ask for a little leaning away from the rules of conduct, so be it." Martha said firmly.

"Speaking of such circumstances," John said, "I'm in the middle of one now. I will be calling to set up an appointment with your office a little later today to talk about it with the two of you. It involves a very nice lady and a baby."

"Since I'm going to be leaving at the end of the week, Rhyma will be handling it," Martha said. "Does the lady live here in town?"

"Yes, but she hasn't been a permanent resident until a few months ago. Martha you might know her. She's Mrs. Kincade's granddaughter, Elaine Colby. After her grandmother died, the house was left to her. Before that she spent most of her summers here with her grandmother while she was growing up."

"I knew Mrs. Kincade. She was such a gentle soul," Martha said, "but I can't say that I remember her granddaughter."

"I could give you a date right now." Rhyma said taking a small book from her purse. How would tomorrow at one thirty work for you?"

"It would be fine with me, but since Elaine will be with me, I will have to check with her to be sure she will be free. As soon as I contact her, I'll let you know."

Turning to Martha, she said, "I'd like you to sit in on the meeting, Martha. I'd appreciate your input, if you wouldn't mind."

"I wouldn't mind at all." Martha smiled.

They ate in silence for a few seconds, then John asked, "Do you live here in town?"

"No," Rhyma said, "after college I was offered a job with a social agency in Ohio, but my parents live in Crawford. As they have grown older I wanted to spend more time with them, so after my husband left me, I decided to come and look for a job close by. I had intended to get an apartment our here in the Cove, but my mom and dad have been doing a great job on convincing me that it's not necessary, so I haven't even started looking. I'm driving in from Crawford every day. I imagine you and your wife live here in the Cove."

John laughed. "I guess I have to say you're half right. Yes, I live here in the Cove, but I'm not married. My wife died two years ago. I have two teenage boys to keep me busy and alert," John said ruefully.

As they were getting ready to leave, John said, "It's been nice to meet you in spite of losing the partnership of a good friend."

"Oh John, you'll no doubt see me spending time around town now and then," Martha said.

Back at the office, John called Elaine and she agreed to the one o'clock appointment for the next day.

When he called Rhyma at the social services office, he asked if she had wanted them to come to her office or was she intending to go to Elaine's house.

"I will eventually want to go to the house but I think until I know the whole story, we better meet in the office."

The next day when elaine and John arrived at the social services office, they were instructed to go right to Mrs. Benson's office where Mrs. Benson and Mrs. Vale were expecting them.

After introductions, Rhyma Vale looked at the chief. "Now what can we do for you?"

"I'll make this as concise as possible but I think it's necessary to give you some background information," the chief began.

Rhyma Vale nodded and opened her desk drawer, removed a large notebook, took pen in hand and waited.

"A short time ago you may have heard about a drug bust here in Carson Cove."

Rhyma and Martha both nodded.

The chief continued to share details of the lengthy and entwined accounting. Each detail led both women through a dark string of events arriving at today.

"I know this is a very condensed version of the facts we have learned and feel free to ask any questions.

"Are you married, Mrs. Colby?"

"No, my husband was killed in a car accident about a year ago. I was pregnant at the time, but I fell down the stairs that same night and lost my baby." Tears rolled heedlessly down her cheeks.

"I see and where did you think the baby came from?" Rhyma asked, her voice soft.

"I didn't know. I thought some poor mother must have been in desperate trouble to give up her beautiful baby to a stranger."

"But now you know?"

"Yes. Now I know."

Elaine nodded, "the main reason I want to get everything out in the open is Jim and I are engaged to be married and we would like to do everything right, so we can adopt both baby Aaron and Greg. I know I should have done this before it went this far, but I was so afraid the baby would be taken away from me and Greg. I love them both so much," Elaine said, the tears once again sliding down her cheeks.

Rhyma reached over to her desk and grabbed a tissue from the half empty box and handed it to Elaine.

Standing she said, "I want to thank you Mrs. Colby for coming in and you too chief for giving us some of the background information. I can assure you that Mrs. Benson and I will discuss the circumstances very thoroughly and we'll be in touch with you."

Reaching over to Elaine she laid a reassuring hand on her shoulder. "Don't worry too much. I'm sure something can be worked out." Then turning to John, she said, "I imagine there will be other questions we'll need answers to, so we'll be calling you soon."

As he drove Elaine home, he was thinking about Rhyma Vale. Elaine was more relaxed. "She seems to be a very nice lady and beautiful too," Elaine said with a glance in John's direction.

"Yes, so I noticed. I don't think you're going to have too much trouble with all this." John said, smiling at Elaine.

Chapter Forty-Five

Later in the week Rhyma Vale called Elaine for an appointment to inspect her home. She complimented Elaine on her lovely home, as she was escorted through the house.

"For now, I have Aaron's crib and dresser in my bedroom," she said as they were about to enter the room. He's taking his morning nap right now," she said, lowering her voice to a whisper.

Rhyma tiptoed over to the crib and peered in to see the baby. "You weren't exaggerating, he is a beautiful baby," Rhyma whispered as they left the room.

"Do you have children" Elaine asked.

"No, sadly I was not able to have children. It's one of the reasons it's so important for me to help young people with their parenting. So many of them are so ill equipped to be parents."

"It must be difficult for you sometimes to witness a neglected child."

"Yes it is, but also rewarding when I see the successes we have in changing their lives."

Elaine opened the door to the next bedroom as they walked down the hall. "this will be his room after Jim and I are married."

Elaine explained. "When my grandmother was alive, this was the guest room, since I was here so often when I was young, I referred to it as my room. The baby's room is only a short distance away from my room and I have a baby monitor so I'll be able to hear him is he fusses."

"I understand from what the chief said that the young boy took care of him before he was brought to you. He was in pretty bad shape when he came to you?" Rhyma inquired.

"Oh no, not at all. He was clean and healthy and his clothes were worn but in great shape. All of the extra changes were folded and neat. I would not have guessed that a young boy had been the one taking care of him. There were no signs of neglect. None at all. Since I've had him, I've taken him for a checkup and his shots are up to date. The doctor made a change of his formula. He is a very good natured baby."

"You mentioned when you were at the agency that you are engaged to be married. Will that be soon?"

"We haven't set a date yet but I think it will be soon."

"Your house has passed inspection. Mrs. Benson and I discussed the odd situation here and we agree if everything else is in order, we will leave the baby here but there are some things to be done to meet the requirements of the agency. You will have to fill out the required papers just as if you are petitioning to obtain a child. If all goes well with that, we will be glad for the baby to be in your care

Elaine beamed, "I love him so much, I feel as though he's mine. I want you to know that he will be very well cared for."

They walked back to the dining room where Rhyma had left her briefcase, she withdrew two packets of papers. "These are the papers you have to fill out" she said, handing them to Elaine. Well will have to approve them. I brought a packet for your future husband to start work on too, since it will be required when you start the adoption process after your marriage. The chief said they hadn't found any evidence of relatives but there is a chance that one may turn up. If they meet the requirements, it would be possible they could claim the child."

Seeing the dismay on Elaine's face she added, "It's not too probable in this case, but I wanted you to be aware of it."

Rhyma looked over her notes. "You said you have a job waiting for you in January?"

"Yes, part time at the library."

"Do you have a babysitter in mind?"

"Yes. Marge Keller, my future mother in law, has agreed to baby sit. She has been so kind and thoughtful from the first day I arrived here in Carson Cove."

"I will have to interview her too. Would you give me her address and phone number please?" she asked, taking out her notebook. "Now we have to consider something else. Usually before a child is placed in your care, you would be required to take a parenting class to meet the guidelines set by the county. There are quite a few odd circumstances in your case but I think it would be a good idea to have it on record, since you intend to adopt. The papers I have given you and your husband to fill out are an extensive life profile from birth to date which includes all family members and all health history, jobs and marriages up to the current time. This information is very important, so fill them out carefully. You have already passed your home inspection so you don't have to worry about that. I would tell you that when the time comes for you to adopt the boys, it may be quite expensive and you should obtain a lawyer that specializes in adoption. Sometimes depending on the circumstances, he or she may have a new set of things to be done. I want you to know I'll be glad to help in any way I can."

"Thank you, I appreciate it very much."

As Rhyma prepared to leave, she stopped and looked around the yard. "What a beautiful setting for your home, here on the banks of the river. Do you have any problem with spring floods?"

"Never in all the years that I can remember."

"And your yard is so beautiful too," Rhyma said. "If I remember correctly Greg Roberts did your yard work."

"Yes, he's quite a boy; so smart for his age. Have you met him?"

"No, but I plan to coerce the chief into arranging an introduction, if I can."

They both laughed. "I'm fairly sure he would be glad to do it. Greg is down at Farrell Dunn's house for now. Greg took care of quite a few yards here on Barber Road. When Farrell was on crutches for awhile, Greg did a few odd jobs for him and they became good friends. He's here often. He still thinks of Aaron as his brother. We discuss books he is reading quite often. He reads way beyond his grade level. From little bits he's told me, he was never allowed to have friends, so he probably turned to books. I admire him so much. Most kids who are left to their own devices and abused as he was, could be expected to be quarrelsome and violent, but he sure isn't anything like that."

After what John had said about the boy and now Elaine was giving him enthusiastic approval, it was making Rhyma very curious. Since the boy had a father who was providing for him, the agency would have no reason to be involved. There wasn't much chance she was going to come in contact with him through these channels.

Chapter Forty-Six

John Redding sat having his second cup of coffee. His sons had left for school. It was the first time since his wife had died that his mind was totally occupied with another woman. It was as though Rhyma Vale had opened a door to his loneliness and walked into his aching heart. So many years had passed living with a comfortable and loving wife, raising a family. Then living for two more years without the easy atmosphere, he had now accepted the emotional emptiness in his life. Did he want to start a new relationship? What was even worse to think about was, did he even remember how to go about it?

Glancing at his watch, he walked to the coat rack and placing the car keys in his jacket pocket, walked out to the garage. It was time to go to work.

After the morning meeting with his men, he pulled out Dora Roberts file and began taking notes of details that still had to be done to bring the case to a proper close. Calling Delmont's lawyer would take care of some of the questions.

Placing the call, he waited to be connected. He told the lawyer the reason for his call and gave him the information about the bullet. The chief said he would send him a copy of the report.

"While I have you on the phone," the lawyer said, "I need to know the whereabouts of Martin's son. I need to talk to his caregiver." John gave him the information.

"When I last talked to Martin," John said, "I told him about a couple who want to adopt the boy. Did he say anything to you about it?"

The lawyer hesitated, "Yes, he did but even though he agreed to it, I discouraged it and I'll tell you why. There's a lot of paperwork involved and of course he would have to give written consent, which he is willing to do. Adoption is a more complicated process that just being a caregiver. Sometimes it takes years to accomplish. The boy being the age he is, it seems almost futile to attempt it. Tell them to contact me or their own lawyer so it can be explained to them in more detail. Martin has allotted some money for the boy's living expenses as well as college tuition."

"Well," the chief said, "let me explain the situation here. The people involved are trying to become a caregiver for Dora Robert's baby and Greg, Delmont's son, has thought of this baby as his brother since he was born and for the most part, has cared for and protected him. He is very close to the baby and is literally the baby's caregiver as well."

"So you are telling me Martin's boy is living with the caregiver now?"

"No, not yet. At the present he is living with a close friend of his, but I know as soon as the caregiver is married, they plan on adopting both boys if possible."

"Ah yes, now I see. I imagine social services has approved of both houses."

"Well I haven't heard as yet, but I assume it has been taken care of by now." The chief hedged, feeling a little guilty for straying off the path of truth. He would take care of that as soon as possible.

"I can't tell you much more than that. When they are ready to move forward on it, tell them to contact me or their own lawyer."

"Thank you for your help. I think they will be in touch soon."

When he finished the phone call, John sat back in his chair, thinking. This whole situation is quite a mind bender when you come down to it, he thought. He wondered what Farrell Dunn thought about the whole thing. He knew Farrell was fond of Greg too. He sighed. There was something else too. He had found out the house did belong to Dora Roberts. He would imagine the house would rightly go to Aaron, but who was responsible for making arrangements for the baby? Pulling the phone towards him, he dialed the office of social services. The secretary directed the call to Martha Benson's desk.

"Hello John, what can I do for you?"

"I've got some questions for you. I'm trying to wrap up some of the details left over from our drug /murder case. You know about Greg Roberts and the Roberts baby. I'm assuming Rhyma Vale discussed the case with you."

"Yes we talked about it thoroughly. When you and Mrs. Colby were here in the office, you gave us an outline of the situation and when Rhyma inspected the house, Mrs. Colby filled in some of the details."

"Well then," the chief said, "if it wouldn't break any rules, can I ask if the house passed and the baby is still there?"

Martha laughed. "Yes to both questions. Rhyma said the house was in excellent condition and the baby was happy, healthy and absolutely beautiful. She will have to do a little catching up on some paper work but outside of that everything is fine."

"Very good," the chief said. "Now I'd like to ask you another question."

"All right but Rhyma is free now so maybe you should ask her, I'll put her on."

"Hello? Martha says you have a question?"

"Yes," John said. "I've been trying to clear away some of the details of the Roberts case and she owned a cottage. The DEA put a lock on her bank accounts but not the house. I'm assuming it would belong to her baby since he is the only known relative. Do you know who should be notified in this situation?"

"Yes, in a situation such as this the state would appoint a trustee to dispose of her state which would include anything belonging to her and it would be sold and the money put in a trust until the baby is eighteen or possibly twenty-one. If you would like me to, I would be glad to notify the officials and get it started.," Rhyma volunteered.

"I would appreciate it. Thank you very much. There is another piece of property that I believe belongs to her too. I'll check it out and let you know."

"If you have a few more minutes, John. I'd like to ask you about Greg."

"Sure, go ahead," John was smiling to himself. She had called him by his first name, it was a start.

"I gathered from things you and Mrs. Colby said that Greg is not related in any way to Dora Roberts and he has a father but he is not with his father. Am I right?"

"I'm so sorry. We have given you bits and pieces without realizing it must be difficult for you to put the pieces together. Let me see if I can fill in some of the spaces. Greg's real mother died when he was under three years old. Before she died she turned over her bank account to her best friend, Dora Roberts, with the promise to take care of her well loved child, Greg."

"Roberts knew that Greg's mother wanted to tell Martin Delmont about Greg before she died, but she died before that could happen. From what we have learned through our investigation, Dora knew but had no intention of telling Greg's father he has a son for fear she would lose the money and properties, even though she worked with Martin for many years, not only in Crawford but later out her in the Cove. Greg's father is Martin Delmont and he didn't know until recently that Greg was his son. Are you with me or have I lost you?"

"I'm here," Rhyma laughed, "I'm taking notes."

John went on to provide Rhyma with the information to allow her deeper understanding. The story was complicated, filled with several twists and turns.

"Wow! What a story," Rhyma said. "Where is the boy now?"

"When he came home from school that day, he found his mother dead and called an ambulance and then immediately called his good friend Reverend Farrell Dunn. He came right up to be with Greg and when we got there I sent Greg home with Dunn. He has been there ever since."

Rhyma sighed, "What a horrible thing for a boy his age to go through. Is he all right?"

"It was one of the things that baffled me for awhile. He was shaken but nowhere near as upset as you would think he might be."

Glancing down at his notes, it reminded him that he intended to go down to see Farrell Dunn and Greg.

"One of my men, Jim Keller, plans on adopting Aaron and Greg. I don't know how that would go over with Farrell, but when I mentioned it to Martin Delmont, he said he didn't have a problem with it, as long as Greg was happy."

"Yes, Mrs. Colby mentioned their intentions. It's going to be quite a project but as things stand now, I don't foresee any big problems," Rhyma stated.

"You haven't met Mr. Dunn or Greg have you? I'm going down to see them today, would you like to go?"

"Oh I'd love to go. Do you have any idea what time?"

"It would have to be sometime after three thirty when school lets out for the day. So it would be about four o'clock."

"Perfect," Rhyma said, "I'm done work at that time."

"Good ," John said. "Of course I haven't called Farrell yet, but I will and call you back as soon as I know."

"Thank you John, I appreciate it."

As they approached Farrell's driveway, John recognized Jim's car.

"It looks like you will meet Jim Keller too." John said to Rhyma.

After the introductions, Jim said "I'm not staying long chief. I came down to see if I could recruit a small work force for this weekend. I'm putting an addition on Elaine's house. We're expecting to add a member of our family shortly after we're married."

"I don't know how much help we'd be," Farrell spoke up, "but we're trainable, right Greg?"

Greg laughed, nodding his head.

"If you could use a few inexperienced hands, my sons and I would be glad to help," the chief said.

"We sure could," Jim said. "I've conned a real carpenter into bossing the operation. Jack Denver built his house so he knows the ropes."

"You know, chief, we've been a little busy lately and I don't think I've told you the good news," Jim said "I'm the luckiest person on the planet. The Good Lord saw fit to send me two fantastic fathers in one lifetime." Stretching out his hand and laid it on Farrells shoulder. "Farrell Dunn is getting ready to marry my mother."

Farrell smiled up at Jim. "With the exception of when your mother agreed to marry me, I think that's the nicest thing anyone ever said to me. Thank you, Jim."

"Well, I'm going to be on my way and let you and the nice lady here take the floor. I'll see you tomorrow, chief."

After he was gone, Rhyma asked Farrell, "Is the lady you are marrying Marge Keller?"

"It sure is. Do you know her?"

"No, not yet but I have an appointment to talk with her tomorrow afternoon. Mrs. Colby said she will be doing some baby sitting for Baby Aaron and I have to look her house over."

"She makes the best cookies in the whole world," Greg said, "and a lot of other stuff too."

Rhyma smiled. "Maybe she'll let me sample some, do you think?"

"Sure, I do some yard work for her and every time I go there she always gives me some. She brings stuff over here a lot too, doesn't she Mr. Dunn?"

"She sure does and if she misses a day or two, we make a point of going over to get it." They all shared a chuckle.

"Well Chief, I understand you have something to discuss with us so maybe we better let you get at it," Farrell said.

"Yes I do, but it's not too earth shattering. I understand you and Greg have been down to see Martin."

"Yes, it went very well. I think Greg feels a little better about accepting his father now, but it will take some time. Greg and I have had many talks on subjects concerning God's view on things. He's a great listener and learns quickly." Greg smiled up at Farrell. It was easy to see the love and respect between the two.

The chief nodded. "I came to tell you that Martin's lawyer will be in contact with you soon. Martin set up a fund to care for Greg and for his education. He'll tell you about the provisions that have been made."

Greg bristled. "I don't want any of his drug money. I can earn my own just as I always have."

Farrell reached out and grabbed Greg's shoulder. "We haven't had time to touch on the things of this world that have been tarnished by the way people have used them. Money is one of them. There isn't anything wrong with money. It has to do with how we get it and how we use it that makes it good or bad. Maybe you could turn the hateful drug money into something God would approve of. We will discuss this more later."

Greg nodded.

"How is your school work going?" Rhyma asked during the short silence that followed.

"School has always been easy for me," Greg responded. "and Mr. Dunn has kept me going so I wouldn't get behind while I've been home. I'm back to school now and I'm working on a science project right now." Turning to Farrell he asked, "Would it be alright if I take her up and show her?"

"It certainly would," Farrell smiled. "As a matter of fact, I was about to suggest the very same thing"

After they left the room, John asked, "Did you know that there is a possibility that Greg will be going to live with Elaine and Jim after the wedding?"

"Oh yes, Jim and I have talked about it. He will make a great dad for those two boys. Greg belongs with his brother. I will sure miss him, but soon I'll be moving up with Marge and we can play at being grandparents for both boys. I'm not rich, but I'm not hurting for money either. I'll see to it that both boys go to college if that's what they want when the time comes."

"I'm glad. I know the kind of man Jim is and I thought he would probably talk things over with you, but I wanted to be sure. I wouldn't want you to be hurt by this whole mess. I know how close you have been to Greg all through this thing. I'm glad you will have a relationship with the whole family soon.

"That's very thoughtful of you. Thank you. What about you chief?" Farrell asked. "Greg tells me you have two sons but no mom for them. Is this young lady interested in that position?" John smiled. "I haven't known her long enough to find out yet. Being a police officer, I'll use one of our best forms of dodging an issue. I'll say she is a person of interest."

Epilogue

Greg stepped out of the car and looked around. So many memories came flooding back. The high school he graduated from looked so small now after so many years away at college and divinity school. Now it was Aaron's turn to graduate.

Greg had been given a position to minister to the same church he and Grandpa Dunn attended each Sunday so many years ago. He was home again. This was where most all of the people he loved and admired lived. He knew they would all be here today.

Greg hoped he would be a good minister to the people of Carson Cove and maybe be able to help some people who didn't yet know their living God. He smiled thinking of his sessions with Farrell Dunn. He would be forever grateful that Mr. Dunn had seen something worthwhile in the young drug runner and had instilled in him a life of faith and love. They were all one big family now. Farrell Dunn had married Marge Keller and they became Grandma and Grandpa to Aaron and him. They had been adopted by Elaine and Jim Keller who eventually gave the boys two beautiful sisters. They could not have had two more loving parents.

Greg glanced at his watch. He was early enough to walk around to the back of the schools sporting fields. He remembered the two Redding boys and he and Grandpa watching the games together, along with their parents, John and Rhyma Redding.

Jack Denver and his family were there when his schedule allowed it. They were always around for many occasions and hosted many fun times at their house.

Family and Friends are the most important relationships in anyone's God given life here on earth.

As he walked back to the front of the school, he thought he saw his real father, Martin Delmont and Grandpa Dunn's relentless pursuit of Martin's soul. He had been right to insist that Greg should go to visit that first time when Martin was in jail. Mr. Dunn had told Greg that he should give Martin a chance to change. He owed him that much. Greg had gone to see him many times after that. Now Martin was back here in Carson Cove, where he would see him more often.

Greg silently thanked God for allowing him to have so much joy and comfort in his life, freely given by all of these people. He would be forever grateful.

Greg was so deep in his memories, that when someone behind him asked, "Are you Reverend Keller?" he was startled. Turning he said, "Yes, I am Reverend Keller."

"I'm David Boles, a reporter from the Carson Cove Daily News."

Greg smiled. "What can I do for you?"

"I have a program for the graduation ceremony and I see you are the guest speaker."

"Yes I am." Greg was wondering where this was going.

"It also says you are the Reverend Gregory Collins Roberts Delmont Keller. Can you tell me why you have four last names?"

Greg laughed, "Well sir, that's a very long story."